PALI

Steven Grossman

2021 White Bird Publications, LLC

Copyright © 2021 by Steven
GrossmanCover design by
Isabella Russell

Published in the United States
by White Bird Publications, LLC, Austin, Texas
www.whitebirdpublications.com

Hardcover ISBN 978-1-63363-506-7
Paperback ISBN 978-1-63363-507-4
eBook ISBN 978-1-63363-508-1
Library of Congress Control Number: 2021933971

PRINTED IN THE UNITED STATES OF AMERICA

Dedication

As a journalism student at NYU, my father grew restless and decided to audition as a writer for Sid Ceasar's Show of Shows. After waiting for hours, he soon decided to leave, and rather than complete his remaining years in school, he enlisted in the Army. Eager to pursue his love of writing, he became a speechwriter for the General on base and created a company newsletter. He was editor, reporter, cartoonist, and sometimes the man on the street interview. Upon his discharge from the military, he soon got married and, with a child on the way, decided the uncertainty of a writing career was incompatible with a mortgage's responsibilities, stay-at- home wife, and a newborn.

He dabbled in writing PTA plays but never pursued his dreams. While in his early fifties, his business took a tumble, and with the stress of starting a new venture, his heart gave way, and he was gone: He died with eight post-dated checks in the breast pocket of his jacket and an equal number of writing projects that remained unwritten. The checks were never cashed, and writing projects would never see the light of day. So much for taking the safe route. I am sure he thought about the "what if's" of a writing career, which would have allowed him to pursue his passion.

So this book is for you, Dad.

Acknowledgment

After decades of business travel and a sales career's ups and downs in the insurance field, I decided to become serious and pursue writing. I knew I had desire, but knew little of the sausage-making of books. Fortunately, I found an online group headed by Kathy Ver Eecke which imbued its members with the skills they needed to market books and see their dreams to fruition.

I found an excellent editor, Teresa Kennedy, who taught me the ropes. She had a sharp razor wit, an ex-hippie Texan with fiery red hair, and encyclopedic writing knowledge. I learned a ton. She has since passed, and I owe her an enormous debt of gratitude.

It took years, but thanks to Kathy and the many friends across the globe, from her group, too numerous to mention, the dream is a reality.

Many childhood or adult writing friends offered to beta read my rough versions, each making the next draft better.

My forever wife Magy never hesitated to support me in this endeavor. My son Andrew who pursued his creative dreams as a music engineer, and my son Bryan, an attorney, have always inspired me to keep the dream alive.

I hope you enjoy this story.

PALIMONY

**White Bird
Publications**

Chapter One
Getting out of Dodge

Ross checked his watch. He was three hours into a meeting that would determine the trajectory of the second half of his life. The divorce mediation was Ross's Hail Mary pass, two attorneys, and their warring clients. The sides were light-years apart. Miles, a three-hundred-and-fifty dollar an hour mediator would act as an interlocutor. The entire proceeding was on Ross's dime at a thousand an hour, lawyers and mediators included, worth the money only if he avoided court, and for now, that seemed impossible. Getting out of the mediation spending five grand or less would be ten cents on the dollar compared to settling things before a judge in court. Having to pay for both would be like leaving a generous tip for the very processintent on fucking him over.

Twenty-five minutes elapsed before Ross heard the footsteps down the hall. Miles, the mediator, entered the room. His raised eyebrows said it all. "It doesn't look good."

Becky, Ross's intrepid attorney, put her reading glasses low on her nose and perused the notes on their offer. Her furrowed brow revealed her exasperation.

"Miles, this is a nonstarter," Becky said, her tone indignant. "One hundred percent of the equity in the house? She can sell the house and get a townhouse in the same school district. My client downsized. She can, too. Split the pension? Let the house be her pension. Stay married for two years so she can stay on his health insurance? We're the only ones making sacrifices here."

"Well, counter with something," Miles said.

"We want a completed divorce decree when they reach a year of separation. That's six more months." She paused. "For Chrissakes, she'll be earning an income by then and can get her own damn health insurance."

Ross nodded in silent agreement. His life would be ruined forever.

"We agree to pay the daughter's medical bills, but she can pay her own deductibles," Becky said. "She has a medicine cabinet full of happy pills. Getting out of the house and working will do wonders for her psyche. My client has been paying for her drugs every time she sends him receipts. The dosages are off the charts. She's no model of stability. If Counselor Burbank doesn't play ball, we'll play the psychologically unbalanced card in court."

"What's with the venom, Becky? It's not like you," Miles said.

"Ms. Burbank doesn't help her clients," Becky said. "She doesn't empower them to take charge of their lives, to get a fresh start. She just has them buy into a victim narrative which does as much harm to them as it does to the ex-spouses she fleeces. Every lawyer in town knows her games and yet here we are. It's time to call her out on her bullshit."

Miles sighed. "What should I tell her?"

"She can be a fifty percent beneficiary on the 401(k) and get half the equity after selling the house when the daughter graduates. Here's our proposal—half of Ross's income for a year, two thousand monthly for another year, and a grand for another five years. She has a healthy amount of child support. I'm being more than reasonable. Walk it back, Miles. Tell her I'm not playing. I'll not have you wear out a pair of shoes and an entire legal pad with this nonsense."

"I'll see what I can do," Miles said, looking pessimistic as he closed the conference room door behind him.

"Becky, what the hell just happened?" Ross leaned forward, hands clasped in front of him. "This is blowing up, isn't it? It's going nuclear."

He had been prepping for this day for more than a month. Stoic and resolute, Ross was a reluctant warrior ready to tilt the settlement towards a fair equilibrium. His ex would insist on one hundred percent of everything, and Eunice had her believing it was possible.

Just hours earlier, Ross had stood outside, a disheveled mess, sipping the remains of his lukewarm coffee. Before entering the lion's den, he repeated his mantra—*You got this.* He didn't sound convincing, even to himself.

The meeting took place at the Langley Building, which was historic by Charlotte standards. The lattice work on the brick façade showed the workmanship of a bygone era bulldozed to near extinction in a banking city that preferred shiny new glass-encased structures.

The building stood next to a flat-surfaced parking lot and hollowed out construction site destined to be a multistory tower. The building once housed law or accounting firms, involved in the defunct textile or furniture trade that once dominated the Queen City.

Now, it stuck out like an infant's first tooth from beside the flattened parking garage and leveled construction site surrounding it on three sides. From what he'd heard, it would soon face its executioners: a wrecking ball and a bulldozer. Ross could relate since ex Stephanie and Eunice, her attorney, would soon deliver their own one-two punch.

Just outside Ross spotted Becky, struggling to walk under the weight of two accordion files.

"Oh, they're just for effect," she said. "I have client files in there. Let Eunice think I have mountains of depositions. While the mediator meets with them, I can work on other clients and save you a few dollars in billable time."

Becky seemed to look out for Ross, although at three hundred and fifty dollars an hour she was an expensive guardian angel. Genteel yet plucky, Ross admired her intellect and guidance and she seemed uniquely qualified to rebuff the onslaught of his soon-to-be ex-wife's man-eating attorney.

Becky and Ross waited in a gigantic conference room with a hickory table that could have seated thirty. It was well crafted, an exquisite piece carved during the heyday of North Carolina's furniture boom. Ross wondered whether he too had a heyday that had come and gone. Ross caught himself tapping his fingers and stopped. No nerves before the opposition. He hoped to leave today with a smidgen of hope. All his chips were on Becky.

Fumbling noises emanated from the hallway as Eunice's sausage-like fingers gripped the doorknob. She was large and tall as expected with a broad frame. She wasn't so much obese, but possessive of large girth, and the warmth of your average headstone.

"I'm Eunice Burbank, and I'm representing Stephanie."

Who else would she be? "Ross, but you can call me Dickhead if you prefer," Ross said, using the nickname Stephanie said was her attorney's preferred moniker for him.

Stephanie was the first to laugh. Miles, the mediator,

chuckled, as did Becky, at the retort Ross had been practicing in the mirror for almost a week. Eunice's dehumanizing nicknames were legendary in Charlotte's legal circles.

His sarcasm disarmed the moment. Eunice had to follow her client's lead and acted amused, but she wasn't. Ross drew first blood. Becky gave a nod as if to express her pride. But it was a pyrrhic victory, as Eunice proved as headstrong as he had feared.

Eunice Burbank, Esq. was six-foot-two with a chiseled, permanent scowl. Her well-oiled make-the-bastard-pay pitch resonated with bitter housewives intent on revenge rather than a just settlement. She focused on those who did not work, referring to them as displaced homemakers, like they were refugees from the Congo or war-torn Iraq, and her MO was to maximize the settlement by arguing for rehabilitative alimony, the maximum allowable.

She proposed career choices that required lengthy schooling, during which her client would receive up to sixty percent of the spousal income. To compound matters, the couple remained married and eligible for spousal health coverage. Because the couple would continue to file jointly, it prevented the deductibility of alimony. Ross did the math, and if he fell prey, he would be in a hole so deep he might never recover.

Before he even met her, Ross dreamt of Eunice as Godzilla, a towering, fire-breathing figure with tiny T-Rex arms causing cataclysmic destruction to all Ross worked so hard to achieve. Anything of value was in her gun sights. There was a house, some savings, and a few possessions, but Eunice went to war as if she were a prosecutor in search of laundered money.

From what he gleaned, her reputation was not for her sharp legal mind, but endless petty squabbles that left the meter running on billable hours. According to Becky, when the dust settled, her clients thought of her in one of two ways: as a fierce advocate who went to war for them or a bombastic grifter whose actions left a mountain of legal bills and little in the way of assets to split. Either way, Eunice got paid.

After searching for weeks and unsuccessfully interviewing two attorneys who flat out refused to deal with the curmudgeonly Eunice Burbank, he found Becky. Rebecca Harrington worked for Haddon, Piper, and McCorkle, one of the city's top firms. A handsome woman, she cut a striking figure with her flowing salt-and-pepper hair, tailored suit, and stylish bifocals. Becky Harrington seemed the answer to his prayers. She had a keen intellect disguised under a syrupy Southern veneer. Her barbed comments to opposing counsel sounded as if she wrapped them in velvet.

Smartly dressed yet conservative, Becky was in her late forties, her graying hair conveying wisdom, professionalism, and certain contentment with her station in life. She tempered his tendency to ramble as she jotted notes on her legal pad. Becky asked about his daughter, the only attorney he talked with that mentioned her place in all this mess. After their initial meeting, Ross sold his beloved Fender Stratocaster and part of a cherished coin collection passed down from his grandfather to pay Becky's retainer.

In dire circumstances, sentimentality becomes a luxury trumped by survival. Now it seemed destined to run out shortly as the two rival lawyers locked horns, parsing his material possessions, income, and complicating the relationship with Nicole, his only daughter.

After Miles revealed Eunice's intransigence, Ross was on the verge of an anxiety attack. His breathing became labored, and his throat parched, the overwhelming thirst a result of his cold turkey effort to stop taking Zoloft. As he feared, the mediation was not going well. He spotted a water fountain on his way to the bathroom and gulped the water like a racehorse.

Ross hated the antidepressants as they numbed his

moods. His estranged wife had a medicine cabinet full of them. They left her lethargic and dependent but were hardly enough to undo a decade's long assault on her self-esteem by a domineering and controlling mother. Her failure to deal with the root causes of her fragile ego made her increasingly bitter. Ross swore he would never end up like that. He quit the pills two days earlier after being warned by his doctor about the side effects he was now experiencing.

Ross's only sexual experience after the separation was with a co-worker at a team-building dinner three weeks after starting the pills. After too many Japanese Saki Bombs, things with a sales assistant got frisky. They groped one another in the elevator and tumbled into her room.

Sure it was the pills that made finishing the act impossible, he disposed of the condom in a manner that made his paramour none-the-wiser. He flushed them down the toilet upon returning home. He had hoped his initial foray would leave him somewhat excited about what lay ahead. Instead, he felt guilty and empty inside.

Ross accepted he would lose most of his assets and the lion's share of his income. He realized his relationship with his daughter would have additional complications. But, after a marriage that had grown void of physical intimacy, the divorce at least had the promise of greener pastures ahead. If the pills caused dysfunction in that area, better to be miserable with a functioning libido.

Whether his jitters resulted from the abrupt pill stoppage, the Red Bull he gulped down on his way to the mediation, or lack of sleep, Ross was paying a thousand an hour with no signs of progress. Everything was converging all at once in the form of a monster headache.

"Eunice asked for the moon just like I anticipated," Becky said.

"But I thought…"

"This is how she plays. Miles knows she's out of the ballpark here. Let's see what happens." Becky's lilting Southern inflection soothed him. He had nothing but respect for her legal acumen.

Ross heard the opening of a door down the hall. A shrill but muffled voice said something to the effect, "I'm supposed to be provided with the same lifestyle I had before." That voice was clearly Stephanie's as was the tone-deaf sense of entitlement. The rhythmic staccato of shoes in the hallway meant Miles was returning. It had been less than five minutes. Either they had caved or remained obstinate.

"Becky, she shortened the marriage and health insurance to two years but insisted on leaving the rest intact. She seems to have her client convinced she will get everything. The client's mom has been on the phone, too," Miles said.

Becky sat forward. "You know this isn't fair. She knows this isn't fair. We can live with her changes to marriage and income if she moves the alimony down to two thousand. The house has to go, and my client will need seed money, so half of the equity. Walk it back, and it's the last time."

"Here we go again," Miles said, retreating.

"Becky, my flight leaves in two hours. I have to split. Are we okay? I'll be in the air for five hours. Get this under control, please. They're coordinating with my mother-fucking mother-in-law. Know this, she will blow everything up."

Whatever swagger Ross had in his step that morning disappeared. He bid Becky farewell, as she grabbed his hand in a gesture of solidarity.

"It'll be okay, trust me. I have a hard stop at two-thirty. It won't go further. If they come back with enough changes,

I'll deal. If they don't get serious, I'll walk out."

"I hope you know what you are doing," Ross said.

"I do. Now go catch your flight. You look like shit," Becky said.

"Is that your legal opinion or your personal opinion? Because I'm not paying for your personal opinions."

"Well, I checked with accounting and you aren't paying for my legal opinion either."

"Don't mess with me now. There has to be some retainer left."

"I'm kidding, Ross. You can't lose your sense of humor during this. It's your most endearing quality. It'll get you through this and enable you to start fresh. But we have to get through this first."

"They cut my power this morning of all days," he said. "My ex conveniently forgot to tell me that the final bill showed up to the house before we switched the account to her name. I'm certain she told them of my new address and to disconnect my power for non-payment rather than hers. Typical Stephanie."

His chest expanded. "Got dressed in a pitch-black apartment. I was hoping to iron my shirt and suit to look crisp, but in my Amish apartment that wasn't possible. I feel like a wrinkled mess," Ross said. "I was so pissed after calling Duke Energy I threw my shoe in a cavernous walk-in closet, and it took fifteen minutes to retrieve. I left with mismatched socks and a few shaving wounds, which stopped bleeding shortly before arriving here." Ross ran his hand across his throat.

"They wanted two-hundred for a deposit plus two-fifty for the past due balance. Screw that. It's my spending money for the trip. When I get back, I'll have a warm freezer full of putrid meat and if my neighbors catch wind of the smell, I might become a suspect in a few missing person cases. Today has not been going well, Becky. I'm counting on you to give me a ray of hope."

"You are pathetic, Ross. Go enjoy your trip to

California. Maybe take some time and drive along the coast. You need to clear your head. I got this. Eunice Burbank's bark is worse than her bite," Becky said.

"I almost forgot. I got a flat tire on the way here. I had to change it myself. Luckily, I had enough time to stop at a gas station to wash up on my way here. My hands were so dirty it looked like I just jerked off a coal miner," Ross said.

"That's the sarcastic wise-ass I'm proud to call a client. Your luck will change, maybe even on your California trip. Let me take care of the lawyering. I promise I'll fight for you. You have my word."

"Becky, no matter what, I want you to know I appreciate all you are doing for me."

Ross's relationship with Becky was professional, but also like that of an older sister, despite being similar in age. She could sense this once-proud man with a wounded psyche needed a confidence boost. Shortly after he signed her retainer agreement, Ross spent a nervous weekend trip with his daughter, Nicole, in Myrtle Beach. A trip he hoped would solidify their post-separation relationship. After dropping Nicole off at her mom's house, he found a Father's Day card in his mailbox from Becky. There was no stamp, like she had dropped it in the slot herself.

"Just keep being a good dad," she wrote. He texted back, "Thanks!" and assured her the weekend went well. She called him back immediately, off the clock, part pep talk, part friendly chatter, as they spoke for almost an hour. When wrapping up, Becky let Ross know she didn't do this for all her clients. It was a small gesture, but one Ross never forgot.

As Ross exited the conference room to walk to his car, it was obvious Becky and Eunice had some bad blood. When the blood feud of divorce attorneys coagulates, it inevitably turns into billable hours, way more than Ross could handle. He was disappointed and nervous but mostly glad to be out of that tension-filled room and on his way to catch his flight.

Ross walked the two sets of stairs rather than wait for the elevator. He retrieved his car, paid the fourteen bucks to the attendant, and headed to the airport. In a perfect world, Ross would nix his trip to LA to focus on the mediation, but Ross wasn't living in a perfect world. He needed his job now more than ever and rescheduling a trip of such importance would jeopardize the one source of stability in his life. It was also a chance to live a week on company plastic and temporarily remove himself from the collapsing house of cards that was his personal life. A spacious leather seat with unlimited drinks at thirty thousand feet for a full five hours sounded like a Club Med vacation, given the circumstances.

Ross's thoughts shifted from his shrinking assets to Nicole and how all of this would weigh on the shoulders of his teenaged daughter. Their Saturday morning chocolate chip pancake breakfasts at the Broken Egg Cafe had been part of a father-daughter routine since moving to Charlotte. He knew she would eventually outgrow their ritual, but he hoped not because of a divorce decree. He chaperoned Nicole's class trip to Washington DC on the last weekend they would spend together before he broke the divorce news, shattering her fourteen-year-old universe. It took a week of tense pleading with Stephanie to give Nicole one last weekend of quality time before springing the news on her. He'd kept the facade intact while dying inside for the duration of the trip.

The gleaming towers of Uptown were now fading into the rear-view mirror. It was a metaphor for his life, as was all he had hoped for when moving to his expansive suburban home in this New South Mecca where McMansions on quarter-acre lots sprouted up like crabgrass. That vision was fading fast.

As he entered the highway heading to the airport, he could not help but think of his exit from the marital home just a few months earlier. The visions of Nicole on that day replayed in his head like a horror movie of a typical suburban family imploding.

"Get your fucking shit out of here, you bastard!" Stephanie heaved a few suits and ties out of their daughter's window. Some ties didn't clear the overhang on the garage and were dangling precariously, much like his dignity. A suit fell in a mulch pile near the garage while another one hung loosely from the crepe myrtle on the side of the driveway. A few shirts decorated the grill of the U-Haul. Assorted sporting goods adorned the lawn. Golf clubs were strewn about, one bent at an odd angle, a baseball glove, a bat, tennis racket, and even some books, along with some vinyl albums thrown on the lawn in an earlier rage. The open garage revealed the cartons he had packed the week before.

The day laborers he'd found at Home Depot had been poker-faced. He knew Juan and Hector must think *these Gringos are nuts*.

Nicole stood beneath the portico, clutching her jean jacket in her hands, head hung low. "Let Daddy stay. Mom, stop."

"By the time my attorney is through with your father he will have nothing. A nobody with nothing!"

"Mommy, stop saying that. It's not fair. Daddy didn't do anything." She stomped her feet.

"Yes, he did. He's an asshole."

"Stephanie, watch the language, okay? She's fourteen."

"She's heard the language before, Ross. Plus, it fits, so fuck you."

Stephanie was screaming, and Nicole did not hide the fact she was crying. While his two helpers loaded the U-Haul, he walked to the portico to comfort his daughter.

"Don't you set one foot in this house, or I'll call the cops," Stephanie said.

"It'll be okay, babydoll; your mom's just upset. We

12

will see each other over the weekend. We'll go to Target and you can help me get stuff for my new place."

"I don't want you to have a new place. You already have a place...here... I don't want to wait until next weekend to see you. It's not fair. Just try to work it out with Mom."

"Nicole, she's just upset. I know it seems bad now, but we'll get through this, sweetheart."

"I want to see your place...now."

Against his better judgment, Ross stepped back and called out to his soon-to-be ex.

"Stephanie, can she come with us to help oversee the move?"

"Absolutely not. She doesn't need to be further traumatized by your exodus from this house. Nicole, get in here," Stephanie yelled.

"Nicole, go with your mom. Give me a kiss. I'll see you Friday night. I need you to help me fix up the place."

"It's not fair," Nicole shrieked.

Life's not fair, thought Ross, but his daughter shouldn't be forced to learn that lesson now.

Nicole was sobbing. Ross was on the verge himself but had to hold it together for his daughter. Juan and Hector were dutifully putting each of the cartons in the U-Haul and had even collected the golf clubs strewn across the lawn, using the putter to fetch the ties dangling from the garage overhang. It was as if they had done this before.

A few neighbors had gathered on their front steps, watching to see if police should be called but not wanting to weigh in on a domestic matter. Others were peering through windows. Next, there would be lawn chairs and popcorn.

Stephanie slammed the door, but he could hear his daughter scream, "I hate you," at the top of her lungs.

Juan pointed to the closed door. "Your wife, she furious."

Ross nodded his head sadly. "Sí."

"Your daughter will be okay?"

"Yeah, I hope."

"That everything, Señor?"

"Yep, let's do this."

Juan and Hector offloaded his stuff to his spartan starter apartment. Although he imagined them to have far more vexing problems in their own lives, the pair consoled him over tamales and beer at Zapata's Cantina. The night he spent on the hastily purchased air mattress was his loneliest. As he imagined his daughter muffling her cries into her jean jacket, he knew what transpired was far worse for her.

Ross couldn't shake the image of Nicole from his head. He'd been on dozens of week-long business trips, but this time he didn't know how he could make it 'til Friday without consoling her. Stephanie would spend the week trash-talking him, sparing no details from the couple's daughter. No amount of California sunshine would brighten the dark foreboding gloom swirling around in his head.

At last, the familiar statue on Billy Graham Parkway indicated he arrived at the airport exit. Within minutes he was at long-term parking where he spied a BMW with taillights that had just come on.

Primo space. He waited, drumming his fingers on the steering wheel as the driver styled her hair and applied make-up in the rear-view mirror. He debated whether to call out and ask her to move on, but he had an hour and thirty minutes until his flight. He had time. Let her do her thing.

The worst part of the day was over. Godzilla had not destroyed the world, at least not yet. He'd be thirty thousand feet from the maelstrom below and then three thousand miles away from her path, a brief respite from the battle ahead. This was, at worst, a petty annoyance compared to what he had faced. In a few hours, he would be comfortably reclining, drink in hand, and incommunicado with the world.

Chapter Two
Up in the Air

Ross schlepped his bags and hopped off the terminal bus. At least his airline status allowed him to avoid long lines. One perk of his former life remained intact. Before long, he would take his shoes off and put his laptop in the bin while clearing security.

Passengers milled about: vacationers, business travelers, military personnel on leave, families reuniting, and families splitting apart. Most appeared weary while changing planes, but none as weary as he.

A family from hell passed him as they called for boarding. The husband carried luggage in each hand with a carryon and laptop slung over his shoulders. His two kids fought over some gaming console while walking to their gate. The wife strolled unburdened by anything heavier than her pocketbook while ripping into her husband for not keeping the kids from fighting. He had the look of a man void of hope and identity. Ross knew that look well. He was looking at his former self.

He thought about the goings-on just a few miles away. His phone had less than ten percent power with no outlet in sight. He wanted to do a quick voicemail check and call Becky, who remained in a thousand dollar an hour pissing match. But, as if on purpose, every outlet was being hogged by a millennial with multiple electronic devices.

As they called for first-class, Ross skipped the normal indignities due to his elevated status. He walked to his seat in the front cabin, and the attendant offered to take his jacket. Ross focused on plopping into that wide leather seat and downing a drink, and then more when the plane became airborne.

His divorce had created a dichotomy that pissed him off. His Plutonium level status afforded first class air travel, drinks-a-plenty with hotels, and dinners unaffordable on his dime. When sucking the corporate teat, he felt accomplished, undeterred, but while paying the bills for two households he felt as if his financial house of cards would collapse.

The suburban LA offices on his schedule were a viper's nest of rivalries and interpersonal conflicts. Traffic was always oppressive, and he had to go to each of the far-flung suburbs on appointments: Inland Empire, Orange County, Redlands, Glendale, and Ventura, navigating a maze of highways throughout So Cal. An airport hotel would be his home base to avoid a nomadic existence. He gulped down his VO and soda and passed it to the attendant before takeoff.

His cell was officially dead, and it would be another six hours before he could charge again. It would seem like an eternity unless he got buzzed. His first appointment was at 2 p.m. tomorrow. He could rent his car the next morning if he arrived too inebriated to drive.

"Hey, excuse me; I think I am in the window seat."

Ross scooted to the side to allow the man to pass. A travel stranger had spoken. Ross was in no mood to talk. He had too much on his plate to act normal, and he wasn't even sure what normal looked like anymore. This guy seemed accomplished, well dressed. He probably had a perfect family—a wife, kids, and a pet dog. His kids were on their way to Ivy League schools after winning the science fair. His beautiful wife had a megawatt smile and big, shapely tits. They flew to exotic vacations in picturesque locations, thanks to their perfect two-income lifestyle, which paid for their perfect home. He didn't want to hear about them.

He wanted to talk to someone with problems, insurmountable problems, but who kept soldiering on like Ross hoped to do. You didn't find that in first class. First class existed so you could avoid people with insurmountable problems. Ross was an anomaly, and airlines don't like anomalies. If he were outed, the airline would kick his ass back to coach, if not throw him out of the emergency exit from thirty thousand feet.

"You from Charlotte, LA, or just changing planes?"

Travel stranger talks. Please, no perfect family stories...

"I'm from Charlotte. You?"

"I'm near the lake."

"What area?"

"Huntersville. It's just temporary, I hope. Had a house on the lake, but that's all in the past,"

Whoa! Did the perfect family separate?

"Same here," said Ross.

"You live up near the lake too?"

"No, Ballantyne, but I'm living in an apartment, which I hope is temporary," Ross said.

Ross liked what he just heard. The guy in the next seat sounded as if he had his own troubles.

"Kids?" Ross asked.

"No, never had them. We thought about it, but then me and the wife split."

This guy had no wedding ring on his finger, but a well-worn groove showing one had been there. It was a groove

Ross knew well. He had one, too.

After the separation, Ross had scant social interaction. Some friends wished him well, though not out of sincere concern. An introvert, he'd never been much for social networking. Ross rarely ran into people from his neighborhood anymore. He didn't know how to talk about divorce with others. It was akin to discussing venereal disease. Just as Ross was figuring out how to bring it up, Traveling Stranger spoke again.

"So, by temporary, you had to leave the marital home? Because that's what I'm going through. It's a bitch."

"Jeez, yes. I know what you mean. My apartment is surrounded by new college graduates and couples waiting on the construction of their custom golf-course community homes. Or guys like me. You know, divorced or separated."

Did that sound pathetic?

Ross had been at his new residence for five months. Ballantyne Meadows consisted of transplants waiting for the completion of their McMansions, fresh out of college millennials, and the saddest group of all—divorced middle-aged males.

These men once had manicured lawns, spacious decks for grilling, perhaps even a hammock. Now parenting was relegated to every other weekend. They shouldered the bulk of the expenses for children they only saw occasionally, trying their best to fashion a home by stocking their kid's favorite cereals, or fruit roll-ups. But fake plants, artwork from Target, and IKEA® furniture were no match for the marital domicile.

Now each time he headed through his Ballantyne neighborhood with its gleaming new offices, and finely manicured lawns attended to by hired gardeners, his feelings alternated between beckoning and mocking. On one hand, his mind told him he still belonged, but on the other, his brain rejected him as an outcast no longer welcome.

Designer lattes now out of his budget; his one vestige

of normalcy was his daily walk to the adjacent Quickie Mart for a coffee and the morning paper where, on a good day, he might chat with the clerks who recognized him.

"Buddy, you have no clue. My ex is an attorney. I worked for my father-in-law, head of a pharma company. Do you've any idea how many attorneys a pharma company keeps on retainer? They toyed with me like a cat with a mouse. I've been living, eating, and shitting lawyers for the last six months. They tied me in knots, while my father-in-law fired me after I busted my butt building his company. Excuse my rant."

"No, please go on. Two hours ago, I left a mediation costing a grand an hour. I faced an attorney I nicknamed Godzilla who calls me The Dickhead. My ex wants one hundred percent of everything. I'm surprised they haven't asked for the gold fillings in my teeth yet."

"Dave Morrison. Pleased to meet you. Not sure if this is Candid Camera, or if you are my long-lost brother from another mother."

"Ross Cameron. Thank you for not making me the most pathetic person in first class."

"I'm going for a week-long training for a job which was better suited for my skill set fifteen years ago. It's half my previous pay. They had me on the fast track at Merck, but I threw myself into my father-in-law's startup. I'd have been so much further ahead career-wise if I stayed with a brand name. His generic knock-off company took me out of the game. It pisses me off," Dave said.

Ross nodded empathetically.

"No one understands what it is like to get knocked down peg after peg. I haven't been able to share this with a soul, but it is like you are my guardian angel or therapist," Dave said as Ross loosened his tie.

Dave explained he'd just completed the mandatory one-year separation required in North Carolina. Without as much as a prompt, he recounted his journey to divorced status. His wife came from a moneyed Atlanta family, prep schools—the works. Against his better judgment, he took a job as a professional son-in-law.

The advantage of being a professional son-in-law is that you have job security as long as your marriage is secure. The disadvantage is that Thanksgivings, and virtually all other holidays, are with the boss. If your marriage dissolves, so too does your job.

Dave's wife, an attorney, needed to make her way and wanted no part of the family business. He made a good living in pharmaceuticals with Merck and was on-track to make product manager. His father-in-law needed his expertise and contacts. Dave thought he'd be an integral part of the family business. Since his wife Julie refused to step in, he was the logical successor. This was no Lilly or Roche or Pfizer rather a small manufacturer of generics called Balsar. Dave worked hard, as hard as if it were his company, and he made sales to firms that never would have been on the old man's radar. That never stopped Julie and her daddy from reminding Dave that he married into his job.

As if just for humiliation, Julie got a stipend for being on the Board of Directors that rivaled Dave's salary. Dave pointed to an exponential growth in sales fueled by a strong and well-thought-out marketing plan, enabled by his extensive contacts with hospital executives. Dave's contact list opened doors, quadrupling sales in the space of ten years. Going back to Merck was not a viable option, and now neither was going back with Julie.

"I spent three months last year subsisting on pizza and Chinese takeout in a Travelodge off Hwy 77. Now I have a one-bedroom in Mooresville. Nothing fancy, but at least I don't have to worry about police finding dead hookers in the trunk of the car next to mine,"

"The lawyers," he said, "will eat you alive."

As an afterthought, Dave added, "Never ever divorce an attorney."

Julie didn't practice family law, but her firm did, and

since Daddy's company remained their most valued client, they spared no expense to do her bidding. By his calculations, Balsar paid at least a million dollars in retainer fees. The client and his daughter deserved the full royal treatment. Catering to Julie's legal needs was a small price to pay to continue to represent the growing company of Balsar Pharmaceuticals.

Dave made an epic mistake by taking the job. It changed everything. Julie's career took off, thanks to her talents as a skilled litigator but also because of her connection to Balsar. She proved to be a competent attorney, but no better at her job than Dave was at his. It weighed on his manhood and he strayed.

A thirty-five-year-old sales assistant with a knockout body and appreciation for Dave's marketing acumen seemed like just the tonic he needed. After several business trips, the flirting grew bolder. Dave needed an ego boost and things got frisky.

Dave had messed around not only on his wife but also on his father-in-law and their arsenal of attorneys. Julie's fling with a married real estate developer was swept under the rug while Dave lost his job and his self-respect.

Ross listened to Dave's tale with rapt attention. Just finding a kindred spirit gave him some solace. Dave's ex sounded nothing like Stephanie, and yet the results were identical: an endless abyss of economic downturn and dashed expectations. It was as if they traveled in different directions and yet arrived at the same spot. The odds two such anomalies would meet must be infinitesimal.

In the space of an hour, with three scotches apiece, Dave had barfed out the entirety of his marital woes with no social inhibitions.

"I'm sorry. I have been going on for a while. I should give you a shot." Dave leaned back in his seat and grinned. "So," he said, "tell me about Godzilla."

"Godzilla? Where do I start? Well, she is the size of a Panthers linebacker with Mike Tyson's sunny disposition, and it took me three tries to find an attorney willing to take her on." Ross stopped to take a swig of his drink, anesthetizing a painful memory. Ross continued while placing his drink on the center console.

"After moving out I'm talking to my ex about when I need to pick up my daughter from volleyball practice, wanting to keep it brief, but she taunts me about all the ways her new lawyer will fuck with me, how she is six foot two and has a well-earned reputation for breaking the will, spirit, and finances of ex-husbands. How her lawyer has named me The Dickhead and when she gets done with me, I'll have less than nothing."

"Dude, no way."

"Yeah. My ex says that as a displaced homemaker it entitles her to the same lifestyle she has now until she can finish schooling for a new career. Then she says that her lawyer only represents women clients because she is a lesbian as if being a lesbian automatically makes her want to destroy men. Who is the most famous lesbian you know? Ellen, right?"

Dave nodded, "I would say Martina Navratilova, but only because my ex is a tennis nut. But okay, I get your point."

"Everyone loves Ellen. She is one of the most likable people on TV. She doesn't have any animosity towards men baked-in because of her sexual orientation," Ross said.

"Dude, exactly. I am repulsed by having sex with men, but it doesn't make me hate them. I didn't choose to be attracted to women. It just happened. If I wasn't attracted to women maybe I wouldn't have to give away all my shit and start from scratch after ten years of marriage," Dave said.

Ross chuckled "Maybe I wouldn't have to buy a house for someone that hates my guts or worry if I was peacefully sitting watching sports that my wife would bring up some misinterpreted conversation from six years ago that I don't even remember and start crucifying me until I admit I was wrong for saying something I don't even recall saying."

"Yeah, I can't imagine two guys doing that to one another," Dave said.

"I know, right? My accountant Les Pelzer just had a horrible divorce that dragged on forever. His opposing attorney was a six-two woman. Tells me her name-Eunice Burbank. Now I can tell the lawyers I'm interviewing who they will be opposing. Figure I have to get a major league attorney now. This isn't fixing a parking ticket. The first appointment is with some white-shoe firm in Myers Park. Who would be better connected?" Ross said, referring to Charlotte's Old Money enclave. "Seersucker suit, bowtie, grey hair, looks like Orville Redenbacher but with a voice like when Herman Munster played the judge in 'My Cousin Vinny'."

"The two yutes…" Dave said. "I loved that movie."

"He turns and says, 'Son, I think I speak for every attorney in the firm in stating we would rather not have anything to do with that woman.'"

"Seersucker suit rejected you?" Dave asked.

"Yep. But said he would only charge me two-hundred of the four-hundred-dollar consultation fee," Ross said. "So, I go to some do-gooder, ACLU-friendly firm on East Boulevard near the Greek Church, located in one of those restored turn of the century houses. I figure maybe they might have worked with Godzilla on some issues. The guy says, 'You're going to court, guaranteed.' Tells me I am better off screwing up my job and getting **a** job at a Home Depot and declare bankruptcy after biting the bullet for two years and throwing myself on the mercy of the court without a lawyer."

Ross swirled the melting cubes in his drink glass. "He adds, 'But I never told you that.' Godzilla's MO is to come up with some career path that requires lengthy schooling to extract the maximum percentage of income. Sometimes she succeeds and sometimes not, but her involvement guarantees a protracted fight with endless squabbles. Lawyer says he'll pass. He even said 'Bless your heart' at the end which meant..."

Dave chimed in, "You're screwed."

They laughed at the gallows humor, having lived it and being familiar enough with Southern nomenclature to know when the ubiquitous saying was in fact, sarcasm.

"So now I know why Stephanie, my future ex, signed with her. She has a history of unsuccessful employment, and she loves being vindictive and playing the victim. She's Godzilla's perfect client," said Ross. "I used to dream about this fifty-foot tall-monster with tiny T-Rex arms breathing fire and taking all I've worked for. She isn't fifty feet tall, but she's a pain in my ass, and I hope my attorney gets her under control."

"You must be freaking. But you have an attorney now?"

"Oh, I was a mess. My last hope was Rebecca Harrington. She said she knew Eunice Burbank—Godzilla—well, and that she slapped her hand a few times when she was out of order. Becky was a teacher and got into law because she noticed the effect bitter divorces had on some of her students. She is with Piper, Hadden, and McCorkle and a show pony when high-profile cases get contentious and kids are involved."

"I've heard of them," Dave said.

"I must have been as nervous as a germaphobe in a Waffle House, and had butterflies in my stomach the size of pterodactyls, but Becky kept me focused, asked about how my daughter was doing, and how my relationship was with her. She would do all she could to keep her out of the line of fire.

"Then I tell her about this Dickhead nickname I have, and she says Godzilla hands them out as meteorologists do for tropical storms, to dehumanize the exes. I don't want my daughter to hear that crap."

"Losing money is one thing, but if my daughter Nicole comes out of this scarred, I'd be beside myself. So, I tell Becky about my Godzilla dreams. She tells me 'I'm your dragon slayer.' I signed the agreement in a New York minute. She is smart as a whip and one hell of a lawyer."

Ross shook his head. "Let's get the attendant to get us more drinks and I can tell you about my day so far. It's a doozy." Ross hit the call button and the attendant replaced their drinks.

"I have been counting the days until the mediation. It's my one chance to avoid court. Tons of pressure, but I have this business trip that can't reschedule. Three huge California clients want to restructure their entire risk management program. Studying for my meetings, and dreading the morning, praying it would get under control by noon. That didn't happen." Ross shook his head and sighed.

"I get to bed early. I'm tossing and turning, and my phone alarm goes off, but everything is dark. I mean everything." Ross said as he recounted his ill-timed interruption of electricity.

"Now I'm a wrinkled mess heading to a meeting that will determine the trajectory of my life."

"I hope your attorney ripped Godzilla a new asshole," Dave said as he cut into the cold chicken breast served for lunch and broke off one prong on his plastic fork.

"For Chrissakes! Fuck Osama bin Laden! Before 9-11 there was actual silverware in First. Flight attendants who would mix Caesar salads for you, an ice cream sundae cart. Now I'm cutting some piece of rubbery chicken with the plastic you get at Wendy's salad bar. For fuck's sake! Can they give you a piece of chocolate bigger than a postage stamp? It's not like I'm pushing the call button for surf-n-turf," Dave exclaimed. "I'm sorry. How did your attorney handle Godzilla?"

"Oh, she was masterful. Godzilla was trying to paint my ex as a hapless victim, but Becky was crackerjack. My ex has started and quit so many things I have lost count. One of her unfinished ventures was massage therapist, and she quit just before the exam. So they planned to say she would study physical therapy. Takes about four to five years. Becky gets her to admit she could work part-time during school as a masseuse, rather than admit she has no intention of doing so. Godzilla knows where this is going. She can't get Stephanie to shut up about how lucrative this part-time job would be and how she is eager to work. I kicked Becky's high heels under the table to let her know how much I was digging it. Stephanie admits she could make fifty G's a year with either career, and I shoot Godzilla a look like we are on to her BS. She gives me the stink eye."

"Wow, what happened next?" Dave said, stirring his drink.

"We split up to prepare a proposal after a fifteen-minute coffee break that I realize is costing me two-hundred and fifty dollars but with no coffee. I tell Becky she shredded Stephanie. 'Well, she was having so much fun bragging on herself I thought it would be downright rude to interrupt.' We laugh. I thought we whipped them. Becky in a TKO. They dug their heels in, and it shocked even the mediator. We huddle two times. They don't budge." My mother-in-law is on the phone. She and Godzilla make quite a pair. I split and don't have a clue what went on afterward."

"Dude, you need another drink."

The buzz settled in, and Ross could feel the tension lifting slightly. His airline row had become a safe space. "It's all so surreal. When I left the mediation to get to the airport, I was freaking out. I have no phone service because my battery died, and my fate is being discussed as we speak."

"The weirdest thing is my family dynamic is like a photographic negative of yours."

"This I got to hear," Dave said.

Dave was fully attentive, as Ross opined about Stephanie, the monster-in-law that helped shape her dysfunction, and bolting from the mediation after it went awry.

Dave and Ross were global travelers that arrived in the same spot by traveling in different directions. Julie was driven to excel, while Stephanie was determined to do the bare minimum and always blamed others. While Ross's father-in-law was henpecked, Duncan ruled the roost with business acumen. While Ross's mother-in-law was a cold shrew, Dave's was his biggest protector, warm, elegant, and kind. These different paradigms produced the same catastrophe: VP level executives in their mid-forties in economic free fall, casualties of divorces gone nuclear.

Ross exhaled as if preparing for bench presses at the gym and described his soon to be ex-wife. Stephanie grew up in Silver Spring, Maryland, with a very established pecking order by subdivision. For the status-conscious, one's neighborhood determined their social strata.

For those unaffected, economic diversity was a source of pride in the mixed community. Stephanie's mom Mildred consumed herself with status. Those a rung above were snobs, while those below were trash. With most hatred, there was an element of envy. Mildred's sister Candice had married a plumbing supply magnate whose good fortune allowed her to move to Oakview from Woodside. Stephanie hated receiving hand-me-downs from her wealthier cousins. The jealousy flourished in high school as designer labels were all the rage, and her parents were in no position to keep pace with parents in the more affluent parts of the school district.

College compounded Stephanie's social insecurities. A new breed of nemesis invaded College Park: spoiled New Yorkers or Philadelphians who were oblivious to the frugality her mother preached. She hated them but wanted to be them. Stephanie swore someday she'd get even with those that thumbed their nose at her...

Mildred pushed her daughter to run in elite circles while making her feel unworthy of their acceptance, to achieve by marriage what her sister had done. Thus Mildred would be on even footing with her sister. She controlled her docile husband. Cecil had been so deflated by her continued nagging he never stood up for himself at home or work. It consigned him to a mid-level government job void of opportunities for advancement, but which came with a pension. The effects of Mildred's domineering were different with Stephanie as she copied the mannerisms and mores of the group she envied but always felt an outsider. Stephanie vowed to live a life of leisure without adult responsibility. She loathed her mother for making her feel inept and self-conscious. But as with those who follow powerful and occasionally benevolent bullies, Stephanie imbued her mother with an intellect and street smarts that didn't exist.

Ross confided he felt a measure of anxiety seeing the woman with whom he once shared his life. A few months of living apart had brought a modicum of clarity. She was self-absorbed and void of any sense of fairness. He no longer felt obliged to do her bidding. His very survival depended on standing his ground. Ross feared that might increase the level of vitriol it would subject Nicole to and thus damage his relationship with his daughter.

Ross sighed. "I'm getting perspective. Love really is blind. Often, you're the last one to see things." He continued, "When we first met it was the summer after college. A lot of my friends moved back home, and I got a job in Maryland. My social life contracted. Stephanie was in a battle of the bands. She sang and was cute too. So it probably wasn't enough talent to get a record deal, but if you quit, you'll never know." He paused. "She was one of two talented singers in high school, in garage bands mostly. Her mom pushed her with singing lessons, criticizing every missed note. It never really was fun for her. The year after college, that rival became a backup singer with the Dave Matthews Band. It was like Stephanie lost. She would never be the most famous singer from her high school, like it was all about who could go to the next reunion with the biggest success story. It was always 'Marci Simmons got the gig because she fucked the drummer.' She had no sense of doing things for enjoyment, and so she self-sabotaged."

"Abe Lincoln said, 'People are usually about as happy as they decide to be.' It's true." Ross took a swig of his drink, a gulp's worth of painful memories.

"When we started dating, everything I said was funny. Every time I listened to one of her stories, she said I understood her like nobody else. Every time I said something I thought was profound, she nodded in agreement. I was her soulmate. It was intoxicating. Her mother barely warranted a mention. It was like she knew to keep her away during the courtship, because she'd be a red flag if you were contemplating marriage.

"There were signs, but I just didn't see them. The adulation, 'you're my soulmate,' was a courtship ritual that convinced me to sign on the dotted line.

"When it becomes more infrequent, you think if I only try harder, like a rat in a lab experiment frantically pressing a lever to get a pellet, but they eventually become so infrequent you stop pressing the lever. My friends started getting married, and I thought that is just something you do when you hit twenty-six. I went from being perfect ninety percent of the time and being criticized ten percent, then fifty-fifty, then twenty-five seventy-five, which is when you try to do whatever you can to get back in good graces. When it's five percent, you realize it's rigged.

"The first part was just courtship behavior, and now

you're dealing with the actual person, not their facade. They say a woman marries a man hoping he will change, but he never does. While a man marries a woman hoping she will never change, but she always does. Look at the girl's mom. That's who you are going to be married to in twenty-five years. It's wild."

"It's wild alright," Dave said.

"No, I meant Oscar Wilde. 'Every woman becomes their mother.' He actually said that."

"That's deep, dude," Dave said. "I like my mother-in-law."

Ross shook his head. "Not me. Hurt people hurt people. She gets off on conflict and making you feel bad. It's like wrestling with a pig, after being muddied, bloodied and exhausted, you realize they are enjoying themselves."

Ross smirked. "My ex has aversion to work," he said. "I'd love to meet a woman driven to excel, and capable of handling her shit. She taunted me on the phone last week 'You'll never meet anyone like me again,' and you know what I said? 'That's kind of my goal.' Click."

"Good for you for standing up for yourself, dude. Shoot, I'd be happy as a clam if Julie met someone and got married. I'd even coach the person on what to say, but she's so damn independent I doubt she'll get remarried."

"I need to get through this mediation bullshit first before I even think about dating, but I'd love it if my ex got remarried. Hey, have you heard the one about the ninety-five-year-old couple that goes to a divorce lawyer demanding he divorce them immediately? He says 'You've been married over seventy years. What possible reason could you have after all these years for divorcing?' 'Well,' they say. 'We were waiting for the kids to die'."

"Good one. Have you dated at all?" Dave asked.

"One date, a fucking disaster. I met a divorced woman at the pool in my complex and invited her to dinner at my place. I go to Whole Foods because she's big into organic stuff. Sixty bucks in groceries, my card gets declined. I'm in the longest line. You should have seen the looks. Do you know how judgmental a line full of Whole Foods customers can be? It's like I waterboarded a free-range chicken. I was pure evil for delaying their health-conscious purchases for five minutes.

"Now I have a twelve-hundred-dollar expense check, but the bank is holding it because I bounced a check the week before. I got three hours to put dinner on the table. I have twelve dollars in checking, not even enough to take out an ATM withdrawal."

Dave laughed. "Been there."

"Desperate, I drive over to a blood plasma place on South Boulevard and sell my blood. One of my old neighbors is a phlebotomist. I'm trying to cover myself with a sweatshirt, so she doesn't see me."

"I get sixty bucks for my first donation and have twenty minutes to get dinner ready. I go to Dean and Deluca to make it look like I prepared something. It comes to seventy-three dollars and I paid for it with the preloaded blood donor Visa, eleven of my twelve bucks in checking, and four quarters I had for my clothes in the dryer. I get to the house. Throw the shit in pots and pans as if I cooked it and forget I have a bandage on."

"She's asking me what happened to your arm. I say I had a physical. It's a blood test."

"She says, 'It's Saturday. What doctor gives physicals?'" Ross said, pointing his finger in accusatory fashion. "I'm sure she thought I had hepatitis or was on methadone." He mimed an addict shooting an imaginary syringe into the crook of his elbow.

"It's a clinic for busy executives. She's sure that I'm full of shit. Then she sees the plastic Dean and Deluca containers in the trash. Knows I faked everything. Asks me recipes. She wants to make it at home. So, I play along because I don't know she's seen the containers. I'm balls-deep in a whopper of a lie and figure out why she keeps glancing at the trash bin. Leaves after dinner. I see her with her friends at the Labor Day pool party. She was snickering at me with her friends. Thank God the pool is closed for the season. That's my bachelor's dating life. Some sex life."

"So, you haven't gotten laid since…"

"There was another incident at a sales conference."

"This had better be good."

"Well, we have a team-building dinner at a Japanese restaurant next to the hotel and there is this sales manager from Seattle. I just needed to unwind, and I guess she did too. Next thing I know the rest of the gang is gone, she's sitting in my lap, and we're doing shots."

"Ross, you player you," Dave said.

"We make out and stumble to the hotel, groping in the elevator like high school kids. But I had a problem."

"You couldn't get it up or something?"

"No, just the opposite. I couldn't finish. I'm sure it's the anti-anxiety pills my doctor prescribed. I'm thinking she's at the point where she wants to roll over and sleep, so I fake it."

"Men fake it?"

"Hey, my arms were tired, and the rubber was tired. So, I pretended, took the condom off, and got rid of it before she could see it was empty."

"Dude, way to go."

"Yeah, except I get back to my room and there is no way I can sleep. It's like the Seinfeld Contest."

Dave laughed. "I loved that episode."

"Well, I'm thinking there is only one thing between me and sleep. I debate getting online, but it's a work computer and the last thing I need is for them to find porn on there."

"What did you do?" Dave asked.

"I started channel surfing. Hoping for some skin on HBO. Game of Thrones. Dear Lord, give me something. And then Marissa Tomei in 'My Cousin Vinny' appears like some angel sent from Brooklyn."

"Great movie, but what is with you and 'My Cousin Vinny'?"

"Hey, she won an Academy Award for that role, and she deserves another one for letting me rub one out and go to sleep."

"So, you weren't Master of Your Domain?"

"I folded like a cheap card table," Ross said.

"You are a sick man, Ross."

Dave raised his glass for a toast.

"To 'My Cousin Vinny'."

"And lesbians, except Godzilla. Also getting through our divorces in one piece."

The PA system announced the initial descent into LAX. Soon the attendant would collect their drinks to prepare for landing.

"You want to swap cards, maybe grab a bite in LA?"

"Where are you staying?"

"Crowne Plaza, near LAX," Ross said.

"I'm up near Century City. Not far."

"This has been nice."

"Yeah, me too. Cathartic. For some time, I felt like there was no one else to talk to. They tell me to move on. Easy for them."

"You don't just get over losing everything you worked for."

"Exactly," Dave said.

"So, we pick a restaurant on the expense account and grab a nice meal?"

"Sure, I'm in. Call me."

Chapter Three
Paradigm Shift

Ross grabbed a rental car first thing the next morning. Wonderful news. He had no hangover. He had arrived for his appointment in Irvine with a minimum of aggravation. The typical southern California traffic had cooperated without bumper-to-bumper mayhem.

Back in his airport hotel, Ross hustled through the lobby. He passed the queue of flight crews, business types, and vacationers all eager to check-in. His hotel status had him on the top floor concierge level, accessible by a special key. Munchies, wine, and beer were provided nightly at the Platinum Lounge. He had fond memories of his bartender, Marcelo, with whom he chatted in Spanish and who always took care of Mister Ross.

He inserted the key into the elevator that allowed him access to the upper floor, feeling again like an outlier.

A few doors down from the Platinum Lounge he spied Marcelo, always upbeat despite his hardscrabble existence.

Ross had no desire to engage with the business types and their lives of comfort. He wasn't in their world anymore. Marcelo's life, however, intrigued him.

He went to the room and dropped off his computer bag. He loosened his tie and headed to the lounge.

"Hola amigo."

"Mister Ross, ¿Cómo estas?"

The two shook hands and struck up a conversation while Ross piled chicken wings and meatballs on a plate.

"How's the family?" Ross asked.

Marcelo regaled him with how his spouse Maria had a new job in human resources for a rival hotel, using her bilingual skills to bridge the communication gap between maids with limited English and management. She managed this while shuffling her son to school in their gritty neighborhood, and she always made sure Marcelo arrived to a home-cooked meal.

Ross couldn't decide between the cold beer and the bottle of Merlot. He needed both. He put the two drinks and his plate on the small table and fetched another plate of veggies and dip. So few things in his life were free. He took advantage.

As he fumbled in his pocket for a few bucks to tip his amigo, he ran across the business card of his new friend. David P. Morrison, Sales Director with some handwritten scribble on the back about the hotel in Century City. The memory made him smile. How odd it was to find someone in similar circumstances knocked down a few pegs by a brutal divorce, living well on the road but drowning when on his own dime.

More than a day had gone by, and Ross felt timid about calling. Did their bond wear off with the booze? Ross's social skills were rusty. Was their chance meeting even memorable? His insecurities were playing tricks again.

Dave could be a much-needed confidant. Ross's friends listened, but most of them disliked Stephanie from the get-go and now freely admitted it. Their advice was to move on. Easy to say. Hard to do. A friend who really understood his situation was hard to find.

Ross dialed the cell number listed on the card.

"Dave Morrison speaking."

Ross explained that he was the guy on the plane and enjoyed their conversation and had gotten back early from Orange County. The split second of silence seemed like an eternity, while Ross desperately waited for Dave to speak.

"How could I forget? Hi, Ross, I was thinking about calling you. I'm not good at these things, and I was looking for your card. I couldn't find it. I was freaking out and thought of going to the Crowne Plaza to find you. I was afraid we'd never connect. It's been a while since I found anyone willing to listen who wasn't charging me by the hour."

They exchanged small talk about how their trips had been going, and Ross felt comfortable to suggest a get-together. "Are you up for dinner tonight? I could use the diversion. I can invent a few names for the expense report and use corporate plastic."

"I'm in. I'll make up a few names myself. We'll split the tab and order a feast. I know an impressive steak house and cigar lounge nearby."

Dave's steak place was near Wilshire. The joint reeked of testosterone. Dark wood paneling adorned the Wilshire Chop House, known for its huge portions of aged Kobe beef. Finding a place that even allowed smoking inside was difficult in California, but Dave knew of a cigar bar off Santa Monica a few blocks away.

If the 405 was cooperative, he could swig the last of his red wine that Marcelo refilled without prompting and be on his way for the seven-thirty reservation. Oddly, he needed the male bonding more than that of a female, but a gorgeous flight attendant glanced at him from a few tables away. She was so attractive he thought of ditching Dave.

"Take a picture, it'll last longer," she coyly said as she busted Ross for staring at her. He couldn't help it. She looked perfectly coiffed and dressed in her attendant uniform.

"Australia or New Zealand? I have trouble telling the difference. Either way, very endearing."

"Australia. New Zealand accents are more like the baaaaaa sound of a sheep. I hope there are no Kiwis around. Ask what comes after five and someone from New Zealand will pronounce it as sex. That's the easiest way to tell."

Ross told her he too would be in for the balance of the week and could give her tips on where to explore. He asked if she would be back in the lounge tomorrow, and she said yes. Ross summoned the willpower to leave and have the valet fetch his car.

"Off to a business meeting, wish me luck." Ross said, hoping that the self-deprecation would leave an impression. She was quite the looker. Was she out of his league? Ross had the clean-shaven look of a successful executive unless she pulled a credit report. Six feet even, with a full but somewhat graying head of hair, deep blue eyes, expressive smile, and a body that looked as if it was athletic twenty-five pounds ago. If he could keep his self-esteem above sea level, his divorce problems three thousand miles away, and be reasonably witty, maybe he had a shot.

Back at the bar, he beckoned Marcelo. "Marcelo, here is ten bucks. Call me if the Australian woman is here tomorrow. This is my cell number. You do that, and I'll owe you big time. What do you drink? I'll get you a bottle of whatever you want."

"I can do you one better, boss. I'll let the restaurant, lounge, and reception downstairs know. I can get you her name from my amiga at the front desk. Booze won't be necessary, boss. Okay, maybe Jose Cuervo if you insist."

This Australian woman seemed so down to earth, even while drop-dead gorgeous. They seemed one of the few countries left that liked Americans. He was hoping to be that American.

Fifteen minutes on the 405 and Ross arrived at the

Wilshire Chop House. He flipped the rental car keys to the attendant. Valet parking lots were a pet peeve, an unneeded extravagance, and a rip-off, like designer coffee houses, but unavoidable in status-conscious Beverly Hills.

He envisioned film moguls talking financing and real estate tycoons talking deals with powerful attorneys. He sidled up to the bar and waited for his trauma-bonded brother. It was time for the hard stuff. "Crown and soda, with a twist."

No wine, no beer, and no candy-assed drinks with cute names or umbrellas. This was a man's territory. Ross shouldn't be holding anything less potent than whiskey when Dave arrived.

Dave arrived at eight on the dot. He looked crisp and polished. Ross let out an "Ah" as the drink hit the spot. "Hey, what's up? Want a drink? Scotch or something?"

"Sure, Johnny Red with a splash."

Just two divorced guys enjoying straight liquor with little more than a splash to dilute the taste. This was how real men rolled.

The attentive staff readied their table just as they finished their drinks. They followed a shapely hostess to their seats.

"So, how's the mediation deal?"

"It sucks balls. My attorney was there 'til three. Thought she could reason but didn't accomplish anything. Here is the fun part. I'm paying her under the interim agreement 'til something gets worked out. That's five grand a month, half my income, except I can't deduct a penny in alimony 'cause the tax laws have changed. Add a grand for child support and I'm looking at keeping less than thirty percent of my pay.

"I can try another mediation, but why would that work? My attorney said it's a trick. The rehabilitative alimony stops if she quits school if it's decided in court but can be non-modifiable in a side agreement like at a mediation. I can petition for divorce as soon as my twelve months are up, but it could be delayed if agreed to in mediation. Godzilla was trying to get me to agree to terms in mediation that wouldn't fly in court. I'd just be flushing another six grand down the shitter. So, looks like I'm heading to court. Twenty-five grand minimum with Godzilla the lawyer and Mussolini, my mother-in-law, pulling strings. Fuck my life."

"Sucks to be you dude. We're here. We got excellent food, good booze, forget all that. Let's have a few laughs."

The server interrupted Dave. Her tuxedo outfit did a poor job of hiding her curves. She had a Hollywood bleached smile to match her dyed-blonde hair and ruby red lipstick. She did a perfect reading off the day's specials involving various cuts of meat. Marbleized steaks aged in a special locker. While she had memorized the spiel at a staff meeting, she seemed to relish the role of an actress. Most wives would dissuade their husbands from ordering such gargantuan slabs of cholesterol, but here there were no wives to temper their behavior. Besides, her tip rested on the night's total.

Fuck the diet. What's the point in squeezing out a few more years of life by eating healthy if they will suck?

"I hope you're hungry and in the mood for some serious food. I only had time to grab a burger for lunch," Dave said.

Both of their stomachs were on Eastern time.

There was shrimp to start, a ridiculously fattening fried onion dish, a lettuce wedge with bacon crumbles and Scotch and Canadian whiskey.

"I've at least four names of business contacts to put on the expenses as guests... I may need more by the end of the night," Ross said.

"Not a problem dude, I've got six business cards from a client whose offices are down the street, as long as we keep this under six hundred, we can sneak it past the bean counters."

The food was exceptional, and the liquor was flowing.

It was a working dinner of the fraternity of screwed ex-husbands, and it produced some comedic moments. *Dave sure uses the word dude a lot.*

"Right now our exes are sleeping. If only they knew." Ross chuckled gleefully, as if he was pulling one over by enjoying a magnificent meal without having to give her seventy percent.

The table had five-hundred-dollars in food on it, with top-shelf wine and whiskey, as they talked about how broke they were. *First world problems.*

"What we need is a paradigm shift." Ross couldn't decide if his speech was slurred as he cut into his steak, bloody and a few degrees north of mooing. Naturally, he thought of Stephanie.

Stephanie was dating a guy twenty years her senior, as Becky predicted, assuming she would go for a fatherly type for security. Becky saw so many divorces she knew how things unfolded afterward. The arrangement gave Stephanie security and Henry got arm candy. It was a job that required little actual work, so she was game. Boost the ego of a sixty-something while draining his 401(k). She was self-conscious at the mere mention of his age, and it sent her into a tizzy. Ross had nicknamed him "Wilfred Brimley," after the aged spokesperson for things senior. Dave was smiling while chewing, saying dude for emphasis whenever Ross said something profound.

"Fuck, I'd like her to marry the guy, but he's been married just once, for six months. He's been single ever since. She'll overplay her hand and scare him back into the arms of someone closer to his age."

"Dude, my divorce will probably be complete when I get home. It's been a year. I have the standard cohabitation clause, if she lives with another guy, I'm off the hook. Why would she? She's independent; she has a career, family money, my alimony. She'll date for fun and will be on my payroll for ten long years. Dude, that's over half a million bucks. She doesn't need the money. It's about winning. She and her old man. Be thankful you aren't divorcing a lawyer," Dave said.

"Be thankful your ex's lawyer isn't Godzilla." The liquor was amplifying the comedic effect of each comment.

The conversation took a darker turn as the table next to theirs had a Tony Soprano look-alike with three associates direct out of mobster central casting.

"I bet those guys could solve our problem," Dave joked. "Did you ever see *The Sopranos*? I miss Tony. He got things done." Dave raised his fork and punched the air for emphasis. "Did you ever see *Strangers on a Train*? Get someone to murder for you, and you for them. Perfect alibis."

"You're fucking kidding, right? I'm not capable of that, besides I have a daughter. With my luck, I'd be on death row rooming with a well-hung cellmate who would make me his bitch, while my daughter languished in foster care."

"I'm joking. But there must be a way to solve this problem and get our lives back. Do you ever notice how it is with the wives getting revenge in movies and popular culture? A woman gets a poor settlement, and she's a hapless victim. A man gets a bad settlement and he's an idiot or had it coming."

"Men shouldn't be victims either. You hear about a woman driving over her husband or poisoning him, and they say she's crazy, but she always gets a pass. It was her hormones, or she was jealous."

"Being treated fairly is a two-way street. What about manipulative wives? What about the dad who gets to see his kids every other weekend while paying for everything? What about when the man gets a raw deal? We need to fix this."

"Okay genius, how are you going to do that?"

"Maybe I can plant drugs in her car and then get someone to drop a dime to the cops to pull her over."

Julie worked within a thousand yards of a school, and

Stephanie picked up Nicole at school most days, which made penalties for drug possession stiffer. How hard would it be to score a pound of weed, or an ounce of coke, and get a lowlife to stash it in the car? An anonymous caller witnessed a drug buy? The plan had its sound points, but it relied on too many variables. What would stop the accomplice from just stealing the drugs he was about to plant? What if the police didn't stop the vehicle? With Stephanie's self-centered narcissism, she'd blame Nicole. And if Ross got caught planting or buying the drugs or bought them from an informant or during a sting, it was a felony. Stupid idea.

"As bad as she is, I don't want my daughter's mother in jail. If she blamed Nicole, I'd never forgive myself." Ross shook his head.

"So, we wait for them to get married? Part of me wants to take her boyfriend aside and tell him how stupid he is, but another part of me wants to urge him to marry her. Maybe even write him a check to sweeten the deal and another one when they move in together."

Ross's imagination was on a roll. If he could only get the guy in a one-on-one setting and have a heart-to-heart talk with him. Maybe he could convince him her parents were rich spendthrifts. Her parents lived frugally and were such bumpkins though, it was a stretch to paint them as eccentric millionaires.

Ross sighed heavily. The weight on his shoulders was crushing. It was a fun evening and diversion from the pain, but facts were facts. They were check-mated. Doomed to scratch and claw their way to a mediocre existence slightly less shitty.

"You said it before, dude."

"What?"

"Paradigm shift. *Strangers on a Train*. They don't have to marry. Just live together for a month. That constitutes cohabitation. You tell me what to say to woo her. I'll steal her from Wilfred Brimley, and I'll coach you on seducing Julie."

Ross choked on his steak. It was a combination of laughter, and the subsequent realization the plan had merit. Dave looked deadly serious.

Who better to coach someone on how to win the heart of a woman than someone who had two decades of inside information and a vested interest in getting her off the payroll? It seemed so damn logical.

Favorite song, favorite vacation, favorite color, favorite pizza topping, favorite movie, favorite everything. What do they like? What do they hate? With planning and ingenuity, it's a way out. Ross would save five grand a month. At least that's how things were when he split from the mediation. Over the life of the divorce, half a million, like Dave.

For all her bravado, Stephanie couldn't survive without a man. Her mother told her so almost daily. And the photo that Dave showed him of Julie looked hot. Perhaps when the effects of top-shelf liquor wore off the flaws in the plan would seem obvious, but from Ross's current vantage point, it was brilliant.

Now the booze was slurring his speech. Ross was using dude for emphasis in every sentence, just like Dave. "Fuck, you are a genius, dude. I may not be sober, but I'll give you the roadmap you need. We'll get that fossilized fuck out of the picture in no time. She's paranoid, to begin with. All we have to do is convince her he's cheating on her. She's so incapable of being alone that she'll be all over you like a nasty case of poison ivy. Move-in and move out a month later. Stephanie is easy, but Julie? She seems more complicated. How do I pull that off?"

"Ross, listen. Think about it. That chick has a million things about her that make her unique. You know all one million in advance that makes you a one in a million guy. Study and prepare like it was your biggest presentation, but if you can click with her, it's a high percentage shot. She's multifaceted? Her facets are an advantage. Your foreknowledge will seem like the hand of God himself is screaming for her to sleep with you. Just don't fake any orgasms and watch "My Cousin Vinny" on Netflix afterward like last time."

"What's next? I'm ready to start."

"Let's swap pics of our exes. We need to know what we're getting into, or at least trying to get into."

Both swiped at their phones searching for some representative photo of their formerly intact family. Julie had a cute face, petite but curvy figure. Stephanie was a tad taller, and trim. While her smile looked a bit forced, and her figure a bit boyish, she was reasonably attractive. Both men nodded a presumptuous nod as if to say *if push came to shove, I could go through with this.* They could and would sleep with the other's ex if duty called.

This plan was still a long shot and in its infancy. The Scotch said otherwise.

"Get the check, and we head to the Cigar Lounge to sketch this out."

The meal ended with a strong coffee and a brisk walk to the cigar bar. Ross was in no position to drive and needed an hour of club sodas to even approach sobriety.

He wanted to flush out this novel idea with a clear head. Kick the tires on it, ask questions. There was a Vons on the way to the cigar bar. They could buy a few legal pads and make notes.

They would note ground rules, timelines, and code words like a military operation. The devil was in the details. The scheme involved outwitting the most complicated and oft-misunderstood entity in the universe—The Female Mind. Careful planning and tons of inside information could crack the codes to win financial freedom.

Finally, they were changing the paradigm and being proactive.

Ross felt his mind racing as he crossed the first of three crosswalks on the beautiful Southern California night, cool with no humidity and not a soul on the streets.

The cigar club had an obligatory twenty-dollar membership to get around the smoking ordinance. Its interior had rich paneled walls and a collection of books, leather high-back chairs, and oil paintings behind a mahogany bar. Cigar girls dressed like 1920s flappers. Each went through a well-rehearsed ritual as they hawked cigars of various brands. They clipped the cigar and then put it in their mouth, puffing and blowing an O-ring before handing the lipstick-stained cigar back to the patron. Freud would have a field day.

"How did you find this place?" Ross asked.

"A client told me about it. Closed an enormous deal over Macanudos and brandy."

"Brandy the drink, or Brandy our waitress?" Ross laughed aloud.

Dave ordered another Scotch. Ross needed to clear his head. He realized that this was a watershed moment. Vetting with a clear head would be essential. He needed to assess the plan's chances of success.

"Okay, let's shake on this idea. We will explore, share intelligence, and poke holes. We'll try to think of everything we can. We make up ground rules and timelines and agree to give it our best shot. If only one of us is successful, we tip our hat and move on. Agreed?"

Ross was in South Charlotte, Ballantyne, a twenty-year-old high-end suburb of Charlotte still within city limits, populated by transplants. Dave was on the other end of town, near Lake Norman, where everything revolved around lakeside activities. Both were pricey enclaves but on different ends of the city, with different restaurants, bars, and shopping malls. Each was a dozen miles from Uptown. Social circles rarely intersected as the two locales were affluent bookends of the same metropolitan area.

"My ex is a nosy SOB. She bugged my computer, stole my cell phone bill. She's paranoid. If you are courting her the surest way to mess up the plan is to bed some bimbo you picked up online. She'll join every dating site with a fake name and spend hours of her pathetic, miserable day to bust you." Ross made sure Dave knew exactly what he was signing up for.

"Julie's no dummy either. We'd better make sure we remain faithful to our targets until move-out day." Dave was lapping up the conversation, writing the bullet points furiously on his pad. The rules part of the conversation flowed smoothly. Like the whiskey at the restaurant. Dave recorded each of the agreed-upon rules on his legal pad for posterity.

"Dave, after living in a sexless and lame marriage I've missed out. I've earned a few mulligans. As much as I enjoyed our get together, there was a Qantas stewardess I met at the hotel. I need a window of time to sow wild oats. Just a month or two. This project could take a year."

"Ross, it will take at least a month to study our prey. We chase skirts, sew our wild oats, and start fresh afterward. No falling in love during the period, recreational sex only, with no serious relationships. Agreed?"

They puffed cigars with satiated bellies. This was getting good. A good night's rest would determine whether the notes were brilliant or the disjointed ramblings of wistful middle-aged men, longing for a former life.

The two parted company. Dave walked the five, or six blocks back to his hotel. Ross went in the opposite direction to fetch his car. He momentarily forgot the make and model of the rental, then remembered how he fumbled to fit his luggage in the compact trunk of his Mustang convertible. He wanted to test that big Ford V6 on an open stretch of US1 along the Pacific Coast Highway. A scenic drive along the ocean would clear his head.

Ross fumbled for the claim check. Dave's card popped out. He grinned. The duo would take on the system that wronged them and no longer feel emasculated.

The Mustang roared as it made its way from the garage. Ross looked forward to the drive. It was after midnight, and traffic was minimal. He felt sober, perhaps not legally so, but enough to shoot down Wilshire to the highway and the safety of his hotel room. In thirty minutes, he'd be in bed contemplating the night's events and would awaken with a sense of purpose.

He wanted to see Dave's legal pad with the benefit of a good night's sleep. Finally, Ross regained a whiff of confidence and didn't feel alone. He recalled the Qantas attendant and wanted her. She was here for three days, then back to the other side of the globe. They would have an ocean between them, a three-day whirlwind with no future. He wanted to lie down next to her, to start his funfest now.

A few more exits to the Sepulveda turn off, then on to Century and the hotel garage. He reeked of cigars and booze. The faint taste of steak was in his mouth. It was the middle of the night, Eastern Time. Ross's body begged for rest. The lobby was abuzz from a large flight arriving from the Orient. A cacophony of languages he couldn't discern filled the air.

He headed to the elevator and inserted the key to go to his special floor and entered his room. He flicked the light, unwrapping the chocolate on his pillow, while admiring the swanlike figure of washcloths adorning his bed. He had to get up at six to make sure that things were under control on the East Coast but had time 'til his 11 a.m. appointment in Glendale.

At 5 a.m., the phone rang. Ross couldn't locate his mobile device. Fumbling, he could grab only an alarm clock and a lamp. His cell was in his pants pocket, slung over the chair on the workstation across the room. Who would call at this hour?

He got the phone on the fourth ring.

"Dude, it's me, Dave."

"What's up?" he asked in a baritone voice that conveyed the partying done until just hours before.

"Last night wasn't some kind of joke? It's real, right? I woke up and needed to see what I had written. I'm obsessed. I had to call to just see if you were still in one-hundred percent."

"I'm a hundred percent in Dave. It's early, and my head is pounding, but definitely in. Amazingly, I feel hope."

"Last night I tried to sleep, but I went downstairs to the business center. Thought I'd be there for maybe five minutes. For hours I couldn't stop. I have the cheat codes, the road map you need. You follow it and I'm off the hook."

"Cheat codes?"

"Did you ever play video games? It's the way to get to the next level of a video game. The playbook. With all this stuff, I know we can waltz into their lives and sweep them off their feet. I made a list of favorite stuff, inside jokes, and a list of pet peeves. I was up to one hundred eighty-seven things at 4 a.m. when I quit. I was waiting 'til morning to call you but couldn't wait any longer."

"Buddy, go back to sleep. I'm in."

"Cool, talk to you later. Sorry to wake you."

Ross couldn't help but get caught up in Dave's enthusiasm. He was tired and his mouth had a film the consistency of paste. Ross jumped in the shower and made his mental list. The Plan passed the sobriety test and was coherent in the morning light. It was all systems go.

Chapter Four
Wonder From Down Under

Ross's cell vibrated. A two-one-three area code, LA's original. Surely, this was work bullshit. Either it's a client needing something ASAP or a future meeting with complications. It demanded that Ross violate the California ordinance on talking on a hand-held device while driving. Just one exit short of his airport hotel, he answered.

"Meester Ross, Meester Ross! Rosalia called me from downstairs. The Australian lady from the airline just sat down to eat. Rosalia is holding the table next to her. You ask for her and she'll seat you there."

"Marcelo, you devious bastard, I had no clue it was you. I forgot you have my cell number. Thanks for having my back."

With all that had transpired since Ross left the Platinum Lounge, he had almost forgotten entrusting Marcelo with his cell number. He may have forgotten his exchange with Marcelo, but the easy-on-the-eyes Aussie with the flaxen hair and exotic accent was unforgettable.

Their brief banter had gone well, and yet it was Ross who pulled the plug to meet with Dave for their dinner. Their plan-in-progress gave Ross a spring in his step. He wasn't the beaten pound dog that boarded the plane for LA a few days ago.

"I'm maybe five minutes from the hotel. I'll park and go right to the restaurant. You thank Rosalia and tell her I'll sit down to eat in a few. Don't give up that table. How'd she look?"

"Meester Ross, tan bonita. She's a nice lady. We talk after you leave. I told her you are always kind, a good person. Funny guy. She ask about you."

"Don't mess with me. Really, what did she say?"

"She says she always deals with executives in first class. She knows how to read people and you are fair dinkum. She teaches me Australian words. It means you are a real person. Not plastico. She could tell. I tell her we're friends. Boss, she's funny. Don you worry. I said all good thins about you. She very beautiful."

"I owe you big time. It's 5:15. Maybe we stop by after dinner. I thought you were a pain-in-the-ass client and almost didn't answer. My luck's changing Marcelo, and it's due to you. I promise I won't forget you."

"No te preocupes, Meester Ross. We homies. Marcelo always takes care of Meester Ross."

Ross pulled into the lot and took his ticket. Things were changing, he could feel it. As if by divine intervention a primo spot opened near the entrance to the garage, a quick hop to the lobby, while the Beatles "Here Comes the Sun" played on the radio.

He popped a breath mint for good luck and locked the door to the Mustang. He had his laptop bag slung around his shoulder, and removed it to put on his jacket, making him look more like the executives Ms. Qantas might encounter on a twenty-hour flight. He combed his hair for good measure.

Rosalia asked if he was dining. He said yes, and that Marcelo had instructed him to ask for her. He winked.

"Oh, Señor Ross, I have a fantastic table for you. Marcelo tells me to take good care of you." In coquettish fashion, she winked back.

Ross followed the petite hostess as she sashayed to the corner of the restaurant.

"Will this be satisfactory?"

"Yes, Rosalia, it's perfect. You've been an angel."

"My pleasure. You're, after all, one of our most esteemed guests."

Ross reached into his pants pocket and pulled out a bill. It was a five, but he would have given her a c-note rather than fish for another.

The Aussie grinned at him from one side of the booth, "Hey, you're the bloke running off to a meeting. Your friend Marcelo was telling me about you. Do you know everyone in the hotel here? You're like the mayor of this place."

"Coming from someone that takes care of first-class travelers, I'm very flattered you would say that."

"Some can be a gigantic pain in the ass, to be candid. I love my job. I'm dining alone. Your friend told me lots about you."

"Oh, Marcelo's a wonderful guy. He always takes care of me. We talk. I think he appreciates my attempts at Spanish and taking an interest in his life, but he has a good heart. Seeing a familiar face on the road takes some edge off. So much of travel is solo or business meetings where you are playing a role."

"I just ordered. Care to join me? You can put our tables together if you like."

Marcelo had already earned his tequila.

"I'm Victoria. Vicky to my friends. How'd your meeting go?"

"Ross. The meeting? You wouldn't believe it if I told you. Life-changing. An amazing exchange of ideas. Ever have one of those?"

"Yes, when I say ba-bye to an obnoxious passenger. Now I'm intrigued."

"Ever met someone in similar circumstances when you had been walking around thinking I'm the only one going through this? One thing when jetting around for work, and another when you get back to reality."

"I can relate, mate. Tokyo, London, Paris, Seoul, Bangkok, New York, Fiji, all in a month. Sounds impressive, right? Great hotels, varied tuckers, amazing sights. Love it—but the average bloke in the forward cabin plunks down more for his round trip than I make in a fortnight. The last thing he wants to hear is that a Qantas hostie is dealing with her bludger of a partner back home who's out on the tiles dipping his wick while she's away. And they think being on your feet for sixteen hours serving brekky and booze to the Figjams in the forward cabin is a piece of cake when it's exhausting. I get back home, slip into tracky-daks, and I'm down to Aldi buying meat that's on special 'cos its use-by date's up. Like that?"

"I think I got the gist if you meant the dichotomy of living on the road. Like you appear to have a problem-free life and return home to an idyllic situation. As for the Aussie lingo, anything past G'day, and shrimp on the barbie, will require an explanation."

"We call them prawns, not shrimp. That was for the movie so you septics would understand," she said.

"Septic? That's a new one," Ross said.

"Comes from septic tanks, which rhymes with Yanks."

"I thought you liked Americans," Ross said.

"That depends on how the rest of our conversation goes," she said.

Ross couldn't believe his ears, but that sounded flirtatious.

"So, this person you met, who is in similar circumstances, was a chick, a woman?" Vicky asked.

"God, no. A guy I sat next to on the plane. We are

going through some similar woes."

"You want to know what your friend Marcelo told me? He said in a room full of tall poppies, you're always taking the time to talk to him. I deal with a lot of Figjams in my job and…"

"Excuse me, but what the hell is a Figjam? You've said it twice."

"Fuck-I'm-Good-Just-Ask-Me. It's Aussie slang. Tall poppy is someone who thinks they're above everyone else."

"I've got to visit Australia one of these days. There seems a real aversion to people too full of themselves."

"Consider yourself invited. Says you are going through some stuff but are fair dinkum. That's a genuine guy. I like that. A girl traveling by herself meets a lot of weirdos, and I've got to be cautious. You seem easy to talk to."

Ross smiled. "I guess being humbled can do that. Long story. Crazy divorce, being there for my daughter. Just sorting stuff out," Ross said before hesitating. He knew talking about divorce wasn't a great prelude to getting laid.

"Well, that's a healthy attitude."

The two visited the lounge to continue their conversation.

Victoria was a senior flight attendant with almost twenty years of experience with Qantas starting right after completing her degree. Her magnetic personality and quick wit made her a favorite with the airline execs, and she served on some advisory board. She was attractive, polished, and no shrinking violet.

During dinner, Vicky confided that she, too, had been going through some turbulence of late. Not the thirty thousand feet kind, but with her on-again-off-again ex. Reginald, rugged jack-of-all-trades, had developed an increased reliance on alcohol, which morphed into a few violent outbursts.

Confiding to the Flight crews she traveled with was a "no-go." It might screw up her job and having her work schedule reduced was the last thing she needed. There was an element of embarrassment with friends and family as she was the jet-setting, glamorous Victoria visiting more continents in a month than most see in a lifetime. Marcelo's words about Ross had her thinking he might be the empathetic stranger with whom she could offload some of this crushing private burden. She too could be an attentive ear for the problems Marcelo hinted Ross was dealing with.

Ross's misfortune would soon be his greatest asset. His Dad once told him 'don't look down or up to anyone' and 'it costs you nothing to be kind. You never know where it'll lead.' Ross shared his tale of woe but also listened to Marcelo about his kids having to navigate gang-infested streets on their way to school. It moved him. Most customers just wanted their Merlot and cheese cubes and were more curious if they would serve those little quiche things than how some Hispanic in a starched uniform was doing. It seemed to hit a responsive chord with Victoria.

Taking the elevator to the Platinum Lounge, the two were not alone. Victoria looked at Ross while a few European tourists stared at the buttons.

Traveling seemed a blessing to Victoria, now, but extended time among strangers was not without costs. It was doubly hard on a woman, particularly an attractive one. Unbeknownst to Victoria, Marcelo had a bottle of tequila riding on a successful introduction. He spoke of his friend Ross and would have done so without prodding or the offer of Patron. He was interested in two friendly people feeling less lonely thousands of miles from home.

"I'm so happy you two saw one another and are here. My two friends, what can I get you?" He asked, while giving them both firm handshakes.

"We ate downstairs but thought we would say hi, or should I say g'day?"

"I know. She teaches me Australian slang too, boss."

Ross gave Marcelo one of those knowing glances, which said there was Patron in his future.

They found a table in the far corner of the lounge near

a table of some loud execs from a healthcare company.

Victoria shot Ross a glance and in a hushed whisper said, "Loudmouths like that make up the two percent of passengers that make my job difficult."

"I have to present insurance proposals to CFO's," Ross said. "Most are nice, but some have bean-counters humanity while intoxicated with an inflated opinion of their own importance. You know, a Figjam."

Vicky laughed. "You're an Aussie now. Welcome, mate."

Her smile melted him, an enormous radiant smile that projected an aura of inner beauty. If she was a ten before, she was now an eleven.

A sympathetic listener was worth big points to Victoria. Marcelo was right; Ross was "as advertised." They talked and drank wine, imbuing one another with the "halo effect," looking for angelic qualities rather than flaws. Both were yearning for an attentive ear after dysfunctional judgmental and critical relationships. The chemistry was not stationary. It depended on context and timing.

Ross realized that Dave's statement the night before had a kernel of truth. A cornucopia of coincidences and inside information on a potential partner's mindset was powerful.

There was nothing manufactured about what Ross was feeling. Vicky was an attractive woman, a catch under any circumstances. She was also responding in a way that delighted him. Whatever Marcelo said worked, and now with his foot in the door and her coquettish giggles, he tapped into dormant feelings. He didn't just want to bed her, he wanted them to comfort one another. He wanted to feel a soulful embrace that tells you, "It's okay now; the worst is over," and in some intuitive way, he could sense she wanted that too.

Vicky excused herself to use the restroom, and Ross walked up to the bar to refresh both glasses.

"You both nice people," Marcelo said. "Boss, she's

going through tough times. She needs a friend like you. I tell her you too tienes cosas duro en tu vida."

When speaking from the heart Marcelo reverted to Spanish, or at least Spanglish, something Ross figured he would never do with the Figjams.

Days earlier Ross had been sweating bullets, as the mediation turned nuclear. Some cosmic force had shifted.

Vicky returned to the table.

"So, before I left the other night, I promised I'd give you some ideas on where to go exploring. LA is a city with several places within striking distance. It's not blessed with a stunning skyline like Sydney or Hong Kong, but the beauty within a few hours rivals even yours," Ross said.

"Ross, that's so sweet. Was that the wine talking? Are you a closet Figjam? A root rat?"

"Root rat?"

"I believe you call them horn dogs," she said.

"Guilty as charged. I mean, I'm not a cad if that's what you mean. But having separated after a lengthy loveless marriage, I hope to have a partner who isn't counting the tiles on the ceiling during sex, ya' know? After we had our first child, my ex said 'this is excruciatingly painful. I feel sick to my stomach and never want to go through such a nauseating and disgusting experience again'. That was just during conception."

"My God. You're a bloody comedian. A lot of men don't realize that humor will get a lot more knickers on the floor than big-noting yourself. You already knew that."

"Victoria, I'm new at this. I guess I can be funny, but it's a defense mechanism. Just trying to get back out there, a little at a time. I've had a lot on my plate. I have a lot of self-discovery left to do. It's not the life I was living earlier. I've been knocked down a few pegs, but in some respects that life was a lie." Ross furrowed his brow. He was getting deep. "Pared down expectations or not, I'd rather be true to myself. Here I'm sitting next to you. This is the part where a guy tells you how they have life by the balls, and I'm laying it out there that I don't have my shit together."

"Can I confess something? The first-class cabin, the travel, has been an escape mechanism. People see me and they think it's a life of glamour, but…"

Vicky sighed as if she was hesitant about revealing more.

She gulped her wine. "I got an ex off the chains, drinking out of control. A neighbor saw him casing my house, and he probably ripped me off. I haven't been lucky in love. I went for a rugged, handsome bugger, and he turned out to be a fuckin' nightmare. Right now, I need someone to talk to." Her hand trembled as she held her wine glass.

"I read people for a living. You've puppy dog eyes and something that tells me you've had a little rain in your life. I don't need a boyfriend. What I need is a friend," Vicky said.

Ross grasped her outstretched hands. She was having a hard time.

"If I told Dad my shit, he'd either have a heart attack or track Reginald down with a cricket bat. I'm ashamed to tell you the truth. Who was that footballer from California, OJ something? I look a little like his ex-wife, and I saw a pic of her with bruises and I could barely compose myself for work. I cried for a solid hour looking at her pics. Those two were separated. Was I looking at my future?"

"Victoria. I'm here for you okay? I've needed a friend for a while. Hey, I have an idea. Let's drive up the coast. We can make a day at a winery in Santa Barbara and then walk around the town at night. It's gorgeous. I've got a Mustang convertible. The coastal drive is awesome. We can clear our heads. Talk on the way. I feel like we communicate better than I did in twenty years of marriage. We live too far away to allow for complications, but with emails and cell phones we can be awesome friends no matter where we are. We can be each other's get-shit-together life coach."

"To friendship, my new mate."

"To my amazing Aussie friend." They clinked glasses. She swallowed and gave Ross a closed-mouth grin, both joyful and sad.

"Well, this is fuckin' awkward, knowing we both have hotel rooms a few yards away, wouldn't you say? Boy, did that come out wrong? I mean, I don't. I can't. People think flight attendants and assume we jump into bed with anyone, anywhere. The stuff I'm going through. I don't think I'm ready to…"

"Shh. It's okay. No pressure. Give me an enormous hug and let me drink in some of that perfume you're wearing and gimme a smile. You have the most beautiful smile and eyes I've ever seen. We can go to our rooms and talk on the phone like teenagers. We can tell each other everything. We will wake up tomorrow early and have a glorious day."

"We'll look ridiculous giving an over-the-top hug here, won't we? Let's walk around the lobby and find an alcove or meeting room for a proper hug." Vicky sniffled and dabbed her eyes. "Damn allergies."

The two went hand in hand and took the elevator to the second floor. They found a vacant meeting room and had the most emotional embrace, deep eye contact, and a "From Here to Eternity" kiss. It was obvious Ross's Down Under was enjoying the proceedings and would need a time-out before entering the lobby.

"I promise you, love, I'll make you happy in that way soon. Now, I need to talk. We go back to our rooms. Talk on the phone like teens. I'm looking forward to getting to know you, Ross."

"This has been the weirdest and most exhilarating few days of my life. There aren't even words for it. My attorney said my luck would change. Boy, was she right."

They walked through the lobby, inserted their cards into the elevator, and realized they were mere yards from one another. Ross thought about how easy it would be to jump into a room together and hump like rabbits. But it would detract rather than add to what they were hoping to do.

At their respective rooms, Vicky gave a demure wave. Once inside Ross pictured Dave chiding him for being the dumbest guy in the history of horny post-divorce men and against everything they stood for in some soliloquy that began with "Dude, what were you thinking?"

Despite decades of deprivation, something was satisfying in being gentlemanly. If all went as planned, in twenty-four hours he might have the emotional, physical, and sexual bonding that would make it into his internal highlight reels.

Vicky flicked off her high heels and plunked herself on the bed. Within an instant, the phone rang.

"Hi, stranger," Ross said.

"Are you that pervert that sat next to me in the restaurant?"

"Afraid so. Is this the part where I'm supposed to breathe heavy?"

"No, that's tomorrow night."

"So, what's going on, Victoria. Tell me about all this stuff you are going through. What kind of idiot can't appreciate his good fortune to have you in his life?"

And so it began—a solid two-and-a-half-hour conversation about their life, their hopes, dreams, disappointments, and regrets with no pretense or hesitation. Ross even mentioned the content of his meeting with Dave, the chance meeting in first class, and The Plan. He thought it risky, but she thought it clever and urged him to think of how to best neutralize Reginald. They reluctantly hung up the phone after bidding each other goodnight. It was 1:47 a.m., according to the clock radio on the nightstand.

Ross went to the bathroom to brush his teeth. His erection throbbed, and he was debating how to deal with it when the phone rang.

"Room 1635. Give me a few minutes to get myself ready and I'll be waiting. But promise me you'll hold me close all night long."

Ross was elated, surprised, and nervous as hell but not nervous enough to bail on the proposition of a lifetime. "Sweet Victoria. I'll be over in ten minutes."

Time for a quick shower, some cologne. What to do about Little Ross? He was at attention and would stay in the fully locked and upright position until landing. He was out of practice but would have to take his chances.

"Vicky?"

"Yes?"

"So, I guess it's true what they say about hosties, you know, being easy."

"Get over here asshole before I change my mind, and you'll spend the rest of your life thinking of me and kicking yourself."

"Be right over."

He knocked on the door. She had on a sheer blue nightgown. It was classy but not something one would use to greet room service. They quickly embraced, but she asked him to hold on a second and went to the dresser to take off the strand of pearls she was wearing, and to brush her hair. She leaned forward, cleavage overflowing her nightgown while looking in the mirror. Ross thought if he lived to one hundred, he wanted to remember that exact moment. He had never seen such beauty. This was the intimacy he'd craved in his marriage.

Ross didn't want to think about her being a few days away from the other side of the globe. This was tonight. She loosened the spaghetti straps from her shoulders and let the loose-fitting gown fall to her feet, shimmying ever so slightly as it caught first her breasts and then ample hips. Ross helped slide her sheer panties down her legs. Victoria was magnificently naked.

He fumbled to undo his pants and belt, trying to kick off his sneakers in a coordinated manner but not quite pulling it off. They kissed, and then with a coquettish glance she patted the bed inviting him to sit down.

"Just hold me for a while and look in my eyes. Okay? We have all night. We have talked so much. I just want to feel your closeness. It's been a while."

The two now faced each other, stroking each other's hair, touching cheeks, eyes locked. His hands roved up and down her back as they embraced, lingering on her soft buttocks, feeling her breasts pressed against his chest.

After what seemed like a half-hour of just smiling and gentle touching, Vicky said, "I want you. Make love like it's our last night on earth."

How was this even possible? The eye contact and extended embrace made nonverbal sexual communication reach a higher plane. She prodded and guided him on what she wanted, where and how to touch and lick and caress with little more than gentle moans. She guided his hands and face by the movements of her hips and a quivering of her legs. He thought about uttering a Down Under reference when she guided his head to where she wanted him but didn't want to spoil the moment.

The foreplay must have lasted another half hour before she patted the pillow, signaling he lay back for her to straddle him. She climbed on top slowly, guiding him inside her before stopping to savor the momentous instant of their bodies merging. There was a slow rhythm at first, and then faster, with momentary interludes to savor the intensity. He sensed the movements and pressing of her pelvis against his. She was close to climax and nearing a finish. Their moans became louder.

"I'm almost there. Come with me, yes, yes, that's it. Oh God, yes!"

Ross and Vicky were just two quivering bodies, holding one another. She dismounted, and the two lay on their backs, holding hands and telling one another how amazing it was. There is sex and there is making love and sometimes if you are lucky, a third category that has no words.

The two fell asleep, legs intertwined while holding hands and grinning. It was past five.

Vicky threw the drapes open when the wake-up call came at eight, proclaimed what a beautiful day it was, and invited Ross to shower with her. Sliding his hands on her soapy curves while the water cascaded over the two of them was a great start to the day.

Ross scooted to his room and rendezvoused with her at the lounge for breakfast ten minutes later. Life was grand as he put the top down on his Ford Pony. They would face traffic getting to the Pacific Coast Highway. Ross was impervious to annoyances. They soon were passing Malibu and Ventura on their way to Santa Barbara. Ross had Googled two vineyards in Lompoc. The two had a glorious afternoon walking the properties of Arcadian and Bridlewood, putting a distance between them and their troubled romances. They ate seafood on the pier in Santa Barbara after meandering around town, stopping at the galleries that dotted Anapamu and Anacapa streets.

Ross suggested that when back at their hotel, Vicky could get in her airline garb and pretend he was a first-class passenger who wanted to join the mile-high club. She admired his creativity and promised to comply.

He had juggled his Thursday appointment to Friday and had a full day, with little chance of making adjustments. He would be back from Redlands perhaps at 10 p.m. and she had to be out the door at 5 a.m. with her crew. She gave him an extra key and told Ross she'd be in bed naked waiting but wanted him not to get up when she woke so they wouldn't have to say goodbye. They promised emails and weekly calls and to be as good at being long-distance friends on opposite sides of the planet as they were as forty-eight-hour lovers. Ross feared he would never replicate the feeling. Vicky held a different opinion and wrote as much on the note she left on the nightstand.

"I think we have proven that we can have loving feelings despite licking our wounds from the past. We can help one another, you and me, on this journey. I want you to always be in my life. I'll cheer you on to find love and hope you'll do the same. I'll never forget this as long as I live."

Chapter Five
Rules of Engagement

Dave proved more organized and paranoid than Ross regarding the plan. They devoted a day to consider each excruciating detail. Comparing travel schedules, Richmond seemed most convenient. Both had clients there, and it was a five-hour trip. They juggled their calendars and decided on the weekend before July 4th. Travelers getting an early jump on the holiday would leave hotels mostly vacant. Ross used points for a Crowne Plaza, and Dave booked the Embassy Suites. Both were within an easy walk to Shockoe Slip, an historic cobblestone area that had the city's best restaurants.

The Tobacco Company was Richmond's signature restaurant. It would be a perfect place to get a buzz on and hammer out the details of their devious partnership.

A former tobacco warehouse, they remodeled the Tobacco Company with exposed brick, brass, and a turn of the century décor. It had private booths for dining. The

Palimony

downstairs had a bar, with free hors d'oeuvres, and roaming cigar girls. They wore all black, were attractive, and a major draw for patrons. After their LA meeting, the cigar angle seemed perfect. Stick with what works. Ross joked that a former president, notorious for his sexual exploits while in office, probably visited before his dalliance with his infamous paramour.

The downstairs filled with urban professionals getting off work and a smattering of coeds from the nearby University of Richmond and VCU. A guitar player crooned mellow, soft rock tunes from the 70s and 80s, as diners waited to take the antique elevator up to their floors and waiting tables. Victorian decor abounded on the lower level.

Ross imagined a scene a hundred and fifty years earlier with railroad barons, war profiteers, scallywags, and carpetbaggers all drinking whiskey. Card games with silver dollar chips raged and occasional gold pieces adorned card tables while saloon girls clamored for the players' attentions. The decor, garish red wallpaper blended with exposed brick and the exquisite wooden stairs, exuded the ambiance of an elegant bordello from the mid-1800s with cavalry officers and colonels asking ladies in hoop skirts for a twirl as fiddlers and an upright piano provided musical accompaniment.

Dave booked a private booth. The two brought portfolios with notes: likes, dislikes, and pet peeves along with ideas on how to first meet. Theirs was a different reconstruction after a brutal civil war, a war between spouses, now being methodically plotted in the former Confederate capital. Hopefully, things would end better for them than they had for Jefferson Davis.

Dave had a stack of categorically sorted index cards. He handed Ross a disc that was password protected to download to a cloud account before destroying. Ross arrived with twenty pages in a spiral notebook and photocopies. It was voluminous, requiring transcription.

The two grabbed some free spread, sat down, and conversed.

The final plan was to devote six weeks to gathering intel, searching the exes' online footprint, and sewing wild oats.

"I'd love to get laid a few times before we go balls deep. It's been quite a while."

"Simple, go outside the geography. Go for enclaves surrounding Charlotte. Statesville, Gastonia, Monroe, places like that. Where there won't be anyone in common. Get a NASCAR loving redneck girl from Gastonia, a lady from Monroe. Go line dancing or bull riding or go to a Fish Camp for Chrissakes," Ross said.

"A what?" Dave asked.

"A fish camp is a place, near a stream or lake, where you used to take the fish you caught to the kitchen and they prepare it for you. It's a redneck thing. Those women aren't in our social circles."

"Ellie May Clampett types, Daisy Duke, women like that?"

"I took Nicole to one coming back from Girl Scout Camp and this attractive country girl yelled 'I dropped my fish plate. Damn!' I thought if I ever get free from my marital hell, I'd date someone just like the fish plate girl. She had a pair of tight jeans on and had gotten out of an abusive relationship worthy of Gerry Springer, but she and her friends were laughing and having such a good time. She had an adorable accent, and I pictured her being impressed with men having white-collar jobs, college degrees, wearing ties. I want to cross fishplate girls off my bucket list. Uncomplicated, not demanding, appreciative."

"Dude, you're out of your fucking mind. The average redneck girl can out-drink, out-shoot, and out-fuck you. Do her wrong and she'll shank your ass in a Wal-Mart Parking lot! If that doesn't kill you, one of her twenty-two cousins will run you down with a pickup and finish you with a thirty-aught-six."

"I'll take it under advisement. What's your unfulfilled fantasy fling?"

"Maybe a Mexican girl. Ever go to the flea market in Pineville? There are some hot Mexican women there. I'd love to date one for a few weeks. They're sweet, sexy, down to earth and low key. They're the polar opposite of my ex, Ms. Career ball breaker."

"Let me tell you something. Sexy? Yes, but you've been so out of practice she'll be leading you around by your dick in a week. They know how to work it. 'Oh, Latin women aren't the least bit jealous,' said no logical man ever. Watch a fucking soap opera on Univision. There's screaming and crying with drama the entire time. Good luck with that. Remember Dorena Sonnit? Do you know what her husband did wrong? Came too early."

"I need to get this out of my system. I've had time to think about my bucket list before settling down. Maybe I'll borrow some of your Zoloft Mr. My Cousin Vinny."

"We will need to clean the pipes. We stay out of our socio-economic strata or geography. No overlap. Leave a clean trail when you engage with the exes. Whether Fishplate or Flea Market, we better be careful. Break it off at the first sign of boiling rabbits."

"I'm going for low hanging fruit and low maintenance. We date in that pool and we won't be going broke on dinners, etc. Both of our exes will require us to take them to nice places. Four to six-week hall pass. Agreed?"

They summoned the cigar girl and had her clip two Partagas and light them.

"I think I want to add a cigar girl on my bucket list too."

"Dude, we meet once a month, coordinate schedules, and pick a city. We create dedicated email accounts using public computers. We buy burn phones where we leave messages and texts, hiding them when not in use."

"Think your ex is on a dating site? We use fake profiles to search for them. They call one Plenty of Fish.

I'm sure there are plenty of fishplates for you on it. I'm sure Julie isn't on any sites. She has been into martial arts of late. Weird, huh?"

"Mine is still dating that guy twenty years her senior. I can't see it lasting. We'll get them to break up first," said Ross as he stirred his drink.

The Scotches were kicking in. After she-crab soup and prime rib, it reduced the table to some coffee, a half-eaten key lime pie, and two legal portfolios filling with notes as they talked.

Dates would be in a neutral location, unlikely to run into neighbors. Noda, Plaza Midwood, The South End were artsy enclaves and were unlikely to have suburbanites from Ballantyne or Lake Norman. Day trips were also a good means of ensuring there would be no unwanted attention.

Dave seemed confident he would succeed with Stephanie. She was less challenging than Julie and vulnerable to compliments. From what he could tell, she appeared to be a self-absorbed wannabe sophisticate. She wasn't bad looking in the pictures but would need to be told she was a goddess. Ross called her high school friends, 'the Nattering Nabobs of Negativity,' and they would judge Dave at each step. Get past them and he was home free.

Ross wasn't as sure. While Stephanie hated to be uncoupled and single, Julie was more self-reliant. The Julie that Dave described was a tough cookie. She had taken up martial arts and for the last six months had been training like a banshee to channel her angst. She had a tough exterior and lofty standards.

"Dude, I don't know how to say this delicately. You're a wrinkled mess sometimes. Julie, her entire family, they dress impeccably. Even the hippie brother looks put-together fashion-wise. Kind of Trust Fund Hipster Chic. When you get back to Charlotte, go visit Revolve or Jillian's on East Boulevard. A lot of the high-end bankers and real estate developers put their custom suits there. My girl Marcia at Revolve or Tony at Jillian's will hook you up. When you approach Julie, look sharp. Trust me, it's important."

"I promise to clean up better," Ross said.

The two went to their separate hotels and digested the voluminous data. They had spent a good four hours and would meet again at Boychick's Deli in the Fan district for some breakfast. Dave logged on to his laptop, browsing through profiles in Match.com until finding what he was sure was Stephanie. She was highlighting her maternal skills and her love of travel, listing all the destinations Ross had taken her to, only to hear constant complaints of jet lag. To the trained eye, her profile gave subtle hints of bitterness. "No phony's, liars, or manipulators." Dave assumed that meant Ross. If Dave was unsuccessful in meeting her via the gym, Match.com would be Plan B.

Ross fired up his laptop and scanned Plenty of Fish for a fishplate. He was out of practice. There was no online dating when he last dated. Ross thought of the fishplate girls, flea market attendants, and what it would be like to bed one. He searched profiles while creating a mock profile for himself.

He spent ten minutes searching for Julie and felt confident she wasn't online. The easiest way to meet was to enroll at her dojo. He could spend a month getting in shape and use the time to chase Fishplates or Flea Market Mexicans, but he'd never find another Victoria.

The ubiquitous availability of online dating made Ross feel like a kid in a candy store. It was tailor-made to the societal shift towards limited attention spans. Ross had a way with words and writing gave him an excellent shot at roping in someone above his pay grade after completing his assignment with Dave. There were so many women looking for a partner.

He could tee up his eventual rendezvous with Julie while pursuing his Fishplate fantasy. A low maintenance NASCAR-loving fishplate woman would be a novice's way to reenter the dating world. The endless pics made him ebullient. He planned on three dates a week for the next month. With Julie a devotee of martial arts, he needed the time to get in shape. Hopefully getting shanked in a Walmart parking lot wouldn't interfere with his training.

The dating world wasn't like this when Ross was single. He might never have gotten hitched so soon after college. Instead, the outbreak of weddings among friends prompted him to tie the knot. Ross read several profiles. The atrocious grammar and level of bitterness on some profiles jumped off the page. It was easy to see who hated men. "Liars and manipulators stay away!" No thanks.

Ross tried to provide his formulaic assessment of the odds of success within a certain time. His inner risk manager was coming out. Poor grammar eliminated half the profiles and hostility eliminated others. Some were too far or too close. He didn't want gold diggers. What little gold there was would be needed for Julie. It would be hard replicating Vicky's flawless body. He already knew he got lucky right out of the chute and would spend a lifetime trying to recapture the feeling he had in LA. Regardless, Ross penned about a dozen snappy emails to potential dates. He finished for the night.

Chapter Six
Bye Bye Wilfred

Dave's notes on Julie were voluminous: index cards classified by dining preferences, musical tastes, clothing, hobbies, etc. Ross pictured Dave commanding a pharma meeting, with a PowerPoint detailing some drug, its efficacy, and side effects.

Ross struggled to keep up with his penchant for perfectly constructed documents and details. Each packet of information was a collated, graphically pleasing dossier.

Ross flew by the seat of his pants but had come up with dozens of rules. Stephanie was simple but quirky. If you viewed her as some overarching personality, you could fill in the blanks.

There had been only one minor spat during the two-month planning stage, and it was about Ross clueing Vicky into the plan. Dave hated anyone else knowing. Ross disagreed. Vicky lived in Australia, an ocean away. There was no chance of her running into two Charlotte ex-wives.

Vicky had become a confidant of Ross, his feminine voice of reason. She also was fascinating. A sequel to their fling in LA was improbable, but he treasured their friendship. Void of the capacity to confide in a woman for most of his marriage, she scratched a much-needed itch, and the two exchanged frequent witty emails. Men and women could be platonic best of friends even when physically attracted. You just needed a six-thousand-mile partition.

Vicky got to the US perhaps two or three times a year but assured Ross that if he ever found love again and tied the knot, she would be on the next plane to be there. He promised the same, a running joke between the two.

Vicky was also hilarious. She was a prankster. It seemed only natural to confide in her the ultimate joke he hoped would turn the tables and reverse his misfortune.

Vicky's emails were like Christmas gifts from exotic locations Paris, London, Kuala Lumpur, Manila, or Tokyo. She often had him laughing aloud as she told her fish out of water stories, cultural missteps, or about her quirky passengers. Her difficult passenger stories were the most entertaining. Quick on her feet, even at thirty thousand feet, Vicky got the best of the exchange with Figjams unprepared for her wit.

Ross finally enlisted her help in this little scheme.

Stephanie was a bitter onion, each layer just as bitter as the one beneath. She was paranoid, vain, and entitled, with her insecurities requiring constant stroking. Stephanie also loved finding out dirt, hoping to hold it as a chip she could use to get an upper hand. She always looked for a person's bad side, which somehow made her feel better about herself, and she was about to get a dump truck load of dirt on Henry, courtesy of a mysterious Australian.

The sixty-eight-year-old car salesman was in love with Stephanie. Dave's path to cohabitation was blocked with Henry in the picture. According to Facebook, the two were inseparable.

Their relationship was symbiotic. Henry got a woman

a quarter-century his junior, and Stephanie got a docile boyfriend to shower her with compliments, with economic and emotional support. In exchange for having a man two decades her senior, Stephanie would get a handyman around the house, capable of yard work, and who knew his way around under the hood of a car. Henry was not rich, but by remaining unmarried for the bulk of his peak earnings, and being only minimally involved in raising his kids, Henry had few, if any financial burdens.

The mere mention of "Wilfred's" age sent Stephanie into a tizzy. At first, Ross was amused, but the after-effects of her rage weren't worth the momentary satisfaction. "You're just jealous I'm in love. You need therapy." Said the woman with a medicine chest's worth of pills.

When Ross heard of their coupling, he was hopeful it would result in marriage, but Henry hadn't been married absent a few years in the seventies. The odds weighed heavily against Henry marrying Stephanie. Ross was upset, not out of jealousy, but because she was dating a commitment-phobe.

The Plan changed the calculus. Dave needed a clear shot to Stephanie, and that meant Wilfred must go. Now seemed as good a time as any to engineer Henry's demise. Vicky was more than happy to help pitch in to separate Stephanie from her senior-citizen boyfriend.

Stephanie salved her insecurities about her age by pairing up with a man twenty years older. She was insecure about her intellect and sought to mask these insecurities. But what if she discovered Henry was having an affair with a stunningly beautiful, accomplished, and intelligent younger woman? It would just about kill her.

Henry worked the Hendricks family of auto dealerships, owned by Rick Hendrick, owner of a legendary NASCAR team. Engineers, drivers, and their wives shopped for high-end vehicles, trucks, and sports cars with regularity.

On orders of Rick Hendrick himself, Henry provided

concierge service whenever needed. It was not uncommon for Henry to have to interrupt dinner or Sunday watching football to get on his computer and crunch numbers for a driver's wife or pit boss who needed a custom vehicle.

While Stephanie thought NASCAR crude, Henry's rubbing elbows with the racing elite in town gave her the status she so craved. She was jealous Henry might meet someone in that social strata that felt Henry might cut a better deal, with some sex thrown in as a down payment.

Vicky would be an anathema to Stephanie. Her erudite Aussie accent would seem exotic and classy. Vicky exuded worldliness. With enough coaching, Vicky could push all of Stephanie's buttons. Ross came up with a minor project.

Ross left Vicky a voicemail to look for an email about advancing the plan. First, Vicky would call Stephanie's cell phone, making up some ruse about finding a page of his cell bill after spending the night. She just assumed the most frequently called number was his office. Then she'd say, "You must be his daughter, Loretta. He's told me all about you." Stephanie would play along to satiate her morbid curiosity—why she spent the night, and how she knew his daughter. She would keep it together while angry to pin down the date so she could bust Henry in as airtight a manner as possible.

Ross knew her proclivities and was sure she would not call out Henry's paramour but hang on the phone to get as much evidence as possible. By using a Tracfone Vicky could avoid the possibility of a caller ID popping up.

After two hours of careful planning, scriptwriting really, Ross emailed Vicky a lengthy list of what to say, which she read during a layover in Bangkok. She responded by assuring Ross she would nail the call and snapped a few racy selfies that had Ross reliving their one night of passion in LA.

The call would go down in one week. Ross would signal her WhatsApp that Stephanie successfully dropped Nicole off at school. Vicky would then call the number.

Vicky studied Ross' notes as if she was rehearsing for *Evita.* Ross became as precise in his planning as Dave. They planned three dry runs of the call on consecutive nights while Vicky was in the Western Australia town of Broome, inaugurating a new direct service from Sydney for the burgeoning resort city. Vicky ran through a few mock calls in the mirror of her Bangkok hotel room before her trip to Northwest Australia.

Ross reacted differently in each of the three rehearsals, and damn if Vicky didn't nail them. Her improvisations were better than the scripts Ross took hours to craft. She knew of Stephanie via Ross's emails and the exact best way to get under her skin.

Vicky's Broome trip had her meeting with airport officials, some members of the business community, and travel agents. When it was time to make her accidental phone call to Stephanie, she dialed the two dozen digits necessary to connect halfway around the world. Broome's Cable Beach was the original spot where the first Trans-Oceanic Telephone Cable arrived on the Australian continent, connecting it to Asia and Europe. Now satellites connect the world. She recited the name Henry Graves aloud to minimize the chances of inadvertently blurting out "Wilfred."

"Hello, sorry to bother you but perhaps you can help me. I'm looking for Henry Graves, please."

"Who is this?" Stephanie asked while trying to place the accent between England, Australia, or South Africa but not from the Carolinas.

"It's kind of a long story, love. I'm trying to locate him. I was at his place, and he's supposed to help a friend of mine get a car. He wrote quotes on a piece of paper on the nightstand, a page from a cell phone bill. I figured since this was the most frequently called number, it was his voicemail at work. I'm assuming you are his secretary, then?"

"He doesn't have a secretary," Stephanie said.

"The owner of a car dealership has no secretary?"

The snippy tone in her voice told Vicky that Stephanie was fuming.

"You didn't reach him at work."

Before she could get in another word, Vicky sensed an opportunity to raise her ire.

"Ah, you must be Loretta. Henry has told me all about you. The apple of his eye. Your Dad is quite a character."

"He's a character, all right. I forget your name again. I recall him mentioning something about you," Stephanie said.

"I'm Diana." The name was a word association exercise. The one woman Stephanie wished she could be was Princess Diana. With elegance, grace, and intelligence, her tragic death froze her youthful beauty in the minds of the entire world. The mental picture was too painful. Vicky even tried an upper-crust accent for the occasion.

"I saw your picture on the breakfront with you and your dad with NASCAR's Dale Earnhardt a few weeks before he died. Must have been hard losing a close friend like that."

Being confused with a Redneck ignoramus was one thing; NASCAR was anathema to Stephanie. She knew of legendary Dale Earnhardt and she knew Henry wasn't friends with him.

Vicky was over-the-moon when she heard a gasp, and the subsequent attempt to regain composure.

"Diana, how did you two meet again? Daddy told me but I forgot." Stephanie said.

"Well, your dad likes to shoot pool on Wednesday nights."

Wednesday nights were the nights he stayed to close up the showroom which Ross had told Vicky would be the one night he could guarantee his ex could pick up Nicole.

"Yep, you know Daddy and his pool."

"We had some Jack Daniels with the race team engineers. Imagine that, my first week after moving to the states. I'm used to the Formula 1 cars. I love talking about cars with your dad. He knows NASCAR, but his Vietnam stories... My uncle was in 'Nam too. He met lots of American GIs. Never flew choppers like Henry though."

Henry had come of draft age in the latter part of the war but remained exempt from the draft by spending two semesters in college. A motorcycle accident in Myrtle Beach after exams caused him to miss school, but an orthopedist certified to a poorly healed fracture, giving Henry a 4F deferment.

Not a day in uniform. Now the lying shit was claiming he was a Vietnam veteran and a pilot no less. The bastard is screwing a sexy Australian Aeronautical Engineer? The woman sounded half his age and had an engineering degree. Vicky fought hard to keep from laughing as she checked off box after box of Stephanie's insecurities. Ross knew Stephanie would obsessively search for a digital footprint of the make-believe Diana, but it's hard to find what doesn't exist.

Vicky fed into Stephanie's fears for over thirty minutes before she thrust with what she hoped would be the fatal blow to Stephanie's relationship with Henry. "Whatever happened with that annoying bitch he met on e-harmony, you know the Pilates one you make fun of?"

That annoying bitch was her! Stephanie shook like a leaf and ran in the house to get Klonopin. She couldn't do any more of this call and abruptly said in a strained voice, "Gotta go. Delivery guy."

With the call disconnected, Vicky laughed. She had accomplished the first step. More was to come. Vicky would send a racy photo and emails from a newly created email address. Henry would look at them and assume it was spam. "I've been thinking about our lovemaking." Henry would think they were ads for a porn site, but to Stephanie, snooping via spyware, the racy pics, and sexy notes would be damning evidence of an affair. If Henry even opened the emails or responded, he would be busted. Either way, Henry was screwed.

Every day for a full week, there was a new Aeroaussie email. Long enough for Stephanie to plant keystroke monitoring software, and hack into his emails. Ross knew Stephanie. She would make up an excuse for staying over Wednesday as Henry closed the showroom. Ross volunteered to have Nicole stay over and drive her to school.

Ross chuckled, imagining poor Henry trying to deny the irrefutable truth, and a mountain of evidence and looking guiltier with each denial. If Henry knew her like Ross did, he'd thank his lucky stars later. Ross was doing the old guy a favor.

The Chinese philosopher Sun Tzu once said the grandest victories go to those who receive no credit for achieving them because their methods were so cunning, so enigmatic, done so adroitly, that the tactics never surfaced.

Vicky had e-mailed Ross after the call using codes, grading the relative success of the outcome on a scale of one through five.

> Call went much better than expected results, buyer very interested, and seemed to find additional information fascinating. I expect you should know something within a few days as the parent company will inform subsidiaries of new info. 5+. Ba Bye WB.

Now, Ross just had to sit back and wait for the fireworks. It took a week from Vicky's call for Nicole to call Ross regarding her mom's mental state.

"Mom broke up with the old guy because he pissed her off. She says he screwed her over. Oh, and all men suck. That's a direct quote. I need to spend more time at your place for a while."

Ross's spirit soared. The Plan was working. Henry was toast. The coast was clear. The next day, Dave enrolled at the gym where Stephanie took Pilates.

Chapter Seven
Sparring

Approaching Julie was the motivation Ross needed to get in shape. Working out post-separation had been a series of fits and starts—jogging, sit-ups, and pushups. Each diet had him dropping and then gaining thirty pounds and winding up with some variation of dad bod. Julie's newfound interest in martial arts would be the easiest avenue for the two to make their acquaintance.

Thousands of things could go wrong after joining Fighting Fitness Gym: injuries that would sideline him from the gym, or an embarrassing humiliation that would make him undesirable to Julie.

Ross was neither jock nor uncoordinated. It had been close to thirty years since he lettered in baseball, a left-handed pitcher whose quirky motion and southpaw delivery proved effective, but at other times, wild. He was, what his coach called, a head case, on his mark when he had confidence and unable to hit a barn when he didn't. The

Yips they call it. Ross had talent unless he started to overthink. He did well in brawnier sports like football but never lettered after a ski accident mangled a knee.

Nerves preceded Ross's entrance to the gym. His legs were powerful yet not flexible, arms somewhat flabby but strong. Ross lacked conditioning, footwork, and confidence: the holy trinity in combat sports.

Ross wasn't a fighter. Two decades of acquiescing had killed that instinct. Ross was conflict averse. Perhaps the controlled aggression would rebuild his alpha side, which oozed slowly from him during the marriage.

The last three weeks he had jogged a few miles daily but never got beyond hating it. He did a hundred pushups and sit-ups and a few weights each day but never grew to like the routine. Ross merely tolerated the discomfort with greater ease.

Given the devious nature of his planned courtship, his moral compass seemed conflicted, making it difficult to discern whether guilt added to his anxiety about his initial approach. Grifting was not in his wheelhouse. Ross's conscience didn't have an on-off switch. His ex-wife had no such limitations, and as Ross discovered, a conscience in a bitter divorce can be a liability.

Ross now had to act like Stephanie in pursuit of self-advantage. His friends were telling him to move on, to ignore the rear-view mirror in favor of a new future with a clean slate. The therapy proved somewhat insightful in better managing Stephanie's quirks, but ineffective in changing the choking financial nightmare she left in her wake. Circumstances demanded he move forward.

Julie sparred in a variety of ways: legally, emotionally, corporately, and for the last eight months in a dojo. She had captained her high school tennis team. The tony prep school, which she attended, Buckhead Country Day, comprised a rather eclectic mix of Old Money Atlanta, relocated Yankees, and a smattering of bohemian types. The school, unlike many Atlanta private schools chartered in the seventies, courted African Americans, athletes also suited for rigorous academics. Country Day thrived in the league of preparatory schools with whom they competed. In a city with a black population as large as Atlanta, proactively looking for such students while others did not, helped give the athletic program a competitive edge. Country Day sent several athletes to prestigious schools that also excelled at academics like Duke, Clemson, Vanderbilt, and the Ivies. There was a pair of NBA players, and three drafted by the NFL.

The school's reputation solidified when former Georgia Governor Jimmy Carter finished his term. Many former Carter staffers were among those whose children attended the school. Julie felt comfortable with jocks, the most diverse of the cliques in her prep school. She knew blues, funk, jazz, and Motown, which was foreign to many of her white classmates, but introduced via her brother. She felt a kinship with minority students.

Julie was immune to the superficial barometers of the social construct that are measuring sticks in high school. The Old Money group held no sway with her. The offspring of legacy alumni were less capable, achieving by familial connections what they could not by merit. Julie all but ignored them. They had long-established mores designed to maintain dominance. She had no desire to be in their good graces. They thought her brash and hot-tempered. "Julie Rican," they used to say derisively, confusing her mom's Panamanian heritage with that of the Caribbean island. Julie paid it no mind.

Julie's tennis teammates admired her tenacity. Her one quirk was her trademark grunt when hitting a hard backhand or serve. Quite out of place for a petite girl, few tormentors attributed unladylike behavior to poor breeding. Some boys said she must be wild in bed, but it was a gritty determination and an admiration for Monica Seles who had risen to stardom with a trademark grunt. A few baseball players, whose practice facility abutted the tennis courts, chided her but appeared to admire her spunk. Athletes seem to appreciate those who give one hundred and ten percent.

Ross showed up to Julie's dojo to begin his pursuit of her. There were two dozen people in the Muay Thai class, mostly men with a handful of women. Their outfits ranged from ratty tee shirts and shorts to those breathable under armor outfits. Some in the class were barefoot; others had jogging shoes.

It was nothing like the fashion show at Ballantyne gyms. After signing the release forms, Ross agreed to the one-year membership with unlimited classes at ninety bucks a month. A thousand-dollar investment hoping to end Dave's asphyxiating alimony for the same in return.

Muay Thai combines boxing with kicking and the use of elbows and knees. It was a good steppingstone for beginners, with a solid foundation for striking, fighting while on one's feet. According to Dave, it was Julie's favorite discipline and involved frequent sparring after a requisite training period.

Students stretched, jumped rope, hit bags with bare fists and feet. Ross surveyed the students gathered until he heard a grunt, just as Dave had predicted, followed by a pop of what sounded like a firecracker as Julie's foot hit a leather pad at just the right angle. The juicehead holding the pad against his thigh recoiled. Ross winced. Julie cocked her leg again, grunted, and replicated the exact sound. Julie repeated it twenty times at which time she switched legs.

Julie wore what appeared to be form-fitting yoga pants and a t-shirt. She was petite but sported a shapely behind. There were four newbies, including Ross. They stood to the side of two instructors, a diminutive female, and Trahn, who Ross assumed to be Vietnamese, and observed punching techniques.

It was an eclectic group, diverse in every conceivable

way. Gender, ethnicity, social status, from the corporate elite to pure redneck. Javier, a former Golden Gloves boxer from the Bronx, pummeled a speed bag with merciless efficiency. An Israeli woman, judging by the Hebrew lettering on her t-shirt, demonstrated a choke on a larger student, imploring him to attack at full speed. She seemed fearless, impervious to the size advantage, and discarded him with ruthless efficiency. Impressive and scary. *Just how dangerous is Julie?*

Despite the controlled violence, it was welcoming. There were no matching uniforms, nor cult worship of a sensei. Age, gender, race, and economic station seemed of minor concern. Individualized self-improvement was the only currency of value, from what Ross could tell.

Mike, the instructor asked the novices to say a little about themselves and what they hoped to gain from the classes. Ross chuckled as he thought of a suitable lie that would spark Julie's interest. He mentioned he enjoyed skiing, wanted to get rid of his dad bod, and his daughter, whom he hoped to teach to defend herself. And he confessed he was a southpaw.

Being left-handed is an enormous deal in martial arts. Referred to as unorthodox, instructors hated teaching moves from the opposite side. Ross shared this affliction with Julie.

"Which one of you two oddballs wants to be a training partner for the Southpaw?"

Julie claimed Ross. "I'll take him."

Her voice was raspy, which Ross found sexy. She demonstrated proper stances, pad holding, and techniques for kicking and punching. *So far, so good.*

Next was cardio: running in circles in all conceivable ways, followed by sit-ups. He struggled to keep pace while huffing and puffing. His arms felt wobbly but functional. They ended by planking, a yoga pose, remaining stiff while on elbows and toes.

"Jump rope," shouted the instructor. The class grabbed

the jump ropes hanging on pegs. Several students were proficient at doing crossover moves with fancy footwork. Ross could string together perhaps fifteen seconds of consecutive jumps and then would screw-up. He tried not to look clumsy when restarting. Julie did crossovers effortlessly.

Then came shadowboxing, followed by a game of shoulders and knees. The rambling mass of students would roam around trying to touch each other's shoulders and knees with an open palm. The exercise required agility, peripheral vision, and hand-eye coordination. One of the other newbies clunked heads with another student. The game taught hypervigilance and situational awareness. Ross was winded but enjoyed himself.

"Okay, pair up," the Israeli woman shouted in a booming voice.

Julie trotted away, giving Ross a fine rear view of her petite, curvy bottom and sturdy, toned legs.

She grabbed some pads and extended a hand to introduce herself. "This is a lot of fun, you'll see. It's a wonderful group of people."

Ross pushed the conversation towards other commonalities. "Well, after my divorce, I need stress relief. Too many lawyers."

"I'm divorced, so I know how that goes. I'm also an attorney. Perhaps if I was defending you?"

"You're late to the party, maybe next time. Not that it'll ever happen again," he said.

"You should try Krav Maga. You'd like that class too."

She referred to the Israeli martial art taught to soldiers. They focused on real-life situations and had a no-holds-barred approach to self-defense, increasingly popular with Hollywood types.

"The one where hitting below the belt is encouraged? Sounds like my divorce." Ross chuckled.

An above-average first exchange. Witty, self-deprecating, and interested in self- improvement, he laid the groundwork for future interaction.

The Bronx Golden Gloves guru demonstrated hip movement while hitting a bag. Students punched slowly, then rapidly. They expanded the drill to include punching from one's knees and then on their backs. Julie's shirt rode up, exposing her toned belly. Ross tried not to stare while standing above her and straddling her body. She was powerful, but the next drill showed her prowess.

Julie was barefoot. Ross wore jogging shoes. The snap of her bare feet hitting the leather pads sounded like the crack of a whip. Julie grunted as if to signal maximum effort. Ross's kicks were a hit-or-miss proposition. Some felt okay, but others caused sharp pain because of unnatural hip flexing.

The class ended with students sprinting to the end of the mats, kicking and punching at full speed. They'd then switch and become pad holders, panting like golden retrievers as they exerted maximum effort. The drill ended with the class lined up, followed by bowing to the instructor.

Ross filled his water bottle near where Julie put her gym bag. He wanted to quench his thirst while thanking her for assisting him. The class was more enjoyable than he expected. Julie was a few slots over on a bench, lacing her sneakers.

"Marshall Tucker, huh?" She asked while staring at his T-shirt. "I did legal work for those guys. They're from Spartanburg, you know. I'm an Atlanta girl raised on the Allmans, ARS, Little Feat, and The Georgia Satellites. It was quite a treat."

Ross was flummoxed but blurted out a reply, forgetting her love of Marshall Tucker was on one of Dave's index cards.

"Aren't you too young to be listening to that Old School Southern Rock? It's the late seventies."

"My older brother, Brad. He was big into the Allmans and then the rest of the stuff, Outlaws, Atlanta Rhythm

Section, and Little Feat, etc. I went to the University of Georgia and everyone was going nuts for the local bands B-52s and REM, and I enjoyed that too, but my older brother shaped my musical tastes. I never grew out of it. My tastes are maybe a little dated for someone in their early forties."

"You look younger than that. I guess all the working out helps. I hope one day I can get the hang of this. I graduated in nineteen-ninety, Penn State. Time sure flies."

He felt tentative trying to compliment her, but it was sincere. She appeared younger than her age.

He was enchanted but sweating like a Sumo wrestler in a Zumba class. The class was exhausting but exhilarating. The conversation seemed natural.

Dave had warned Ross about her deposition mode, where Julie would rapid-fire questions and throw in one to trip up a litigant, making you say something you wished you hadn't.

"One of my favorites in college was: 'Can't you see'."

"Lemme guess, it's your new divorce anthem?"

"No, although there are times I felt like jumping off a mountain. I'm doing my best to move on and keep positive."

"She left? You want her back?"

"God no. I'm trying to keep it civil and my daughter out of the crossfire from my ex-wife and her attorney. You don't practice family law, do you?"

"Contract law. I hate family law. It's designed to bring out the worst in people. My area is cut and dried. Figure out what the law says and apply it. Divorce is emotional and too contentious. Sounds weird. Here we are punching and kicking, and I complain about something being too combative. This class helps you get rid of a lot of those frustrations once you get into it."

"Your divorce, was it combative?"

"We didn't have kids, so no custody issues, but it's complicated because he worked with my dad in a family business. I had to get the best outcome for my dad, so I got the best outcome and locked in the agreement. It wasn't bitter. We just weren't in sync. He wasn't a bad guy. I'm not here 'cause he beat me if that is what you are thinking."

"God no. That would be horrible. You beat him?"

"Good one." She laughed.

"Well, my ex and her attorney tried to make it contentious. I wanted calm. They wanted conflict. Just trying to keep things civil and be there for my daughter."

Ross wondered if he was revealing too much. Talking about divorce was the surest way to not get laid, but it somehow worked with Victoria. *Women are complicated creatures. This is going too fast. I might fuck things up.*

"You'll find that fighting can be like yoga. It's relaxing once you develop the ability to breathe. It has calmed me. I'm far from inner peace, but I'm less on edge."

"Say Julie; ever go to Manifest Records on South Boulevard? Vinyl shopping?"

"Wow, I love that place. I sometimes go there looking for a particular album and walk out with two dozen. I still use my turntable all the time."

"We should go there sometime," Ross said, pleased with his initial conversation.

Julie seemed downright friendly. This was a surprise. Dave got the whole competitive thing right, but Julie seemed approachable. Perhaps it was the twelve hard-fought pounds Ross shed in the last month or two.

"Well, Julie, I'll see you later in the week. It was good to meet another southpaw."

"Likewise, Ross, you take care. Tuck your chin like I told you."

They walked through the doors, Julie to her Lexus and Ross to his Audi, eight years old but respectable, his first used car since graduating college. As she walked away, he couldn't help but stare at her butt, which was a work of art.

At bedtime that evening, Ross downed two ibuprofens with a light beer, hoping to avoid the revenge of dormant muscles.

The next morning, Ross woke up sore, but not as bad as he feared. He put on shorts and a t-shirt and went for a morning jog, adding another mile to the two that had been his routine. He was on autopilot, buoyed by his conversation, putting one foot in front of the other while mindlessly replaying his conversation. Along the tree-lined streets of Ballantyne Commons Parkway, Ross contemplated Julie and tomorrow's class.

Wednesday's appointments ran late. A lunch meeting and a late request for a proposal kept him in the office until six. He grabbed a salad and headed to the South End towards the gym.

Julie's drive was five minutes from her uptown office to Ross's half-hour. Ross packed a gym bag so he could arrive in business attire. He wanted her to see him dressed for success. A starched shirt, new tie, and pressed pants unveiled for the occasion.

Ross arrived about ten minutes after the six-thirty starting time, spotting Julie's Lexus as he pulled into the parking lot. He grabbed his bag and straightened his tie. Women love a sharp-dressed man. It wouldn't hurt to showcase his devotion to work, either.

He located her as she hit the heavy bag with her pink gloves. Ross pretended not to notice her as he walked to the men's locker room. He had four t-shirts specially devised to engender commonality as per Dave's index cards.

A Hard Rock Cafe shirt from the Bahamas was a loaner from Dave, who figured she'd never suspect it was his. Dave had recounted to Ross a memorable vacation with Julie, who had gone native, complete with braided cornrows. She tried parasailing and scuba diving and liked both. Though Ross had never been there, he Googled Nassau's attractions and should be able to hold his own in a conversation.

He had sweats from Vanderbilt, her law school, and

some Nashville paraphernalia. Ross's timetable was a week to three weeks before asking her for a drink. If successful, dinner would follow. He scanned which bands were in town to keep apprised of future concerts.

When Ross returned to the gym, the Israeli woman was demonstrating an escape from a headlock. The students would grab her from the side around the neck, and she would make a Karate chop motion to the balls while webbing her hand over her opponent's face, thus forcing them to fall backward. The key was a singular index finger under the nose. Pushing that one finger backward could neutralize a much larger opponent. The petite woman dispatched the students like a lumberjack might fell an enormous tree. She then feigned a groin kick to end the maneuver.

Three goons choked her against the wall. The instructor tucked her head into her shoulder. She then lifted her arm, trapped their hands and delivered an elbow to the face. Her maneuver was matter of fact, requiring minor effort. This must be the Krav Maga that Julie mentioned. It was raw and ugly but practical and efficient.

There were other students rolling, slang for Brazilian Jiu-Jitsu. Two people were locked on the floor, jockeying for better arm or leg position. It was hard to follow, but he would hear "Tap," which meant someone was about to break a bone or blackout from asphyxiation. Smaller people were dispatching larger ones, ladies throwing men to the floor. Julie was one of the better examples.

Ross checked his protective cup. Testicles would be an essential part of completing the enterprise he and Dave had embarked on.

He made eye contact with Julie after she finished pummeling the heavy bag and was taking a sip of water. She smiled as if she hoped to see him.

"Hey, southpaw," she said. "Back for more?"

"You know me, can't wait for a battering by an attorney."

The students lined up to do the traditional Thai bow before the cardio portion of the class. Julie was half a dozen slots to the right. Ross didn't want to force things. The first class had gone well. Best not push the envelope.

The class followed much the same format as the first except this one had groundwork, lying on his back, protecting himself from an opponent who was circling him to tap a part of his body. His cocked leg was his weapon, sending a kick when needed. His abs worked to exhaustion trying to move counterclockwise and then back to position against his attacker. A minute seemed to Ross like a thousand sit-ups. Julie spun like a top, tireless, and impossible to tap, outdoing much younger students who probably wondered how this middle-aged woman made them look ridiculous.

The next activity involved escaping from a bottom position while being mounted. For women in the class, this drill approximated a rape scenario. He now understood why the classes were empowering. Julie's spunk was laudable. As the class lined up, she stared at his Bahamas shirt and smirked. He held a grin in check. Too bad he couldn't see into her mind. He'd bet she recalled the trip with Dave.

"Wow, you were good out there; I could barely keep up." He wiped the sweat from his face with the tail of his shirt.

"You looked fine; it takes a little time. You did well."

"I feel like my stomach is in knots. If I laugh or cough within the next week, I'll be in pain. But I liked it. I want my daughter to learn this stuff before she goes away to college. Imagine someone trying to get grabby with the instructor over there." He pointed to the pint-sized woman making minced meat out of her students while encouraging them to attack her.

"Oh, that's Tzipora, but we call her Sippy."

"Well, I for one will wear my sippy cup."

He didn't hit it out of the park but got the intended response. Julie chuckled, perhaps politely.

"She's nice, but she takes this stuff seriously. She's the Krav instructor and taught in the military. Tough on the outside, but a softie inside. Because I'm smaller and female, she took a special interest in making sure I was comfortable. Thanks to her, I believe I could replicate this in real life. Whenever there are new guys, big ones, they can't believe it when she takes them down so easily. Her husband works for Teva, an Israeli firm that does business with my dad. We're friends. I'll introduce you."

Fighting Fitness was not some haven for steroid gobbling meatheads. It was egalitarian. Male, female, big, small, fat, skinny. What mattered was improving yourself relative to your previous self.

"She scares the shit out of me now, but I appreciate the offer of a formal introduction. I'm sure eventually she will kick me in the balls."

She glanced back at his shirt. "Bahamas, huh?"

"I was there for an insurance convention."

Total bullshit, but Ross knew enough facts to start a conversation before letting Julie talk. He knew some hot spots and beach names but little else.

"Have you been?"

"Yeah, family vacation: dad, mom, brother, nieces and nephew, and my ex. A nice time. We went to Atlantis. I para-sailed but my favorite was scuba diving. All those colors just beneath the surface. It's like another world. I'd love to explore the world's majestic dive places. That's my dream, anyway. Life gets in the way."

"I was on business, a few tours, some leisure time but lots of meetings and had to keep the beverages to a minimum to avoid embarrassing myself. I snorkeled a few times in Cancun and Puerto Rico and liked the colorful fish. You seem like the ocean, which is even more colorful under the surface."

He flirted. She smiled demurely. Despite all the index cards, she was fascinating. More approachable than he was led to believe.

The banter continued for ten minutes. Insecure about being a novice at the gym, he threw in a few high school baseball stories, and some travel destinations to appear interesting.

He had searched his old vinyl collection for every southern rock album he could find and even hooked up the turntable from the garage. He would save that for another day when he could wear his Allmans tee, the Vanderbilt sweats, and Nashville shirts he picked up from a recent trip.

The reality was that they were two divorced, professional, forty-somethings in a class that was on average fifteen years younger. They were also lefties, which made them a natural pairing.

After three weeks Ross figured he was ready to ask her out for a drink. He summoned up the courage one Wednesday evening.

"Left-handed training meeting at Lebowski's after class. Can you attend?"

Julie shook her head, "I have a deposition. I need to leave at five to get to Raleigh by eight. Some other time, perhaps."

Ross had grown up in Pennsylvania and since moving south had difficulty telling when one was being strung along by southerners merely acting polite. Meetings in which the client had no intention of moving forward were always friendly. This extended to flirting. Rejection might come in the form of "perhaps some other time," and they expected you to take the hint. It confused Ross.

He knew Philly girls, and when they shot you down, you knew it. Crude, but at least you had closure. He hung on Julie's smile at the end, hoping she had a deposition.

He parsed every word for the next four hours, internally debating until bed. Ross questioned whether to include this blip in his weekly reporting to Dave. Julie attracted him. He wanted more. He contemplated calling Vicky before nodding off at about 1 a.m.

He had Nicole for the weekend, but she didn't want him around much, a movie Friday night, a friend's house all day Saturday. They grabbed some Mexican food for lunch before he dropped her off, but she was uncommunicative. It tempted Ross to pry, but with teens, that is often counterproductive. If Nicole was distraught, he wanted to know.

Monday's class couldn't come soon enough since the weekend with Nicole had him skip Saturday's class.

When the alarm rang on Monday, Ross packed a Nashville Cats t-shirt in his bag, and Vanderbilt sweats. It was best to stay calm and not push the issue about the date. No questions about the deposition, and the jealousy it might imply. He got to the gym early, hoping to interact with Julie and talk after the aborted leap from training partners to socializing outside the gym.

He pulled into the lot at six-fifteen, but no Lexus. He changed from his business suit. He hoped to be on the mats when Julie arrived and in a further show of dedication would ask Sippy to show him a few moves. He double-checked in his shorts to make sure his Sippy cup was in position.

Sippy knew of Ross. Julie must have talked to her. They began with the choke escape against the wall. After throwing Ross away perhaps five times, she let him have a go at it. Her thumbs pressed against his larynx. He couldn't talk. He dipped a shoulder, tucked his chin, raised his arm, and twisted his body. First one, then two of Sippy's hands became trapped under his arm. He then threw his elbow and had her off balance. He pushed enough to tumble her to the ground, enabling Ross to escape. He felt the rush of confidence from mastering a new skill.

"See, it's easy. A little sloppy but not too bad," she said in her guttural Hebrew accent. At this moment Julie walked in and seemed pleased to see Sippy tumbling to the ground and Ross facing the pint-sized pugilist.

"I see you met my friend, Sippy."

"Yes, if you call being thrown to the ground a few times meeting."

"Ross, you up for a rain check? I felt bad about last time. Maybe after class?"

Julie was asking him out. He was elated but wanted to contain his enthusiasm with Sippy nearby.

"Sure, that would be great." Surprised, he could think of nothing better to say. Ross thought of places nearby conducive to getting better acquainted.

Tonight was the first sparring session in which Ross could throw actual punches and kicks with more advanced classmates. The sleeve-tattooed kid seemed as if he was itching to pummel someone. There were three or four goons, which Ross felt might get out of control. He was nervous if only because he needed to both survive and remain mobile afterward.

Julie and Ross paired up to train. Fueled by the enthusiasm, Ross punched and kicked his way through in a manner befitting someone more advanced.

"You have improved. Your kicks are stronger and more accurate. Nice job." She professed an affinity for the Nashville and Vandy paraphernalia and blurted out that she spent more than a few nights on Lower Broadway listening to live music during law school. Not much time for chitchat during the class, but it was a perfect tee-up for their date if he managed to not get killed while sparring.

"I like this," he said as he toweled off the dripping perspiration from his brow before swigging some Gatorade.

"I told you," she said, sounding more familiar than Ross expected. "Don't worry, you'll be fine," she said, alluding to the sparring. "The instructors will make sure you don't get overwhelmed."

"Thanks, I'll try to make it through without looking like a Picasso with my nose on the wrong side of my face."

Dwayne, a squat, powerfully built instructor, was

leading the sparring class. His neck was like a tree trunk, as were his thighs. Thin in his lower legs and stomach, he was soft-spoken and patient with beginners. Dwayne was an expert at giving tiny but impactful adjustments to your technique. He did not tolerate show-offs. In keeping with his tenets, he instructed the class that there were two newcomers, Ross, and a chubby twenty-something who was working hard but with little athleticism.

Javier, who was assisting Dwayne, was a Golden Gloves boxer from Puerto Rico by way of the Bronx. He was lanky with long, well-defined arms. He showed the newbies how to put on shin guards and headgear while helping to insert their mouth guard when combatants were gloved.

There would be a round robin where one individual would go three rounds, each with rotated opponents. Ross wasn't sure if he would face Julie. Sippy was also in the mix, although she trotted in late after finishing a private lesson.

They instructed the class to go slow with the newbies, that for them it was about learning and getting comfortable. They could signal if they wished to go harder. He was glad that the other newbie was not a natural and appeared even more bewildered than Ross felt.

The instructors offered feedback after they dispatched each student. Ross listened, hoping to pick up useful tidbits before being sent into the lion's den. He counted on the fact he was new and not known as an unorthodox fighter. Keep to the right, they told him, and keep your hands up. Remember to breathe and not tense up, which takes much more energy than staying relaxed.

The first opponent was the dude with the sleeved tattoo. Ross tried to get in close and was greeted by a jab to the padded forehead of his headgear. Much to his surprise, it didn't hurt and gave him a rush of adrenaline. Ross landed a kick to the thigh and swooped underneath to get in close. There was a tussle of arms jockeying for position, and he traded a few quick jabs to the ribs while getting a few in return. Those hurt far worse than the shot to the head. Dwayne barked to separate, and the two resumed their distance. A few jabs here, crisp exchanges there, and an accidental head butt were all part of the next few moments.

Somehow Ross had cornered his opponent, who was oblivious to Ross being left-handed, and for a moment, had the more experienced fighter trapped. Ross was worse for wear, however, when his partner fought his way out of the corner. The buzzer rang, and Ross felt a sense of satisfaction with having held his own.

Julie was up next. She bowed and would say, "Nice" or "Good one" if hit. Her strength was her legs, and she kicked one guy smack dab in the ear without him having a clue what was coming. She was under control and looked kind of cute with her pink gloves. Javier peppered her with jabs, and he urged her to get in and get out. She dodged a jab and burrowed underneath for a quick strike to the ribs. She even got a kidney shot that made Javier wince and say, "That's what I'm talking about."

"Still have the energy for a drink?" she asked as they walked to their gym bags.

"I need a drink more than before."

"Good, meet you at Lebowski's in about fifteen."

Ross shuffled to the locker room and put on his work clothes sans tie. In the parking lot, he searched for her car but realized she had already left.

The drive on East Boulevard went past several restaurants, but passing Becky's side street, it reminded him of something he hadn't thought about tonight. This Julie woman was Dave's ex, and the date was part of an alimony scheme. Some of the air escaped his balloon.

He passed the sparse weekday crowd and walked up the stairs to the rooftop lounge. A combination of hockey, college basketball, and baseball games were on TV as he approached the stairs. Seated and still looking fresh, Julie sipped her beer and had ordered one for Ross.

"You were impressive out there," he said and sat next to her. "If you spar like that in court, I feel sorry for the opposing attorney."

"Thanks, but it's no big deal. It's not a competition. I try to improve. You were great for a virgin."

Julie blushed when she realized she had left herself open for a counterpunch of cliched sexual innuendos.

"That's the best compliment I've had all day. Other than not being able to breathe, I enjoyed it. I got hit and thought, 'This isn't so bad' and just tried to make it through and do what they told me. I was glad I was getting feedback, or I'd feel lost."

"Southpaws have an advantage in that we're a novelty and when you train for something for ninety percent of the time, the force of habit makes people do dumb things. You'll always have that as an advantage. Experienced fighters take notice and adjust, but it's a plus."

"Makes up for all that time using the wrong scissors and writing on desks designed for righties."

"Exactly." She giggled and took a swallow of her beer.

"So that guy was aggressive. Did he hurt you?"

"No, it's just his thing. I don't pay attention, just cover up and hit him back. Sippy says that's how a fight on the street would go down. Otherwise, it's just unrealistic choreography."

"So, Vanderbilt, huh? I was just in Nashville. Love what they have done with the music scene there. Lots of rock bands, the Alternative Country in East Nashville, the Bluebird Cafe."

"Yeah, went to law school there. I love the vibe. Everyone converging on the town, pouring their hearts into their music, trying to make it. Songwriters, live bands, they're incredible. Don't get there much anymore."

"You should go. It would surprise you how diverse the music scene has become."

They shared beers, ordered wings, and went on about music for a good fifteen minutes. The talk steered towards in a more personal direction. Ross had a rotation of about four index card items to inject into the conversation, movies, books, TV, stuff like that, but felt as if things were doing fine on their own.

Ross talked in general about his daughter and his ex-wife. He didn't want to seem bitter or reveal too much in the way of personality lest she finds out that Stephanie is the woman Julie's ex is chasing.

Julie told him about her lack of social life due to her work schedule. "I decided on a whim to enroll in a class for martial arts after seeing a TV ad for a women's rape prevention seminar. I work late a lot, live by myself and I'm in hotels. I didn't want to be a statistic. I love the adrenaline rush of martial arts. I quit the whole Lake Norman scene and am in the city, Fourth Ward. I can walk to work. My apartment is a smaller place, which I love."

She didn't seem bitter about the divorce, but she got the best of it, so why would she be? He could see why the marriage disintegrated. She was the doer, and while Dave was organized and meticulous, he was not as driven since he would always be the son-in-law and not blood.

She told him Dave liked his job when he was on the road but hated the office and family politics. She made more money and got a huge stipend for being on the board of directors, which he felt was emasculating. With Julie's competitive streak and kids no longer a possibility because she was infertile, it was a combustible combination.

Ross volunteered that he too was growing fond of city life and more disconnected to suburbia. It was a lie, but it was something to plant in her subconscious, should cohabitation ever enter the picture. After frequent visits to Becky's office, he felt there was a definite vibe in the city's uptown region with the influx of newcomers, restaurants, and luxury high-rises.

Ross glanced at his watch, and it was nearing eleven. He wanted to be respectful of Julie's time. Asking for her number would not be too forward. She pulled a business card out of her purse, which he read as a bad sign until she wrote her cell number on the back.

The elephant in the room was the kiss. He was now dealing with the should-I-or-shouldn't I? Erring on the side of caution. They walked separately to their cars. Ross said he had an enjoyable time and bid her goodbye as Julie followed with "Me too." He wanted to text her as soon as he got home and debated whether it would appear desperate.

Dating rules: did they even apply in the information age? Better to move slowly. Ross needed to update Dave and stopped in the all-night Kinko's to drop him an email. Ross preferred to go home, but this couldn't wait until their meeting in Charleston the following week. He would drop Vicky a note about the big news, that he survived sparring, and a first date. She would undoubtedly have advice. The sparring and subsequent date tired but energized Ross. His joints creaked, like a tin man, but he was happy.

Chapter Eight
Rambo Gets TKO'D

Ross had survived sparring, and a mini date afterward. Waiting the three days 'til the next class to try again was excruciating. He imagined helping his standing by sparring well. Ross watched MMA on TV, imagined teen toughs trying to get the best of him in a dimly lit parking lot. He was working way too hard trying to get into a mental frame of mind for what would be ten minutes in a two-hour class.

Julie arrived first and spotted Ross pulling into the parking lot. Julie liked how he acquitted himself in the ring as a newbie. Ross exchanged pleasantries but had a more somber tone, like a man on a mission. He obsessed about being an alpha male in the ring, missing the basic goal of a self-defense class. What seemed lost on Ross was his social progress with Julie was based on being humble. A guy eager to learn, while climbing up the pegs he got knocked down while maintaining a quirky sense of humor.

"Ready to mix it up. I've been waiting for the sparring

all week." Ross said.

"Try to learn something each time. That's how you get better," Julie said in an encouraging fashion.

Ross was hoping they called his number first but didn't. Each match had him analyzing how he could have gotten off a clean shot if it were him fighting.

Julie was next while Ross waited eagerly to show his fighting chops.

She drew pint-sized Derek, a pugilist with a Napoleon complex and often wild. Since they weren't much different in reach, fighting close or staying out of range favored neither. What Julie had on him was her ability to kick. She drew him in with a feigned punch to the midsection, waited for him to drop his hands to block, and landed a roundhouse kick square on his jaw.

It was an impressive maneuver, which in the spirit of competition, should have drawn an "Atta girl," but Derek went apeshit. Hers was a clean shot. His grabbing her by the arm and rabbit punching her in the back of the head was not. He was swinging wildly afterward.

Dwayne the instructor implored him to calm down. Sippy was at the other end of the room, a stroke of luck for Derek, who would surely sing a few octaves higher if Sippy had been in range. Julie recovered as if nothing had happened with a look that said, *"Is that all you got?"*

Ross somehow thought it a splendid idea to jump in the ring and exact street vengeance on Derek. It took a few split seconds for the instructors and Ross to realize the extent of his stupidity. Apparently, this is a contingency for which they prepare. Ross landed a sucker punch to Derek's temple with little impact because of his headgear. Within ten seconds Ross was on the ground, in an armbar, wincing, and decided his forearm broken in a show of bravado was ill-advised.

Dwayne marched him to the office where Trahan and Sippy had gathered. Ross glanced at Julie as he turned the corner, and she shot him a look filled with scorn for trying to fight her battles, and disappointment that he didn't have his shit together as much as she thought. Their verdict: A one-week time-out and no sparring for two weeks as well as a written apology to Derek who they agreed was the second biggest douche in this tragedy.

"You realize Julie would have kicked his ass within the next sixty-seconds?" Sippy said confidently.

Ross fucked up. BIG TIME.

Chapter Nine
Career Suicide

Ross stared at Julie's business card for twenty minutes, hoping to gain clarity and undo his colossal inept attempt to rescue a damsel who could handle her own distress.

Do flowers work on women who know how to throw jabs and solid left hooks? It was worth a try. Googling her home address would seem stalker-ish. He would have to send them to her office. Emailing a lawyer's office might piss her off more since they would monitor the communication, and catalog it for eternity.

He would send the flowers then text, hoping she was in the office to receive them and wouldn't quickly tell him to fuck off. He had five hundred characters he could put on the FTD card. They better tee up his apology.

> Julie, I want to apologize profusely. I know you can handle your own stuff. I had no right to jump in to save you when you were more than capable. I learned my lesson. A

knee to the groin, a kick in the head, a punch to the gut. I'll take whatever punishment you deem appropriate, but please give me a chance to make it up to you. I'll do my best to be a model citizen in the gym.

Remorseful Ross.

Ross: Julie, I hope you got the flowers, and they are as pretty as you are. Please let me have another chance. I won't let you down.

Julie: WTF, were you thinking, asshole?

Ross: I just lost it. I'm not used to women who can take a cheap shot and not lose their cool. I'm an idiot and hope you can see it in your heart to let me make it up to you.

Julie: That gym is like home. I'm not happy. I look stupid too. Did you really think with black-belt instructors you could just be Rambo and rescue me?

Ross: Dinner? I promise I learned my lesson thanks to you, Dwayne, Trahan, and Sippy.

Julie: Dinner and a knee to the groin, with a kick in your thick male-chauvinist skull.

Ross: Deal.

It was a turbulent week in Charlotte. A small but virulent protest movement against the Marriage Equality Act maintained a daily vigil outside the Mecklenburg County Courthouse and they were growing hostile. Mecklenburg County had the largest number of marriage licenses for same-sex marriage in the state. Therefore, the Disciples of Adam and Eve maintained a constant presence.

A recent news story emboldened the group. A married same-sex couple had adopted a child and allegedly sodomized the child. There were questions whether the police had properly interviewed the child or whether the child's religious grandparents had coaxed the child to testify by scaring the child with threats of eternal damnation. Before the first day of testimony, the child, while in the temporary custody of the grandparents, went missing. A week later his body was found: A drowning fatality in the Alabama River.

Protesters and counter-protesters blamed the other. The police called it an accidental drowning after they found the child's bicycle near a creek bed. The couple insisted that someone murdered the child because he would not testify and renounce them. Religious groups implicated the parents; saying they murdered the child to avoid conviction. The DA quickly had a media circus outside his office every day, while under enormous pressure to bring charges against someone from both groups. A criminal conviction favoring either side would throw a match into a powder keg. Washington wanted the FBI to take the lead, further complicating matters.

A group supporting Marriage Equality booked space in a Motor Lodge in town and someone threw a Molotov cocktail through the motel window of a New York LGBTQ activist, legal advisor to the local counsel arguing for acquittal.

Less than twenty miles from Selma, an infamous location in the Civil Rights movement, an amalgam of liberal groups were planning to retrace the steps of the March to Montgomery to draw parallels to today's turbulence. A candlelight vigil for the murdered activist drew several counter-protesters, and in the ensuing melee, a member of a gay activist organization had thrown acid in the face of a church deacon, disfiguring his face, and blinding a local police officer not wearing riot gear to avoid optics reminiscent of the Selma march.

The story leads the news for a week and showed no signs of subsiding. The protests grew. Just as the story waned, a blast went off inside the Mecklenburg County Courthouse, despite security measures. Everyone suspected an inside job. They killed a magistrate who officiated weddings, along with a judge in a nearby office. The bombers knew where to strike. One judge was in critical condition, as was a court stenographer, and a bailiff. They targeted Becky's mentor, Judge Everett, who vowed the week before on TV protesters would not intimidate him, He was advising opposing attorneys in a nearby room when the second blast hit. The contentious story had now shifted to Charlotte.

Becky was distraught. She had been in the building and heard the noise. After four long hours, she was unsure whether Judge Everett survived. For Eunice, a prominent LGBTQ attorney, this was a perfect time to court media attention for her solo practice. She went to the site of the blast, angling for an interview. She reasoned that the media would connect the dots to the Whitcomb case, where she represented the estranged wife of a prominent Charlotte banker. It was front-page news and ugly. Eunice prodded her client to weaponize the daughter in the divorce, and with millions at stake, Rhonda Whitcomb was happy to oblige. Their daughter, Melanie, on heavy doses of antidepressants, pressured to testify against her dad with false accusations of abuse. She refused, in the most dramatic terms possible, by throwing herself off the Bell Tower of the University of North Carolina before stunned onlookers. Eunice's spin had not a kernel of truth, yet it didn't stop her from continuing to slander the once prominent executive. The grieving father was in no mood to fight back bare-knuckled as he had during the Senate Banking Bailout hearings. He left banking altogether, a broken man.

After its orderly evacuation, Becky left the courthouse

and headed to her office on foot as car traffic was halted. Her lot was being swept for explosives and evidence. She gathered her belongings and went home, advising her assistant to cancel the day's appointments.

Becky took a cab to her house, a small, well-maintained Dilworth ranch on a leafy side street. She flicked on the TV to CNN, intending to switch to local coverage when there she was, larger than life. Eunice, the presumptive spokesperson was outraged at the goings-on. "How dare she!" cried Becky, knowing full well the moral turpitude and hypocrisy of her rival attorney.

Eunice railed about the inept police, and failure to protect the LGBTQ community while fostering an atmosphere of hatred. The national audience was unaware of her disreputable past or shoddy legal reputation. Eunice wanted to promote her abrasive personality as the only voice that could protect those in the LGBTQ community. Becky's fumed with indignation.

Her phone was already in hand when Mindy called. "Are you OK, Babe?" she said. Becky was not okay, but pissed. "I'm okay, but guess who the de facto spokesperson is now for Marriage Equality in Charlotte? Turn on CNN. That lying bitch is on the goddamn national news. The building is still smoldering. I don't know how or when, but I'll shut her down. We must go public, to give truth to the situation. She shouldn't have anything to do with marriage on the front end or back end. She's a reason not to get married!"

"Becky, I think we need to get married. Let's not kid ourselves, we've been together for ten years, and times have changed. I can try to get a position at a Charlotte Medical Center, sell the house and we will get a fantastic place in a high rise with a sweeping view. We can get your friend the judge to marry us, and you'll be the human face of this story. It'll be important to atone for not going public before Melanie's suicide. If we get married, you wouldn't have to testify that I shared Melanie's therapy notes with you. What do you say, Sugar?"

"I'm in. I'll call Judge Everett right now. The news would have said if something happened to a judge right? Dear God, I hope he is okay. He put his life at risk and I would want him to marry us. I was nauseous seeing Eunice on TV before you called, but now I feel calm. I want to make this official and to atone for that poor girl. We could have done something." Becky pounded her hand on the end table. "We can bring closure."

"I want to get on the Raleigh News and ask forgiveness from Grayson Whitcomb and the soul of his daughter for not doing enough to prevent her death." Mindy said.

The suicide of Melanie Whitcomb, like a dormant virus, would bubble to the surface with each related news story. Now it was omnipresent.

"That kid in Alabama was in the same situation, being coerced to testify against his parents. He rode his bicycle to the river and drowned himself. Both sides are screaming for blood, and they will charge someone with murder and start holy hell. They'll never rule it a suicide. Both sides want to make a murderer pay. Someone could have said something, and no one did. Now the kid is dead." Mindy said 'kid' but it was Melanie in her thoughts.

"Mindy just don't. Not yet. Hang tight and see how things play out in the media. I'm just saying wait a few weeks. We still have time."

Judge Everett was not picking up his phone. Was he injured? What about his clerks? Becky sent him a text not knowing if the septegenarian even used texting. "Guess who the new spokesperson is for Marriage Equality in Charlotte? Turn on CNN."

There was a dust covered bottle of scotch in the cabinet. After the call with Mindy, Becky had a headache. She needed to nap and remembered a leftover Percoset from a root canal nearing its expiration date. A Scotch on the rocks plus the pill would put her out for a good four hours. It was a blessed and cursed day. Terrorism had visited Charlotte, but she and her long-term partner, Mindy, would finally marry, purging a secret both had kept bottled up for years.

Becky, still in a business suit, changed into sweats, heated leftover lasagna, and poured herself a scotch on ice. Next, she fetched the pill from the medicine cabinet and set it on the napkin she'd used to cover her mouth upon seeing Eunice. She switched to Charlotte news to get the local coverage. They canceled all local programming to bring the big news to the Piedmont.

Eunice appeared again, the absolute worst advocate for peace and reconciliation any community could have picked. This time the screen said: Women's Rights Activist/ Attorney and Concerned Member of the Charlotte LGBTQ Community. "*What horseshit!*" Becky thought. Judge Everett texted: "Just saw her. Got your message. Let's talk! Call you in a few." At seventy-five years, Judge Everett was proficient in texting. Within a minute the phone rang.

"Hey, are you okay?"

"Yeah, I was in a conference room a hundred yards from the blast. They blew my entire office to smithereens. If I was inside, I'd be dead! They were after me, but I won't shut up. And you?"

"I was in the building; Family Court, Room 3220, and heard the blast. How are the people in the hospital? News says three critical, with a few others with minor scrapes."

"I think all but one will make it, serious shrapnel injuries. Like a war for Chrissakes. The mother of four, thirty-seven years old is critical. The cop will survive, although he might lose an arm."

"Dang. Are you ready for some pleasant news?"

"I can use some today."

"I'm getting married, and we want you to officiate."

"You know I'd be happy to."

"I want the media to see it, and I'll speak my mind afterward."

"Are you sure about that? I took a stand to let the loonies know they would not intimidate us. You don't have to. I now have a squad car outside my house twenty-four seven. Think about what you're doing, Becky."

"I've already decided. I had a suicide under my watch I could have prevented. Mindy remains convinced the kid in Alabama killed himself to avoid testifying against his parents and you know, the Whitcomb girl."

"Come to think of it, it makes perfect sense. I hadn't thought of that. You're haunted still?"

"Yes, we'll always be asking ourselves if we could have done something different. The suicide makes perfect sense to everyone except the DA and Law enforcement. They need a scalp or neither side will be satisfied."

"Becky, that's interesting. By not having to testify against your spouse, it'd be a tough case to prosecute either of you. Your access to her notes from the girl's therapy would never come up. Your firm would have to slap your hand for revealing information on the case. You'd be open for disbarment, but I'd say you have an eighty-twenty shot at beating that rap. Not a good career move, but I'd say it would be tough to bring criminal charges against either of you."

"What about Eunice taking a civil action against me or Mindy?"

"She could, that's her right, but you have the facts on your side. You get her on the witness stand, and she won't practice law either."

"I was on the verge of quitting before. I could drop this career in a heartbeat. It's burning me out." She sighed.

"What the fallout will be for Mindy, I don't know. She might lose patients or get a slap on the wrist."

"We have a few weeks to figure this stuff out. She wants to go public. We might know which direction the media circus will take by then." Becky had enough news for the day.

"Well, we both have a lot of thinking to do. The media has been hounding me all day; I don't know what to say. I don't like seeing Eunice enjoying her fifteen minutes of fame while there are dead bodies barely cold."

Charlotte had a day or two in the spotlight until some Iranian saber rattling topped the national news. The Charlotte City fathers were lucky to get off the front pages for something negative and were searching for a silver lining. A recent ESPN story announced that major league baseball wanted to add two unknown cities and shift two lower performing teams to other markets. This meant four cities that didn't have a team could receive franchises. The Knights were in an AAA Championship Series that would have its last game on Friday night. Typical aspirational, Charlotte. *"We get terrorist bombings like Atlanta, Boston, and New York. Why shouldn't we get a baseball franchise too?"* Such was the mindset of city leaders desperate to be thought of as major league.

Chapter Ten
Fireworks

The bomb set off in the Mecklenburg County Courthouse that had killed a magistrate and seriously injured several others had caused a lockdown of the businesses close by the building. Ross's attorney had been in the building when the blast rocked through it, but she had not been injured. The protests between the LBGTQ community and religious groups escalated. Ross's martial arts classes were canceled on the Monday the incident happened. Ross watched the news reports with avid interest. Had Julie been in the courthouse and injured by the bomb? When her name failed to be called as one of the injured or dead, Ross relaxed. He would see her at class on Wednesday.

They canceled martial arts again on Wednesday. CMPD set up checkpoints throughout Uptown. Two principals of Fighting Fitness taped interviews on the evening news about situational awareness and terrorism. Ross grew impatient with the delay in his and Dave's plan until the gym emailed a phone list of students and urged everyone to start a phone chain regarding the cancellation. A perfect excuse for Ross to call Julie.

After a perfunctory discussion of the bombing, Julie's experience in the courthouse, proximity to the bomb, and continued apologies, the call shifted gears. Ross introduced a few of Dave's scouting intelligence nuggets.

They talked for an hour and made a date for Friday to stroll through uptown. Julie's firm had a coveted baseball box, and Ross would try to pull a few strings and get tickets to the Alabama Shakes, one of Julie's favorite bands. They'd dine uptown, and go to the game or concert, and play the rest of the night by ear.

The Alabama Shakes were sold-out. StubHub had tickets, but they were beyond Ross's reach. He pulled strings with a work friend, a manager of the fan page of the Double Door Inn. The venue hosted Clapton and Stevie Ray Vaughan, among blues greats. According to Cheryl, the Alabama Shakes lived just a few miles from Friday's featured act, a Muscle Shoals-based band called the Pinched Nerves. It was a certainty that Brittany Howard and her bandmates would show for a late-night impromptu concert.

For Ross, this would be even better than tickets. Getting the inside scoop, and surprising Julie would create a bonding moment, as the two could dance the night away.

The festival at Bearden Park was called a Fan Appreciation Night, with scheduled local bands and local celebrities. Thanks to a greased-through permit, and donated corporate jet, the famed Grucci family of New York would put together a spectacular fireworks display.

After a moment of silence to the fallen, the show would stress a united community. Eunice, however, didn't see things the same way. She was, according to one councilman, "An unwelcome skunk at a funeral" decrying the city's failure to address the festering issues of sexism and homophobia.

Eunice wore on even those in her community or those who should have been political allies. Deborah Collins, the left-leaning Councilwoman from NoDa forgot to say, "Off the Record," during an interview with the Observer. She stated, "When I see Eunice Burbank, I see an uncouth media whore. She's doing irreparable harm to the cause, and I wish she would shut the fuck up."

Her comments were at first stricken by the copy editor but made for good copy. The Observer ran with the story. Other council members soon added juicy quotes.

Julie brought a change of shoes to work and an outfit for her date. Ross suggested Bentley's, a restaurant on the thirty-third floor of the Park Plaza Building. Views were romantic, and he wanted to pull out all the stops to make this evening seem magical. The plan was to meet for drinks, work their way over the Epicenter for some Mexican food, and then walk to the park. Julie's office was a few blocks from Bentley's, but she had never been there.

Ross took the light rail up, leaving his car at the Archdale station. Their bar table had a view of the stadium and the western side of Uptown. Ross had a champagne bucket already set up when Julie arrived. He greeted her with a kiss on the cheek, which she returned. Gentleman Ross pulled out her chair.

"Wow, I like it in here," Julie said just as the waiter brought some crab dip.

Ross filled the glasses, took the single rose from its perch on the windowsill ledge, and said, "A toast to a great evening."

"That's so sweet."

If only Dave could see his appreciative ex-wife, such a

far cry from the ball-breaker that caused Dave grief.

"I missed the class so much," Ross said. "I'm growing to enjoy the stress relief," he said, while hoping for another kind later that night.

She nodded, "It's been better than yoga and has calmed me."

"Was anyone from your office in the courthouse?"

"I think we had a runner there to file documents, no one near the blast. I go to the building a fair amount and have been in the courtroom right next to where the judge was."

"Yeah, my divorce attorney knew the guy, and she's pretty shaken up. You know that heavyset woman on TV a lot, the attorney from Charlotte, that is my ex's attorney."

"Wow, she seems like a piece of work. Not a good spokeswoman, not in this town where civility is the Charlotte way."

"Well, from my experience she's no picnic to deal with."

Ross needed to shift the conversation, and fast. He wanted nothing that could connect the dots to spill out. Loose lips sink ships, especially when involving alcohol. He told Julie he had made a reservation at Vida, a high-end Mexican place at the Epicenter where they could grab a margarita or two, dine and walk over to Bearden Park next to the stadium. Ross adopted Dave's meticulous obsession with planning.

After a few glasses of wine, Julie excused herself. Ross glanced at his phone, now in silent mode. *Texts from Becky. How odd. Best not to look now.* He didn't want distractions. Ross worked in a few tidbits from Dave on music, politics, and movies. The conversation was deep and engaging. No longer a tough as nails attorney, nor a dedicated martial artist; this was just a middle-aged divorcee enjoying herself.

Ross grabbed the check, and the two took the elevator down the thirty-three floors as sexual tension filled the elevator cab. He wanted to feel the small of her back or exposed skin between her shoulder blades. If not for the other couple in the elevator, he would plant one of those Hollywood-style first kisses. He imagined what Julie might think. *This is a guy I have lots in common with, who even enjoys martial arts.* Clearly, she thought of herself as an outlier. A pang of guilt penetrated his psyche, as he realized the meeting was contrived, planned to mitigate the financial burdens of a stranger he met on a plane.

Ross caught a whiff of her perfume and looked at her legs. They were fit and toned from working out and yet silky smooth. His guilt subsided. The sundress she now wore had him enthralled. A text from Vida showed their table was ready. They began the brisk two-block walk to the Epicenter. A leisurely dinner and walk to the stadium would put them in their seats for the eight o'clock start. They ordered a pitcher of margaritas with two straws like college coeds. The crowd was at least a decade younger on average, but Ross felt equally youthful and Julie looked it. She confided that she sometimes worried about her image, an attorney doing martial arts and that underneath it all she had a softer side. It now showed through like the pastel colors of her sundress.

"Julie, your dress looks amazing, and no, I think nothing bad about the martial arts. I get it. It's like therapy. It gives people a kinder disposition than people who have no outlets for their aggression. It's empowering for women," Ross said. "As for the lawyer thing, it's great you are so independent. A woman handling her stuff is a huge turn-on. You've accomplished a lot and looked good doing it."

Was that too forward? Ross was caught up in the moment. He held his breath while Julie chewed on her enchilada. He waited for her reply after she swallowed.

"Ross, that was sweet. My ex was in my dad's business, and so I always felt as if I had to prove myself. To be more accomplished than my brother Brad, or my husband. It made me lose sight of some things." She paused. "Funny how the dojo allows me to channel my competitiveness and get more in touch with the softer side. Sounds stupid. Guys always go to the gym or roughhouse when they're younger. Girls keep everything inside. Some spar with gossip. They use words to channel aggression. I did tennis, but it didn't satisfy me. I viewed my career as a statement. The divorce has forced me to reevaluate this toxic need to compete. I've mellowed."

Ross blinked. She had remorse for the past.

"It contributed to the marital rift and I take ownership. You can't love someone you're competing against. I'm glad we're getting to know each other. You're easy to talk to. The margaritas are running through me. Will you excuse me?"

His phone now had texts from Becky urging he call her back. He replied stating he was out and would get back with her tomorrow. Becky was normally the calm one, and Ross the nervous wreck. Why now, when he was making progress with Julie?

He spied Julie walking back. She was fifteen years older than most of the other women in the place, but looked every bit as fresh, with a depth the younger ladies would never develop. The girls, slurping their Dirty Martinis or Cape Cods, were squeezed into form-fitting hooker clothes to look attractive. Julie had style and substance. The others were barely old enough to drink, while Julie was the whole enchilada. The Plan seemed oddly irrelevant.

She didn't pick at a salad, pretending she had never eaten before. She became animated at the suggestion of a Tres Leches cake for dessert. The check arrived, signaling it was time to think about when and where to plant that first kiss. The question of if was settled. He positioned his chair closer to share their dessert. He was touching her shoulder, neck, and while a trained counterpuncher, Julie offered no resistance.

They made their way to the stadium through the network of walkways, first through the Bank of America lobby. The walkways lined with stores, and lunch places that catered to the nine-to-five business crowd, were now all closed. Ross searched for a deserted nook for his historic first kiss. An alcove just above Trade Street provided just the opportunity. Julie was an impressive kisser. They continued their ten-minute walk with the tension abated.

Bearden Park was crowded in anticipation of nightfall and the fireworks. A band was already playing the ubiquitous "Freebird."

They sat on a ledge to rest and entered the ballpark after the guitar solos had subsided, to search for their seats before the fireworks started. He kissed her again and she reciprocated. He threaded his fingers through hers, and they held hands and rubbed each other's backs. Julie seemed at ease.

"Julie, I feel comfortable with you. The dating thing has been awkward, and I don't always mesh with others. I'm picky, but you're quite a package."

There was little pretense or inhibition. She looked beautiful but challenging, with wry humor. It was a welcome change from the smarminess he had endured. She was flirty with depth. Ross felt as if his confidence had emerged from its dormant state. The humility of all that had transpired tempered it, but he was no longer a beaten pound puppy.

They meandered to the box in BB&T ballpark, avoiding PDAs for fear of running into work associates. Their glances spoke volumes. The first of many salvos launched in the air, each time followed by ooohs and aahs. Julie clasped Ross's hand during the national anthem and didn't let go until hearing the customary, "Play Ball."

Ross did a quick scooping motion in his pants pocket, applying just enough pressure to the touch screen to scan for recent texts. There were easily a dozen from Becky, unreadable, with Julie at his side. His attorney was having a meltdown when he could least afford to respond.

The Knights' players trotted out to their positions, and

Ross asked Julie if she wanted something from the concessions. Neither were hungry, but Ross needed a few minutes to read Becky's texts. Becky was Ross' rock. Now she was hyper, frantically texting and endangering his perfect evening. While rusty on the rules of dating etiquette Ross knew reading texts in the presence of your date was a buzzkill.

Walking to the concessions, Ross read:

> Ross I need to talk to you, and Ross, where are you? Ross I've reached a decision I need to tell you about. Ross, I've decided something I need to share with you.

Ross was reading the text trail when he felt a thump in the middle of his chest, and then the wail of a spoiled child upset at his spilled popcorn.

"Watch where you're going. How rude."

"I'm sorry ma'am."

"It upset my child. Don't you look where you are going?"

"Look, here's five bucks, sorry for the inconvenience."

"I'm not waiting in line again, buy me another."

What a bitch. He would have given her a twenty just to have a few minutes to assess the Becky texts.

"Yes, Mommy, that man needs to get us a new one."

Yet another spoiled generation being groomed. But in no mood for the drama, he told them to wait while he got another.

He picked up Cracker Jacks for Julie and stuffed them in his back pocket before the little demon seed demanded those as compensation for her pain and suffering.

Ross typed out:

> Becky, I'm with the girl, big night. Can't talk now, perhaps later or tomorrow morning. Might meet you for B fast.

He handed the mom the replacement popcorn with a snarky look. Now he had to go to the bathroom, with no time for a call. *What is wrong with Becky and just how serious is this?*

Julie gave Ross an endearing glance upon his return. She wasn't monitoring his time. This burgeoning chemistry with Julie was unfamiliar terrain. How did he win her affection? Becky's freak-out texts added to the anxiety. The little blue pill in his pocket was reminding him he needed to be at his best while anxiety was stalking him.

The game was boring, as baseball often is: no home runs, and except for an off-the-wall double to drive in a run with a play at the plate, a pitcher's duel. Of significance was the game's 2-2 tie in the bottom of the ninth. Extra innings were not factored into the spontaneous concert at the Double Door with Brittney Howard. The timing required Swiss watch-like precision. Extra innings would throw off the timetable. The Richmond Braves had rallied to push a run across in the top of the ninth inning. Unless the Knights scored, the game could last all night.

It was the worst part of the batting order to expect offense. The Knights' number seven hitter was a Dominican teen starting at shortstop to fill in for a pro prospect now in the big leagues. The number eight hitter was a defensive outfielder, thus prompting a pinch hitter, and the Knights' number nine hitter. It would leave a lanky middle relief pitcher to bat so as not to leave a depleted bullpen.

The Dominican kid, Cesar Semilla, fouled off about four pitches. But with a one-two count, he beat out a slow roller to third and was on first base. Rolland Gaines, the next batter up showed a .211 batting average on the scoreboard. He flew out to centerfield but moved the speedy Cesar to second base. Eddie Campos, the lanky pitcher, was hitting an abysmal .126 but did Ross a favor and grounded out on the first pitch. Semilla needed only to advance two bases to make Ross and the crowd happy.

With a one-two count, he hit a screamer down the first baseline that went over the first baseman's head, enabling Semilla to round third. A relay from the right fielder to the second baseman arrived a split second too late as the throw to home arrived in the catcher's mitt as Semilla's foot hit the plate. The crowd erupted in cheers as the PA system crowned the Knights champions and thanked the fans for their support.

Ross tugged Julie's hand to make tracks outside the stadium. They angled past the crowds. Ross said a coworker could get them in the Double Door and was raving about this alternative band worth checking out. They flagged down a cabbie with an East African accent. Ross doubted he knew where the Double Door was but the cabbie nodded, he was familiar with the Red Sea, the Ethiopian place next door. Julie held on to his arm.

Ross mentioned Carol, the club's social media manager, to the bouncer. They were quickly ushered in, and they waived the cover charge.

"Nice going," Julie said.

Ross felt good to have his competence praised.

The Double Door was little more than a dilapidated turn-of-the-century wooden house near the downtown campus of the community college. However, it had a lengthy history, and tonight would provide another photograph on the wall. The place was packed as the band performed its first set. Pictures of celebrities that had jammed in the club adorned the walls and dated wood paneling gave the room a nostalgic feel.

Julie was content with a light beer. It pleased Ross she seemed immune to the microbrew craze. Ross grabbed two beers as the Pinched Nerves worked through their fresh material. They were tight, hailing from legendary Muscle Shoals, a musical hot spot.

They found a ledge to perch their beers. Ross waited to acclimatize before asking Julie to dance. The crowd was eclectic, a large contingent of twenty-somethings and a sprinkling from each age category, including some graying ponytails that Ross guessed were blues musicians. Ross felt occasional vibrations in the pocket from his phone. *More texts from Becky.* At some point, Julie would need to use the restroom and he would then read them.

Ross rarely did shots, but tonight was special. He asked Julie, who shuffled her hips as if to show she was in rhythm with the music before nodding yes. Ross saddled up to the bar, ordered two Patrons with a few limes, and a shaker of salt. He walked back to their expanse of the wall. Julie took the shaker, dipped her finger in her beer, dabbed the beer on her neck, and then put salt on it. "I figured you would rather lick the salt off my neck." Ross downed the shot, bit hard on the lime, and put his arm around Julie and licked her neck. She let out a purr as if she was a contented cat. She took her shot, chewed her lime, and licked the salt off the space between her thumb and index finger. Julie then planted a kiss on Ross's cheek. The night was going swimmingly. Ross asked Julie to dance, as the band began another set.

A few minutes into the song, the band's lead singer announced he would like to introduce a few friends and neighbors. Muscle Shoals neighbors, the Grammy-winning Alabama Shakes, would join them and asked his friend Brittany Howard to take the microphone. She and a few band mates took the crowded stage.

Julie gave an incredulous look as if she couldn't believe her good fortune. Ross told her he had received a tip they would head over to the Double Door after their concert. She hugged Ross as if he had just come back from a yearlong deployment as the band launched into their song "Hold On."

Julie kissed Ross's lips and said, "Thank you!" Ross confided that he hadn't felt this happy in eons. She drank her beer while enchanting Ross with her undulating dance moves.

"I saw so much live music when I was at Vanderbilt. It was my guilty pleasure. I'd plan hour-long study breaks in law school and go down to Broadway or Printers Alley and check out a band or two. I missed having that close by and twenty-four seven. I forgot how much I miss hearing bands live. You think I'm crazy?"

"Quite the contrary. The ex wasn't one for seeing music. She thought everything had to be age-appropriate and as soon as she became a mom, she would insist we were too old to enjoy venues like this. I'm making up for the lost time."

"That's great, Ross. It's not the booze talking. I hope you don't think this too forward, but there is an outdoor music festival at Shelton Vineyards, about an hour north. I was thinking of going myself. Do you want to get a picnic basket or cooler, go for a tour of the winery, and then catch the music? There is a fantastic shag band. I don't want to pressure you if you've something to do, but it would be fun." Julie choked on her words. "I can't believe I said that."

"Julie, that sounds great. It's sweet. I need to get to my car and stop at my apartment. But it sounds wonderful."

Trouble at high noon. One of Stephanie's Bunko mates was in the house. A frizzy-haired small-time editor of a South Charlotte Paper. She was a Northern interloper who derided everything in Charlotte from pizza to bagels, and intellect, which she viewed as inherently inferior to her beloved Boston. Brenda was bitter and snarky, qualities Stephanie enjoyed. Her husband could never get a word in edgewise. Her kids were a hot mess, but that didn't stop Brenda from passing judgment on everyone else in the neighborhood. Best to be proactive.

"Hi, Brenda," Ross said.

"Go fuck yourself. I hear every day what a despicable human being you are from your ex-wife. You're scum." She was drunk but parroting what Stephanie told her.

"Being a two-bit small-time editor, do you examine the veracity of your sources to check credibility, or whether there is another side of the story? I mean, that is the point of journalism, isn't it? Otherwise, you are just a jerk with an opinion, right? Have a wonderful night and nice talking to you. Give my best to Stephanie."

"Asshole," she said flipping Ross the bird for good measure.

"Very classy. Love you too, Brenda. Don't forget to tell Stephanie I said hello."

"What was that about?" Julie asked.

"Oh, she's just some troll my ex knows. Part of her bitter housewives' collection. I call them the nattering nabobs of negativity."

"What an asshole, and your ex-wife, she's awful too?"

"Yep, you get a sense she has moved on with her life, huh?"

"You know that Bonnie Raitt song? Let's give 'em something to talk about. Grab my ass like it's spring break in Daytona. Make her head explode," Julie said, demonstrably fawning on Ross, winking then blowing a kiss to Brenda to get her goat. Word would get back Ross was doing just fine with the ladies.

Despite the fortuitous evening, Becky concerned him. Ross hoped to meet her for breakfast when this long date ended. Now it might take the entire weekend. Ross mapped it out in his head. His car was at the Light Rail station. *Was Julie asking him to stay over? Was he supposed to pick her up in the morning? Was she going to stay over his place?* These were all good problems.

Other than saying yes to the winery music fest, there were loose ends. It was after one, and there were maybe five songs left. He needed to talk with Becky.

Ross looked at Julie's sundress swaying as she moved her hips and had visions of it falling to the floor as he unzipped the back. The last song could be as little as an hour or two away. No time for an early breakfast with Becky. At some point, Ross would broach the delicate subject. Was this a sleepover? Would they go their separate ways and reconnect in the morning? Asking would kill the spontaneity if he misread Julie's invitation.

The flickering lights signaled for last call. The Pinched

Nerves and The Alabama Shakes did their obligatory bows and launched into their last song with the house lights up. There was a line of cabs outside and which prompted some serious logistical questions.

"Julie, what an outstanding night. Let's get your car and grab a cup of coffee at the Midnight Diner. We can relax at my place while I change, and head up to your place, maybe grab a breakfast, fill a cooler with sandwiches, and get on the road."

He knew the Dobson exit. He had enough points to get a room comped at the Hampton Inn, off the highway.

A day of picnicking and wine tasting might be conducive to staying over. They found their Uber and climbed in.

"I got to change the destination to the garage at College and Third." Julie seemed unconcerned about any logistics as the two were kissing like teens in the back. She seemed fine to drive as it was a quick hop to the South End where the diner was and then just a straight shot down South Boulevard to the train station. The cup of coffee would give them a chance to talk and get at least a beer or two out of their system. It was about ten after two. He had forgotten to down the Viagra but could do so in the bathroom of the Midnight Diner. Ross pulled out a ten spot as it seemed more impressive than tipping on the app. They scurried to her car, one of only three in the parking level, and her keys made a chirping sound as the lights flickered and the door unlocked.

The car was immaculate and smelled scented. It was a far cry from Ross's bachelor car. They crossed over seventy-seven and into the South End, passing bars that had just closed and a smattering of twenty somethings either paired up or going home alone.

Julie had asked Siri by voice for the address of the Midnight Diner on South and then used the address to program in directions. They were a mere five minutes away. It was busy for two-thirty as they walked up the stairs to the door. The crowd was bleary-eyed hipsters, burgeoning bankers, and dressed to the nines club goers. Security guards scanned for rowdy drunks. The waitress passed out menus and asked if they were ready to order. "Just some coffee for now," Ross said. Something was comforting about the clanking of silverware on plates, the animated and often inebriated conversations and bright diner lights punctuating the darkness of the deep night.

Julie poured some creamer and said she wasn't hungry. Ross got a bagel. He figured they could split if she changed her mind.

"So, tell me about the music festival. I've been to Raffaldini Vineyards, but not Shelton. I pass by there all the time when I go to Roanoke."

"It has beautiful grounds with a large grassy area and a pleasant restaurant. We can go there for lunch before the festival, my treat."

"Julie, I'm all about this. Watching you spin like a top on the dance floor got me swept up."

"I love to dance. My ex, not so much. He just never liked to go out much. He liked movies or watching sports or checking out restaurants. Had to be planned to a tee. I guess working for my dad kind of ruined our relationship." She was wistful and sipped her coffee before continuing, "Dad felt disappointed after I got a law degree and didn't work for the family. I studied patent law and did the entire coursework specific to the pharmaceutical industry in law school. Dave had a hard time. Once we split, my dad circled the wagons. I had to play hardball with him. I kind of regret it. The guy lost his job." She sighed. "My father purported to get Dave a job for a competitor, but it was a contract position so he could show high income during the divorce, higher than mine but no benefits. His contract ended when the settlement was final. I feel bad about it. I have this unhealthy competitive streak. Wow, we started out talking about dancing and look where I wound up."

"Most divorced people you meet have this narrative,

they're the victim and the innocent one. That can't always be the case. It speaks volumes for you to say you have regrets. You still have feelings for him?" Ross wanted to gauge if he was scoring points or was just a rebound relationship.

"Not those kinds of feelings. Like I said, working for my dad was a gargantuan mistake. He wanted so bad to get out, but it would have been an enormous breach of loyalty in the family. It trapped him. We might have been victims of circumstance and a poor decision, but over time the feelings died. I'm sure he resents me for dragging him into a dysfunctional family business. Without kids, there isn't much reason to communicate after a divorce. I'd be conciliatory, and if he was open to it, develop a friendship. I'd like to think I'm a different person now. The resentments got in the way."

"I can understand how that can happen," Ross said quietly. "You want half my bagel? We can get out of here afterward. Let's get my car at the station. It's not the Ritz, but if you are up for it, we can relax till nine then head up to your place. I have a big beach cooler we can fill with stuff from the Teeter."

"Ross, it's been a long time since I've been with a guy. If you think I have my shit together, you're wrong. This is new for me, too. Just don't screw me over, okay? Don't make me kick your butt."

Ross chuckled. "Funny, it's been a long time since I've been with a guy, too. So, we're even. I like you too, Julie. We have a lot of stuff in common."

"We do," she said, smiling.

"So, to be upfront, I had a procedure that removed some vital parts, and made relationships difficult, if not impossible."

The mood got somber.

"Seriously? What happened?"

"It was a divorce, and I had most of my assets removed. Bad joke."

"Phew, you had me going. Real funny."

"Check, please."

It was happening. The words looped in Ross's head as they strolled to the car, a tiny nip of autumn now in the air of the pre-dawn hours. He had his hand on hers as she drove down south, passing the car dealers and ethnic stew of stores until reaching the train station at Archdale. He was not sure he made his bed. Ross had dishes in the sink and unfolded laundry on the couch. Grabbing a coffee with Becky should be the last thing on his mind, but he needed to figure out what the texts meant.

"Julie, let me get your address. I'll go home, shower, change, shave, and pack a cooler full of stuff for our picnic. You won't have to do a thing. I'll drive if you like. I figure you want a few hours to freshen up. Tonight has been beyond perfect, and I want it to continue. Two hours sleep and I can be at your place at maybe 10:30 and we'll get to Shelton by noon. I don't want to rush things in some two-hour window and have an entire day running on fumes."

"Ross, I know this is where everything is code words and rules, but to tell you the truth, I was expecting you would ask me to your place, and we would be together, and maybe sleep half the day away. I too would prefer to get a little sleep. I want to be awake when you know... This is awkward. I want things to be special. You don't have weird stuff going on at your place, do you? Cabinets full of porn or S&M stuff? God, I sound so paranoid. Am I making an ass of myself?"

Julie seemed so vulnerable, so unlike the tough cookie, Dave described. Ross felt the need to reassure her without hesitation.

"Julie, no dead bodies under the floorboards, no woman's lingerie hanging in the shower stall, no porn stash, just a messy bachelor pad, and a guy who wants to get rest before another perfect day. As an attorney, may I ask you a question?"

"Sure."

"Are there any statutes in Mecklenburg County against making out at a public train station?" Ross grabbed her close, and they embraced. His hands roamed all along her back and down to her shapely rear. She offered no resistance. The two came up for air with a mutual, "Wow."

"See you at 10:30, Julie."

She blew a kiss and winked as she got back in the car. *Damn she is sexy.* He wanted to find out more about her. How could Dave let her get away? He pictured the clean sheets of the Hampton Inn at Shelton after a glorious day and the excitement he would feel as clothing fell to the floor. He figured it was a good idea to text Becky and tell her he could meet her at a Dilworth Coffee at perhaps 8:00 and head on up to Julie's after grabbing picnic items at the nearby Teeter. He shot her a text and headed out as the first stirrings of daylight were visible on the horizon.

Chapter Eleven
The Winery

He got in at 5 30 and could think of nothing but plopping on the bed after setting his alarm for seven. An hour to shower, get clothes together and head up to Dilworth to meet Becky. Ross scribbled a note of what to buy as he dozed off: some cheese spread, those high-end crackers, and some baguettes, gourmet sandwich meats, some gazpacho, croutons, ham, salami, nuts and some exotic fruits like mangos, or papayas. Dessert could be tricky. He'd play that one by ear; he wanted this to be perfect.

She practically said she'd sleep with him, but this wasn't about conquest. He wanted her to like him, but not to complete Dave's end of the deal. This called for an impressive picnic basket.

Working on an hour sleep was risky. Often, you wound up waking up more tired than if you went without, but Ross leaped out of bed, unusual as he wasn't a morning person. His rigid state reminded him he downed a blue pill at the diner. Hopefully, it would still provide the needed enhancement a day later.

Next step, pick out clothes, iron them, and have a travel bag ready at seven-thirty. Becky signaled that an eight-thirty cup of coffee at Caribou on East Boulevard would work. He grabbed a gym bag and the cooler in the garage and threw them in his trunk.

Becky looked maternal in a cable-knit sweater. She was like a sister. She was troubled, and he felt it only fair to provide a sympathetic ear. What a role reversal. Ross was a psychic mess when he approached Becky for representation. Now he needed to reassure her. They both looked as if they hadn't slept.

"Well, look who is here, Romeo," Becky said.

"I guess I have a way with female attorneys. If you weren't representing me, I bet I could turn you straight," Ross said.

"Your ex was right. You're a pig." Becky continued the playful repartee.

"Did Eunice make you a job offer? Sounds like you might fit in at her firm," Ross said.

"Ross, there isn't anything funny about that woman. I wouldn't walk across the street to piss on her if her heart were on fire. We need to talk," Becky said in a somber tone. "You may not even remember when your accountant called a family court judge on your behalf to find out the short and skinny on your ex's attorney. It was Judge Everett, who almost got killed in the bombing. You were trying to narrow down who your ex hired, and all you knew was she was gay, with a sizeable frame."

"I remember it. He told me about the attorneys he knew to be lesbians, and if it were the heavyset one, I'd be screwed big time. Another was an African-American lady just out of law school. I kind of guessed you were the well-respected one he said worked for the large firm. So what?"

"My long-term partner is a psychiatrist. She was treating the Whitcomb teen when me and Eunice were facing off in a high-profile divorce. We were sharing notes to help the girl. It's an ethical breach, but if we get married, we won't have to testify against one another. Eunice was pressuring the girl to testify against her dad, to say he abused her when he didn't."

"We were talking about the Whitcomb suicide and your case. We have decided we will help you, but you'll be my last client." Becky nervously fingered the cardboard sleeve of her coffee.

"Eunice and I have unresolved business from that case. At the end of this, I'll expose her for what she did. Painting Bank of America's top exec in such a negative light would have been worth millions. We need to come clean on what we knew, how we knew it, and what Eunice did to that poor child."

Becky drew in a deep breath. "We'll use it to help your case and help your daughter to not become a pawn." She sipped her coffee, "I want to expose Eunice as a fraud. We're getting married. They can yank both of our professional licenses for violating attorney-client and patient-doctor stuff, but no criminal stuff can stick without either of us testifying."

Becky picked at the opening of her coffee cup. "Mindy can write books. I might try politics. I've got some powerful friends in this town. I might help Grayson Whitcomb run for office. All this bullshit about the sanctity of marriage. I see the marriages when they're terminally ill and there isn't anything sacred about how they pull the plug on them."

While Becky was on her soapbox, this was a far less confident version than the lawyer he saw as his rock. She had reached a breaking point. The realization shook him.

"For all too long I've kept my private, professional, and public lives out of the public eye, but with that bitch hogging the limelight I'd be a hypocrite if I didn't come clean. She'll alienate everyone in this city who might pull us together. Our livelihoods have been primary, but it's time to throw them under the bus for something nobler. You were at the intersection."

"Whoa Becky, you seem so…" Ross paused, searching for the right word "Resolved. Like you are at peace with yourself. I'm touched that I might be part of such a big decision. Would it be selfish to ask if this could mess up my case?"

"Ross, by the time this stuff hits the papers, she'll have her mask peeled off and will have the credibility of a turd. You'll have one of the state's preeminent psychiatrists calling her out as having precipitated a teen suicide, weaponizing a kid to get an advantage. She's reduced one of Charlotte's most respected business leaders into a recluse; grieving and blaming himself for something that rests on the shoulders of his ex, and her attorney. If given the opportunity, she'd do the same to your daughter. Optics and politics are on your side."

"Is it an awful time to tell you? I'll probably be sleeping with Julie, the girl from The Plan tonight. I swear I'm falling in love with this girl. I'm getting food for a picnic basket but can't decide whether to go to Dean and Deluca's or a Teeter around here."

"Go to Reid's uptown. They do all our catering. Jimmy, the catering manager, owes me. Tell him to put it on the firm's tab. By the time anyone scrutinizes my expenses, I won't be practicing law. A picnic arrangement from Reid's will make her fall for you. Thank me later."

"Thanks, Becky," Ross said.

"Men. I'm happy for you. You deserve happiness. We all deserve happiness. Your daughter deserves happiness. I need to sleep. Ross, you and your daughter are the beneficiaries of this decision. We have a plan to clear our conscience and make sure Nicole is off-limits in the divorce."

"Becky, I got to go. Bring it in for a big hug. Anything I can do to help you. You've done so much for me. I love you like family. I'll vote for you, or Grayson Whitcomb. I'll help in any way I can. My life turned around thanks to you."

Life was happening at warp speed. Things hadn't sunk in yet. Ross drove on the deserted streets to Reid's and sought the catering manager. As if by magic Jimmy appeared, gushed about Becky, loaded him up with some crab cakes, chili lime shrimp skewers, a low country boil, a variety of salads, side dishes, and beef tenderloins. It was three hundred dollars' worth of gourmet stuff, which he marked down to two-hundred and gave him the receipt to put on the law firm's tab. They packed it in dry ice in special cartons, beyond elegant. The icing on the cake was the checkered tablecloth and linen napkins thrown in for free.

Ross was on cloud nine as he approached the Fourth Ward bungalow that had a view of the skyline. The eighteen hundred square foot ranch was done in modern decor. She greeted him in a casual yet stylish outfit. She smelled delicious and had primped as her hair had the curls that can only be achieved by an hour's worth of prep work, based on his experience with Stephanie. This was obviously an enormous deal for her. She had prepared a breakfast spread: fresh coffee, his third cup of the day, and a professional attempt at Eggs Benedict, freshly squeezed juice from her food processor, and some potato dish like hash browns but with more spices. The smell was enticing. He was ready to cohabitate immediately.

"If you would rather, we can go to McDonald's," Julie said, knowing full well it made an impression.

"No, it's okay. It's eerie because I splurged on our picnic stuff. I hope you can put away some food, but I wanted everything to be perfect."

"Ross, eat your breakfast and shut up or I might not let you leave this house and then we will miss the festival."

Ross savored the Hollandaise sauce and last forkful of Canadian bacon and grunted that he wanted more juice. He kissed her as she bent down to pour.

It was a pleasant hour and a half drive. There were moments of silence, but it was not uncomfortable as one might expect with a new couple. They drove past Lake Norman, and both commented on the clear blue skies with just a hint of autumn. Julie's hand more often than not was on top of Ross's on the shift knob. He debated telling her he got a room at the Hampton but thought it might be wise to wait until they entered the grounds.

The turnoff in Dobson was just a mile away from the winery. The crowds still filed in and they secured a suitable parking spot and spied a pleasant place to spread out. Together they set up their blanket and tablecloth and unpacked their cooler of goodies.

"This smells even better than breakfast," she said.

"That was hard to top. Let's say it was a tie. No competition here. Just happy we're together."

They uncorked the Chardonnay and toasted to a great weekend. Ross decided he could tell her about the suite, and that driving wouldn't be an issue.

"You are just too much, Ross. I hope you got rest because I don't know how much you'll get tonight."

The sexual tension was palpable, the anticipation intense.

"Why? You snore?"

"I don't know. No one there to tell me if I did."

"I hope I wasn't being presumptuous with the invite."

"Depends on what you are presuming," she said with a coy smile.

The first band, a shag band, took the stage while the front row danced to the Carolina Beach Music Medley. There would be plenty of time for dancing later. Being on a blanket was about as perfect a spot as Ross could imagine. The first date had lasted a day, which seemed like some kind of record.

Some secret glances and touches signaled what was to come while maintaining middle-aged respectability to the nearby patrons. Ross felt young again. His life had become a series of responsibilities. At long last, Ross felt the flutter of butterflies as he savored each moment like fine wine.

Like the vineyard itself, the two had been cultivating their grapes, borne not of wrath, but middle-aged longing. A bond that took him by surprise sweetened its fermentation.

As Julie went to the restroom, Ross thought of the genesis of this relationship. How could something that started as a con job become so beautiful? Somehow, he'd have to relieve his conscience but racked his brain for how he could do so. That was not a struggle for today. The day was rainbows and sunshine with no harsh realities. Ross did, however, wonder how the secret would gnaw at him in the coming days.

Ross uncorked the second bottle of chardonnay. Surely it would quell all thoughts of the great deception. As she walked down the sloped lawn, he could see her pearly white smile looking right at him. He felt wanted and accepted for who he was and was elated. If only she knew.

"I couldn't keep my eyes off you as you made your way back." The wine had disabled Ross's edit button. He could only say what he was feeling. Julie gave a coy smile and a kiss.

"Ross, you make me feel happy. I feel like a teenager," she said.

"Me too," said Ross, echoing her sentiment.

The band did a spot-on rendition of Little Feat's "Oh Atlanta" and Julie jumped up like a Jack-in-the-box and dragged Ross towards the grassy dance area at the foot of the stage. It was getting darker, and the two gyrated like tops. The wine said their dance moves were more in tune with the rhythm than they were.

"Ross, have you ever listened to music with someone and felt as if they heard it the same way, feeling the same sensations you were in your ears, in their mind. Shit, you probably think I'm weird."

Dave never told of her passion for music. He listed

bands she liked, and Ross made notes, but in the pre-intelligence meetings, they were the CDs she played in her car. She was letting loose and the music was helping things along. He searched for words to convey he felt likewise.

"It's telepathic."

There were suggestive comments, pats on the ass, a glancing boob touch, either by accident or with intent, Julie's right hand on his crotch as they embraced. He'd never been on a date where sex was a foregone conclusion but where hours of anticipation preceded it.

"Last Dance for Mary Jane," a Tom Petty cover was, in fact, the last dance of the night. Julie batted her eyelashes as they walked with the picnic basket towards the car. There were shouts from passersby who recognized the couple who had been dancing. They were quite the hit when Julie jumped onstage with three or four other middle-aged women and sang the female chorus of "Stop Draggin My Heart Around." She was the most animated in a group of forty-somethings and got a t-shirt from the band's merchandise table as a thank you.

In the lot, Ross popped the trunk and threw the picnic basket in. There were still leftovers. If all went well, they could have lunch tomorrow at the Harvest Grill and head home.

Like a teen, Julie lifted her shirt to reveal a boob.

"Coming attractions," she said. "And there is another one there."

"They usually travel in pairs. You are a nasty girl," Ross said.

"Well then, spank me later."

"I might."

She kept cool as they walked into the hotel lobby. He shuffled with a purpose to the Honors section of the line, which had other Shelton visitors. Their suite was at the end of the first-floor hallway and the two were intertwined and getting grabbier with each step down the narrow corridor. Ross fumbled with the key, and Julie undid his belt. The two groped and fumbled their way inside as Ross tossed the two gym bags on the floor and fell with her onto the king bed.

"Hang on, relax, and let me do this. Lay down, baby." She flipped her shirt and bra off as Ross was laying his head on the pillows waiting for her to take charge. Julie undid his pants and pulled them down to his ankles and took him into her mouth.

Her pants and panties came off in short order. Ross returned the favor and buried his face between her legs. She was guiding him and moaning to give her feedback. It was like a dream as they changed positions, and she prepared to mount him.

"Are you?"

"I can't have kids, no worries. Just hope you're…you know."

"I have none." The disease questions. The responsible thing to ask, but lust was driving the conversation.

He looked at her on top of him and reveled at the newness of it all. He wanted to drink in every drop of the experience. The rhythmic movements were in perfect sync as if guided by some life force greater than the two. She had the body of a woman much younger with the maturity to let go.

"Did you? You know…finish?" It was perhaps a faux pax, but after years of Stephanie feeling indifferent to her pleasure, Ross questioned his prowess.

"Amazing, Ross. Multiple times, if that's what you are asking. Give me a polygraph. I'm a happy woman," she said. "You need to visit down there more often. It has been a long time. I was worried about being out of practice."

"Would you like my best attempt at a full body massage? Then we will soak in the Jacuzzi until we feel like boneless chickens," he said.

"Holy shit. A Jacuzzi. Didn't even see it. You thought of everything. You're something, Ross Cameron."

He took the lotions from the bathroom and motioned

for her to turn on her stomach. He rubbed her shoulders, taking time to smell her perfume on her neck and savoring the smell of sex on the sheets. Her skin was silky smooth and without blemishes. She was a petite china doll, but powerfully feminine.

Ross rubbed her feet. When he finished up, he told her to relax and filled the tub.

"You'll sleep like a baby," he said as he turned the water on.

She acted drunk on happiness, obeying, and trusting his commands.

He had two glasses of wine on the ridge of the tub and a pair of candles on the nearby dresser. She glided toward the Jacuzzi, holding his hand, the candlelight flickering on her naked form. Ross couldn't believe his good fortune. All those days imagining what was beneath the yoga pants and tee shirts. She was toned, and yet voluptuous. His hands roamed around her body, delighting with each touch. Every square inch in its way was an erogenous zone, mainly because of her smile and expressive eyes.

She gazed into the blue-hued windows to his soul. He hoped she would never see the dishonesty that was the original sin of their relationship. There was no turning back.

They fell asleep, arms and legs intertwined, like children clutching a favorite stuffed animal.

Ross became aroused a few hours after their initial slumber. Julie responded to his arousal and awoke seconds later, and the second round of lovemaking began—semi-slumbering sex, a primal urge in the middle of the night. They spoke no words, nor were they needed. Telepathic intuition guided the activities.

Once again, they collapsed in satiated bliss after the movements reached their crescendo. Ross, a middle-aged male, had his obligatory middle of the night pee run. He didn't mind getting out of bed to relieve himself. He thanked his penis for its extraordinary efforts at doing the second of its most important biological functions. It was a job well done, perhaps enhanced by chemicals and perhaps slowed by alcohol; it provided the perfect balance to cap off a perfect day.

As he walked back to the bed Julie stirred and motioned as if to ask him to keep holding her. Whatever her facade before, she was not shy about needing him. She nuzzled his shoulder with her head as he inhaled the smell of her hair and perfume.

Sunlight hit the curtains. Ross blinked against the brightness and had no clue what time it was. Julie looked angelic as she clutched a pillow while she slept. Without makeup, her beauty was even more impressive. He could wake up to this every morning and not feel deprived. Her eyes opened to him staring at her.

"I hope you don't mind, but I was just looking at how beautiful you are. How everything, down to the way you breathe, is just so beautiful."

"Aww. It was like a dream. I slept so well, still tingling all over. What time is it?"

Ross glanced at the clock on the bed table, surprised to see they had slept a good eight hours, even accounting for the midnight activities. The two made a run at the leftover picnic basket in the fridge. There were only a few scraps left. They must have downed another bottle of wine, although neither could recall when.

Ross picked up the phone and asked for a late checkout. "Let's chill and head over to the winery for a Sunday brunch."

The room was theirs till noon and the vineyard was a scant five minutes away. Brunch and a leisurely walk around the grounds would put him back in Charlotte at five. It had been a marathon date but probably best if he spent the evening working on the week's proposals. If he stayed at her place, he might never leave.

They strolled into the lobby at eleven-thirty with an ear-to-ear grin and knowing glances as Ross picked up the bill comped by points. It was a quick stroll to the car and a few minutes to the Harvest Grill. The day was crisp but sunny, and impervious to cold and warmed by a fireplace, they decided on a table in the screened-in porch area.

Julie ordered crab cakes and Ross a lamb stew with some unfamiliar ingredients. They picked at a plate of cheese and grapes, feeding each other before deciding they would look cringe-worthy to other patrons. No longer in the cocoon of their hotel room, they were adjusting to the outside world like a newborn. They walked hand in hand to the pond and made a sweeping last look of the grounds, kissing under a willow tree.

Ross navigated the rural road to the exit off the interstate while Julie searched for something suitable on her Apple playlist. She pleasured Ross at seventy-miles-per-hour on the interstate. She unzipped his trousers and undid his belt and pulled his pants down just enough to take him in her mouth. The road was wide open. This was an unimaginable bliss for Ross, who had grown to find such spontaneous expressions unimaginable. Julie went at it for much of the rural portion of the trip.

Julie had buried her passions in her career, tennis, music, and now martial arts. Ross had opened the key to romantic possibilities. The relationship would provide balance in her life. Genuine love was one of life's greatest gifts.

She hoped he was the one, not for marriage but love. Without kids, she wanted to know unconditional romantic love for once in her life. For all the bravado of her sparring, either in the ring or with opposing attorneys, she bought into the Prince Charming mythos. She didn't need a man for financial security, but a soul mate was always good to find.

They passed Interstate 40, signaling there was perhaps a half-hour left in the ride.

"Ross, we both were in long-term marriages and you know the breakdown starts far before you can put words to it, so you rationalize and justify and bury your wants and needs under the rug, thinking the growing distance is normal. You feel lonely, lonelier than you feel when there are no people around." Julie turned the stereo down a smidge. "For me, going to family wasn't an option because my husband worked for the family business, and I'd jeopardize his job. I did all the right things and wound up lonely, with no one to talk to, and I threw myself into things that would toughen my skin. I'm not the woman you might have thought I was."

Her heart fluttered while she waited his response. What would he say?

"Julie, I feel we have something telepathic. Like in the Eagles song, l lived my life in chains never knowing I had the key. I felt used and manipulated and lost track of who I was. I went through the motions. I was a zombie." He paused. "If I traveled, I could be myself with work associates, with high school and college friends, or perhaps with a few neighbors but felt like a neutered cat. I wanted to be with a woman who wanted me for me. I wasn't faithful in my marriage. I'm not proud of that."

"Being upfront with you is unfamiliar territory. We both have baggage. I knew the other side could be better. That was just a theory until this weekend. It's hard to put your feelings out there, for fear of harsh judgment, but I want you to know you're everything I want."

Julie sniffled. "Fucking fall allergies." Except it wasn't allergies, and they both knew it. She took his hand from the console and squeezed it. "My mom is from Panama, and I don't know if you know that in Spanish there are about a dozen ways of going from like, to love with nuanced words. English needs a few more, but let me say I more than like you."

"I more than like you, too."

Julie thought of her mom, Blanca. The Army stationed her dad in the Canal Zone during Vietnam. The daughter of a prominent banking family, Don Ernesto eventually gave

Balsar the seed money it needed to manufacture its first generic drug. The family had been hesitant at first to approve of the marriage but became convinced the couple was inseparable. Cultured and elegant, she became a counterweight to Julie's dad's hard-charging business mentality. But for all their cultural differences, they had a passionate, unshakable bond that Julie doubted she would ever replicate.

The skyline of Charlotte was visible from the rise in the highway. Julie dabbed her eyes and Ross patted her back.

The tree-lined street on the Fourth Ward seemed more than just two blocks from the bustle of downtown. He pulled in her driveway, and they walked up to her bungalow.

Everything was as it was over a day ago. So much had happened.

"Julie, let me walk you to your door. This has been an unbelievable weekend."

"You can relax here, I'll put on the game."

"I don't want to go, but reality calls. It's Sunday night, and I have a full day tomorrow. I feel like my soul has been on a two-day vacation, and I'm twenty years younger than I was Friday. We can text. I'll call. I want your voice to be the last thing I hear when I doze off."

"Me too. I miss you already. Please don't break my fucking heart. I can kick your ass if I need to."

"I'll try to keep that in mind." She walked him to the door and under the portico she threw her hands around his neck and the two had a five-minute make-out session like a prom date, and then he stumbled down the stairs with his chemically enhanced hard on now protruding from his chinos.

He avoided the highway on his twenty-minute drive to

Ballantyne and wound through the tree-lined streets of Myers Park, through Southpark, where he decided he would write to Vicky and Dave. He pulled into a FedEx and typed his abbreviated description of the weekend.

Chapter Twelve
Coming Out

Eunice's TV appearances infuriated Becky. She needed to "do something" to assuage her conscience about the Whitcomb suicide. Mindy and Becky could put a reasonable face to the Marriage Equality debate. The public needed to know how Eunice comported herself during the Whitcomb divorce, whatever the cost to Becky's career or that of her girlfriend.

Becky had the respect of the legal community. While feeling she let down Grayson Whitcomb and his daughter in the most egregious way possible, Grayson did not blame her in the least. They were close, although with sporadic contact. He somehow pieced together the fact that his daughter's shrink and his lawyer were a couple, before either acknowledged it. He assumed they kept their professional knowledge separate, never thinking in a million years it might have saved Melanie's life.

He was introspective after her death. What role had his high-profile job, or the departure from the marital home, played in her suicide? During the trial, Becky apologized for not having done more to chastise Eunice for soliciting false testimony. Grayson wasn't having it. "However imperfect my ex-wife is, she is a grieving parent too. She is in a prison without bars for the rest of her life. For my sanity and hers, I need to let this go," He said. "You did your best. One day Eunice will have to answer for what she did, in this life or the next. If you or your partner stop doing what you do, how many other families will be worse off legally or mentally?" They kept in touch afterward, but the contact grew sparse.

Becky couldn't help but think of Grayson's reaction to the public spectacle of seeing Eunice as a spokesperson. She was so contemptuous of his marriage and indifferent to the child the couple shared. Surely, he was enraged. Grayson split his time between Charlotte and Central America, where a micro-lending NGO started in Melanie's honor was empowering women to start their own small businesses.

Becky and Mindy both felt compelled to speak out publicly about Eunice now championing a cause they felt passionate about. As prominent professionals personally affected by the Marriage Equality debate, and who in their professional capacity saw the depths to which Eunice stooped as an attorney dissolving a prominent marriage, they could not allow the wanton disregard for the couple's teen daughter to remain a secret. Eunice bore responsibility for the child's tragic suicide, and both Mindy and Becky wanted the public to know.

Mindy had seen anorexia, cutting, depression, and even suicide in her practice. Eunice did not treat marriage as an exalted institution. She made sure they ended in the most contentious way possible, maximizing collateral damage.

By professing her love for Mindy in a civil ceremony, and receiving the legal immunity from testifying, Mindy and Becky would have free license to knock Eunice from her perch as a Marriage Equality champion. Karma seemed destined to weigh in on the matter and offered up a two-for-one.

They could surely get a reporter to cover their nuptials at the courthouse and its connection to one of Charlotte's most storied divorce cases. An investigation of their breach of professional ethics would paint Eunice as a fraud and a hypocrite, thus ending her law practice. If it saved another child, and perhaps Nicole, from being used in such a manner, it would be a small measure of contrition for their failure to save Melanie. It would help cleanse their universe.

Mindy envisioned a new career writing books on children's issues from her house in Ocracoke, or out big pharma on the abandonment of old-fashioned cognitive therapy in the name of a cheaper and quicker fix via pills.

Becky was toying with some form of public office, at first a seat on the city council, or perhaps as a state assemblywoman. She was fed-up with the state's direction of late and had several influential friends beyond Grayson. If he was open to running for mayor, she would be happy to take a secondary role. He could bridge the city's divides as a respected business leader and provide an empathetic face, given the hell he endured. His standing in the business community could bridge the political divide.

Would Becky survive with the firm? Would they have her back or discard her for the breach of ethics? Revealing privileged information would cause professional censure for both, but with the spousal exemption from testimony, criminal charges were unlikely to stick. If Eunice pursued a defamation or libel suit, Becky would counterpunch until her disbarment. It would be a tactical mistake of epic proportions by the ego-driven and self-aggrandizing Eunice.

With Eunice discredited, Mindy and Becky would make a far more palatable face to the Marriage Equality debate. A long-term stable and professional couple could advocate more effectively. Eunice would be in no position to try her vile tactics during Ross' case with a media circus. Under such scrutiny, Stephanie would have to behave responsibly.

By triangulating Eunice's ethical shortcomings, Becky could be an effective advocate to win over those on the fence about this contentious issue and therefore increase support.

While somewhat secular, Mindy wanted to take the time between Rosh Hashanah and Yom Kippur, a traditional time of soul searching, to reflect on how she could be a better person and atone for previous mistakes. She had met with a Rabbi, sought counsel on the matter, and would offer her *mea culpa* in some public forum for not having spoken out earlier. She had done too little to make the authorities aware of Melanie Whitcomb's tormented last few months. The timing and manner of this revelation was an ongoing matter of much discussion between her and Becky.

Becky wanted a full-page ad in the Observer as a tell-all. This would spark a bunch of media attention in Charlotte, and perhaps statewide. The story had all the elements of tabloid fodder while also allowing the moral arc of the universe to lurch forward. She first needed to speak to Grayson and get his blessing. He needed to be on board, but she hoped he might consider a run for mayor. It would be cathartic, giving voice to his passionate concerns for teen suicide prevention, and the need for reform of the family court system.

Perhaps Grayson would find his groove again, sharing his pain to help others. Becky could advise him on Family Court Reform, while Mindy could strengthen Ad litem protections. Grayson could be a bridge between government, business, the faith community, and an increasingly polarized electorate.

Becky was sure they could make a go without practicing their professions. They now spent hours talking about leaving the rat race, and what life would be like afterward.

Becky put a lot of thought into her proposed Observer ad, and the fallout it would cause. It would be a hot news story because of its connection to a high-profile sordid divorce, and how a once-mighty executive fell in unimaginable ways. Enough dirty laundry for a reporter to take the ball and run with it. Each word of Becky's ad would be scrutinized and taken out of context for the benefit of those on the extremes.

It needed to be beyond the pale of reproach and appeal to reason. To cast Eunice in a negative light, but not the movement, which she was championing. It needed to paint Becky as a voice of reason and mainstream, while admitting her most egregious failure, to protect Melanie Whitcomb. Above all, her motives needed to be pure, as a small but vocal minority that saw her relationship as perverse according to their strict interpretation of the Bible.

Becky needed to thread a needle. For many, the subject of Marriage Equality was uncomfortable. In a city wrestling with its image as progressive new south or bastion of old-fashioned family values; a tolerant haven or bulwark against moral decay, it called for a high-wire act that had Becky hoped her writing skills could encapsulate.

There was the matter of Mindy's blessing. Mindy wanted off the treadmill and envisioned a quieter existence. Becky could teach but questioned if she would miss the rough and tumble of law. Mindy was tired of the pressures of psychotherapy and a department chair in a major teaching hospital. She wanted to spend weeks at a time on Ocracoke watching the tides, writing, or painting. Her most recent hobby was carving decoy birds from wood, but she had little time to pursue it. Becky was unsure how she would spend the increased leisure time and looked to politics to fill the void.

After almost daily complete rewrites, she took a glimpse at the manifesto she hoped to put in the Observer.

Fellow Charlotteans

My name is Rebecca Harriman, Esquire, a lifelong resident of the Queen City. Like many, I'm troubled by the divisions in our city, which for so long had been noted for its ability to foster moderation. We stood as a beacon to which more polarized cities looked when they wished to settle divisions amicably, and now we are at a crossroads where voices looking to ratchet up acrimony, are as many as those promoting harmony. We were the gold standard for integrated schools.

I've practiced Family Law for two decades with one of the city's most prestigious firms. I have experience defining this institution we call marriage. Like a homicide detective, I'm brought in when that cherished institution is little more than a corpse. I depose litigants to find out how something so beautiful became so ugly. We often treat the institution that many of you call holy with contempt. We often treat the children born of this holy union as little more than pawns. That is far more dangerous than expanding the definition to include those of the same gender. One particular instance of this perverse contempt haunted me for years and resulted in the tragic suicide of a child. Because of professional confidentiality, I kept quiet about what I knew. I now feel no such restraints.

My partner practices psychiatry as a chair of a department in one of the state's most prestigious hospitals. She has dedicated her entire adult life to helping those struggling with mental illness, particularly children. One of her clients committed suicide. It was the teen daughter of a law client in a high-profile divorce case. We shared information, in violation of privacy statutes, not for tactical advantage, but because the teen faced an unimaginable choice: falsely testify against her father to tilt the settlement to favor her mother. She could not, and faced with such a choice ended her own life. We shared this information because we are humans first, and attorneys or psychiatrists second, and we hoped to help her. Medicine and the Law are similar in that they are supposed to protect people. To us that child was a human being, to my opposing counsel, she was a pawn to be used for tactical advantage. The system failed. I can no longer remain silent while this debate rages. I cannot stand by as a welcoming place, tolerant to others, becomes drowned by the dividers. That's not who we are. Dividers, those who would turn the city against one another, or pit a child against a parent, are not welcome in this debate. I'll speak out against anyone on any side who inflames hatred for personal gain.

Despite seeing how ugly divorces can get, I'm a fan of marriage. I'm blessed with the love of a life partner, accomplished in her profession but whose passion for her job colors her life. My life partner is a woman, but my love for the institution of marriage is no different from anyone. It's rooted first with my parents. They gave me an example to follow. I think of them each time I'm confronted with the wreckage of once loving marriages filled with vitriol and need a reminder of its beauty.

This debate is about who gets to sanctify their love via marriage. It's being championed in this town by someone who urged a child to testify falsely, hoping to gain a tactical advantage. Melanie Whitcomb no longer has a voice. I intend to be her voice. In her voice, I say a person so compromised has no business leading a debate on morality, on legislating any aspect of what makes up a family.

I spent countless hours talking to my client, a beloved member of our business community. Imagine for a moment her pain of knowing her only daughter ended her life, rather than bring false accusations, and undeserved shame to a person who had done nothing other than be a loving dad. Imagine the pain he felt having to put that first shovelful of dirt on her grave. Imagine the pain of my partner reading the notes of her file, a teen girl urged to perjure herself.

Had she lived and succumbed to the pressure, a grieving father might have been in jail as an innocent man, and the opposing litigant would've gotten a settlement more tilted in her favor. There should be consequences for those who would torment a child in such a way. Spokespeople for a cause should be pure of heart. A person who views marriage as a chess game using such despicable tactics has no business professing to know how to define it. We need someone who brings our communities together, not one who tears our community and individual families apart.

I'm a proud Charlettean and North Carolinian. Mom and Dad weren't rich, but we never lacked for anything, including love. My dad sold cars, and my mom was a seamstress in a mill. They may not have had much but what they were wealthy in traits like empathy and compassion. They drew me to politics with their embrace of Terry Sanford, who as the governor made it his life's mission to make North Carolina as a progressive beacon that would afford opportunities to everyone.

He's a personal hero, and the reason I have an interest in public service. Because of his vision, we have a Research Triangle where there was once a tobacco road and the skyscrapers that now define Charlotte. The enlightened self-interest that created those gleaming skyscrapers also provided a peaceful transition from the shame of segregation. Our city leaders were out in front of integrating restaurants, lunch counters, and schools without outside pressures from courts forcing us to do so. They knew then what we seem to have forgotten: leaders should inspire the best in the citizenry, not appeal to their most base instincts.

People like Hugh McColl helped make Charlotte a place where talented newcomers could put down roots. The leadership of our state and our city have departed from those ideals. For me to honor my parents I must fight their fight, sometimes at the cost of friendships and ostracism in social circles.

I'll marry and imbue it with the same qualities of love that helped strengthen my childhood home. The time for silence has ended. For me to speak out against the injustices in our family court systems I must speak out against those who mock its protections. Those who shatter families and cause lasting damage to the bonds of parenthood by using children as pawns. People who merely want to have a loving union and its protections are no threat to anyone. People who mock it by their actions are not their advocates.

To those skeptical or not on board with equal marriage rights, we have values, and we're people just like you. Please accord us the chance to imbue this institution with the same respect you purport to value. Challenging long-held beliefs can be hard, but it's how we grow as human beings.

We all need to live together, and how we go about that will shape what will become of Charlotte during the next generation. If you are interested in healing and unity and not division, I urge all of you to join me at #onecharlotteforall and let's make our city an example again.

Chapter Thirteen
Planet Fitness

Dave had googled, "Charlotte Mature Single Adventurers," and joined by paying the fifty-buck membership fee. Ross suspected Stephanie was going on a singles trip to hike Chimney Rock and another trip to Lake Lure with a boat ride and cocktails. Nicole had blurted out something on a recent weekend visit that clued him into her mindset.

"Mom vowed to fill every non-custodial weekend with adventures because she is dying of boredom. She is pretending to be all into outdoors stuff, to meet men. She hates it though. Her idea of the outdoors is a strip mall," Nicole said.

Dave reported he had been to Stephanie's gym a handful of times without seeing her. Only a week remained before the Chimney Rock excursion, so Dave signed up for the hike.

"Look, Dave, it's going to be far better if you meet her at the gym first. Then your coincidental meeting on the trip will seem cosmic. Suck it up and get your bod to the gym every day if you have to."

Dave sighed. "Alright, dude. I'll step it up."

On Wednesday, Dave spotted Stephanie on a Stairmaster. He rushed back to the car to get the Cozumel hat as a conversation starter. He spotted her moving to another machine and took residence on an adjacent machine.

"Hi. Are you familiar with this machine?"

She nodded. "Having problems?"

"Yeah. Can't figure out how to get this function to work."

Stephanie moved over and adjusted the machine. "Been to Dewey Beach?"

"Huh? Oh, my shirt. Yes. You been there?"

"I spent like four summers at Dewey Beach. I graduated from the University of Maryland and went on my honeymoon to Cozumel."

"That's kind of strange," Dave said.

"Some of my best summer memories are on Dewey Beach. Did you go there?"

"A bunch of college buddies decided it would be a good central place to have a week of debauchery near the shore. We hit the bars by the Bayside every night and pretended we were back in college."

"That's so weird. I was a waitress at the Rusty Rudder for three summers."

According to Ross, she worked a week, spilled a plate of spaghetti on a customer, broke a tray of drinks, and walked out to the parking lot to confront a customer who didn't tip. The patron knew the owner and insisted he fire her.

"Yep, I remember that place and catching bands at the Bottle and the Cork," Dave said. "I was one of your obnoxious customers." Dave imagined how he would react with a plate of spaghetti on his lap. "Cozumel. You had a honeymoon there?"

"It was nice except for my shit for brains ex."

Bitter much? "You practically foamed at the mouth when you said that."

"Sorry, I know I shouldn't say stuff like that. I come off bitter, but he's an idiot, and I moved on."

People who moved on didn't start discussions of their ex with expletives. "What was so bad?"

"Lying, cheating asshole, loser. I got the most man-hating attorney I could find to make his life a living hell, and now I'm doing a reboot. You know like a butterfly that reemerges more beautiful."

"So, this guy did drugs? Drank too much? Beat you?"

"No, just wasn't honest, cheated, caught him red-handed. I have a sixth sense, and I always get even. I enjoy revenge. But I'm a friendly person as long as you're nice."

"Hope I've done nothing to bother you yet."

"No more about him. You're right, he's the past. I'm getting in the best shape of my life. I've had such a burst of energy since the divorce."

"What did you do before?" Dave continued his work out and waited for her response.

"I was concentrating on my daughter. She's fifteen now. I wanted to make sure she had proper parenting, and I was a great mom. I think it's sad that kids have no parental involvement these days. I was there for her. I could have been a successful singer, but I devoted myself to my daughter and now it's time for me."

"So, you were like Suzy Homemaker?"

"Well, no. I don't like to cook if that's what you mean."

She was self-absorbed, prompting all kinds of red flags. If this was a normal first interaction, he would have challenged her with more than playful jousting, but Dave wanted the conversation to continue until she was comfortable.

"Yep, you deserve your me time. With all the activities kids have and driving around, playdates, it's hard to keep up."

"It's been hard on my daughter, you know, with her father gone, but we're managing."

"Must've been tough for both of you. Kudos for making something good out of a terrible situation."

Ross had relayed the narcissist playbook from Becky's partner. Compliments are intoxicating. Her head nodded in agreement every time he stroked her ego. It entitled her to life, liberty, and post-divorce happiness.

Growing bolder, Dave suggested an outing when they were finished. "Let's grab a smoothie after the workout so I can delay going back to my lonely bachelor apartment. You seem so interesting."

"Interesting" made Stephanie melt. Dave was thinking shallow, self-absorbed, and negative. The compliments hit her like a Cupid's arrow in the rump.

The compliment stuff worked like a charm. Dave decided his best course of action would be a pleasant conversation, without asking for her number. It would make a meeting on the Chimney Rock excursion seem like a twist of fate. According to Ross, she was going alone from what Nicole had said. There would be no way to just ignore him, and the two would have an entire day together.

"I'd like that. It's so hard to find people you can open up to. Most people are so into themselves," the projecting narcissist said.

Dave nodded. He was familiar with projection. He would do the work to make her swoon.

Fifteen minutes on the elliptical and Dave signaled he would hit the locker room and change. Stephanie finished with her circuit but feigned some additional medicine ball exercises to appear busy.

His plan was to offer scant details on his life but try to flush out hers, highlighting areas she embellished: her career, her industriousness, and the things she appeared most defensive about.

Dave sat at the gym's juice bar. He ordered his drink first then ordered her a passion fruit and mango smoothie, with kale for good measure. As the blender stopped, Stephanie emerged from the locker room. She appeared to have made a supreme effort with her beauty regimen while she changed into her street clothes.

She had over-applied eye make-up, to accentuate the effects of the plastic surgery that Ross confided was paid for by pissing away his hard-earned bonus.

Still, Stephanie had a pleasant figure and, like a Monet, looked far more alluring from a distance. She was neither curvy nor boyish.

"Have a seat, I ordered a smoothie for you, passion fruit because you seem so passionate when you work out."

She chuckled, and he steered the rudderless conversation to Stephanie and her heroic journey as a divorced mom making her way in the world.

She asked about his ex, but upon his mentioning the words high-powered attorney she feigned indifference. Dave pivoted adroitly and went into compliment mode.

"I think it's great you are preparing for a career but spending time with kids is as important a job as any."

After twenty minutes, Dave had a well-crafted playbook to work with at Chimney Rock.

"Listen, Stephanie, it was great to talk with you. I better get back home. I hope to see you around again." He was careful not to ask for her phone number. He wanted the singles trip to appear to have been a complete coincidence. "I have a commitment over the weekend I can't shake, but see you Monday maybe?"

"Sure. I have something too. Monday then?"

Dave stopped at the SouthPark FedEx to log on to a computer and drop Ross a note.

> Major progress today, dude. I think I'll administer Vitamin D within a few weeks.

Ross had already written a cryptic note.

I've bagged the Tiger and got it in the sack.

Ross had slept with Julie. Dave couldn't decide if he was jealous of his conquest or elated that he was closer to removing the alimony shackles.

Stephanie was at home ignoring Nicole, writing emails, and IM'ing her friends while imploring her daughter to order pizza from the magnet on the refrigerator. The emails were all about Dave.

> He seems so nice, but he didn't ask my number. Why is that? Could he be married? Was he playing it slow?

Her group chats on Facebook encouraged and explained away her paranoia.

> You have residual trust issues. Go with your gut on this one. I'd go to the gym every day to run into him.

The suggestions ranged from practical to ridiculous.

> Wear perfume. They like that.
> Get one of those lycra® bodysuits.
> I don't have the boobs for it.
> Tie up your hair.
> Wear an iPod and pretend not to see him.
> Play hard to get. Make him work.

She couldn't resist calling the front desk of the gym and insisted she took the wrong keys by mistake and that it belonged to a man meeting the description of Dave.

"You can drop them off here if you like, but we cannot give out information on members," the assistant manager said.

When that maneuver failed, she searched for social media, address, credit rating, criminal past, employment records. Her mind raced with ways in which she might find out all his vitals without appearing like a crazed stalker. After Henry's betrayal, she wasn't about to get burned.

She hated the old man. How dare he lie to her? She was the younger, prettier thing on his arm, doing a massive favor to his ego. She missed having a boyfriend. For all their problems, boyfriends make life easier. Each day was a maze of decisions, without a local confidant to bitch to or to offload errands. However flawed, Henry could still be counted on for compliments, so she let him stay connected on social media.

Her mind raced even as she realized there was no way to investigate Dave further. She didn't have enough to go on: lived near the lake, some kind of pharmaceutical work. She worked the angles in her mind, but all came up dead ends.

Dave digested the day's events with heated leftovers. Things were going smoothly, and the apex would be the trip to Chimney Rock. He would arrive early, hanging around with a cup of coffee in shorts and hiking boots, looking nonchalant and alone. The gym workouts, despite some aches and pains, were getting his body toned. He spied the mail at the far corner of the dining room table. Bills, bills, more bills, lawyers, utilities, credit cards. He was sliding backward and only Ross could prevent it from getting worse.

Dave vacillated between incredulity and envy that his partner in this enterprise bedded his ex. He missed his house on the lake: decorated and homey. His apartment was transient and utilitarian. There was barely sufficient space to move about. The lake house had man toys, jet skis, gigantic TV screen for sporting events, a fireplace to relax by with an adult beverage. His apartment was a way station for a shitty chapter in a life that might never improve.

He skipped the gym Friday, as a tease, to make Saturday more of a surprise.

Stephanie showed up at the gym, dolled up for the occasion, yoga pants, iPod, scrunchy, and new sneakers, but no Dave. Disappointment ripped through her like a cold wind. She had hoped he would ask her out. She now regretted booking the hiking and lake excursion. She hated the outdoors stuff, and she would be stuck hiking with complete strangers.

Everyone in her circle had bailed on her. If the trip ended an abject failure, Sunday would be an abysmal day of laundry and commiserating with her college buddies online. Nicole would be with her father, fortunately. She was in no mood to dispense cheery anecdotes to a hormonal teenager when experiencing a crisis herself.

Chapter Fourteen
Take A Hike

Dave sprang out of bed for the trip to Chimney Rock. His cargo shorts and hiking boots were laid out, but he couldn't decide between the Dewey Beach sweatshirt, and Sanibel Island windbreaker. Both had relevance for Stephanie as she spent summers at one and had a memorable vacation at the latter. He found a George Thorogood T-shirt, musical regulars at Dewey Beach, and pulled the Sanibel windbreaker over the T-shirt.

Stephanie struggled with the alarm on her iPhone, pushing snooze three or four times. Shaking off the lethargy, she walked to the bathroom to brush her teeth before climbing in the shower. She filled her travel mug with instant coffee and slipped into jeans, comfortable shoes and a top she picked out haphazardly. With so much energy put into Friday's gym appearance, she cared little about impressing strangers.

Dave grabbed a *venti* at Starbucks drive-thru with none of the weekday lines. There were still variables. What if Stephanie had a girlfriend with her? Would he have to hang with both and await an opening? If she was alone, he could play a shy guy, asking if she would mind sitting with him. *You got this.* He settled the coffee in the cup holder and drove toward the tour location.

The huge SouthPark lot was deserted. Dave arrived first, staying in his car sipping on his coffee. A second car arrived, then a third, both with middle-aged women. He fiddled with his phone to look busy.

At five minutes to eight, Stephanie whipped around the corner. He looked away, feigning indifference to her arrival before counting the twenty paces she needed to walk before eye contact would be unavoidable. She glanced in his direction. Pay dirt.

Her casual clothing showed a reasonable figure, and she smiled. This was an excellent sign.

"Wow, I didn't expect to find you here," Stephanie said.

"Neither did I. Not stalking me, are you?" Surprise colored her face. "I'm kidding," Dave said. A friend kind of talked me into this and backed out on me at the last moment. To tell you the truth, I don't know another soul going on the trip. Do you want to sit together?" Her posture relaxed, and a smile lit her face. The Plan was looking good. It was ideal hiking weather, cool and clear. The sky was a deep Carolina blue.

"So, do you mind keeping me company?" Dave asked.

"Not at all. I was supposed to come with some girlfriends, both wimped out. I like to hike and so I'm here."

She hated hiking, but guys like outdoorsy girls, right?

After all that worrying about whether Dave would show up at the gym, here he was, and a whole day to get to know him, maybe even walk trails together. Her mind raced. *I can do cute and flirtatious, and there is no way he could resist. Is that a Sanibel Island Crest on his windbreaker? Holy shit, I have like a half-hour story about the trip there. No more bitterness. I'll be funny. Guys like funny. I'll be like a guy, joking around, hiking but cute, damn cute for a forty-something, pretending to like sports. My hair came out shitty. What if he notices? I wonder if I can sneak a trip to a bathroom to put on makeup.*

She smiled. "I need to walk to the CVS to use the ladies' room and maybe get gum. Do you want anything?"

"No, thanks, I'm good."

Dave knew tons of gum-snapping girls from college, New Yorkers mostly it was a pet peeve, but not a relationship killer. This was different. He was on a mission.

Dave took a window seat with the view facing the CVS. He wanted to see her walking to the bus. There is something in a woman's gait that reveals her personality. Dave realized how much he loved watching women walk—the click-clack of high heels on a woman comfortable wearing them, the swaying of hips, butt cheeks shifting with each step like Roy Orbison sang about in "Pretty Woman." It fed his libido.

He spied her leaving the pharmacy. Her walk was nonchalant, nothing too feminine, no arched back, or exaggerated sashay. She filled out jeans nicely, he would give her that. Her smile was infrequent and forced and didn't emote much.

The tour leader got on the PA just as Stephanie boarded the bus. She slunk past him while her body language betrayed embarrassment. Putting her bag in the overhead rack, she assumed her seat. Stephanie was snapping gum and drinking vitamin water. She offered Dave a piece. He hesitated before saying yes, thinking of his coffee breath and the possibility of a first kiss. The bus got rolling on the two-hour journey to Chimney Rock.

Stephanie suggested they make up stories about various passengers. Ross mentioned her cattiness, but the crueler the descriptions, the more Stephanie reacted. Their seatmates to the side were, according to Stephanie, from a South Carolina suburb, perhaps Rock Hill, and she classified them as local-yokels. They had alcoholic exes that beat them and were looking for someone classier.

The girls looked sweet. One had a kind of syrupy drawl but with an educated bent to it. She had big, straight, white teeth that radiated, and teased hair with blonde highlights. Dave figured the one in the outer seat to be a teacher but dared not say, and the inside seatmate to be perhaps a nurse or something healthcare related. She had her hair in a tight bun like nurses often wear.

It seemed they were strangers but began chatting loud enough for Dave and Stephanie to overhear. One talked about her son, who was in third grade. Dave expanded on Stephanie's analysis.

They didn't get alimony or child support from the deadbeat exes, and therefore had to work double shifts, leaving their kids with their mothers after school. Stephanie added that the one with teased hair got pregnant in high school, kept the baby, and smoked and drank throughout the pregnancy.

Dave realized the more judgmental and mocking he was in this sick game of hers, the more Stephanie responded. Her concept of humor was projected insecurities and acting tall by chopping off the heads of others.

Next row up, a girl and a guy, strangers engaged in small talk. The girl was thin with a big nose but coiffed hair. Dave created their narrative. "She seems like a social worker type."

"Yes, couldn't get dates because of that big nose and is attached to her career of helping people. No sense of humor, invites girls from work over for dinner parties, comprised of vegan stuff from Whole Foods. She has six cats and fish that she talks to. She has lots of plants in her South End walk-up apartment. Drives a hybrid."

Dave was wise to the shtick and added a few zingers of his own.

"Parents asked if she wanted a nose job but she refused. Buys free-trade coffee, maybe a loft in Noda or Plaza-Midwood where she brags about it being eclectic but is petrified since getting mugged at knifepoint. Got a tiny clover tattoo on her ass, hoping to surprise some guy with her wild side but hasn't been with a guy since the Bush administration. Speaking of bush, she doesn't groom down there."

Dave waited to see if the bush comment was too much too soon.

"You are so intuitive. You get me. Not everyone does."

Not everyone wants to.

His cruel descriptive rant on some poor lonely girl who wanted to save the world, who was kind and cared about the homeless, and the environment and whales didn't deserve ridicule, but Dave wanted to prove himself to Stephanie. This was feeling forced.

"The guy," he said, "works in a cell phone store, but is viewed as a screw-up by his family because his parents spent big money to send him to Davidson and warned about his unmarketable major in English Lit. He thought growing a beard would make him seem intellectual. He enrolled in a spin class but mostly to spy on girls in bicycle shorts. He has feminine tastes in music, new age, and shit like that. Perving on the girl next to him right now."

"Wow, impressive, I can't tell you how many people just wouldn't get the humor."

This went on; row after row but it passed the time.

"I see the Sanibel logo on your shirt. You go there a lot?"

"Just twice, extended a business trip from Jacksonville

and another time when I went for a weekend in the fall."

"Me too, I went with my ex. I liked the place except I got sun poisoning. I thought I could put baby oil on my face and use a reflector like in college, but boy was I wrong. I also had a shellfish allergy and my lips got swollen, but despite it all, I liked the place. I got to lay around, and there were nice spas and cute shops."

According to Ross, it rained, and she insisted it was a sign from God that she should spend the day shopping. She got her period on day two of a five-day trip. Despite being shut out on the sex part, Ross felt it was almost a relief because she was crawling out of her skin one minute, crying at other times, and was pitching a fit about him watching college football on vacation. Once the period came, she had calmed down somewhat. He got to go fishing while she nursed the sunburn. Dave wanted to hear her spin.

She recounted that Ross watched football most of the day Saturday and wanted her to go on some charter fishing thing that involved other couples who loved to drink. She refused and spent the day shopping. Had a few enjoyable meals, and the hotel was nice. No mention of PMS.

Dave had revealed nothing about himself when Stephanie proclaimed, "You get me, don't you?" It was an odd thing to say after such limited, unnerving time together. Now she seemed clingy. She didn't know his getting her was some intel from Ross. He saw through her facade and just wanted to complete his mission without collateral damage to their daughter Nicole.

He was girded for about a three-month courtship and after doing the Christmas-Valentine's Day loop would be free to go away on Memorial Day, unencumbered, in time for a summer romance.

He was getting queasy. What was he getting himself into? This would be a twenty-four-seven life of deception, being someone he wasn't, enduring hour-long phone calls when he preferred watching TV. And there would be whining. Say what you will about Julie, she never whined.

She might voice her opinion, or be stubborn, but it was never the whining female he so hated. He could tell with Stephanie there would be lots of nagging and whining.

Stephanie would look over every so often with a forced smile. Dave revealed precious little about himself. She was talking more than listening but being too agreeable. It felt weird spending eight hours with someone you didn't care for. Time to man up.

You got this. Your buddy is already in your ex-wife's pants. Suck it up and be charming and move your part along.

"So, I'm kind of looking forward to this hike, fresh mountain air. I was last at Chimney Rock, maybe three years ago. Late fall day, chilly but nice waterfalls. The weather today is perfect. Plus, with all that climbing, we won't need to be on the Stairmaster for a while."

Her earbuds dangled from her neck. "So what were you listening to if you don't mind?"

"Just a mixtape from spin class. Why don't we ask each other questions? Like what do you do for work? Any kids? What's your first impression of me? How old do you think I am?"

Her knack for turning the focus of the conversation to herself was a red flag under normal circumstances, but vis-à-vis The Plan made things easier. Armed with the knowledge of the narcissist cheat codes, Dave knew where things were headed.

"I'd say you are mid-thirties, maybe?" He knew this to be a decade below her actual age. "My first impression is that of someone healing from a dysfunctional relationship and is finding herself for the exciting second act of her life."

"Wow, that was uncanny. I've been reinventing myself, like a butterfly, free to pursue things like this trip. Impossible when I was a wife and putting all my energy into being a mom."

Dave heard about the absence of home-cooked meals,

the single socks that seemed to multiply after each load of laundry, and other homemaker inadequacies. His job was not to check the veracity of her statements but to provide an echo chamber of praise.

"Well, you're doing a superb job and not at all bitter."

"I have some unresolved issues with my ex. He's doing a number on me and my daughter, but he's feeling my wrath. Did I tell you about my powers of revenge and karma? Get on my bad side, and you're miserable forever. I'm your worst nightmare."

Lovely. The relationship hadn't even started, and he was having anxiety about ending it. *One thing at a time, Dave. Don't put the cart before the horse.*

"Chimney Rock," the tour leader said. "Take your passes on the way out of the bus. We will meet here at four-thirty. There are maps at the ticket booth."

"Care to walk together?" Dave asked. He didn't want a group complicating his pitch for her affections.

This was music to Stephanie's ears. She wanted him to herself. It was difficult coming to terms with Henry's departure. Stephanie never saw it coming. She hated to be alone without someone telling her she was the most important person in the world.

A proper boyfriend would never give her the look. The stand-up-straight look, the you-don't-know-how-to-put-on-makeup look, the you-put-on-weight looks her mother dispensed with regularity. This Dave guy seemed like he had wounds that needed nursing and had him a bitch of an ex-wife. By the night's end, by sheer force of personality, she would make him want her. She needed to seem vulnerable but not helpless, agreeable but not wimpy, funny but not overpoweringly so, not focused on the past but willing to put it in perspective.

"What trail do you want to go on?" Dave asked.

"Don't care. Why don't you decide?"

"Here is one with some waterfalls. We should be able to get excellent pictures."

The mountain air was pleasant and fresh, a good ten degrees cooler than Charlotte. The air smelled of pine. Dave was ready to take things to the next level. He would be the alpha male, leading the trails, pushing her to experience more of the park but not pushing too hard. Dave hoped to impart a man in charge right out of the gate.

The first twenty minutes were an uneventful climb up a series of terraced logs, leading to wooden stairs two hundred feet higher. They reached a ledge with an iconic view of the valley below, and a huge majestic American flag waving from the large rock from which the park took its name. The view was panoramic and grand. The cars below looked to be the size of ants and the farmhouses like little Monopoly pieces on the checkerboard of farmland.

"Dave, this is amazing. I've never seen this view before. Thanks for picking this trail out." It was a flirtatious quip, which, while telegraphed, still felt good to Dave.

It was too early to try the initial kiss. There were others on the trail, although he felt as if he set the table. "I love it too. The air is so fresh up here. The valley below looks tiny. You're close to nature here."

"You know when my husband dragged me here, I never felt like doing anything that he enjoyed. I rejected it because the thought of spending a day doing what he wanted made me feel queasy. After a while, you don't want to do anything the other person wants. If I wasn't happy, why should he be happy? It's different with you."

She was asking for absolution, for selfishness. Dave's job was to give it to her. "That makes sense." This was one of those innocent quips that made him feel for Ross. She would rather stay miserable herself, deny enjoyable experiences to her family because it was something her husband suggested.

"If you weren't happy with your husband, why would you want to spend an entire day doing something with him?"

"It's doing something with him and feeling like I had to enjoy myself. Then I'd get an I-told-you-so. He loved being right and damned if I'd do that. I made enormous sacrifices to move. I have resentments."

"Well, we're here now, and it's a beautiful day. We have a clean slate, so we can enjoy ourselves." Dave swallowed hard. This would be painful, but he knew it would move things along.

"He sounds selfish. It's amazing how you've moved on and now you can enjoy all those things."

"I'm glad I'm here with you. I'm enjoying myself."

After a few outcroppings with decent views, the trail descended which, while not as tiring as going uphill, did a number on middle-aged knees. According to Dave's map, they were a quarter mile from a waterfall and could stop, soak in the view, and chat. He could steer the conversation away from bitterness and towards the fresh beginning he hoped would blossom between the two of them. Dave would suck it up and feign agreement with Stephanie, that yes, Ross was the schmuck she made him out to be.

"Okay, I hope you don't take this the wrong way. I'm enjoying getting to know you. I have baggage from my ex. We all do. No one gets divorced because they got along with their ex. No one thinks their ex is blameless. You know what? That's the past, and we are here in the mountains, and all that stuff should be as small as those cars when we were on that ledge."

"Agreed, I'm not bitter and you're right, we should leave that for another time, I mean there will be another time? Sometimes I get like that, but it's not me. You're a likable guy. If your ex was bad to you, I'm sorry. I'm sure you didn't deserve it."

Stephanie seemed flummoxed but was adjusting course.

Almost as if by divine intervention, the trail opened and spectacular falls of perhaps a hundred feet cascaded into pools of rocks, creating a circular pond. A few brave souls waded into the center and were about waist deep. Others sat on rocks, their pants legs rolled up and shoes off, feet dangling in the cool water. It might have augured for a kiss, but Dave was dead set on waiting to let the anticipation build.

"Dave, this is just the stuff I enjoy with the right person. I'm glad I'm here with you and thanks for being a trail guide. Thanks for making me forget about the past. It's a beautiful day and there is no need to look backward."

Dave glanced at his watch. It was about four and the hike back was a good twenty minutes. "Best we start back to the buses. We can take another trail rather than backtracking. It looks scenic."

"Okay, you're the best tour guide."

The trip back to the bus was full of small talk. If Stephanie took umbrage at being called to task about bringing up her ex she didn't let on. It appeared she wanted to be on her best behavior.

Stephanie seemed to try to talk about everything except Ross, so as not to be put in that basket of bitter divorcées. Dave tried to summon up some intelligence Ross had provided him and attempted to work in favorite movies, concerts, and vacation spots but was drawing blanks. Perhaps it was the rarified air in the mountains or just one of those middle-aged moments where the neurons weren't connecting with the memory. Maybe it was his subconscious saying, walk away.

Their hands interlocked on the trail. There were glances. A part of Dave felt elation he might just pull this plan off, and that he might enjoy a relationship with regular sex. He cued another antenna to the red flags.

He thought of Ross's daughter Nicole, and whether she would be affected if suddenly he was the boyfriend only to disappear within weeks. Then there was Stephanie and her obsession with getting even. Dave hadn't even gotten into the relationship but wondered about the difficulties of extricating himself. The realization that this was a scam would creep into his head at odd intervals. He boarded the bus, holding hands, trying to enjoy the moment.

The drive down the mountain took twenty minutes. They passed by a biker bar, with tons of Harleys parked along the street, Native American craft stores, and quaint shops. As the road wound towards the lake, it flattened. The weather was picture-perfect, with a gentle breeze cooling the fresh mountain air just enough so that the heat of Indian summer was no longer noticeable as nightfall approached.

Chapter Fifteen
Teen Hormones

The trip to Chimney Rock left Dave emotionally spent. The gravity of what lay ahead was sinking in. As the bus returned, he knew he'd have to suggest grabbing a drink to solidify the day's progress and couple-hood. The wine bar at the Piedmont Center was a stone's throw from SouthPark and despite the autumn chill, they grabbed a table outside. Warmed by space heaters, they listened to acoustic crooning. Stephanie talked of her journey of self-discovery and mid-life metamorphosis.

She invited him over, but exhausted, Dave politely declined, citing a work project and the physical demands of the hike. They hugged and made out as he walked her to her car in the vacant mall lot. He had crossed a Rubicon, and they vowed to see one another during the week at the gym. At her urging, he would sign up for the Lake Lure trip in a few weeks.

The following week they met at the gym three times,

each evening ending with Dave inviting Stephanie for a drink at the adjacent Hickory Tavern. They talked about Stephanie mostly, and Dave felt confident with Nicole's presence in the home, she wouldn't ask him over. He wanted sufficient build-up to the inevitable sleepover.

She insisted on talking each night, marking her territory, mindless blather mostly. He tried to pivot to texting with nominal success, thinking it less intrusive, and more conducive to witty sexual banter. He trod lightly, building up to the Lake Lure Cruise. He didn't want to scare her off with suggestive dialogue. But the lake had a storied history of chronicling improbable romances. Lake Lure was, after all, the movie set for "Dirty Dancing."

It was a good week for Dave and Stephanie, not so for Ross and his daughter Nicole. Her PSATs were two weeks away, and she was all but ignored by her mother. Stephanie was texting Dave, having dinner with Dave, or talking to friends via phone or online about Dave. Nicole's father was enthralled with his new partner. She seemed the odd one out, the divorced parent blues. Dave felt sorry for Nicole.

Ross was not averse to Nicole moving in, but the timing was an issue. With a thousand per month in child support, Stephanie would pitch a fit at the loss of what she considered her money. Ross faced engaging Becky to change the arrangement or continuing to pay support to a home where his daughter no longer lived. That would be going the wrong direction. He would go that route, but only after his relationship with Julie had a solid foundation, or Dave was close to cohabitation.

Teenagers are seldom impressed by a parent's timetables. She needed attention whether negative or positive and threw a hissy fit. Her teenage hormones were coursing through her veins, amplified by the diminished role she seemed to have in her parents' lives.

The one positive to her invisibility was a lack of oversight, and Nicole hung at impromptu gatherings at a greenway in Ballantyne office park. She tried pot for the first time, had beer, wine coolers, and Jagermeister and attracted the attention of Jimmy O'Connor, a junior varsity quarterback. Whether starved for attention, or a need to rebel, Nicole decided he would be her first and in twisted teen logic, losing her virginity was payback for being a bottom rung on her parent's priority list.

Ross picked her up on Friday, hoping to grab Chinese and drop her at a friend's house or the movies. His shrimp and lobster sauce was about to come with a side of teen angst.

"Dad, I decided I'm not taking the PSATs," she said, while fidgeting with her chopsticks.

"Nicole, that's not a smart decision. You're doing well in honors classes. You have the grades for Chapel Hill," Ross said, unwittingly stepping on a land mine.

"I'm not going to just blindly follow the plans you and mom laid out for me. I don't want to go to college right away. I want to see the world, not this sanitized suburban Disneyworld. I'm not some stupid lemming that just does what's expected of me, goes to college because everyone else is, gets married because everyone else is, pops out two kids because everyone else is, and then goes to a shrink to pop pills because I'm miserable like everyone else is. I don't know if it'll be backpacking through South America, joining the Navy, or being a carney, but I'm not going from high school, to college, and then to a shitty marriage and live a life full of regrets."

"Nicole, what are you saying? That's what you think my life is? Regrets? What's bugging you?"

"I'm not some robot you just programmed to do as its told. I'm a person, for fuck's sake." She wanted to push buttons.

"Nicole, we're in a restaurant. Cool it with the language. Calm down." Ross contained a groan. The moment the words left his lips he realized his mistake. No woman, fifteen or fifty reacts well to being told to calm down.

"Dad, you're one to talk. You went to college when you're supposed to, got married when you're supposed to, had a kid when you're supposed to. Did it get you anywhere? You're back where you were after college, starting from scratch. You spent most of your life doing what you needed to do so Mom didn't get pissed at you. Just like grandma does to grandpa."

She was on a roll. If her goal was to piss him off, she was succeeding.

"Do you even have any pleasant family memories?" She asked, breaking a Chinese noodle as if symbolic of her parent's marriage.

"Nicole, I have plenty of nice memories and tons of you before you became a know-it-all at the ripe age of fifteen."

"Did you and mom even have sex after conceiving me? Was it for your birthday? Or when Mom wanted Grandma to stay for a few weeks? Or maybe when she wanted a new car? Did you ever even like one another?"

"Nicole, that stuff is none of your goddamn business! I'm not going to sit here and have you pass judgment on my life. There are lots of things you don't know jack-shit about, including responsibilities."

"Oh yeah, a dad's responsibilities. That's a great one. The weight of the world on your shoulders, so you can keep Mom, Ms. Prozac Queen, from having to grow up. Did you ever think maybe if you grew a pair, she might have been forced to do something productive?"

"Young lady, I don't know what in God's name makes you think you have a clue about providing for a family. You're a teenager. You've one person to think about. Yourself. It seems like that is all you are doing."

"Just drop me off at Lizzie's or the movies at Stonecrest. I don't want to deal with you or Mom. You're both fucked up."

"Nicole, I can drive you where you want, but I'm picking you up at ten. Take your pick. No more foul language." He grasped his trousers and wadded them at the knees to keep from slapping her.

"I thought you would be happy to get rid of me, now you're finally getting laid."

"Keep going Nicole, and you will be grounded, and that's one thing your mother and I can get on the same page for."

Ross was pissed. Sure, Nicole upset him with her self-absorbed teen perspective on things, but she hit him where it hurts, and with painful truths. He hadn't grown a pair and thus enabled much of his servitude. She had a point about Julie. Nicole should have moved in, regardless of the math. He needed to stay the course with Julie and shoot for cohabitation. How do you react to your daughter humiliating you and act like it doesn't hurt, while acting like you're in charge?

"I'm picking you up at ten. Pick your spot, young lady, and not a minute late. When we get back, we'll talk."

"You should be happy you've enough time for a quickie with your girlfriend."

"Nicole, another disrespectful word out of your mouth and you're grounded for a month."

Nicole knew just what to say. A smart-ass teen just like him decades ago. She still needed to be grounded, but she fucked him up with some truth.

Stonecrest was the usual mob scene of teens, and Nicole seemed to run to one boy in particular. Ross didn't want to get inquisitive. That would make matters worse. *Fucking teenagers.*

Chapter Sixteen
Lure Her In

There was so much buildup throughout the week to the Lake Lure adventure cruise it felt like a prom. Time to take things to the next level. Dave's thoughts alternated between elation for moving the ball forward and the trepidation of entering a relationship that would test his patience. Stephanie was looking for a marker to confer boyfriend status. They were two objects moving closer to one another for entirely different reasons.

So much was riding on the three-hour cruise. Stephanie spent all afternoon primping and deciding what to wear, obsessing over skin blemishes while plotting to ensnare Dave. She was at two-and-a-half Klonopins and three Zoloft before the fifteen-minute drive to the SouthPark parking lot. Out of superstition, she had scant contact with Dave to not jinx things.

Despite her attempts to project the image of a self-assured woman, inside Stephanie was a jumble of nerves.

The image of a man-hating bitter divorcée was a red flag, and Stephanie knew it. She needed to bottle up her resentment and be jovial.

Before leaving on the cruise, Dave had a leisurely morning at the office, putting the finishing touches on a presentation for a hospital group in Greensboro. He didn't want work hanging over him, should things turn into a sleepover.

They rendezvoused at the lot and boarded the bus. No belittling other passengers, just small talk. A subdued Stephanie was feeling the effects of her anti-anxiety cocktail. While worrying about defaulting to bitter divorce mode, she dozed on Dave's shoulder.

An attractive middle-aged woman managed the plank to the boat. She handed them two drink tickets and a program of activities.

Dave was certain Stephanie felt chemistry but hoped for a sweet side, as yet undiscovered. He noticed two Ballantyne Barbies, blonde, tanned, and surgically enhanced with all manner of Botox and lipo, sipping apple martinis. They eyed him with their professionally bleached, megawatt smiles. The thought of flirting was tempting but risky to the mission. They would have to be fodder for the one thing Dave knew to be a guaranteed conversation starter—cutting others down to size.

"Look at those Ballantyne Barbies. Cougars on the prowl, fresh fake tans, and Botox after a stop at Nordstrom's."

Stephanie heard the statement and couldn't believe her ears, as if Dave was a kindred spirit who knew her thoughts. She sized them up as competition. What was with men and those ridiculous southern accents out of "Gone with the

Wind?"

I must have a case of the vapors, Rhett. It was sickening and phony. Stephanie envied their easygoing nature and the amiable smiles that had eluded her all her life. Weren't they all so superficial with their book clubs, prayer groups, garden clubs, and identically decorated houses?

Men had to know it was an act. Deep down, didn't men prefer smarminess? Dave knew quality when he saw it, and that must be why he commented.

"Oh, my God. I can't believe you said that. They fill my neighborhood. They're so phony. They say, 'Bless your heart,' but can be every bit as catty as the northern women they mock, they're just sneakier about it. Not a hair out of place, manicured lawns, gardens, spotless homes, tanned, thin legs. They're Southern Stepford wives."

Dave grinned smugly. He'd tapped into a rich vein that would sustain the balance of the evening. Stephanie riffed on everything, the way their tanned legs looked in golf shorts, and how giggly they got when they had a little too much to drink at neighborhood parties. If the men acted inappropriately, he would be on pussy probation for days, if not weeks. Shoot, Stephanie sentenced her husband to months, without even knowing what for. To Stephanie, they lacked substance, which meant being jaded and mean-spirited.

They sidled up to the bar while Stephanie riffed on the Barbies. She went for another Zinfandel while Dave nursed a vodka tonic. When she returned, they found a window table. A three-piece combo nearby provided the evening's entertainment.

The more Stephanie denigrated her competition, the better they sounded. Dave decided his first conquest after this mission was a Ballantyne Barbie, high maintenance be damned. However, there was some unfinished business.

"I bet your ex-wife was just like them. Decorating in that same style always dressed up to go to Harris Teeter."

"She was nothing like them. My ex is an attorney. Everything she did, she had to be competitive. You couldn't play tennis with her without it turning into the finals at Wimbledon. Now she takes martial arts. I used to have to worry about her beating me on the court, now I have to worry about her beating me up."

"Wow, I'm so not like that," she said., her voice tinged with jealousy.

Julie would find this Stephanie an anathema to everything she stood for, and the feelings would be mutual. Two women, both college-educated, one determined to compete in everything she did, the other had an opposite goal, to do the bare minimum and shift responsibilities to others. It was as if feminism opened a door for Stephanie that she refused to walk through, wallowing in victimhood while also rejecting traditional gender roles. Julie rushed through the door and never looked back. She thought she was given opportunities and was determined to make the best of them. Victimhood was not part of her lexicon.

Dave looked at the houses dotting the lakeshore. He was thinking about how two women seemed to want such distinct things out of life.

Dave didn't quite know what to make of Stephanie. She seemed to aspire to do as little as possible as if work was the province of fools. She denigrated the accomplishments of others, reserving equal contempt for those who remained homemakers.

He imagined the work involved in this endeavor to be like escorts plied their trade: focus on a positive, get through the hour, and collect the cash. This was a minimum of a three-month assignment. The entire plan seemed implausible. But Ross had already slept with Julie and was moving the relationship towards cohabitation.

Had they emulated "Strangers on a Train," their goal

would be murder. This project required months of interaction for its two principals, and any slipup had the potential to derail the project. Murder, according to most detective shows, required only an airtight alibi, and lots of bleach.

Stephanie wasn't unpleasant looking, and he had already realized she was like putty when complimented, a narcotic she needed at frequent intervals. The constant fishing for compliments was exhausting.

Suck it up. The narcissistic desire to fast forward a relationship through love bombing would define the bulk of their time together. The next phase, devaluation, would be a good pretext for the breakup. Discard was the third and final act of the narcissist relationship trilogy. If intel were correct, Stephanie would take on his interests, fawn on his every action, to convince him they were soulmates destined to be together forever until her demeanor changed, at which time her dark side would emerge. That would be his cue to split. He might bypass Stephanie's most odious qualities altogether.

"Wow, I hope you don't mind me saying this, but walking back I was just so struck by how pretty you are, and how youthful you look. Hard to believe you have a teenager."

"That is so sweet." Stephanie blushed. Dave's syringe hit a vein.

"Being a mom is what I do well. It's getting to where Nicole requires less supervision, and I'm ready for dating. Nicole is a smart, outstanding student. She takes after me. She is entitled, which she gets from my ex-husband's family, but I have a wonderful example of mothering to follow. My mother is always there for me. I guess you could say I'm equipped to handle anything."

"I feel like I have a special insight into your personality. You're beautiful inside and out." Dave reached over and kissed her, opening his mouth and, after an uncomfortable few seconds of getting teeth repositioned,

Steven Grossman

was making out. She wasn't adept at kissing, but electricity wasn't the goal here. It was passing a mile marker. The relationship passed Platonicsville, and The Friend Zone was in the rear-view mirror. The next few exits might be a challenge, but they passed a hurdle.

"Wow, you are amazing." Dave wondered if he was laying it on too thick, but for Stephanie, no such thing.

Ross warned Dave against looking in her eyes, as she would say "What?" as it scared her, which in short order proved annoying. Dave laughed to himself. His head rested on her shoulder. He held her close and his hands wandered along her back. It seemed a tender way to show interest without the eye-lock proclivity. Dave had a full night on his hands and didn't want to screw things up.

The cruise had two hours and an equal amount of time on the bus where they would sit together. He was fumbling for conversation and settled on: "You smell so good."

"Glad you like it. Let's see; the perfume is Fendi, and the shampoo, it's apple scented. Kind of reminds me of fall, my favorite time of year. I used to go apple picking on the eastern shore. Such pleasant memories."

"I'm getting hungry. Would you like me to get you some hors-d'oeuvres?" Dave asked.

"What a gentleman, that sounds great. Maybe another Zinfandel, I'm in the mood to drink."

"Were you ever on a cruise?"

"Never. My ex always wanted to go on one, but I didn't like being cooped up or at sea with no way to get off. Plus, he pressured me into going on some whale-watching excursion, and I wound up not going. I didn't want to go. Do you believe he got on the ship, anyway? I maxed out his card with overpriced vacation clothes just to get even."

It took less than an hour for her to get back on the ex-bashing train. Dave had heard the other side, where Stephanie would be jet-lagged, not in the mood to do anything. If Ross were being honored for work, she would foment an argument to take away whatever sliver of joy he might feel.

"Sounds like some kind of drill sergeant."

"He was, but enough about that jerk, I can already tell you aren't like that, and I shouldn't be bringing him up."

Dave knew this was one of those moments when honesty wasn't the best policy, and while he wasn't much of a drinker, he decided wine would relax his nerves, and allow him to overlook a few flaws.

"My ex could be high strung and liked to do what she wanted when she wanted. I get where you are coming from," Dave said.

"How did you deal with it?"

"We sort of went in different directions. I did what I wanted, and she did what she wanted. It worked out fine until it no longer did. Let's get a bottle and sit down. We can chat, dance, chat, and dance. We have about an hour until dinner, and I'm famished."

"Okay, you get the wine, and I'll go get some cheese and crackers to tide us over. How does that sound?" Stephanie sounded perky.

"Deal, but let's leave our exes on the shore. I prefer not to talk about them. We can toast to new beginnings. What are you drinking?"

"White Zin."

Stephanie wasn't bad looking. Her figure was alluring from behind but without a feminine gait. It was the walk of someone trying to prevent the world from finding out her lack of confidence.

The sun was setting, and the lights were twinkling on both the boats and houses that dotted Lake Lure. It was a pleasant setting for what each hoped would transpire, albeit for different reasons.

Dave downed two additional glasses of wine. Nerves helped Stephanie keep pace. Dave figured he was a date or two away from sex. Perhaps not great sex, but sex nevertheless. A relationship, even a phony one, would fill in empty weekends for a while.

The band was adequate, playing rock with slower ballads. The clanking bell signaled it was time to head upstairs for dinner. They staked out an empty table, like their bottle of wine.

"I rarely drink. I better get something in my stomach. You'll make sure I'm okay, right?"

Dave didn't know how to take her comment. He feared she might signal the room was spinning.

"You don't feel nauseous, do you?" Dave asked.

"No, I don't think, but I'm not a big boat person. I'm sure I'll be fine."

"Okay, but no more wine. Why don't you stay at the table, and I'll get you a plate of stuff?"

Dave went up to the buffet station with two plates in hand. He added ziti, a portion of fish, and some beef. When he returned to the table, a couple and a single woman took up three of the remaining seats. Stephanie appeared to be making polite chit chat but wasn't firing on all cylinders.

"Hey, Dave. Pleased to meet you," the man said.

There was Misty, Bill, and Georgina, all of whom had ventured on the trip solo. Bill seemed like a nice enough guy, a Charlotte prototype, a golf shirt, a slight Southern accent, khaki pants, and boating shoes. He looked on the prowl.

Bill was already talking about the Panthers and how they seemed destined to flounder because Cam Newton couldn't step up as a mature leader. Stephanie hated men like this, but then again Julie would too.

Misty was zaftig, a bit plump but well-dressed lady of perhaps forty years old. She was made up, but not overly so. Her frosted hairdo was rather retro but looked good. It was short, but she rocked it with confidence. She had the lilting drawl that emanated from the coast, perhaps Charleston, and smiled easily.

Georgina was more of a spitfire. Petite and pixyish, weathered skin, braces on her teeth, but like a faded old building, she still looked good. Her frame shaved a few years off her perceived age. She had a raspy voice, neither full-on Redneck nor the educated enunciation that Julie had. It was sexy. Bill appeared to be debating which of the two to focus on. Dave was curious too. Either would have been fun, but Dave was spoken for on this trip.

"So, what does everyone here do for fun?" Dave asked.

Misty took shag dancing lessons, Bill golfed, an enormous surprise there, and Georgina enjoyed fishing. She was trying yoga for the first time, which she credited as enabling her to quit smoking for over two years. She looked low-maintenance and as flexible as a double-jointed limbo dancer, but to Dave, she was off-limits.

He couldn't figure how to get hers or Misty's contact information without alerting Stephanie. Misty was a keeper too. She loved to cook, had a son working on some agricultural NGO in India, and a daughter serving as a trauma nurse in the Air Force. She started as a claims adjuster for a worker's comp firm and completed her degree while working and was a semester away from getting her MBA.

Stephanie grimaced, prompted by envy but partly because it made her self-conscious about her failure to launch. Dave needed to keep things light and avoid picking at sensitive subjects.

Stephanie would work her hand onto Dave's thigh whenever he engaged in conversation to say: "Don't forget I'm here too." Dave tried to think of a topic where she could chime in.

"Georgina, yoga sounds interesting, and Stephanie, I'm wondering, is Pilates anything like yoga?" Misty asked.

Georgina said she did the class for fun, but wasn't steeped in its history.

Stephanie went into more detail, stressing how difficult it was to master Pilates, which caused Bill to tune out. Georgina tried to include Misty in the conversation and asked about dancing and shag music. There were fits and starts of conversation but it seemed as if one topic that included someone excluded another. The other girls were open to talking about local sports, but Stephanie seemed bored.

The emcee started the karaoke program. Stephanie perked up.

People sauntered up to the DJ to request their songs and put themselves out there to sing. Stephanie walked up with a spring in her step, the only volunteer from their table. The table seemed interested in what Stephanie would do. Nonverbal when the table was getting to know one another, either drunk or aloof, but she seemed confident about singing. Dave hoped they weren't in for a horrendous performance.

The first few contestants ranged between mediocre renditions of Nickelback, to a Carrie Underwood wannabe, who must've sung in church. A soulful singer did a very credible job of Gloria Gaynor's 'I Will Survive', a rather shrewd song selection given that this was a single group of middle-aged divorcees, which she nailed.

Stephanie took the mic and announced she would do 'Black Velvet,' an Elvis tribute by Alana Myles. It was the first time he observed her filled with confidence. The song, a Southern girl's homage to Elvis and his transformative effect, was both sultry and sensuous, not qualities Stephanie exuded normally. Singing seemed to allow her to express a side that was suppressed when away from the microphone.

Her performance was a cut above the competition. It was obvious she had training, and the rest were a rag-tag group of nonprofessionals.

She bowed and did a demure curtsy, appearing surprised but glowing in being the center of attention. The table stood and clapped. Bill extended his hand, Misty said, "Wow," and Georgina asked where she learned to sing.

It drew her out of her shell for the remaining hour of the cruise. She was a star and got up another time to sing 'Landslide,' channeling Stevie Nicks.

There were only three contestants with even a

modicum of talent, and Stephanie was basking in the applause.

She drank more wine to celebrate. Ross had said she didn't drink much. Dave wanted to play gentleman, and drunken sex is non-consensual sex, but it appeared she was in no state to drive home. There would be the question of a sleepover.

The dance floor invited adulation from other couples, and Stephanie basked in it. Kudos were intoxicating, as was wine, and tonight she had an appetite for both.

Stephanie had already consumed a cornucopia of pills, for anxiety, and depression. She thought she was sneaking them in, but Dave spotted them, especially as her drinking increased. Continuing to drink was courting disaster. She became grabby, effusively complimenting how well their date was going. She became clingy.

"Your whole wardrobe seems to be from important places in my life. Someone is trying to tell us something." Her words had a discernible slur.

The coincidental wardrobe played with her psyche. The alcohol was revealing their effectiveness. She recited them on the dance floor—Cozumel, Dewey Beach, Maryland, not to mention their chance encounter in Chimney Rock.

Someone would compliment her on her singing, and she would try to prolong the conversation by asking, "What was your favorite part?" or "Was I loud enough at the end?"

Dave knew in pharmaceuticals like in physics, what comes up must come down, and the landing would not be pretty. Even if she agreed to a sexual encounter at this point it was a red line he was unprepared to cross. He needed to be gentlemanly and not take undue advantage. An odd choice of words for someone who had spent months planning to get in her pants through deception.

The table said its goodbyes to one another as everyone filed onto the dock.

Dave's apartment was small and utilitarian, nothing

like the oversized spread he enjoyed as a childless couple in Lake Norman. There was a lot to gain by completing this mission. He would have time to think. Dave was sure she would conk out once they began moving.

Stephanie got a few compliments on the bus. She was subdued but appreciative. She grabbed for Dave's hand making a few subtle grabs of his butt, marking her territory. Stephanie nuzzled in the area between Dave's shoulder and face. She was nose breathing in his neck, and it became grating.

"I had a wonderful time, did you?" she asked.

"It was outstanding." He brushed his nose, a tell that he was lying. He hoped she hadn't picked up on his tell yet. It wasn't a terrible night as nights go. There just were aspects of her that gave pause. He would soon be balls-deep in a relationship with her. It was following a script, but it involved work. He dreaded the endless blather on the phone and texting.

The breathing in his neck continued to grate on him. His arm trapped behind her shoulder was falling asleep. If he jostled her, she would awaken to ask questions.

"You are my special new friend, right?"

"Yes, Stephanie." *For Christ's sakes just sleep already.*

Dave's trapped arm had his watch, and thus he could neither read it nor reach for the phone. She was now snoring. He was torn between nudging her to move, shimmying his arm free, or riding out the discomfort. He replayed all the things he would have to deal with between the bus's arrival and the next morning.

Dave needed to focus on the task at hand, getting her home, comporting himself as a gentleman, later doing the necessary follow up to consummate the deal.

When the bus got to Interstate 85, a half hour from Charlotte, he would broach the subject of her sobriety and ability to drive. He planned to drive to Waffle House, get coffee and greasy food in her, and see where things led. It would give him time to reassess the situation. It would be at least 1 a.m. by the time they finished breakfast, one-thirty before he got to her place. She might be sober enough to drive or decide she wanted him to stay over. In a morbid thought, Dave realized she was a drunk-driving fatality waiting to happen. He could put her in her car and allow her to drive herself home. If she killed herself on the way home Ross would also be alimony-free, and his part of the bargain would be done. An enticing idea but could he live with the death of innocent victims on his conscience if she rammed her car into an oncoming vehicle? He sighed.

"Do you want to get coffee and a bagel or something? Get the wine out of our systems?" He asked.

"You don't want the night to end, do you? I'd love to. So sweet of you," Stephanie said, as she ascribed tender motives to his utilitarian invitation.

It was only a few minutes to the mall as the bus drove through Tyvola. He rated her as moderately drunk. Not well enough to drive, but well enough to handle a late-night Waffle House where virtually everyone was drunk.

"Where do you want to go for coffee? I'm going to take an allergy pill." She got her purse and popped a Klonopin, which would settle her nerves, not sinuses. Dave knew it wasn't Benadryl. He took it as a sign she wanted the sleepover.

Dave offered to drive. She agreed without as much as a peep. He had cleaned his car out and arranged the CD changer with coincidental song choices, but all for naught. As they drove down Park Road to the nearest Waffle House, Stephanie had a smug look and was thinking how she could rub her "perfect evening" in Ross' face when the two next met.

"I've never been to one except one time on the way to Florida with my daughter and ex. It seemed so redneck."

"Think of it as entertainment. You seem to like people-watching;" Dave said.

There would be characters to talk about at Waffle

House at midnight to keep the conversation flowing. Post-midnight Waffle House was America's greatest reality show. There were millennial girls, dressed up as if they had been clubbing, reeking of alcohol and perfume, a stately looking black man drinking coffee by himself, writing something in a journal, perhaps a sermon for tomorrow, a Mexican family crammed around one table eating breakfast and two toddlers fast asleep wedged between parents in the booth. There were a few loud rednecks in MAGA hats and a bunch of stoned twenty-somethings.

Dave was near Stephanie's turf and didn't want a place her neighbors frequented. There were diners for golfing suburbanites. Waffle House at this hour would be safe from familiar faces.

Dave introduced Stephanie to the concept of chunked, scattered, diced: Waffle House parlance for hash brown toppings. She found his take on hash browns humorous but seemed preoccupied with what would go on at her house in an hour. They wolfed down coffee and held hands across the table. He kept trying to maintain eye-contact. Dave just needed to stay the course, and he was home free.

The weathered waitress served their orders. Greasy food is supposed to help ease a good drunk. Maybe there was something to the myth. Stephanie ate ravenously.

"I don't know where you put all that food, with such a slim figure."

Keep those compliments rolling, said the scouting report. *You are close to sealing the deal.*

"Well, I work at it. My ex has put on twenty-five pounds since we split. I feel sorry for the next woman that has to be underneath his ugly body." Like water in a pressure hose, her bitterness towards Ross was never far from the surface and despite her efforts to suppress it, the resentments bubbled over out of nowhere.

Dave laughed, not at what she just said but at the fact that the poor victim was Julie, and from the debrief, their sex was good. Ross had, because of martial arts, added weight in the form of muscle.

During Dave's last year of marriage to Julie, the sex had been sporadic but good. That was not their undoing. It may have prolonged the inevitable divorce. Dave wasn't expecting similar fireworks with Stephanie but would compliment her as if there were.

Dave daydreamed about the woman he might wind up with if he extricated himself from this plan. He had a tin foil covered Viagra to pop in the bathroom, to ensure things went off without a hitch. He hadn't any previous ED troubles, but performing on-demand, with this level of guilt, would produce anxiety.

His conscience wrestled with his genitals. He was sure that after the Viagra redirected blood flow, all would fall into place. Perhaps Ross was just exaggerating her lackluster bedroom habits.

The waitress asked if there would be anything else. Dave requested to-go cups and the check, discreetly popping the pill.

As Dave paid, Stephanie said it surprised her at how tasty everything was. Dave was a pharma guy and knew the hangover-fighting qualities of Waffle House.

He left a five on the table to seem generous on a twenty-dollar tab. They were on their way to Ross's former home. While leaning against the passenger side of the car, Dave began a session of deep French kisses. She was an awkward kisser because of sinus problems. He hugged her and let his hands wander to her ass, one of her better features.

Out of nowhere, and without warning, she barfed. On his back mostly, but there were chunks in his hair, scattered in the small of his back, and behind his ear.

The best-laid plans…

"I'll run inside and get rags," she said. "It must have been something in the food."

All Dave could think about was Ross's admonishment that she never took a morsel of responsibility for anything, and now after a bottle of wine, and a half dozen Klonopin, it was the short-order cook that conspired to make her barf. Unbelievable.

"I'll go into the bathroom and wash off. Just stay here." He was trying not to lose his shit. Fuck this plan. He didn't sign up to be covered in vomit.

Some teens in a souped-up Camaro were snickering. He wasn't sure if they witnessed the incident but was ready to punch one of them if they said anything. He headed to the bathroom and made her wait near the car. They could carjack her for all he cared.

Dave washed while some ungodly intestinal noises emanated from the lone stall. Whatever was going on in there couldn't have smelled much worse. Dave was almost done with the visible pieces, but the stench remained. Now, he would drive to her car, drive it back to her house, and Uber back to his car at the mall. Stephanie was in no shape to drive and driving her to her house would involve him sleeping on a couch or being coaxed into her lair to make out with a mouth that had projectile vomited on him earlier. He just wanted to go home.

Stephanie said the rest of the night would end on a pleasant note. Except, there would not be a rest of the night.

"Stephanie, I have to get back. I'll drive you to your car, and I'll drive you home, but once we get there I have to get back and change clothes. We can hook up another time."

"It was just food. I'm fine, really I'm... You'll ruin an evening over this?"

Vomit was generally a deal-breaker. Worse, he had popped the Viagra and he would have a raging hard-on. He smelled so bad, even the thought of rubbing one out seemed disgusting.

They exchanged no words, both thinking their separate thoughts.

"Keys," Dave said.

She handed them to him. He GPS'ed her address,

eliminating the need to speak.

"Listen. I'm sorry; okay? Let me make it up to you. We have something special," she said, half declarative statement and half question.

"Okay, we'll get together soon and start fresh."

Dave pressed the Uber app on the phone and said he was going to wait on the bench on her portico. She motioned to kiss him, but Dave turned away, trying to hide his disgust. She closed the door. He heard her trudge upstairs.

His driver spied his damp shirt and asked what had happened.

"Dude, you don't want to know," he said. "Let's just say a friend of mine owes me big time."

Dave was back at SouthPark for the fourth time today. He drove home, in fetid clothes with a Viagra hard-on, knowing the next time he would get laid would be with Stephanie.

He thought of firing off an email to Ross to tell him he took one for the team in the form of regurgitated hash browns, but Dave wanted only to shower and sleep. He received half a dozen texts from Stephanie and decided not to engage.

"Just got home. Going to bed. Talk to you later."

"I miss you. Please don't be mad because Waffle House served me uncooked eggs,"

Dave rubbed one out in the shower, changed into sweats, and watched ESPN, hoping that sports would distract his body from producing another erection.

He slept in until noon and then texted Ross. "I was on track to sleep with her…'til she threw up. On me. At a Waffle House. She covered, smothered, and chunked all over me. You owe me. I'll make another date for next week, against my best judgment."

Ross didn't check his disposable cell until mid-week. He was up to his eyeballs in Nicole's teen hormones and having to counter-parent with someone intent on throwing him under the bus. Every joint parenting decision was an opportunity to undermine his authority. Julie was supportive of Ross's dilemma, but Ross preferred to spare her the full extent of their co-parenting nightmare. Julie had no kids and would not easily understand the full impact of narcissistic personality disorder on co-parenting after divorce. It was hard enough for Ross to understand.

By Wednesday the vomit had washed off his psyche. Dave was ready to try again. Nothing too fancy. Tapas at Miro, an artsy film at the theater in Ballantyne Village. Some French chick-flick that got ninety-eight percent on Rotten Tomatoes.

Stephanie limited the wine to one glass. Between the subtitles, there wasn't much of an opportunity to converse during the film, but Stephanie held his hand and rubbed his leg. She was on her best behavior.

She cried three times in the movie. The story of two French childhood friends who reunite after the death of a favorite teacher couldn't have possibly been sadder than wiping vomit from his hair at Waffle House at 2 a.m. a week earlier. She loved the movie, or at least pretended to, imagining doing so would make her seem worldly.

"That was so good. I'd love for you to come over. I can assure you it'll go better than last time." That was a low bar to clear, but Dave felt duty-bound to move forward, part soldier with a mission, part horny divorcee who had spent the latter part of last weekend fighting off serial erections.

They entered the house and Stephanie dutifully offered pie and ice cream, along with coffee. It was not long before they made their way to the living room couch. The room looked decorated but sterile.

What followed was like two teenagers fumbling on the couch. Hands roamed and legs intertwined. Dave debated whether to do the-hand-in-back-of-the-jeans-ass-cup or go for the bra.

He hadn't thought of such things with the handful of women he had been with since his divorce. Things always just happened, but this was a performance. He went for the ass first because she was proud of her butt, sculpted by exercise.

She rubbed the outside of his pants and, thanks to his second weekly dose of performance enhancer, he had a boner of high-school intensity. She couldn't let this erection go unattended. There was only one way that boy was going back down. He reached up the back of her shirt to unhook the bra. She extricated herself from their kiss.

"Let's go upstairs, just take your shoes off for the carpeting."

They walked hand in hand up the stairs to the bedroom. Down the hall was Nicole's room, the room with tears Ross could not dry. He would now lie on Ross's former marriage bed before fornicating with Ross's ex-wife.

They tumbled on the bed and picked up where they left off. He fumbled for her zipper, undid it, and suggested they get undressed. The room was unlit, unfamiliar surroundings for Dave. He watched, by the moonlight that streamed in the windows, her removing her shirt and pants leaving the bra and panties. He was naked except for socks. Undoing her bra, she moved the arm straps to slip it off. She lifted her hips while on her back to allow her panties to slide off easily. This motion is the exact moment men know they're getting laid, a formal invitation to the vagina, and normally a Kodak moment for the highlight reel.

They groped and caressed, and she opened her legs ever so slightly. She took his tool, at first rubbing it. He thought of offering oral sex, but Ross said she thought it gross. He gestured to down there with his mouth and she shook her head no.

"I'd rather you not. It's not my thing."

A no would have sufficed, but now he was wondering what else didn't feel good. Do you know what else doesn't feel good? Being vomited on, also writing alimony checks. *Take one for the team, Dave.*

Ross said Stephanie was never orgasmic nor did she care about their absence. Pills, low libido, and inability to enjoy herself. Ross had come to think, "If she doesn't care, why should I?"

The dialogue had been replaced by hmm and ahhs. Dave was hoping for more feedback from her, but no advice was forthcoming. Her nipples stiffened. Progress.

He mounted her, dry at first, but after some fumbling, the parts went where they were supposed to go.

After perhaps ten minutes, Dave let out a groan and rolled over in exhausted bliss. The absence of dialogue or movement prolonged the act. It had been a few months since he had gotten laid and, despite everything, he felt relief and a sense of accomplishment.

She said, "Quick, get a towel."

Dave asked if everything was okay, to which she said yes, but she hated to have stuff dripping out of her all night as if his semen was battery acid. Not a peep about birth control or any of it. He remembered Ross talking about a partial hysterectomy but needed to check on that. A child together, while unlikely, would be a most unwelcome development.

He fumbled his way to the bathroom and found a towel. She put it between her legs like a diaper. He climbed back into bed and spooned her obligatorily. He was exhausted but didn't want to just turn over. The extra touches would help seal the deal.

He said he had a glorious night, and the lovemaking was the icing on the cake. She said she had an outstanding time too, and that Dave was a tiger in bed. He had done little of anything other than the basic missionary position.

He now knew why Ross was so impressed by Julie's bedroom prowess.

She breathed hard, the result of a sleeping pill. He tried to doze off as soon as possible to become oblivious to her breathing. The hog-like noises of someone trying to scratch their throat were straight out of Old Macdonald's Farm. They stopped and started, as if by design, preventing him from sleep. Each time Dave grew more annoyed. Ross needed to know. He would write him an email asking him what other surprises there were beyond barnyard noises, and projectile vomiting.

There was no clock in the master bedroom. And why not? Stephanie never had to wake up for anything. Nicole got herself ready for school. The abject darkness and absence of a clock made for an interminable night. There was no way to estimate when the throat scratching chortles would begin, or how much more time remained until daybreak. Each time he had to pee was a struggle to find his way to the bathroom without stubbing his toe.

This could go on for months. He had to ignore these petty annoyances. *Man up.* Ross and Dave had calculated the odds of bedding one of the ex-wives to be one in two. Both exes one in six, cohabitation by one, one in ten, and by both one in fifty. They were marching towards victory, but more work remained. Grunting noises be damned, there would be no retreat.

As he thought of the LA flight with Ross, Dave realized that if nothing else happened, he had gained a measure of hope, confidence, and purpose, after having been a broken man. A little over a year ago he was living at a Travelodge, living off beef jerky and pizza, with hookers plying their trade nearby, and unable to access his direct deposits.

Dave could do this. He had to. For the first time since being booted out by his father-in-law, he was making the best of a losing hand.

Dave was unsure whether he slept for two hours or

five. Eventually, the morning light streamed through the Persian blinds. Suburban noises of lawnmowers, families heading to church, and the chirping of birds signaled it was at least eight o'clock.

Brunch seemed an appropriate gesture for such a monumental occasion. They could get a cup of coffee, perhaps a mimosa, and go their separate ways after a "consummated relationship." He had to get out of Ballantyne. Dave was in no mood to be outed by someone who knew Ross. South Park would put him near the FedEx where he could write Ross on a public computer.

Harpers, with its exposed brick, seemed like an excellent choice, Mimosas, and trophy wives, across the street from the mall, would send just the right message. Now he had to wait for her to wake.

The house would be a treasure trove of information. Ross's descriptions were coming to life. Nicole cried tears just down the hall. He'd have to deal with her, perhaps even listen to Stephanie excoriate her dad in her presence. He wondered how many times Henry had stayed over and whether the throaty noises had kept him up. She probably told him he was a cheating bastard from the phone on the nightstand. He pictured Ross at the real estate closing, thinking he would live in this house forever, only to be kicked out permanently.

For all Julie's vengeful retributions after the breakup, she shouldered her share of the financial burdens and downsized to a smaller place close to Uptown. Stephanie had no particular guilt about the disparate living situations. There was no calculus she hadn't contributed to the purchase or upkeep of the house. It was her divine birthright, and if Ross was in a cardboard box outside the library, that would suit her fine.

Dave might play a big part in her comeuppance if he negated the alimony. Would she take responsibility? Probably not. Perhaps Nicole would move in with Ross. Dave might dispense justice, or maybe enrage her further.

Somehow people like Stephanie always wiggled out of their obligations, passing them on to willing dupes.

Stephanie was grumbling in a low morning voice.

"Got any coffee? If you tell me where, I'll make you some," Dave said.

"Sure, I think I've got coffee in the pantry. There is a coffee maker on the kitchen island. Not sure where the filters are. You'll find them."

Dave put on his pants and headed downstairs. The living room had a museum quality as if it had never been used. The kitchen was clean, and also felt rarely used. He found the coffeemaker and just enough milk but had to search for filters. Unable to find any, he improvised a paper towel and arranged it in the top part of the Mr. Coffee while sitting in the recliner that Ross had relaxed in after work.

He poured himself a cup, grabbed a day-old Observer, and read about what transpired the previous day.

"Sugar and lots of milk," Stephanie bellowed from upstairs. No pleasantries, thank you, or please, just an absence of gratitude. Dave gulped down his mug and looked for another to take to Stephanie.

As he climbed the stairs, he heard the TV being turned on. She had put on a housecoat.

"Hey Steph, sleep well?"

"Yes, like a baby. I needed that."

"Vitamin Dave, Right?"

"Yes, it was great. It's been a while and my last boyfriend was older and let's say he didn't have as much stamina."

Ross told Dave that she bragged about Henry's prowess in the sack. Insecure about her lack of sexual response, she worked overtime to paint a picture of a torrid sex life. Ross hadn't bought it.

Dave passed the test while making an impression. It was utilitarian sex with no soundtrack to give feedback. He was used to Julie who would guide, coach, and moan until she reached the finish line.

Dave felt good about his progress with the plan.

"Hey, I should get moving but let's grab brunch, maybe at Harper's."

Dave wanted to sleep in his bed without animal noises and reach Ross.

It was a crisp autumn day with the trees still full of bright foliage as they drove out of her manicured neighborhood. Like his own Lake Norman homestead, this must have been hard to leave. He would have his personal space back in an hour and felt good. It was his first sex in months, and while neither acrobatic nor erotic, it took the edge off. He felt proud at having advanced the plan past a critical marker.

Chapter Seventeen
Home Stretch

Harpers was crowded with the Sunday brunch crowd. A tad more subdued than Ballantyne restaurants, but with plenty of drinking going on, thanks to the relaxed Sunday brunch laws allowing alcohol before noon. Guys in golf shirts and khakis and their toned wives inhabited the restaurant. If there was an official uniform for South Charlotte, this was it. The South Park scene was subtly different from Ballantyne. More old money, more Southerners, and fewer newcomers. It was not as conspicuous as Ballantyne, nor as recreationally focused as Lake Norman. Country club membership and church denomination mattered. Myers Park was the only acceptable public high school, with various Country Day Schools being even better choices. A tad more subdued than Ballantyne restaurants, but with plenty of drinking going on, thanks to the relaxed Sunday Brunch laws allowing alcohol before noon.

The waitress staff was almost exclusively blonde and

attractive. Patrons came adorned in their tennis outfits. Stephanie gave their waitress the stink-eye everytime she approached their table. Dave and Stephanie ordered Eggs Benedict and Mimosas while observing their surroundings. He couldn't get away quickly enough.

The check arrived via their buxom blonde waitress. Dave signed the check and headed to the lot where they had parked in adjacent spots.

Dave leaned down, gave her a hug, and the two kissed deeply at her urging. But he could think of only the projectile vomiting the week before. She made a point of continuing to hold his hand until reaching her car and did a demure wave as she pulled away. He gave a deep sigh and climbed into his car.

The Fed Ex on the other side of Sharon Road beckoned him. He needed to email Ross but wanted to make sure Stephanie wasn't tailing him. He parked near Nordstrom's and after entering the store, walked the two blocks to the FedEx business center. He wrote Ross of the day's many developments.

Hey Dude. First sleepover. Did the deed. Sleep interrupted by her throat clearing barnyard noises. Nice house. I know why you miss it. She's into the relationship. We'll get this to the end zone. I just wanted to let you know where things stood. It's been quite a rollercoaster for the last three weeks. Chimney Rock, Lake Lure, and some sappy French movie. Next morning brunch at Harper's. We are in the red zone. How's my ex? Don't forget to say hi. Let's talk via cell in an hour. I'll leave you a message. Got to get home and nap. We've cleared the biggest hurdle. Do you believe this is

happening? Dave

He went to the drawer for his hidden phone and charger, then texted Ross's number.

Text Message:

> *Lots to discuss. Shoot me some times when we can catch up. I need more inside tips. She goes nuts over them. I have to ask you a few questions about some of her intimate likes, if there are any, and dislikes. Things moving ahead. I can't believe we are almost there.*

Dave lay on the couch with the phone resting on his chest and waited for a text to tell him when Ross could speak. The Panthers were playing their rivals the Falcons, and it was a roller coaster of a season, not unlike the wild ride both Ross and Dave have been on.

Their secretive system to talk to one another seemed paranoid, implemented at Dave's insistence, but with things progressing to a critical stage, it seemed important to take whatever steps possible to maintain secrecy. One slip up and they'd be back to square one.

Ross could send a text response a minute later or in a few days, depending on his availability and urge to check his phone. But after being informed that the two had made contact at the gym, Ross should be very curious.

If Julie were spending the weekend with him, it would be tough to respond, but with Nicole there he had more latitude. She wanted to move in with her father, and Ross wanted it too, he'd told Dave. He just needed a few months after things progressed with Julie. It broke his heart to tell her, "Just give it a little more time. In a few months, I'll make it happen." Now she wasn't too pleased with either parent. Ross urged her to stay more during the week and made time for Julie too. It was a juggling act. Ross was burning the candle at both ends, not to mention his work demands and money woes. Having Nicole stay over more would give Dave more opportunities for sleepovers and to move his part of the plan forward.

Ross called within minutes. "Hey, stud."

"So those throat-clearing noises. What the fuck?"

"Spring and fall she gets allergies, and it's a nightly ritual. Sorry, bro should have warned you. Bring earplugs."

"Oh, and she drank too much last week. Too many pills and threw up all over me. But other than that, I really can't complain. Some of her conversations, jeez. She's so full of herself and she bashes you constantly."

"No shit, Sherlock. Did you sleepover? Tell me all about it."

Dave recounted the day with some detail, sparing few items. Ross offered advice but said to stay the course. She was quite co-dependent and needed a partner. Ross guesstimated she'd urge him to move the relationship forward in a few months, if not weeks. He promised to share other inside tips he could think of, but the sex would remain cold and sterile, although offered with more frequency as an incentive.

The conversation shifted from Stephanie to Julie. Ross relayed that he didn't mind spending time with her, but that she wasn't what he expected. He liked her. but did not reveal he was on the cusp of another "L" word. There was a brief mention of Dave and when there was she used the term: 'good guy'.

"I think she likes you, Dave. Blames the family business on screwing up your marriage. I'm not saying she wants to get back, but I'm sensing remorse at what her dad did to you. She said her mother misses you, thought of you as a son."

"Well, it's easy to say when you had an OJ-like legal team fleecing me, fucking with my job and life. Maybe ask her to get her old man to cough up a severance package. I did more for that company than her hippie brother, Brad. Her mom, Blanca, is a sweet lady. Julie should be more like her."

"Ironically, she said that. She aspires to be more like her mom."

Dave texted Stephanie. He said he was watching football, hoping she wouldn't demand attention.

After Dave's update Ross wanted to bring Vicky up to speed. She was going through crap with her ex and, while dating a wealthy hotel magnate, was still having a rough time.

Vicky was so far away, but yet, always knew what to say, with rare emotional intelligence. She prepared him to love again, making him aware of how the right woman could enrich his life. Look for feminine and maternal instincts, she said. She never judged him for the cohabitation scam and jumped right into the little plot to separate Stephanie from her aging boyfriend. Her friendship was unconditional.

The oceans separating them prevented a romantic relationship, but it didn't stop them from becoming best friends. After so much heartache, Ross was happy she was on her way to the altar. They would always have the nights in California.

It got harder to recall the minute details of their brief fling, the smell of her perfume, the way she took her pearls off and put them on the nightstand, the way she stood combing her hair at the bathroom mirror without a stitch of clothing, so feminine, classy with an impish streak.

He needed to talk to her, to let her know of Dave's conquest, and his own feelings for Julie. He realized Julie, like Victoria, was strong, independent, and an adventurer. He loved that about them both. Surely Vicky could weigh in with some sage advice or words of encouragement.

He dialed her number. "Vicky, how are you? Doing, okay?"

"Colin is a little pissy. He had a few key employees

leave, and we don't have a sizable population here to draw from. He's down a beverage manager, and the gal in HR left. He will have to find someone and move them. It's hard to find people with experience here."

"What about Marcelo, the guy that worked in the lounge in the Crowne Plaza?"

"Your friend? I love that guy,"

"His wife works at the Sheraton next door. She's in HR. It'd be a two for the price of one. He was complaining about how bad his neighborhood was getting. Their son was being pressured by gangs. I've got his cell number. I owe him big time for…"

"For what?" Vicky asked.

"Victoria, you will not believe this. I promised him a bottle of tequila if he would tell me when you were back at the lounge, so I could meet you."

"You devious little shit. All that pleasant stuff he said about you was for a bottle of tequila if you got me in the sack."

"No, it wasn't like that, I swear. He got his friend to seat me next to you at the restaurant and…"

"Why this is quite the revelation now, isn't it? I thought you were some wounded little divorced guy finding his way after being taken to the cleaners. Turns out you're just another root rat trying to get me out of my knickers?"

"I just wanted to…"

A throaty laugh rolled out of her. "Got you good, Ross. I'm kidding. Look at all the wonderful things that happened. Look at how far we've come. You've helped me along, and you're loyal to a fault. A good roll in the hay, as I recall. Go ring your friend up and pass me his number too. I'll give it to Colin. If he's willing to uproot his family, we'll fast track a work visa."

"Victoria, you've helped me along more than you know. I still think about our few days together. I'm thrilled for you. This would be amazing, helping Marcelo and his family with a fresh life in Australia."

"Colin has got a lot of pull. It would help him out too. Hey mate, I've got news for you. I'm engaged. We're planning the entire thing here at the resort. You and that sheila of yours will get an invitation. I can get the airline to get you out here, and we can comp you a room at the place here. I would surprise you but might as well tell you now."

"I'm so happy for you. That's awesome news. Colin is a lucky guy. I'd love to help you celebrate. Take care, Victoria. I'll see you soon, okay?"

"Yeppers, Ross."

Ross thought about how much Vicky deserved an idyllic life. He thought also of Marcelo, and how he had helped Ross in ways he couldn't imagine. How great would it be for his entire family to enjoy a tranquil life in a beautiful resort town? He called his buddy up before passing the phone number on to Victoria.

"Hola."

"Hola, Marcelo, it's me, Ross."

"Meester Ross, como estas?"

"I'm good. Listen, Marcelo, I'm going to Australia for a wedding."

"You marry the Australian from the airline. Felicitones."

"No, but it's her wedding to a big hotel owner. She's thrilled with him. I have a girlfriend who I hope to marry too. It's a long story. You're like a guardian angel. How are you doing?"

"Is a struggle but okay. All this immigration bullshit. Maria lost her job, the hotel is now with a beeger chain, and they put in the new HR department. Lots of housekeepers get let go with no papers."

"Listen, Marcelo, Victoria's fiancé might call you. You and Maria, you'll have excellent jobs in Australia. Beautiful town, good money, very safe. Are you interested?"

"You kidding me? Por Supuesto! ¡Claro que sí! I was very sad today, boss; my boy got beat up walking home from soccer practice. I'm so tired of the bullshit here. Everything expensive, unsafe, and Salvador is even worse. Australia, I just worry about kangaroos."

"Marcelo, wait for Miss Victoria to call you. I will give her your number. You and Maria, good jobs, okay? Your son can play soccer and have a good life, go to college."

"Meester Ross. You fair dinkum jajaja. That's a word she teach me. Muchas gracias for thinking of me. Wow. I'll tell Maria."

Ross felt good as he hung up the phone. He might have just changed the trajectory of an entire family.

Chapter Eighteen
Moving Forward

Becky seemed to have hit a nerve with the city and state
with her *Observer* ad. Ross read through the ad, proud of
being able to say she was his attorney. When she had first
come out about her lifestyle and campaign to change the
way folks in North Carolina reacted to such news, he
worried about his case. What would happen if she dumped
him? She became difficult to reach but paid personal
attention to Ross's case. He relaxed. For all of its extremes,
North Carolina was the quintessential purple state in search
of an identity. For years its brand had been progressive on
social issues, with bipartisan support for education,
essential to attract business and a high-quality workforce. It
maintained a low-tax pro-business philosophy. In doing so,
it transitioned from a textile, furniture, and tobacco-based
economy to research and hi-tech hub. In a diverse state with
pristine beaches in the east and mountain ranges in the
western sector, environmental issues resonate with voters.

There were extremes, like Jesse Helms, but they attributed his longevity to political chicanery, which always seemed to keep him over the fifty percent mark. Senator Sam Ervin, the country lawyer who brought down President Nixon in Watergate, was a shining example of a Carolinian with down-home common sense.

The brand Becky wanted to revive was a folksy, pragmatic intellect. Someone concerned with moving the electorate to listen to better angels to create a more civil society. It embroiled the state in an identity crisis with a legislature ignoring the will of the electorate and veering to extremes. This slowed corporate relocations to a trickle.

Charlotte needed newcomers to maintain its competitive edge in the financial sector. The Research Triangle needed to attract high-tech workers who were moderate and socially inclusive. The urban areas of the state needed a creative class that would provide the art, music, and literary scene to attract those from larger cities. Most business leaders, even conservatives, knew this to be essential. Xenophobia and polarization would scare away urban professionals and immigrants, who would expand the city's restaurant and cultural scene. Doing the right thing had practical benefits.

Becky's association with Grayson Whitcomb seemed to solidify a pro-business, pro-growth agenda. The Marriage Equality movement embraced Becky's plain spoken manner, a sharp folksy lawyer from the South. They liked that she triangulated an abrasive and radical element in their camp. Becky curried favor with voters whose minds were open to change.

Leadership elements of the coalition decided she was in a unique position to influence minds in Charlotte and could do things an army of invading suits from the Northeast or California couldn't. They wanted Becky on TV because she could speak to urban sophisticates, down-home country folk, and suburban moms with their spouses. She was approachable yet had the subject command of a seasoned political operative. How she entered into this fray made her more credible. The reluctant and approachable cultural warrior wading into a fight she would just as soon have no part of, if not for personal circumstances, distraught at seeing her city fracture at the seams.

Within days #onecharlotteforall was a trending hashtag on social media. As a battleground state, any political blip got national attention and political money. They termed Becky's movement on Charlotte's NPR station, "Mayberry progressivism."

Mindy had mixed emotions about the newfound notoriety. Retiring to Ocracoke and hammering out Child Psychology books while lecturing seemed incongruous with this new notoriety. Peace and tranquility might be more elusive after the Observer ad, but the publicity might make the writing more lucrative. The two talked. Their wedding would attract media attention, a power couple committing to each other, and important things to say before marrying.

Becky wanted off the family law treadmill and to take out Eunice in an epic legal battle. She wanted to atone for the Whitcomb tragedy but feared a media circus. She worried about Nicole, who people would assume was a pawn. Would Nicole be collateral damage?

Becky underestimated the coverage #onecharlotteforall would garner. As a moderate state that often drew outside money to its political battles, it got attention. Becky and Mindy had been talking about the toll a lengthy campaign would have on their relationship. Mindy wanted them to say their piece, put wheels in motion, and end their fifteen minutes in the spotlight. She thought there was no compelling need to do more.

"That's my attorney and I'm proud to say good friend," Ross said, in the same tone one might praise a sibling when people mentioned the goings on in the news. Throwing Becky into the spotlight put more scrutiny on Ross and raised the risk someone could connect the dots with The Plan, now at a critical stage. He and Dave continued to move forward. They had gone too far to turn back now.

Dave was getting nervous seeing both attorneys on the news. "Dude, your lawyer's all over the fucking news. Just what we need. The divorce trial of the century with two lesbian Johnny Cochran's. Julie is an attorney too in case you forgot. Do you know how easy it is to get the 411 on colleagues? You think your ex is good at digging up dirt? So is Julie." Dave sighed. "You need to lay low. Your ex is already getting on my nerves." Dave exhaled.

"Stephanie will twist anything you or your lawyer say. I don't need Mindy's narcissism articles to know she's nuts. You and Julie are hitting it off. I'm fucking close to getting Stephanie off the payroll for you and all this shit's making me nervous. It's too Goddamn much. If Julie connects the dots, she'll eat both of us for lunch and spit out the bones. We're in the red zone. Don't fumble the ball. I'm so fucking close to getting my life back."

Dave had never spoken like this before. Just a week earlier he had sent Ross a bottle of twenty-one-year-old Crown Royal to celebrate the first anniversary of their infamous dinner in LA, and Ross sent a box of Macanudos to Dave at his office, anonymously. The two had reason to celebrate. Ross was north of the six-month spot with Julie, and Dave a month or two behind with Stephanie. In another six months, it might be entirely possible that both would be alimony free. Dave had never been terse or angry in his cell phone messages. He sounded either agitated, drunk, or both.

Julie entered relationships for companionship, and attraction. Narcissists enter them for utilitarian reasons. They need supply, someone to assuage all their fears and validate the false mask they show the world. Narcissists speed up the relationship and courtship process. Stephanie needed a meal ticket but also a reliable source of adulation. It wasn't, however, how things were working out.

Ross worried whether Dave would just cut things off with Stephanie. She was getting on his last nerve. He worried about Becky and Eunice now local celebrities. The odds increased that someone would connect the dots and expose them as scam artists.

Ross emailed Dave to check the cell phone for a message. "Dave let me know your schedule. Pick a city from among the following for a business trip in the next ten days. Atlanta, Columbia, Savannah, Jacksonville, Roanoke, Charleston. Let me know. Hear your concerns and I share them. Let's catch up and talk later."

Dave messaged back. Their next rendezvous would be the following week in Charleston. Enough time for Ross to stir up activity in the tourist mecca and prepare for their meeting. Obsessed with what was going on with Stephanie, he hoped Dave would stay the course through cohabitation. Dave worried Becky's celebrity status would blow up everything.

The week passed with Ross and Julie texting each other to bed with suggestive and witty quips. Ross had Nicole for the weekend and Julie was prepping for a difficult deposition. It limited their contact outside the dojo to texts and a quick iced tea at a Showmars. Ross counted the days until they could next be together.

Dave showed up at the rooftop bar overlooking Charleston Harbor just a few minutes after Ross. Two businessmen flipping open binders, looking like salesmen or attorneys. It was a perfect early fall evening with the breeze blowing off the water. They grabbed a seat on the cushioned area outside.

"So spill, Dave. What's going on with Stephanie?"

"Dude, she's a train wreck. She's needy. I'm required to give her reassurance or compliment her constantly. She's gripes about everyone, especially you. And the mother came for a visit. The mother henpecks the shit out of her husband. It's painful to watch. The night before she was to arrive, I tried to spice things up. Shopped for lingerie with her, garter belts, thigh highs—the whole nine yards. We're finally having sex, and she answered the phone in the middle because it was her mother. The conversation is about how she read an article that tilapia is unhealthy and not to eat it. I can't bust a nut because fucking tilapia is off her mother's approved foods list. I told her next time wear a flannel nightgown or ratty sweats, but just don't answer the phone when your mother calls in the middle of sex."

Ross tried hard not to snicker, "Good luck with that one."

"I was so nice when the mother visited. I figure if I get the Hitler seal of approval, I get the green light to move in."

Ross chuckled.

"Dude, she's railing on you. She calls you abusive, unstable, a liar, and irresponsible, trying to turn everyone against you. It's projection, but it is nonstop. She doesn't need help to turn people against her. She feuds with cousins, nephews, and people in the neighborhood. It's getting worse. Remember the neighbor across the street that works for the airline? She backed into his car, dented it, and just left.

Turns out, the daughter was looking out her bedroom window and saw the whole thing. He rang the doorbell to demand she pay his deductible. She responded that he shouldn't have parked on the street, and he couldn't prove it was her. His paint is all over her bumper. Nothing is ever her fault." Dave grew increasingly animated.

"I have to make all the plans. She suggests nothing. I have to have a list of like twenty places to go or things to do before she says okay. I'm doing this for you, buddy, and she's into me. I think more than anything she's into having a steady boyfriend. She just wants a personal assistant to take care of her shit. She wants a meal ticket and someone to blow smoke up her ass. I'm holding on, but by a thread."

Dave closed his binder. "She talks to her mother like a dozen times a day. The mother is a piece of work. A controlling know-it-all provincial simpleton. The mom bragged she cured her husband's cancer by looking on the internet and inventing a diet. I asked what drug protocol he was on. Treatments are ninety-five percent effective, but her daughter thought her mother was Jonas Salk. I do the yard work. I cook. I get vomited on. That mom is downright scary."

Ross laughed through the entire thing. His ex-monster-in-law was the bane of his existence. A bitter, emasculating woman, she inserted herself in their marriage like an oversized anal suppository. When she entered the house, it became her territory. She criticized everything. Stephanie wasn't close to her mother so much as fully dependent.

When they clashed, the mother would become distant and threaten to cut off Stephanie's additional funds. Then would come the tango. The mother wouldn't apologize but acted nicer. Stephanie's fears of cutting the cord had her walk back from her anger, and they resumed talking as if nothing happened. Codependents that need each other but are too stubborn to apologize.

Stephanie's blowups with her mom inevitably left self-esteem issues in their wake, causing Stephanie to overcompensate by feigning confidence. That meant judging everyone. Dave was experiencing what Ross had throughout his marriage to Stephanie. He wanted to speed up the relationship so he could move in and complete his mission and end it. She wanted to snare a man in her nets and train him to do her bidding.

Ross and Dave discussed Dave's need to come up with reasons he couldn't renew his lease, requiring him to move in with her. Ross shared his concerns about Nicole's rebellious attitude.

Dave told Ross that Nicole was a mature and nice kid. He assured his buddy she was a sweet girl, and that side would re-emerge at some point soon.

Chapter Nineteen
New Broome Sweeps Clean

"Ross, how are you?" Something in Vicky's voice always made him smile. Now engaged to Colin, a rising star in Australia's hospitality business, their whirlwind romance led to a mutual interest in developing Australia's northwest coast near Broome. According to Victoria, Qantas had been talking about expanding air service. It seemed to Colin an ideal place to develop a resort. Victoria viewed it as a splendid place to call home.

Broome was a town of about fifteen thousand residents on a peninsula in Kimberly. At the turn of the twentieth century, it was a magnet for those seeking fame and fortune in the pearl industry, drawing immigrants from China, Japan, and Indonesia. With the advent of industrial pearl farming, fortunes took a tumble but transitioned with the help of a new international airport and exquisite beaches, exotic scenery, with colorful sunsets. Broome remained relatively underdeveloped as a tourist destination with huge upside potential. Asians remembered the area as a pearling center before commercial harvesting, but the area's stunning natural beauty, wide sandy beaches, and abundant wildlife made it an appealing destination. Broome has a Chinatown, a feature Colin thought would appeal to the Asian tourist trade. Colin felt the area was ripe for a high-end luxury resort. An expansion of one of the nicest properties near Cable Beach could leverage the area's airport and draw more tourists from the Orient, perhaps Europe, and the Americas. He worked the wedding destination angle as well and set out to assemble support services necessary for bridal packages.

"Ross, something happened. I need your help."

Ross would do anything for Vicky. If she needed a kidney, he would cut the thing out himself with a Swiss Army knife.

In typical Victoria fashion, this wasn't so much an imposition but an invitation to a wild adventure. She became animated, and when riled had an odd habit of reverting into unintelligible Australian vernacular.

"That bogan ran the same lurk on his new sheila as he did with me. She was so narked she tracked me down and rang me up. That root rat has been visiting every town past Woop Woop. A pawn shop guy dobbed in and now he is coming to Kimberly. I had to call my favorite buddy for help. We've got our rort now, Ross."

"Victoria, what the fuck are you talking about. I don't speak Australian. Talk American."

"You know how Julie and you already blocked off two weeks in the Outer Banks?"

"Yes, I put down a two-hundred-dollar deposit on a place. Vicky, what the hell does this have to do with anything? Please, in English this time."

"Ross, listen, stuff has happened, and it's incredible. Colin and I've hatched a plan of our own and you and Julie can help." Vicky sounded close to hyperventilating.

Melba was the now fuming floozy that Reggie, the

drunken louse, had taken up with, and true to his colors had stolen Melba's stuff from her Alice Springs home.

After being unable to locate him in any of his watering holes, and getting dead ends from relatives, Melba called the number of Reginald's ex-wife Victoria. It was quite a conversation. Melba's family had come from a family of miners and had quite a stash of heirlooms that were valuable and irresistible to Reggie. Emboldened, he got wind Victoria would be on an extended work trip and cleaned her suburban Sydney home of its jewelry.

"Then Ross, the most unbelievable thing happened. Reggie booked a room in one of Colin's properties, unaware of my connection to the hotel. He's living it up, fencing her jewelry as he tours the continent, looking for a buyer with cash to take the lot off his hands. The police were on his tail and just missed him in Bondi Beach. By the time they traced his hotel room, he had checked out. The maid saw tons of stuff in the room, silverware, things you might sell at a pawn shop. Now he's on a watch list. There is a jewelry convention in Broome. We're known for cultured pearls and Japanese tourists come here looking for bargains. He wants to unload the lot in one swoop. If he offloads it to someone from Japan or China, they'll pay cash with no paper trail. He booked a room at Colin's resort."

"Victoria, I thought you were over this creep. Why would you want to stir the pot?"

"Ross, he took all my stuff. I was on two weeks of overnights in Asia, and he took everything of value." She said, "You know how you were telling me how Julie is into martial arts? I want a woman to beat the bejeezus out of him. No worries. It'll be safe with security as a backup, but for Reggie, it would be the ultimate humiliation to have some wonder woman kick him in the nuts. You two will have a fabulous vacation, perhaps even you can propose to Julie, and she'll get to play a superhero."

"Vicky, I like the proposal part but don't want her in a

bar fight with a drunken maniac."

"Ross, I'm off to Singapore, just ready to board, I'll clue you in when I get there."

"Okay, Victoria, I'm curious what your mind has cooked up."

"I'm sending you an itinerary. It's all comped one hundred percent. Just show up at the airport with your girlfriend. Same dates as your trip to the Outer Banks. You'll love it here. You have a day in Sydney to get situated and fall deeper in love."

Victoria's skill set for practical joking was as diabolical as Ross's and Dave's combined. Colin had the means to finance this little adventure. Ross and Julie would get to play a part in "The Australian Plan: The Revenge Down Under," just like Vicky had when she punked Henry.

By Ross's calculations. she wouldn't be in Singapore for about seven hours, To Ross's surprise, she had already spelled everything out in an email written in the airport business center. She was giddy with delight the two couples would finally meet, and very much in love.

Melba wasn't the floozy that Vicky was led to believe. Somewhat rough around the edges, she owned a restaurant that had a watering hole attached, standard fare in Australia's harsh interior. Reggie had saddled up to the bar when Melba was slinging drinks after a few of the barmaids called in sick. A drunkard with a charming side, he was ruggedly handsome and jocular. The bar was in stitches after he and some other wandering salesman had swapped tales of life on the road. He was hard living and untamable. Melba fell hard. Victoria could hardly blame her because she'd done the same a decade earlier. Settling down never agreed with Reggie, and it became clearer to Melba in short order, while Vicky's travel schedule delayed her eventual epiphany.

Reggie became meaner and increasingly reliant on the bottle. One day Melba came home from the restaurant to find her house cleaned out. Victoria recounted how she left her engagement ring at home whenever she went on a foreign trip. They scheduled her to go to Mumbai the next week and left most of her jewelry in the box on her dresser. Vicky came to find out he gave her stolen ring to Melba. Now he stole the stolen ring a second time after breaking into Melba's home.

One of the Broome's largest jewelers seemed sure Reggie called. The jeweler requested an email itemizing his stash "to circulate to potential buyers," and sure enough Vicky identified several of her pieces, including her engagement ring. The jeweler told Reggie that these were the pieces that fetched high prices with Japanese gemologists. He assured him of a lucrative sale when they came to town. To make it seem legit, he requested more photos of the items and a ten percent finder's fee to find a Japanese buyer. Reggie was all in and fell hook, line, and sinker.

Melba was a tough woman, as her family lived in the hardscrabble Outback for generations. She had a resilient side that she attributed to living in an inhospitable climate. According to family lore, her roots were part-Aboriginal. She won over Victoria in their hour-long introductory call. They cried together, something Vicky felt she could never do over Reggie. By the next time, they spoke the tears were gone, and Victoria's desire to exact justice took over. Victoria recounted her similar tale of storybook love descending into alcoholism and abuse. Colin, having been versed in Ross' plan, was interested to see how the two ladies could match what Ross and Dave had come up with.

The Australia plan relied on Reggie's weaknesses to pull him into a trap. It was still a work in progress but coming together nicely. If all went well, Colin would get to meet Ross, with whom he had already felt a kinship, and Ross' soon to be wife. He would keep any mention of Ross and Dave's plan from Julie.

Vicky pulled strings to get her employee discounted fare coded to Ross and Julie, picking dates coinciding with their Outer Banks vacation. She was sure they would prefer Australia. Julie was growing tired of the same patriarchal vacations with her father presiding over everything. She was intending to rent a separate beach house a block away rather than all under one roof.

She loved the Outer Banks but, as in her first marriage, grew tired of the business being the focus of so many of their conversations. That would be the case with Brad now assuming Dave's old position as national sales manager. Her father assumed the role of an alpha male and everything revolved around his benevolence. It was barely a vacation.

Reggie was due to arrive in Broome just in time for the Jewelers Convention. This was the same day Ross and Julie were due to arrive. The timing would be perfect. Colin could arrange a fabulous room for the two of them, on romantic Cable Beach. Vicky would tie the knot with her beau the very next weekend, and Ross and Julie would be in attendance. If all went according to plan they too could get married destination style. For Colin, the wedding would serve a dual purpose. He loved Victoria, but the free publicity their wedding would generate would be invaluable. An article was to appear in Qantas in-flight magazine highlighting the nuptials and the new direct service from Melbourne, Perth, Sydney, Canberra, and the Gold Coast with future routes to Shanghai, Tokyo, and Kuala Lumpur.

Who in their right mind would turn down such hospitality? All that was asked was for Julie to give Reggie a martial arts lesson he would never forget. Ross was tentative, Julie was unaware, but Victoria was confident they could pull it off.

Julie had been told about Victoria, minus the incredible sex part. She didn't seem threatened about the relationship, particularly after she found out that Victoria had become engaged. She had several male friends, some from business, some from martial arts, and didn't get worked up ironically because Ross seemed so trustworthy.

The dynamics made sense to her. Their chance meeting occurred when both were exiting toxic relationships. Julie admired feisty women and had grown to love Ross' sense of humor, his most endearing attribute. Ross had shared some of her emails, edited to omit references to the plan. She had amazing travel stories. Her ability to deflect even the stickiest situation with a parry of her acerbic wit was admirable to an attorney. By sharing her growing heartfelt devotion to Colin and how she was sure he was the man she wanted to share her life with assuaged Julie's jealousy.

If Victoria pegged Julie right as a woman who loved to compete, she'd just love to have some drunken creep get grabby and mess him up with a reality-based self-defense system and "Girl Power." There would be security as a backup. Reggie would saddle up to the hotel bar on his first night in town hoping to unload his treasure trove of stolen possessions after being blacklisted at every pawn dealer from Perth to Sydney.

An attractive American would be almost impossible for Reginald to resist. What would ensue would get Melba and Victoria their stuff back, vigilante justice, and Reginald arrested?

Ross read the email with amazement. She seemed to have an attention to detail that was impressive for a two-hour layover. Her plan was every bit as diabolical as the one he helped concoct.

Australia was a bucket list destination, but he figured it would remain there. The trip was virtually free. Julie, an adventurer, would do cartwheels over the possibility to explore such a faraway place. She would jump at the chance to deliver an arsenal of kicks and punches, with one to the balls for good measure. Ross wanted to help Victoria but still wasn't on board with Julie's fight scene. They would pepper the bar with plainclothes security, eager to pounce at the first sign of trouble, but there are always variables in a bar fight. But how many people get to play a superhero in real life? He was sure she would agree but felt it better to keep it under wraps until Broome and perhaps grow more comfortable in the relationship.

"Julie, Victoria got us tickets to Australia at an unbelievable price. It's for her wedding. I want to call and cancel the place in Nags Head. Her fiancé has a comped hotel room for us at a place called Cable Beach in a town called Broome in the Northwest. We have a day in Sydney too. I looked it up on the net. It looks awesome. We can go snorkeling, scuba diving, but most of all just hang out. They have pearls there and lots of other gems and stuff. I didn't want to say yes 'til I ran it past you, but it's less than our trip to the beach would have cost, and Victoria is working at bumping us up to first class. It'd be our first real vacation together."

Julie gasped. "I'd love to go. I'm stunned but excited. I don't know what to say. Our first real vacation together. You were planning this all along?" She bubbled with enthusiasm. "Tell your friend I can't wait, and I'm looking forward to meeting her. Thank her for the tickets and her fiancé for the hospitality."

"The town was a pearling center. Lots of Asian influence. I don't want to say anything, but I'd suggest you ramp up your training activities. I can't say anything more." Ross wanted her in peak condition, even if he wasn't a hundred percent onboard with the bar fight. Let her speculate whether it would afford her a training opportunity with a famous Asian master.

"Wow, now I'm intrigued."

Chapter Twenty:
Wilfred Returns

Henry was despondent and perplexed over his breakup. Perhaps Stephanie had another guy and sent the emails as a pretext. But would she go to the trouble of including racy pictures? If it was a test of his fidelity, he didn't respond to the emails.

Henry confided his dilemma to his daughter Loretta. "Dad, she was high maintenance anyway. Good riddance. She wanted you for a meal ticket. You need someone less demanding."

Henry knew Loretta disliked Stephanie. She was apathetic to the breakup, even giddy at times at Stephanie's departure.

His son Travis would be more understanding. A PI, he could shed light on the emails.

"Travis, I have to ask you a private detective question."

"Shoot Pops. Watcha need to know?"

"So you know how I'm no longer with Stephanie, right? Well, it's for the weirdest reason." Henry said. "Suddenly I got these unsolicited emails from a woman that claimed to have been going out with me. Knew a lot about me too. Claimed to be some Australian NASCAR engineer."

"They don't have NASCAR in Australia, Pops."

"I know. She wrote and then called Stephanie like it was a setup, but who would go to all that trouble? The more I say it was a setup, the guiltier I sound."

"You still got the emails on your 'puter?"

"Yes,"

"Lemme look-see."

Henry logged on to his computer and turned the keyboard over to Travis, who typed furiously.

"Pops, we're in luck. It's from a Yahoo address. They have IP addresses embedded. We got to do a few things, and I can find where it was sent from. That ought to give us a start."

"Broome... Broome, Australia!? What the fuck? Who do you know in Broome Australia? I never heard of it. She didn't ask for money, did she Pops? Like them Nigerian Oil Ministers. You can level with me."

"No, no...it was just like she was trying to fuck with me. Stephanie has already started going out with some guy. I want to sort this out before things get serious."

"And she called Stephanie?"

"Yes."

"I'll pull a few strings and try to get phone records, but you can tell Miss Stephanie that the emails are from Western Australia. That woman was a ways away from Charlotte, and we can prove it. I'm not sure I want you to get back with her, but I don't like the idea of someone fucking with you neither."

"Thanks, Travis. Can you write to me the how's and why's of all this, like you, would for a client? I'll forward it to her. We still keep in touch on Facebook and I can follow up."

Henry logged onto Facebook and typed a private message. "Stephanie, you need to know those letters were bullshit. They are from a tiny Australian Town called Broome, nowhere near here. I can prove it. I don't know why they were sent but I'll find out. All I know is I never met her, and she never met me. Not even online."

Chapter Twenty-One
Aussie Trip

The first leg of the trip to LA was five hours, a lengthy flight by most standards, but a fraction of the time needed to get to Broome through Sydney. Ross glanced at the gates with international carriers jockeying for gate space on the runways.

At this very spot, they hatched a year earlier, a plot that appeared to be nearing completion. For Ross, a courtship conceived for nefarious purposes had developed into genuine love. The wicked secret of the genesis of the relationship weighed on Ross's conscience.

He was not the only person to have harbored a toxic secret. Men and women have hidden their sordid pasts, or deep dark secrets, since the beginning of time. Now Ross was one of them. After flirting with financial ruin, Ross might live his life without choking alimony and with a woman he loved. But the secret would always stalk him. He sighed. Best to get used to it.

Julie was a strong and resilient woman, but it was impossible to tell how she would react if she found out. He hoped to never receive an answer.

Ross printed out several web pages with things to do for their layover in Sydney and the subsequent days in Broome. Colin's resort had wonderful spas and relaxing activities. Broome was a pearling center, and at the turn of the century divers from Japan, China, and Malaysia did much of the dangerous work. There were elements of Asian culture embedded in the town, including shiatsu masseuses and acupuncturists to rejuvenate. There were adventures awaiting Ross and Julie, but with ample opportunities to relax.

They made their way to the jumbo jet that would take them from LAX to the land of kangaroos. One rather curious email was from Becky. "Ross, I'd love to see Australia with Mindy. I need to get out of town quickly. It's a circus. Forward me the info on your friend, her fiancé, and their resort. Perhaps they can help me arrange a trip."

It would be nice to have Becky and Mindy by their side. He would at least have someone familiar alongside to celebrate. The two had given him special attention on two things he needed most, legal advice and some psychological help in dealing with his toxic marriage to a narcissist.

Without their guidance in tandem, Ross never would have been a suitable partner for Julie. He knew their interest stemmed from a blood feud with Eunice, but he liked to think it was also their affinity for him. Victoria also enabled Ross to ready himself for a healthy relationship. One could say it took three women to repair a semi-broken man and get him ready for his soul mate.

Becky had provided so much emotional support through all his trials and tribulations. He remembered her trip to his mailbox to deliver a Father's Day card. What a gracious gesture to make a trip halfway around the world to see him get engaged. He forwarded the contact information with a brief note. He emailed Nicole, telling her he missed her and was up to his eyeballs in meetings.

> RE: Arrival in Broome: Ross,
> Been planning for our big day and looking forward to seeing one of my favorite mates. Colin is going all out, and I'm excited. I've lots of planning to do. Oh, my ex is heading to Broome oblivious that I'm here. I can't wait to see you and meet your kick-ass GF. We will talk more when we see one another. Bye, V.

"Vicky just wrote to me. She's looking forward to meeting you."

"Ross, thank you for taking me on this trip. I'm thrilled. It's a once in a lifetime experience. Thank your friends for making it happen."

"Vicky is a marvelous girl. You know how sometimes it's easier to have conversations with strangers. Well, she was a kind of random person I met when I was fresh out of the divorce. She gave me enough advice to make me a better boyfriend for you, so in that respect I owe her. I was a mess, and she was like a sister. She has had her share of heartache. I'm glad she found her fiancé. He sounds like an interesting guy, and his billion-dollar hotel portfolio doesn't hurt."

Ross smiled at Julie. "All her stories are about interesting cities she has been to, all the distinct cultures, customs, and cuisines. And Colin has experience hosting people from all over the world. They're wonderful people. I'm thrilled for them. It'll be awesome to share their wedding day. We'll have an enjoyable time."

"I'm looking forward to the mix of cultures. It sounds like a small tourist location, but a diverse spot. A place where indigenous people have lived for centuries."

Ross nodded. "Seeing things through the eyes of locals will be an enriching experience. I love how you are open to new stuff. With all the tension in Charlotte, it'll be a welcome break." Ross referred to the bombing and subsequent protests. Now that Becky and Mindy were going to join them, Becky would finally get to meet Julie. Amazing that two lawyers working in the same city, in the same building, had never met.

Vicky and Colin were to marry in the grand ballroom of the hotel complex. Ross had arranged for Vicky and Colin to send a big diamond ring up to the couple's suite by room service, served on a silver platter. Ross couldn't wait. He hoped Julie would say yes.

If she agreed, there would be a double wedding with all minutiae taken care of: tailors available with a dress, hair, and nail appointments, and legal documents at the ready to address all the destination wedding requirements. There would be a photo shoot on Cable Beach. Vicky indicated she would include them in a destination wedding brochure and promotional materials.

It seemed Colin grew increasingly enamored with branding his resort for destination weddings. By having a grand wedding of his own, and another for friends, Colin would further his marketing plan. Becky was the only person Ross confided his intention to get engaged to before the trip.

Nicole was told only of a business trip and convention. Ross promised to keep in touch but wasn't sure of his schedule. She seemed more curious than usual, while Nicole and Stephanie were constantly fighting. Being incommunicado for the duration of the flight weighed on his mind, but it was unavoidable. During layovers he sent emails. The LA to Sydney leg would be the biggest blackout period. Stephanie pumped her daughter for information about her dad, relentlessly, and vindictively. He hated his little lie to his daughter about the trip and downplaying the serious nature of his relationship with Julie. It was just too risky given the critical stage of their cohabitation plan.

His daughter's behavior and attitude weighed on his

mind. Once he and Julie were married, he hoped to move Nicole into their home. Nicole seemed to welcome her dad getting into a relationship. She liked Julie. Stephanie was intent on undermining it despite Dave's influence.

Stephanie's paranoia and intuition could sense Nicole was hiding something about her father's trip. She wanted to emotionally waterboard her daughter. The pressure Stephanie could exact, a trait inherited from her mother, wasn't to be trifled with.

The pair glanced at those in the waiting area. Aussies, a smattering of folks from Europe changing planes, and some Americans, including a college rugby team. Vicky had arranged priority boarding, and the couple took their assigned seats in business class.

A flight attendant came over. "I'm Raelene, the senior attendant, at your service. My friend Victoria asked that I take special care of you two and if there is anything you need please ring your call bell. Victoria and I have traveled the world together. I have a bottle of champagne I'll bring by once we lift off. I can't promise anything, but if we have a few cancellations or no shows in first class, I'll see what I can do. Meanwhile, relax and enjoy your visit to our wonderful country."

"How nice," Julie said. Raelene turned and walked to the galley in first class. Families were struggling with overhead luggage and those in window seats were shimmying past those in aisle seats as elevator music playing in the background. This was such a grand gesture by Vicky and Colin. Ross had maxed out one of his few remaining cards to arrange Julie's ring and the engagement gift. Colin arranged for the jeweler to allow for a payment plan but other than that, the trip had no costs beyond the trip he and Julie had planned to the Outer Banks.

The trip would last two weeks. Dave was now settling in after his first week at Stephanie's address. Three more weeks and Ross would be alimony free, easier said than done. The pet peeves were making poor Dave a wreck. This was the home stretch, and no time to give up. Ross hoped Dave could stick to The Plan.

Ross felt some anxiety. But with a wife earning a decent salary, no alimony, and the possibility of Nicole moving in with him, his life would become infinitely better. Even joint custody would reduce child support and give Nicole a healthier environment. His golf clubs would need the cobwebs cleaned off, but he might get a few rounds in. Perhaps he would take up tennis with Julie. They already sparred in class, what could it hurt to lose a tennis match to your wife? Julie's spunkiness made her more adorable to Ross.

Raelene announced the need to turn off cell phones as the cabin doors closed. She paused and then escorted Ross and Julie to two open first class seats in the forward cabin. Ross grinned. How could Julie say no to his marriage proposal now?

They entered the curtained partition to first class and walked to their pod, a reclining seat, and a large personal TV screen.

The pod had two terry cloth robes, while slippers enclosed in plastic were on the floor below. The area was a mix between a sleeper compartment in a train and an office cubicle with lots of electronic gadgets. Julie, who was not the easiest person to impress, seemed moved by the gesture.

"I was a little paranoid about spending that much time on a plane, but this seems amazing. I'm looking forward to it." Julie perused the menu with lunch, dinner, and breakfast selections, as well as a page filled with both wine and other spirits, all complimentary. "I can't promise when or how, but I'll make you a happy man on this flight." She winked and gave him a coquettish look that was Southern Belle, not tough as nails kickboxing attorney.

Ross could only manage a smile. "Whatever you decide will be fine by me," he said.

"It'll be discreet but memorable," she said. Almost on cue with that, they read the safety announcements as the jumbo jet taxied to the runway for its journey.

As the plane reached its cruising altitude, Raelene arrived with a bottle of Dom Perignon and two champagne flutes and asked for the couple's lunch selections.

The choice of in-flight entertainment was a combination of Netflix and Gamer Console. They decided on a romantic comedy. Ross suggested "Sleepless in Seattle," an older movie he had never seen, but one that seemed to be on every woman's favorite movie list.

Ross's anxiety flashbacks to Nicole and his communication blackout crept into his mind. She had a key to Ross's place that her mother knew nothing about. She could say she was staying with a friend if she needed to stay at his apartment. He had fifty bucks in a pair of sweat socks she could use for food money.

With Dave spending more time with Stephanie, Nicole was little more than an afterthought to her mom. Dave would talk to her in rare private moments, but Nicole resented the romance that made her feel invisible.

Stephanie couldn't be counted on to drive her places. Ross had left instructions for Dave to pitch in and talk to Stephanie, but to stop short of provoking a narcissistic rage.

The upgrade to first class included free wi-fi. "Julie?'

"Yes, babe."

"I'm worried about Nicole."

"Leaving her for the trip?" Julie asked.

"It's not that. I can't co-parent with my ex, tell her my concerns without it turning contentious. I don't want to pump Nicole for info like I'm putting her in the middle. I feel like she's going through some things, and I'm in the dark."

"Your ex is seeing someone, right?"

"Yes, it's not him. Nicole says he's an affable guy and a good influence. It's not that." Ross knew his baby girl was feeling all alone in the world, lost in the shuffle of two parents moving on.

"You have a teen daughter. I'd be wary of any guy

who is spending lots of time with her. If something weird is going on and that's the reason she's upset, you need to know," Julie said.

Ross kept his chuckle to himself thinking she knew the new boyfriend well. Dave wasn't the problem. Things had been going well for their farfetched plan, and Stephanie would force Ross to re-prioritize his life and pick up the parenting slack. Julie would be stepmom.

Nicole was the apple of his eye. Ross foresaw that Julie, childless, would up her maternal instincts and help parent. Dave completed his first week of staying over. It was tense with Nicole constantly fighting with her mom.

Ross was about to enjoy a trip of a lifetime. He would return with a fiancée, perhaps a wife. Julie would be a strong female role model for Nicole. How ironic just a year ago this was all just a scam conceived by two drunks.

"I swore I'd stay off the computer during the trip, but would you mind if I jotted Nicole a note before it gets too late?"

"I understand."

Ross wrote Nicole. She could stay at his place and use the spare key. Told her he stashed fifty dollars in a pair of argyle socks in his dresser drawer. The only caveat was no boys, only a girlfriend whose parents approved the sleepover.

Nicole wrote back within ten minutes. "Mom won't even care, she's one-hundred percent focused on Dave now. I'm a giant afterthought. Arrrrgh! She won't even notice. I may go to the mall with Lizzy if I can get a ride."

"Nicole, I'm going into some meetings and may not get right back to you, but I love you. Use good judgment, you're a young adult. Okay? I'm proud of you. I'm there for you always. Love, Dad."

Stephanie was making her daughter feel she was an afterthought. Nicole seemed to like Julie. She had come over once when Julie prepared her mom's seafood paella recipe and a cassava soup, two bowls of which Nicole devoured. Nicole told Ross she loved that Julie was an attorney. The martial arts seemed cool. Nicole knew in the abstract that girls could be anything they set their minds to. Ross told her frequently. She knew other moms who had important jobs, but Julie seemed like someone to emulate. She wasn't the glass is half empty like her mom.

"Dad, I'm happy for you. Don't screw up with Julie thinking something else will come along. She is a keeper."

Ross folded his laptop and put it in his bin, fired up the personal entertainment console while hitting the call button. Despite warnings against drinking on such a lengthy flight, Ross needed something to take the edge off. His baby girl was in pain. He knew it. Nicole told Ross she was happy for him, but there was something melancholy about it. He hoped to get Dave to take charge.

Ross didn't have the disposable phone with him for security reasons. Logging in to his secret email would be risky with Julie by his side. He would wait until she was sleeping to write to Dave. Maybe Dave could offer to pick Nicole up or drive her to a mall and check his mail on the way back. Ross needed to check that his baby girl was doing okay.

If only he could enjoy this damn trip without all this crap. It was a manifestation of how far The Plan had come.

Becky too had written saying there was something urgent she needed to talk to him about. The whole fucking thing was coming at him from all sides. Drinking wouldn't make it all go away. Maybe it would take off the edge.

Julie had been reading her Nelson DeMille novel and seemed to enjoy herself. Ross needed to shoot out a few emails. She was supportive. Julie was strong yet delicate, fearless yet vulnerable, practical yet loving. He wanted to say something sweet to her but was searching for words. She looked angelic with her reading glasses, devouring a novel.

He took her hand. "I love you so much. You are the most special person in my life. You made me believe the second part of my life would get even better and that my best days were in front of me."

Julie responded with that megawatt smile of straight teeth. She batted her eyelashes with one half of Scarlett O'Hara's Southern Belle and an equal measure of her mom's demure but pure Latin coquettishness. "Don't worry big boy, you're still getting your special gift when the cabin lights are off."

"I have this stupid shit going on at work. I need to spend an hour addressing it in Sydney. I'm going to get it off my plate and then can focus on you one hundred percent. Sorry if I seem distant or on another planet. This trip means everything, and I want it to be perfect. I won't let work get in the way. I'm just worried about Nicole. She's mature, but I think she's feeling neglected by her mom. She likes you a lot. You're an example of an accomplished woman. She needs that. I owe you, Julie. You've changed my life."

"Ross, I feel like I'm learning a lot from you too. To be a better person. I'm not proud of it, but I could be a bitch. I felt like I kept my guard up. You seem comfortable in your skin. It wrapped my entire family up in the business and the patriarchal thing. I always felt like, as the girl, I needed to be competitive. My ex being in the company made it worse. He was in the position I was supposed to fill. I had this weird sibling rivalry with my brother. I love him to death, but he's a slacker. I'm not sure that's a bad thing. I'm thankful you let me be me and aren't caught up in all that bullshit."

"Love you," Ross said.

"I'm going to nap. If you need to talk about Nicole or work just let me know. I'm here. I haven't felt like I was part of a couple for so long, and I'm kind of liking it."

"You read my mind. Let's never take this for granted."

Ross felt better. The problems were still there, but she was giving him space to do whatever he needed and offered emotional support. It was a gesture he longed for. The tough cookie Dave described had a soft and mushy side like a marshmallow.

Another Crown Royal seemed in order. Maybe he could return emails to Victoria, Becky, Dave, and Nicole. But first, he needed to unwind with some mindless TV comedies on his console for a few minutes.

Julie conked out. Ross could fire up his laptop and shoot out emails unencumbered. From his calculations, it would be about two hours until dinner. He could have a nice meal with Julie, converse, and give her his undivided attention.

> Dave: RE When I'm away Listen, I think Nicole is going through some stuff. Feels ignored. I may let her stay in my place but don't want S to know. Talk to her, cover for her. Have to pay more attention. Give N a pep talk or something. The issue was with her mom and not you. She thinks you're a nice guy, just doesn't want to be a low priority. Enjoying things so far with J, and it'll be a glorious trip. You might be off the hook by week's end. Hang in there. By my calculations, three weeks and we're both off the hook! Delete this after reading okay?

> Vicky: Update Vicky, looking forward to meeting up with you and your fiancé. Lucky guy. Still not 100% on kicking R's ass. Have you planned it out? Lemme know. I'm nervous. Ex is ignoring my daughter, and I feel like I need to be there for her and can't be. I asked D to monitor things. Your friend Raelene has been so accommodating. We're in first class. Chilling. Flight is great.

Ross noticed a letter in his in-box from Becky and

figured he had better read it before shooting off his email to her.

> Ross: Our plans Ross, I know you're on your way to Australia. I emailed Victoria to get your details Inquired whether they had any nuptial packages. Mindy and I are all in. About to blow the lid on a certain attorney's evil ways and our knowledge of the suicide and what precipitated it.
>
> It'll end my legal career and cause Mindy professional harm, but no criminal stuff if we're married. As spouses, we couldn't be compelled to testify against one another. We need to get married. This pushes the timetable up.
>
> Guess what? Colin wants to cash in on the demand for weddings with Australia Marriage Equality Now law. Comped us a trip for agreeing to use pictures in advertisements, maybe even crack the American destination wedding market.
>
> Figured you wouldn't know a soul there other than Vicky and Colin. We would love to have you and Julie give us away. It could be at your party too. You're my last client. This has been so liberating. I can say whatever I want, take an active role in city politics and support Grayson.
>
> Mindy is looking forward to writing psychology books. I'm thinking about writing too. You offered me a chance to fight one last good fight and uncomplicate things. I'm grateful for that. Mindy too. The suicide weighed on both of us and now we can make amends. Looking forward to

seeing you soon. So happy for you. Yours,
Becky

Ross knew there was a special interest in his case by both Becky and Mindy. They had taken him under their wing and fed him a wealth of knowledge about his ex and her narcissistic condition. He didn't understand the extent to which this case was a game-changer for them. Perhaps when this story was written, Nicole would see her dad was fighting to keep her out of harm's way and fighting for the kids that came after. Perhaps in some small way, he could influence how the practice of family law is carried out when children were at stake, at least in Mecklenburg.

In a divorce, as in life, there is no such thing as one hundred percent right or wrong. Divorce is a messy business and while attorneys attempt to win for their clients, all too often they're enriched by inefficiency, fueling revenge fantasies, and converting them to billable hours. The woman who nearly bankrupted Dave turned out to be Ross's soul mate.

It was ironic that Becky and Mindy had to fight for the right to marry. They were exemplary people devoted to protecting children. They understood this thing called marriage better than most and yet had to fight to receive its blessings. Those two had trespassed professional boundaries to protect a child and were now giving up their careers to do the right thing. They weren't in the wrong for caring, yet derelict for not revealing their ethical shortcut to prevent tragedy. Now they would re-litigate their shortcoming to assuage their guilt.

How sacrosanct was the Whitcomb marriage? Their daughter leaped from the bell tower. It seemed the only way to escape the incessant fighting and guilt trips foisted upon her. Where was her representation? What God blessed their union only to have it turn out so wrong.

It seemed to him society had soul-searching to do, especially Stephanie and Eunice. As so often happens, those most in need of serious self-reflection were incapable, blinded by hubris.

Ross could no longer purport to exist in a world of moral clarity. He had found love but did so under pretenses. His love interest destroyed her ex because of the urge to win, which had superseded her instinct for fairness. Her ex had betrayed the family and the business and needed to be discarded like a bad batch of generic pills. No one was pure in this gigantic play. Some grew from their experiences, and others remained static.

Stephanie was consumed with her image and ability to maintain a lifestyle. She would stoop to whatever depths or smear campaign was needed to maintain entitlement. Eunice just craved the spotlight and billable hours, regardless of who was destroyed. Such people lack basic self-awareness.

Dave wanted to get back at his ex and her family after helping to build the family business. He had the rungs of the corporate ladder pulled out from under him: an epic humiliation.

Poor Nicole asked for none of this. She wanted to be a teenage girl and go to Taylor Swift concerts and get a second ear piercing at the mall, try sparkly nail polish, or talk with her friends about boys. She just wanted to be a teen without being part of some legal tug-of-war.

Nothing in life was as simple as those touting traditional upbringings had us believe. That lucky fifty percent who can maintain a marital home? A significant amount live with strife, struggles for power, infidelity, and control issues. They struggle, until they consolidate power, whether by threat, nagging, or sheer intimidation, forcing one party to live as a vessel for their partner to live out their dreams.

It seemed there was nothing sacred about marriage, except for the great ones. Those rare individuals who could find a satisfying mate who made them a better person. It seemed ironic to Ross that for him to appreciate marriage he had to witness the inner workings of a shitty one. He found a soul mate, an ideal spouse, but through deceit.

Ross was wrestling with some weighty questions. There was no way to turn off the uncertainty. On the verge of success with The Plan, he questioned whether it didn't make him cynical. His life was racing ahead faster than the plane's six hundred knots of airspeed.

In the adjacent pod slept Julie, affectionate and yet a lioness when such behavior was required. Ross wasn't religious but wished he were. There was no one to talk to about his vexing questions. Could a supreme being speak to the doubts he had about right and wrong? He wondered if perhaps this primordial urge to mate was an animalistic remnant of an evolutionary past before humans added a laundry list of do's and don'ts and called them sins. Yet there is this thing called love, in some an illusion, in others a justification, but sometimes real. We know a lot about how to fall in love but have no Geneva Convention for falling out of love. Marriage is among society's most cherished institutions, yet it's all brass knuckles on the way out the door.

He would ask Mindy for a referral to a psychiatrist and start therapy upon his return. He was ready for self-reflection and could grow from it. In response to his stream-of-consciousness, Ross pushed a call button for another drink. For the next eight hours of the flight, that would be his therapy.

Free airline booze started this rollercoaster of a year. Perhaps it could help him answer some questions. Nothing made sense anymore. He went through the list of song lyrics in his head to find meaning. Julie got that about music. He needed a song that encapsulated the disparity between our expectations for adulthood and the inevitable compromises. No one ever schools you on the compromises you make with yourself to get to the next exit. It's not in textbooks but exists in songs.

This called for the dark melancholy yet life-affirming Springsteen song that makes you glad to be alive despite the struggles and pain. *Yeah, Bruce, life is challenging, but it beats the hell out of the alternative.* He turned off the drivel of sitcoms and searched the music console for the most prolific songwriters he could find, hoping their songs could speak to him and fortify his weary soul, as he embarked on a journey that would change his life. In a world of syrupy pop, he wanted substance, music that could answer life's deep questions, or at least tell him what the questions were. For many of his age, Bruce somehow provided a soundtrack to their life's journey. He would cue "Darkness on the Edge of Town" at max volume on his headphones and let Bruce weigh in with his everyman sensibilities.

Julie looked so good just to his right. He couldn't wait to nudge her and tell her it was time to request dinner. She was multifaceted. There was not one moment of abject boredom with her. Julie made him a better person, and she said he did the same for her. That's rare, a person who makes you a better version of yourself.

It was a novel concept to grow better as one grew together and grew older with a life mate. He peeled away Julie's layers like an onion and found something interesting in each layer, a welcome contrast from the superficiality of his past marriage.

While he didn't want to force Julie on Nicole, she would provide a different example than her mother's self-absorbed nature. All love from Stephanie was conditional, with strings attached. Such a warped view of parental love would cause intergenerational dysfunction. Nicole would see her dad happy, unconditionally loved, and supportive of a wife who was herself strong.

While the stepparent intrusion had been pilloried in movies and folklore, the reality was Nicole had only his failed marriage to emulate when she would choose a mate. Sometimes he felt a pang of guilt for allowing the dynamic of the marriage to be all she knew. As best as he could describe, the descent into blind obedience and the subjugation of his personality to satisfy the bottomless insecurities of his ex was an infinite series of imperceptible changes.

Put a frog in a pot of water as the temperature rises, the frog adjusts his body temperature so that the heat from the burners is imperceptible. The frog adapts and its temporary discomfort dissipates while the body temperature rises to meet the increased temperature of the water. It's not until the water approaches boiling that the frog feels discomfort, at which time the body can no longer adapt, and the muscles become inoperable, and thus the frog is helpless to escape. What did the frog then die of? Of adapting too little, or adapting too much? It died, Ross reasoned, because it focused on adapting to lessen temporary discomfort and ignored existential threats until powerless to meet them. Ross ceased to be Ross but became a full-time support system for Stephanie. Without Vicky showing Ross a mutually empathetic relationship, he'd never have had the skill set to manage a healthy one. She put him on a trajectory to thrive with Julie. Two women reversed the damage of the first. Four if he counted Becky and Mindy.

Ross went from pondering some of the darkest challenges of his existence to his metamorphosis. It was the power of love and a nefarious scam. Ross would try to focus on the good. He was, after all, in first class on a trans-oceanic flight, not bad for a man who was just a year ago venting to a stranger, bemoaning his precipitous slide to financial purgatory.

"Julie?"

"Yes?" she said groggily.

"Thank you."

"For what, Ross?"

"For everything you bring to my life."

"I'm flying to Australia first class. I should thank you."

"That's not how I see it."

The two held hands. He noticed her manicured nails and felt just how polished they and she were. It was one of the treasured moments in his romantic life, at thirty-five thousand feet, the ocean below, somewhere between the Hawaiian Islands and Australia.

Ross felt contentment in his life, courtesy of a comped trip, and a first-class buzz. There was much he could obsess about, but perhaps he had that jolt of gratitude he so missed over the last few years. He had vacillated between free-floating anxiety, deep thought, and blissful self-contentment.

Dinner was a blur. He remembered ordering and putting out his tray for the various courses of the meal, but the lengthy travel got the best of him. He slept like someone satiated. The pilot had just announced they were less than an hour from their Sydney destination and had passed New Zealand and its snowy peaks on the Southern Island. They would soon begin their descent.

"You know I undid your pants and had a go for a while. You were out of it but said the sweetest things. It seemed you preferred to sleep. Almost a member of the Mile-High Club and you probably can't even remember," Julie said. "We land early in the morning, so maybe we can nap, see the city, and get ready for the trip to Western Australia."

The airspeed slowed. Soon the announcement came to put up trays and stow electronics. Next was the familiar sound of landing gear readying the plane for arrival. It was dreamlike, twice as far as he had ever traveled before, looking forward to a probable engagement, everything it was supposed to be in movies or songs.

The two strolled through customs beaming lovers' smiles, hop-skipping the merry dance to baggage claim.

Chapter Twenty-Two
Sydney

The shuttle driver dropped them at swanky Hyde Park Plaza, one of Colin's passive investments. The lobby was plush, the surroundings posh, but there would be time for sightseeing later. They would change clothes and grab a hot shower and enjoy vacation sex.

Ross put the card in the key slot for their upper floor room and as the bellman opened the drapes, which would soon be closed, the two stared at the postcard view of the expansive park, the skyline, a famous bridge, and opera house as if looking at a tourist brochure. He tipped the bellman who seemed surprised as gratuities are not common for such things in Australia, and after some small talk, sent him on his way.

Ross was in Australia with his girl, and she seemed impressed by the change of scenery. Clothes soon fell to the floor as the middle-aged couple fell onto the bed and into each other's arms. It was another one of those moments that he never would have thought possible a year earlier.

The couple came to, mumbling things about what time it was and what day was. It soon became clear a scant three hours elapsed. It wasn't even noon, leaving a day for shopping, exploring, and sightseeing. Like an aching root canal, Ross knew he must attend to email. It could either bring an all-clear sign or a flood of anxiety over issues that couldn't be addressed from eight thousand miles away. He suggested Julie get a massage, facial, and mani-pedi while he knocked out a few emails. She concurred. Rather than balk at the steep price, Ross welcomed the hour of privacy when he could respond and, if need be, instant message should any fires need extinguishing.

The first troubling email was from Dave.

> Dude, your daughter and your ex know where you are. I don't think Nicole meant for her mom to know, and she's grilling her like she's in Gitmo. Not good. I'm driving her to one of her friend's, but Steph is mentioning a guy named Henry and a private eye and IP address in some town in Western Australia.

> He's claiming the email Stephanie intercepted was from there, and somehow, it's tied to your needing to visit. You know how she gets when she is on the warpath. Something will hit the fan, I'm afraid. Threat Code: Orange.

Next from Nicole:

> Dad, I know you went to Australia and I know you didn't want me to know, but I found a few pages of your itinerary and it says your girlfriend is with you. I'm not mad. You didn't have to tell me. I know it was nothing personal. Mom went on my cell phone because she thought my

sleepover was a lie and I was staying over some boy's house, which I wasn't. Now she's freaking out. She's yelling at her BF and even had that old guy over she used to date, the one you called Wilfred Brimley, and his son who is a detective. She thinks you are fleeing to Australia because you scammed her. Can you call me please or text? Get a WhatsApp though. I don't want Mom to know it's you. Threat Code: Red.

"Fuck my life." He hadn't even gotten to the emails from work or Becky. Could things be any worse? He had to make calls and find a convenience store that had calling cards to the States. Julie would be mid massage, and he should have a few minutes to scurry downstairs and attend to things.

"Hello, I'm trying to find out where they sell calling cards as I need to make several calls to the US," Ross said to the hotel operator.

"Hold on, you are on the account of Colin Masterson. We can comp those calls for you."

"Really?"

"Yes. He stays here for business, and we have a corporate account. Anything business-related, faxes, copies, we run through the account. He said you had business with his hotel out in Broome."

"Well then, tell me what I need to dial first. Thanks so much, you're a lifesaver."

The first call was to Dave, no burner phone, no protocols, just a "WTF is happening" and "tell me now." It was around 11 at night, a stupid time to call if he was fulfilling his cohabitation requirements. He might well be a scant few inches from Stephanie.

However, Stephanie was engaged in some kind of monster conversation over the net with Henry, the old dude, and his son, a PI from Gastonia.

"What the fuck did you call this number for?"

"I don't have the other phone here. I'm in Australia. Can you talk?"

"Yes, but you're getting sloppy. Give me a minute, I'm going to the bathroom and put the fan on. One of my few joys is taking a shit without her checking on me. She's a paranoid snooping nut job. I'm not sure I'll last under this roof. Nicole found your itinerary. Stephanie is now bat shit crazy. I don't know how she found out. Nicole didn't tell her, but she's doing everything but calling Interpol on you. Did you know she was still keeping in touch with that dude that V engineered out of the picture? That's just fucking weird. I mean it's like she was two-timing me with some senior citizen she swore up and down she hated."

"Dave, that's part of the dark triad personality traits. Mindy told me all about it. They love to keep their exes around no matter how strained the breakup. For narcissistic supply. You can look that shit up afterward. It's how you can tell if someone is a sociopath or a narcissist. Whether they keep past relationships around to triangulate and whip up supply when they need to create drama. Normal people move on."

Ross regressed to psychobabble. "She keeps these people from her past around like they're marionettes she can play with when she's bored. It is also someone to flirt with when she wants to get back at you. I guarantee that if I go over her Facebook friends list, it'll have every boyfriend she ever went out with since high school, even if she hates them. Kind of creepy, but it doesn't surprise me. He fawned over her. She loved the attention."

"Congrats at getting a shrink degree at Mindy University," Dave said. "Enough with the Sigmund Freud shit. This is serious. She's driving me nuts. This Henry dude, she said he was a creep. Dude, his son is a PI, and the email that did him in got analyzed for an IP address. Guess where it came up? That town that no one ever heard about until your itinerary, Broome. The email that breaks Old Henry up with your ex comes from the same town on the other side of the world. She has all kinds of conspiracy theories, but so far I'm not in them.

"This guy is so eager to get back in her pants he wants to go to Australia with her. I tried giving her an ultimatum, but she said it had nothing to do with me, and everything to do with your lying ass. Swears they're just friends, and she needs to go with him. She made Nicole go with her to the bank to withdraw money from her college fund for the tickets. I think Henry offered to pay for the room. He books one room, not two. Wonder why? And he'll sleep on the couch or floor or head to toe or clothed according to her. I told her I wouldn't give her a cent for the flight. What if she figures out Julie is my ex-wife?"

"Are you jealous?"

"Fuck no. I want out, but I've already got mail here. If they stay ten days in Australia you are home free, anyway. Even if she wants to kick me out, I'm sure I can buy a week to get an alternative place. She doesn't know the clock is ticking."

"Good to know, but I'd hate to win like that. I want to get you off the hook too. Truth is, I want to marry Julie, for real, but if she figures out our little switcheroo scam, she might dump me too."

"She isn't dumping you. I'm happy for you. We had enjoyable times in the past. Just don't work for her father and no matter what you do, don't divorce her or you'll be homeless. No matter what, Stephanie can't find out Julie is my ex.

"Too fucking weird, Ross. Dude, look at us. When I met you, I never would have imagined the shit would get this far, but damn, it was an interesting ride. Just remember that if I get murdered by your ex or my ex, you can do the eulogy," Dave said.

Sweat popped out on Ross's upper lip. "Shit is about to get out of control. If she finds where I'm staying, I'm fucked. I'm the one that might get shot. She would like nothing better than to fuck up my relationship with Julie.

She might be clueless for some things, but she has a Ph.D. in revenge when she gets obsessed. Get WhatsApp on your phone. Nicole has it. Lots of teens use it. Password protect it or something."

"Ross?"

"Yeah?"

"Nicole's cool. I'm glad I met her. She loves you and thinks you're a wonderful dad. I've tried to talk to her after her mom talks shit about you. She knows more than you think. She misses you whenever she can't see you during the week. Spend lots of time with her when you get back. She needs you. Makes me regret I never had kids. If I ever get out of this mess, I'll find a younger woman and have a child. I'll find me someone in their early thirties, late twenties, marry them, and have a kid. Maybe someone from Latin America with more of a traditional bent on marriage. Someone cultured but down to earth. Kind of like my ex-mother-in-law. I'm serious."

"Stephanie might kill you first."

"Or you."

"Or both of us."

With that, Dave flushed the toilet in the bathroom of Ross's former home, the same bowl Ross sat on many times before and signaled that he must hang up. He went downstairs to drink wine, and to contemplate what might happen next.

Twenty minutes were left in Julie's spa appointment. He still had to talk to Nicole. It was almost eleven-thirty, and she was up, but where was the question. He called her cell.

"Nicole, honey?"

"Daddy, where are you? I mean I know where you are, but what's happening?"

"Can you talk?" Ross asked.

"Sure. I'm at your place. Please, I never meant to let Mom know. Please don't be mad at me."

"I'm not mad at you."

"What's going on?"

"I'm going to Australia with my girlfriend. Some friends of mine owed me a favor and got me an all-expense-paid trip for two. For a wedding. I couldn't turn it down. I felt bad about not telling you, but I worried about your mom finding out. She did, anyway. I know it wasn't your fault, baby doll."

"She pried it out of me after she swiped my phone when I was in the shower. Meanwhile, Dave gave her some kind of ultimatum about not going to Australia or he would split. He didn't seem upset though. He's a little dorky, but I think he's good for mom. We talk. He sticks up for you when she tries to tear you down. He's not trying to take your place. He says a girl's relationship with her father often is the relationship all her future relationships are modeled after. He told me divorce is tough, but the important thing is to always have a relationship with each parent. I just wish we could be together more like before. I know I've been selfish. I see your side, I do. I know I acted bitchy sometimes," Nicole said.

"Mom is going nuts. You know how she gets. Something is going on with the old guy Henry. His son is a detective, and they're looking into your trip, and claim email came from where you are going. She thinks I'm over at Jessica's, and I gave her Jessica's sister's cell phone to call. She is a senior at App State. She knows if it's from Mom to pretend she's Mrs. Taliaferro."

Dammit! Of all the many stops on the globe that Vicky made, what luck to have an email sent from fucking Broome. He got emails from Jakarta, Singapore, Taipei, and Seoul. Any one of those wouldn't have focused her energies on Broome. If Stephanie made the withdrawal from Nicole's college fund, she was coming to Broome, and there was no telling how sophisticated a private eye could be, even if he was from Gastonia. Nicole made him proud, though. She acted like a mature, young woman. He needed to have the dust settle on this mess and get back to being a dad and become a husband to Julie. *Nicole needs to live with me.*

"Nicole, I love you, honey. The email was from the same person who is gifting me this trip. I'll tell you more next time, but I have to go. I know about the email. I'll explain it to you later. The guy, Dave, you mentioned. He sounds like someone you can trust that I'd be friends with. I promise I'll call you soon. Keep your phone by your bed, okay?"

He thought about squeezing in a call to Becky, but she was already on her way to Australia. He needed to tell her that Stephanie might come to Broome. There were only a few ways to get to Broome, The US to Sydney, Melbourne, or Perth, and then a connecting flight to Broome.
If they could narrow down her flight out of the US, at least they would know when Stephanie would arrive. There were only a dozen flights to Australia from the US. Atlanta, Chicago, New York, San Francisco, DC, and LA he supposed. That's five airports for two days, each with ne only one or two flights. It seemed doable to narrow it down. He knew Stephanie, and she wouldn't go through Dubai or London, just US Airports.

Perhaps Vicky could help. There were a lot of balls in the air at the moment, and his balls would be in serious jeopardy if his ex showed up. It was all but inevitable. At least she did not know of The Plan—yet.

Dave was just a random stranger to him as far as Stephanie knew but that could change with a PI on the case and a geriatric ex-lover trying to get in her pants. Having them in Broome was a potential tsunami of trouble.

Ross had ten minutes to respond to emails for work. Shout out to Becky to keep her apprised of his whereabouts, to get a WhatsApp account on his phone, and not act guilty when Julie came back from her massage.

"I feel great, babe," Julie said as she opened the door. "You ought to get one of those." Ross thought about it. It would be an excuse to spend an hour at the business center.

"Okay, maybe I'll try to set something up for the late afternoon."

Meanwhile, it was time to walk around Sydney's premier tourist spots and grab some lunch. It might even take his mind off of the shitstorm percolating.

After a remarkable waterside lunch overlooking the harbor and Sydney's famous Opera House, the couple walked the Sydney Harbour Bridge, which seemed a breeze for Julie but winded Ross. They strolled through charming neighborhoods. Friendly people, the Aussies. Ross consumed about six pints on his various stops, but Julie didn't mind. She picked up preppy clothes, a few tourist knick-knacks, and a coffee-table book about Australia. For a woman who wasn't easily impressed, she was in awe of it all. Ross thought of all those company trips that Stephanie ruined with her whining and jet lag. It was a joy to be with someone adventurous.

What kept Ross from a panic attack was that it was the middle of the night in the US. Nothing of significance would transpire. Conversely, the shit was more likely to hit the fan when Ross was sleeping.

He booked a massage for 6 p.m., the last of the day. Julie napped when they got back. Ross indicated he wanted to look around the hotel, perhaps pick up something for Nicole. He had forty minutes to get a handle on a situation. Stephanie had tracked him down in Australia, at the far end of Australia. It boggled the mind. If Vicky could find out what flight she was on, it would give him a better chance of managing things. He called her. To his surprise, she answered right away. "Vicky it's me, Ross, I'm in Sydney."

"Well, welcome to our little island. What brings you here?" she said with a sarcastic tinge.

"Vicky, the flight, the hotel here, everything has been magical. I can't thank you enough, but I've another favor to ask if I can. It's kind of fucked up, but somehow Stephanie got wind of where I'm traveling to, and with the help of some internet snoop matched it to the email you sent to Henry. I still can't believe it. It could ruin everything. My relationship with Julie, Dave's cohabitation. Is there a way of trying to find which flight she's getting on?"

"Love, you know I'm getting married in a week and have things on my plate."

"I know I'm sorry I shouldn't."

"I'm fucking with you. Listen, there are about a dozen flights daily from New York, LA, Dallas, DC, Atlanta, Chicago, and San Francisco. About half are Qantas. Those are no problem to scope. Of the rest, you are dealing with American, United, and Virgin. There are a few bit players like Air New Zealand and Air Fiji or Hawaii Air, and of course a few that go through London or Dubai, but the connections will be terrible."

"I know her. She won't fly through fucking Dubai" Ross said.

"I'm sure I can get associates to scout the other three airlines. We have agreements with them for missed flights. It's not unusual to talk about passenger manifests. I could probably get her luggage lost. It's simple if we look at which fares are cheapest for walk-up tickets. She'll probably be on the lowest cost flights. Once I know which flight gets here to Australia, I can work on trying to get the connection figured out. Most traffic to Broome goes through Perth first, but there are other ways to get here. You're never dull. So, Dave moved in with your ex, huh? I talked to your attorney, y'know."

"Yes, she told me. She's getting married at the resort. You'll love Becky and her partner Mindy. Excellent people." Ross and his long-distance friend got caught up while sharing the latest SNAFU. Vicky let Ross know how eager both she and Colin were to meet Julie and get acquainted. She shared most everything on The Plan with Colin, and he found it amusing. He felt a kinship despite having never met.

"Love, get your arse here with that girl of yours. I'll share everything with Becky, and we'll sort this out. They're not staying in Sydney, so they arrive roughly the same time as you. I have people that can track manifests, and most of the Broome hotel reservation traffic at some point wind up going through the Broome Visitor Center server. If Stephanie books a hotel, we'll know. Give me her email again, and we can offer them a special deal to get them to stay at our place. It'll seem like spam after a Google search."

"I'd rather she stays far away."

"Ross, it's a lot better if we monitor her here. You'd have security making sure she stays out of your hair."

"I guess. Just kind of nervous."

"It might be in the name of that guy you emailed."

"What?"

"The room reservation. Henry, right? Remind me of his last name, but how many Henrys from Charlotte are booking a room in Broome? This is a piece of cake, and I'm happy to help. We need to get her to our resort. We can keep eyes on her, know her comings and goings. I know you want her somewhere else, but if she's a threat, it's better we know where she is. Do you remember how well I messed with Henry and your ex the last time? I'm on this, you needn't worry. You're close to getting your life back. You and Julie will help me with the little caper I've got up my sleeve. This will be fun, trust me."

"Vicky, I think you'll like Julie. She's fearless and fierce. She's a lot like you. This may sound odd, but you taught me the type of woman I could love. Someone who loves life, and challenges, handles her stuff and knows how to be a best friend and partner. Thanks for that."

"Oh Ross, love, you know I feel the same. Colin is a lot like you. Likable, funny, a prankster, still a kid at heart, empathetic, but he also has wheelbarrows full of cash, which is a kind of added plus for this girl. I feel as if a lot of planets had to align themselves to help me get myself together again and be worthy of a man like Colin. You helped a lot."

"Listen, let's catch up soon. I could go on all day. When I first saw you in LA, coming in from a fifteen-hour flight, you looked so put together. One would never know the turmoil you had in your life. You seemed like the most together woman in the entire world, and I thought I was falling apart."

"You looked like a Yank professional businessman. I'd have never thought you were struggling. You had an impish quality, like you had recently escaped from a suffocating relationship and could finally be yourself. You had me cracking up, and you listened. Next thing I knew, I was naked. Apparently, you had more game than you thought. But I have a lot of my mum in me, and you needed some nursing. I saw right away all you needed was a woman to believe in you, not one tearing you down all the time. Reginald loved to make me feel lower than whale shit. It was a wonderful thing for both of us we met when we did."

"Listen, I got to go. Thanks a million, Vicky."

It was just like Vicky to marshal resources from half a dozen airline computer agents and hotel reservation sites to narrow down the flights and coordinate with Becky to manage the situation. There were hundreds of things that could go wrong. If not for Vicky's reassuring voice, he might've been scared out of his wits. Now, Ross felt he could clear his head, grab a massage, reach out to Nicole, make a dinner reservation, and fall asleep in the arms of his future bride before their a.m. flight to Broome. Ross walked to the concierge and asked for someplace nice for dinner. There had just been a cancellation at Catalina, a seafood restaurant with stunning views of the harbor. Nicole wouldn't be up and about until after his massage. He could call afterward.

A stocky Malaysian lady expertly kneaded his muscles until all effects of the flight disappeared. She used elbows, fingertips, and the heel of her palm in expert combination enough to get rid of the knots and tense areas. The soothing New Age music and scents were the perfect antidote to Ross's racing trepidations about things going wrong. He walked out of the spa feeling renewed.

Outside the hotel, a newsstand clerk hawked calling cards, and Ross grabbed one and went to the conference salon for some privacy. He dialed the endless string of digits and got Nicole's familiar ringtone.

"Hello."

"Hey babydoll, it's Dad."

"Dad, I'm just getting up. What time is it there?"

"It's about 7 p.m., sweetie. Listen, do you know Henry's last name?"

"Graves. Why?"

"Just trying to figure out when they arrive. It's all good. Listen, when we get home, I want us to spend time together. Maybe go to the mountains or the beach or something. You're my priority. I know sometimes you feel you are in the middle of mom and dad's crap, and I want you to know I'll make it stop so you can focus on your school, your friends, and enjoying your teen years."

"Thank you, Daddy. How's your girlfriend?"

"Julie? She's good."

"I like her. She's cute, you know. She's good for you and you make a good pair. She seems down to earth but also..." Nicole hesitated, searching for the right word, "fierce."

"Yes, she's a lot of fun, and interesting and smart. This has been new. I want you to know nothing will interfere with us, though. Okay?"

"It won't. Mom drops me like a hot potato when she has someone she's seeing. She shoves them down my throat. The old guy and his family. This new guy, though. He's a keeper. I think you'd even like him. I'm not sure why he likes mom so much. She's smothering him. I think she'll scare him off."

"Babydoll, there is no figuring out men. Even the most powerful ones can get tamed by women, and some women pick guys bad for them. Take your time with boys and make them treat you right. I worry that the divorce will make you think relationships are all messed up when you want to have a family. We need to have a big father-daughter talk when I get home. Remind me to tell you the story of the frog in the pot of boiling water."

"Dad, trust me. I know how to handle boys. They're immature. You don't have to explain stuff."

"No seriously. It imprints the relationship a girl has with her dad on her brain. Dave's right. Your mom and I, we both haven't always acted like adults. I need to make sure we talk through all this stuff. My attorney, she has a friend who's a psychologist, a famous one, and she's been explaining a lot of things. She had patients your age caught in the middle of nasty divorces. I don't want this to scar you."

"Dad, it's okay. Lots of kids in my school have divorced parents. We talk, okay? I know a lot."

"I know you do, sweetie, it's just that I'm learning lots too. I can be a better dad to you, and your mom in her way, will be a better mom."

"I don't want to see a shrink, Dad. I know you're trying. I've always wanted to go camping. I bet Julie would go. It would be fun. Hiking in the mountains, or maybe skiing or backpacking or something."

"Deal. She'll be thrilled too. We'll plan it when I get back."

"Dad, don't let Mom ruin your trip. She's jealous. I think she's obsessed. She doesn't want you to be happy. She acts like she's happy, posting pictures of me on Facebook like I'm a prop. It's not even real. She's all about appearances. Does that make sense?"

"Honey, it makes perfect sense, but she is your mom, and she loves you. Maybe my attorney and her friend can go camping with us too. I bet you could teach her a thing or two."

"Yeah, but I'm not seeing a shrink, okay? Have fun. Take pictures. Maybe get me something. A shark's tooth necklace. I love sharks. Or maybe one of those surfer boys with an Australian accent."

"I'll look for the necklace. The place I'm going has a lot of pearls. If you like, maybe I can get you some."

"That would be awesome. Just remember to enjoy your trip. Don't let her ruin it. It's immature. Enjoy yourself and tell her to keep me out of this."

It was about as good a conversation as he could have hoped for. Nicole was in friendly spirits. He loved the mature, youthful woman she was becoming. She knew more than he thought. She liked Julie, perhaps seeing some things absent in her mom, that she one day aspired to for herself—self-confidence, a career, the ability to compete as a woman without always playing a victim.

Ross was thinking of ways to expose her to Julie's positive qualities as he strolled to the Business Center to see if Vicky had written.

Subject: Flight

Ross, Stephanie Parkman and Henry Graves are going from Charlotte to LA on American and hopping on a code-sharing flight from LA to Sydney, then Perth, and then a Perth-Broome flight. They leave tomorrow but it's thirty-six hours total. You've got two days. I had the Broome Chamber send both emails on file and banner ads on our resort advertising special promotional rates and they took the bait. They're getting a $300 room for $60 US. I have a special message at hospitality to alert me when they arrive, and also, Nir, head of our security. Get this, he's a former Israeli special ops guy, military liaison to

Australia. He'll watch her. The resort is emailing her about complimentary car service from the airport. The driver will be Nir. By the time they arrive, he'll have the whole scoop on their plans. He has electronic gizmos available I can't discuss on the phone. It's better to have them under our noses. We can keep them occupied and out of your hair.

Talked to Becky. What a hoot! Love her! She had a few ideas of her own. Her candidate's going to be mayor of Charlotte. She wants you to be the best man at her wedding or give her away…your *choice*.
Best man at a lesbian wedding, in our wedding party, and getting married yourself. Guess who else will be there? Marcelo and his wife. We fast-tracked a passport and work visa. He's our new Beverage Manager, and she's the assistant in HR. Their boy will be the star of our high school soccer team. It's an improvement over East LA. Lotta love here for you. We got your back mate.

Never in my wildest dreams did I think my wedding weekend would have this much excitement. It's an enormous deal in this town too. You have a who's who of Northwest Australia and West Kimberly. footballers, news crews, local celebs, an Aboriginal chief. Colin is a master promoter.

It was vintage Vicky. Amidst turbulence, she remained calm and looked for the silver lining. Vicky loved thinking on her feet and diffusing tension with her infectious exuberance. When Ross was at low ebb, she made him believe things would work out fine. If only it was so simple.

He headed back to the room to get ready for a scrumptious seafood dinner with a million-dollar view. It was a world away from his two-bedroom IKEA® furnished apartment with condiments and stale Kung Pao in the fridge.

Julie got dressed and applied her perfume recently purchased from the duty-free shop. She smelled incredible and looked even better. After just a few minutes napping she went downstairs and got a facial, make-up application, and hairstyle. She put on the dress she had purchased during the day, which had an understated elegance to it.

Ross put on the blazer he brought for dress-up occasions. Khaki pants, along with a button-down shirt he bought during the day. The shirt was crisp. Julie took a selfie of the cheerful couple. He was feeling good about things, not just fake good but the happiest in a long stretch he could recall, despite the potential derailment.

The Catalina had an unbelievable veranda. Removed from downtown hustle and bustle, but still on the harbor, she sat situated to encapsulate the skyline, the iconic Sydney monuments, and tourist spots.

A glorious full moon cast a golden hue on the harbor, kissing the yachts and vessels moored there. Crane your neck, and the twinkling lights of the skyline winked in nodding approval. It smelled both nautical and yet different from other places he had been. It was a pristine smell you might get if you were in some Alaskan wilderness, but yet, here in a city of millions, no whiff of industrialization.

"Ross, I've been to lots of places in my life. My mom would take us to Panama, and I'd dine at seafood places off the harbor where we would see boats come and boats go, but this place. It's our special place."

"You were going to say the smell, right? This place

smells not just like it's on the harbor but has freshness to it. Like some forests in rural Pennsylvania, it's unspoiled. Reminds me of Vancouver, the greenest city I know."

Julie nodded.

"Let's get champagne and lobsters and oysters. I know we have to get up early, but I want to slow dance with you. You couldn't look more beautiful."

"Do you believe I met you in a sweaty dojo? I must have looked like a drowned rat," she said.

"You looked hot then and now. You scared me, and it still did not deter me."

"Something motivated you, I'd say, almost as if you were on a mission."

"Oh, I was." He had to chuckle at just how appropriate her characterization actually was.

They found a little jazz bar, and as planned stayed for just a few songs. They danced, made out, and hailed a cab back to the hotel by 11 p.m. A 5 a.m. wake-up call, and they'd be on their way to Broome.

They woke up cheery. Ross stumbled to the bathroom and brushed his teeth. He jumped in the shower and, while toweled up, grabbed the bill that had been slipped under the door moments earlier. Colin comped everything. Ross failed to notice the numbers of direct-dialed calls from the room when in a panic he called Dave. He slipped it in with the passports, oblivious to their significance, and put on a shirt and trousers.

If all went well, they could get downstairs just before six, hit the breakfast bar, and catch a six-fifteen shuttle to the airport. They would be well situated for the 8 a.m. flight to Broome. There would be a day before Becky would arrive and another day and a half until the real Tsunami hit: Stephanie and Henry.

Chapter Twenty-Three
OK Corral

The Broome Royal Pearl Resort exuded enchantment. The staff gave Julie and Ross the full red-carpet treatment. Their suite had an expansive balcony and a sweeping view of the ocean.

Ross fired up his laptop to see if Nicole had written and spotted a message from Vicky to call her cell. Ross called from the room.

She invited Ross and Julie to Colin's guesthouse on the resort property. It was a ten-minute stroll through hibiscus bushes and beach paths. While the property was modest, it was manicured impeccably. Vicky greeted them at the door with a kiss on both cheeks and a hug.

"Can I get you something?" Vicky asked.

The pastel living room had a beach feel to it. There was a cheese plate and a chilled bottle of wine next to some glasses on the coffee table. Colin, looking as if he had just played tennis, indicated he'd be with the couple in a moment after showering. He tousled his mop of blonde hair, smirked, and went upstairs. "You will like this. Victoria is quite the prankster."

In a country noted for celebrating its heritage as a penal colony, that was saying a lot.

"Still doing your martial arts, Julie love?" Vicky asked.

"Yes, although not for the past three days with all the travel. I feel disconnected when I don't get to practice."

"Well love, I know of a gym nearby to practice, but I can allow you to put your skills to good use."

"Like for a movie? Tell me more." Julie said, her voice rising with curiosity.

"Even better, love," Vicky said, sounding quintessentially Australian. "I don't know if Ross filled you in on my first husband, but he's a drunken louse. While I was on a two-week trip for the airline he got in my apartment and took my jewelry. Then he cleaned out his current girlfriend. He's about to stay at the resort, with no idea of my connection to Colin. There's a jeweler's convention in town, Japanese, Chinese, and Australians looking to get good deals on pearls. So, Mr. Jewel Thief thought it would be an easy opportunity to fence the goods, get cash from some untraceable Asian buyers, get them out of the country, and make off with the cash."

Julie wondered what this had to do with martial arts. She decided to just listen. Vicky's accent was so enchanting.

"First Reginald checks in. This alerts the staff he is here," she said. "Then he gets a call that as a hospitality gesture we have fifty dollars in drink coupons for him at the lounge. We've taken the liberty to make reservations at the lounge, with a twenty-five-dollar discount at the restaurant. He never turns down free booze. We now have him where we want him."

Elbows on her knees, face in her hands, Julie paid rapt attention, wondering where this was going.

"When he is at the bar, he will fixate his eyes on the sexy American spitfire sitting all by her lonesome. That spitfire would be you. While he is at the bar, a constable will execute a search warrant for his room and recover the jewels."

"That's it?" Julie asked.

"No love, here's the fun part. You will flirt with the lowlife bastard for an hour while they case the room."

"I can do that," Julie said. Being a femme fatale sounded intriguing.

"I'll not have my girlfriend flirt with your drunk ex-husband. It's crazy."

"Not so fast, Ross, look at all these people have done for us. There will be back up. This sounds fun. Don't spoil it, okay?" Julie was intrigued.

"Oh, it gets much better," Vicky said.

"If I know the man, he will get grabby. I want you to wear something sexy, doll. We'll spike his drinks, if you like, to make this a sure thing. I want you to lead him on and then kaboom! Kick the living shit out of him, to the surprise of the patrons. You'll look like an absolute Wonder Woman. No one ever gets to be a superhero in real life but you, my dear, will be a blooming goddess."

Julie just about pissed herself. She could barely contain her enthusiasm. Ross seemed despondent.

"No way. You don't know what will happen. You're five foot five, he has a good eight inches on you and a hundred pounds. This is insane."

A freshly showered Colin emerged from upstairs, still toweling his wet hair, dressed in cargo shorts, Hawaiian shirt, and boating shoes.

"Ross, buddy, I wouldn't let your lady embark on such an endeavor without having all kinds of backup. First, we got security cameras, and Nir, my head of security, will be in the pub with an earpiece monitoring thing. Nir is one of my best hires. He's a former Israeli Special Ops, manages security at the casino, and will give Julie a little refresher, how to take a guy out from a bar stool, all choreographed. The first whiff of trouble he'll be all over the situation like flies on a pile of shit. No chance of anything going wrong. He'll work with Julie for a few hours to make sure we get this right. There will be cops here regarding the warrant for the stolen jewelry. Everything planned out to a tee. She will like this."

Ross was checkmated. There was no way she would say no to the chance to smack down some drunken pig and look like Superwoman. Every student of martial arts has a fantasy, a showdown at the OK Corral where they exact revenge on some evildoer. Few do so. Opening up a can of whoop-ass on a bear of a man, and an asshole to boot, was a dream come true. Excitement sent her adrenaline coursing through her. She pinned Ross with her stare.

"Listen, I'll go on record as having serious reservations, but I've long since learned not to tell Julie what to do. So, baby just be careful, okay?"

"Ross, we got everything covered, we got your lady's back," a self-assured Colin said.

"Vicky, I love you!" Julie said. "I want to meet this guy Nir. I won't let you down. This is so cool. I can't wait. Let's go shopping and find some Honeypot clothes."

The plan fired neurons in just about every synapse of Julie's brain. The sexy part, the revenge part, and the teaching-everyone-who-ever-fucked-with-me-a-lesson part. She would test her mettle in real life. A girl would publicly humiliate a guy who deserved an ass-kicking for the benefit of a friend he wronged. It would bruise his macho ego long after his wounds had healed. His mates would never look at him the same.

"When can I meet your security guy? I'm ready now!"

The girls bonded like sisters. Julie would help Vicky get back her stuff, and teach the asshole a lesson, and Julie was grateful for the entire experience in Broome.

They decided to all go into town to go shopping, with Julie telling Vicky she had a black dress with a slit in mind with ample cleavage. They were giggling like schoolgirls. Ross couldn't recall seeing her happier.

It dawned on Ross, what better time to put a ring on Julie's finger than after Reginald's SmackDown. Ol' Reggie would be beaten-up by Ross's spunky girlfriend while stunned onlookers applauded and I-Phones recorded the entire thing for posterity to be posted on YouTube.

It was a glorious day in Broome, a lunch overlooking the beach walks along Carnarvon Street and then back to the resort. Julie would meet Nir for a few moments at an empty meeting room where he could gauge her skill set, and then the two would reconvene in the closed Cable Beach pub, where he could choreograph the fight scene like Ginger Rogers if she were about to kick Fred Astaire's ass.

Ross walked to the beach, and with reality sinking in, started thinking about all the things that could go wrong in the coming days. The turquoise waters of the Indian Ocean lapped at the shoreline as the bright orange sunset framed the camel caravan trekking across the sandy beach.

Ross took stock of all that had transpired to put him in this place of almost unimaginable beauty. Victoria's wedding, a girl by his side who he was intent on marrying, and Dave half a planet away receiving mail at his old address, just a few scant weeks away from negating his alimony obligation.

It was a success beyond their wildest imagination. Yet, like a cruel joke, there were so many ways everything could get fucked up just inches from the finish line.

Stephanie was on her way, enraged by an email from

this spot, intent on ruining his relationship. If she put two and two together and realized Julie was Dave's ex-wife, it would be lights out. Julie was about to have a bar fight with Victoria's ex, and now, Ross worried about an even bigger problem.

Victoria had asked Julie to bring along both passports when the two went shopping, saying she needed them for the notary as witnesses to her wedding to Colin. In reality, she required them to get the wedding permit for her American friends, while keeping the engagement and destination wedding a surprise.

Folded inside Ross's passport was the hotel receipt from Sydney, listing his call to Dave, a number Julie knew well. He hadn't paid attention when he slipped the receipt in with their passports, but in hindsight, he realized his calls had been listed among their other comped charges.

Worlds were colliding so close to victory. There were too many secrets likely to slip out of the bag shortly, and they could unravel everything. It convinced Ross his entire universe would come crashing down. Panicked, he tried alerting Victoria, but her phone went to voicemail.

Intoxicated with the idea of her staged fight, Julie mapped it out through the eyes of a military man with authentic combat experience. According to Nir, a woman has a tactical advantage, getting closer to a target without arousing suspicion, increasing the chances for success. Surprise made up for deficiencies in physical stature. He told her he would go to the pub and scope the layout and meet her at 7 a.m. to practice the scenario.

The two traded a few chokes and bear hug escapes, which were the staple of her classes. Julie impressed the wiry commando, throwing him to the carpet with ruthless efficiency. They did a little pad work with kicks and punches and the loud pop sound of skin on leather convinced Nir she was game. Julie couldn't stop grinning, bubbling with anticipation, and eager to share her enthusiasm with Ross.

Julie had an adrenaline rush that infused her libido. Ross rested on the bed as she opened the door. She needed Ross badly and wanted to thank him with her body. She wanted to worship him and make him feel like a king to her warrior princess. She wanted him to know she appreciated his grudging approval.

Julie was in love with Ross. She loved his knack of getting to know people, cool and interesting people, and making them feel at ease. It didn't matter if they were a hotel magnate or a bartender, he made others comfortable, regardless of their station in life.

She hoped her dad would see those qualities in him. For all her father's business acumen, her dad didn't exactly follow his parents' expectations when he came back from the Canal Zone with a bride. His worldview changed from seeing military personnel of all races and backgrounds mixing. There was no segregation among the Panamanians off base.

Upon returning, he challenged his fellow Atlanta friends to reexamine their beliefs about societal norms. He could expect no less from his daughter. Her mom left a life of comfort to follow love and start a family. Julie was her father, driven to succeed and a perfectionist, but also her mom, gentle, kind, and loving.

Julie came from a family of risk-takers. It was a fresh perspective that clashed with her previous view, that they expected her to bend to her father's will.

For so long she thought of herself as conforming, but she had a rebellious streak just like her parents. It was an epiphany.

Ross was the catalyst, allowing her to find herself, her

true north, making peace with all that pushed her to go through life with a chip on her shoulder. She felt less of an outcast and more of an amalgam of positive qualities of her parents.

Instead of feeling she defied convention and forged her own path, she felt humility and gratitude for the sacrifices her parents made. Ross helped her gain a fresh perspective.

A wave of gratitude washed over her. Her life made sense as she could see the ancestral influences at work, combining to make her who she was. Her life was no longer about her journey but carrying the torch of those who aided her along the way. Gone was the bitterness and resentments of the omnipresent family business, and its effects on her marriage. Gone was her fear of loving completely.

She lay there snuggled up to Ross in silent bliss, the sheets, damp from sweat. This may have been the most profound love making of all. Ross may have sensed this time was different but did not know whether it was vacation sex in an exotic locale or the pending excitement. It was a self-love of acceptance, and connection shared with her partner.

They put on the hotel bathrobes and ordered room service for dinner, watching the breakers from their balcony and expressing their love as best as words allowed. Julie's thoughts shifted to her early morning practice run with Nir. She couldn't wait.

The two downed a bottle of Chardonnay as they watched a sappy romantic Australian show called "Home and Away." They dozed off in a face-to-face embrace. As Ross rolled over, she spooned him the rest of night, restless with eager anticipation of the coming day's events.

Julie was up a half-hour before the wake-up call at six. She showered, applied makeup, and dressed in yoga pants and a loose-fitting shirt. She grabbed the phone on the first ring to let Ross keep sleeping, then kissed him on the lips and top of the head. She admired the expansive view of the ocean and headed downstairs and. jogged on the beach for a good twenty minutes and turned around to get back to the main building at least fifteen minutes before the appointed time with her handler.

"Good morning, Julie. How are you today? Boker Tov. That's G'day in Hebrew." Nir opened the pub door with some keys and flicked on the lights to the bar and the principal area of the dining section.

She had heard the accent a few times. Sippy, when barking out sparring instructions at the gym, and Israelis hawking make-up from the Dead Sea at SouthPark Mall always promising a special price for you.

Nir had the rugged, chiseled looks of someone who had seen shit but wouldn't let on unless required to reveal his darkest moments. It was a soldier's poker face. He had an air of mystery around him and it seemed he liked it that way.

"I'm doing great Nir, how are you?"

"I'm doing Fen-Tes-Teek," he said in his accent. "I need to ask you if you are a warrior, and before you answer I need to let you know a warrior does whatever is needed to complete the mission no matter what. You have to have that mindset at all times. Nothing can interfere or defeat you. You understand?"

"Yes."

"You need to lose the ponytail. Your hair will be up in a bun. He can't have anything to grab. Understood?"

"Yes, sir."

"So, I'll map everything out for you today. We will cover just about every contingency and we will practice until you feel comfortable, and I feel comfortable. It might take an hour or twelve hours. That depends on how you train. Victoria and Colin are not just people I work for, they're like family. I love them, I love this place and the life I have here. I'm far away from my country. I miss family and my army buddies.

"Victoria and Colin are like my army buddies here. Vicky's life is being invaded by a terrorist from her past.

She's strong, but this man made her live in fear. He had no right. I want you to picture him. Picture your host and friend, Vicky. He took things from her she can never get back. We must get her possessions back and defeat him to prevent others from falling prey. Vicky's counting on you. You are a warrior, a soldier who cannot be defeated. You are fighting for every woman with an abusive man who lives in fear. I believe fate put you in this place, and you are the best person for this assignment. I'm counting on you, do you understand?"

"Yes, I'll do as you tell me. I'm eager to learn. I'll not let you down, and I'll do the job you ask of me."

Julie wanted to convey that she was leaving the planning to Nir. She would not challenge his judgment. It was one thing to spar in a gym, and yet another to have an actual fight with a wild drunk. She needed Nir's guidance to go into this with confidence. Julie felt nervous for the first time as the reality of what was about to happen hit her.

"I've mapped out what you'll be doing. It's simple. You are a pretty girl, and he won't expect what will happen to him," Nir said.

The way he said will, sounded as if he was sure of success. She liked that.

"He'll be so focused on touching you he'll be on the floor before he realizes what happened. The surprise is the great equalizer. It's far more important than strength. You have a technique, and it'll be quick. I'll have an earpiece, and you'll have a wire to hear whatever you say. We will have a word you'll say right before the shit hits the fan. I'll be close by. As long as you are in control, have at him until you are defeating a beaten man. Once the adrenaline starts, you might need me to stop you. You're a warrior, but not an animal. You have a job to do. The goal is to get him down, helpless to defend himself, beat his ass but not seriously injure him. I'll have the police here in a minute or two. I'll guard him until they arrive. Then they take him away like taking out the trash, okay? You're not the garbage man.

You just put the trash to the side of the curb. They pick it up, okay?"

Julie nodded.

Nir unfolded a piece of hotel stationery from his pocket and laid it on the bar. It had circles for chairs and a map of the bar area, arrows, and some scribble in Hebrew characters and English. It appeared he mapped things out from left and right. He left nothing to chance. It was the commando in him.

"Righty or lefty?"

"Lefty."

"I thought so from yesterday. Even better. If this guy had any fights, he would expect the right-hander. But he'll be defeated before he even realizes he's in a fight, his ass kicked by a woman he thought would have sex with him."

"Tell me more."

"Okay, you'll be on his right. You'll be flirting. You'll get his hands on the top of your thighs. The schmuck will put them there, but if he doesn't, you'll put them there. He may get grabby. That's good. In this way, he won't have hands where he needs them to defend or undo the choke you'll have on him in a matter of seconds. He won't think twice if you've your arm around him, on his shoulder, he'll be happy it's there."

With that Nir took out two leather kick pads from behind the bar. He stacked them on the bar.

"We practice now. First, hair in a bun."

Julie sat to Nir's right as she adjusted her hair. He touched his head to the pad as if to test its distance.

"Okay, we're talking. This is the part I leave up to you. Ask Vicky what he likes to talk about. Win his confidence, and then get him to think you want to sleep with him. You play with his hands and put them on your thighs when you feel it won't seem odd. Let him play with your hands so it'll seem natural. Remember, he'll probably be drunk. The bartender will keep giving him shots. His reaction time will be compromised further from the element of surprise, and the location of his hands. They'll be too slow and too far away to stop your choke."

Julie had visions of Nir, in uniform, pointer in hand, going over a replica of a raid, with several grizzled soldiers paying strict attention. Nir was so matter-of-fact. He never once expressed doubt in her ability. She absorbed his confidence. Nir was talking to her as a commander to a soldier. Surreal. She wanted to pay rapt attention and make everyone proud.

As Nir explained things she'd have her arm around Reginald, resting on his shoulder. His hands would be on her thighs, she'd get off her chair and wind up behind him, sinking her arm around him in one swoop into a rear-naked choke, among the most lethal and difficult to break.

Reginald would reflexively try to grab her hands to undo the choke. Next, she would slam his head into the solid teak bar once, perhaps twice or three times, and then kick the chair out from under him, causing the bruised and bloodied Reginald to fall backward on his noggin, his hands still trying to extricate himself from the choke and unable to break his fall. Julie would stomp on each wrist, kick him in the ribs, and the balls for good measure. Nir and the cops would take out the garbage. Patrons would erupt into cheers for Wonder Woman. Nir expected the entire fight scene to take less than thirty seconds.

Nir cleared a few tables from the vicinity of the bar and unrolled a mat.

"We practice as we fight, and we fight as we practice. When you fight it must be like you are the third monkey on the ramp to Noah's Ark. It's you or him, and when it starts, he must think he is dealing with fifty Mike Tysons on crack. Yell, grunt, snort, whatever you must do to make him know he fucked with the wrong person," Nir said.

"Julie, you need to do this hard. I know how to fall. I'll simulate resistance. Don't worry about hurting me, okay? I'll have you miss a few times to plan for contingencies. I'll have an earpiece the entire time. You won't be compromised for a second."

"I need you to learn this using muscle memory. Your mindset must always be that nothing can deter you. You are a warrior. I know how to fall properly. Your target will be a drunk guy falling backward from a bar stool worried about your hands on his neck."

Julie sat down and repeatedly pounded Nir's head into a kick shield after sinking her arm into a choke. She then kicked the chair out from under him and watched him fall backward, breaking his fall with a thud. Afterward, she counted aloud the five kicks she was to deliver before relinquishing control to the garbage men. Wrist, wrist, ribs, balls, and head if it was available. The fifth one was optional as a skull could cause her to injure her foot and stumble.

Nir urged her to go faster, harder, and again. She would do dozens of consecutive dry runs Each time, Nir would pop back up after being tumbled backward, offering resistance and with Julie gauging his reflexive reactions faster each time. She was sweaty but determined to show Nir she was indefatigable. Nir blindfolded her, and after a half dozen tries completed her part by instinct alone. Nir grabbed her leg on the ground for a takedown, and she did the counter move he showed her, mastering the technique after about five tries.

"Again. Faster. Better. Stronger. It needs to be perfect. For Victoria. This is real life," he would shout after she completed the round of stomps. Nir bled from his elbow, unaware until a trickle of blood flowed towards his wrist while pointing to the floor. He grabbed a napkin from the nearby bar and wiped it off like ketchup from a McDonald's table.

He had her miss the choke, in which case she used the barstool as a weapon. Whatever Nir did or said, Julie was bursting with confidence. She would execute her confrontation with Reginald to choreographed perfection, ready to enlist under Nir's command.

Sharing the story with her dojo was for another day. Today was all about mentally and physically preparing for the showdown. Her slit skirt ensemble allowed for more mobility. Vicky had several conversation starters, likely to pique Reginald's interest. Her Doc Martin boots might be a somewhat unconventional pairing from a fashion perspective, but they would have utilitarian value while kicking Reginald.

During one of Nir's tumbles, his t-shirt rode up revealing a rather nasty scar on his right side running from a bottom rib to his hip bone. "That scar looks serious," Julie said, inviting an explanation.

"I'm fine, actually I'm very lucky," Nir said.

"Was it from…?" Julie needed to know if it was a military wound.

"Let's just say, the other gentleman was not so lucky." Nir shook his head as if recalling something painful. Julie knew not to inquire further. She was certain that other gentleman was dead.

After almost two hours of strenuous exercise, Nir said, "Are you ready?" as if awaiting paratrooper wings. "Yes, Nir." A warrior, she was ready to conquer the world.

Nir suggested she hydrate and relax and stretch and invited her and Ross to have breakfast with him. She called Ross, who asked how things went.

"Fucking great!"

Nir asked for the phone and said, "Your girl is ready, she's a warrior now. Come to breakfast with us. Okay? We'll wait at the restaurant for you."

Ross threw on some clothes, swigged a little mouthwash, and headed downstairs. He needed to see what this enthusiasm was all about. He had bigger issues on his mind, however. When Julie had left, he fired up his laptop to check emails. *What a cluster fuck.*

Nir and Julie were engaged in candid conversation when Ross sat at the table. They had each accessed the buffet table and had taken fruit and some cereal, none of the greasy stuff.

"Ross, this morning was amazing. He treated me like a soldier. This is the coolest thing I have ever done. It's not that complicated, and we practiced a ton, even for mistake scenarios."

"Ross, she's an excellent student and was pretty well trained before. She had an Israeli woman as an instructor. The women teach better than men. Julie said you took classes too, right?"

"Yes, and she kicked my ass a few times. I underestimate her toughness at my peril."

"Ross, you know that she needs to step behind him and choke him when his hands are not in close range, stomp him a few times afterward when he falls. I'll be all over him along with three other security personnel. She'll have a wire, and I'll have an earpiece. This will not only be enjoyable for your lady, but it'll be a tremendous favor to Victoria and give the police time to recover her stuff and arrest him."

"Hon, I have to head to the ladies' room," Julie said.

Ross told Nir he would ask her to marry him right after all this shit went down. Nir thought it was a brilliant idea and would arrange for one of his detail to record the entire thing on an iPhone. Ross asked man to man if there was anything to worry about. Nir assured him. As a soldier who had "seen things," he said she's trained and ready. It was a simple plan with lots of back-ups built in.

"We would consider this a low-risk operation with an overwhelming chance of success."

Ross didn't mention an ex-wife and her ex-boyfriend might arrive at the hotel as this was going down. He tried his best to conceal his nervousness about the pending arrival of his arch-nemesis.

Nir told Ross he would allow him to propose to the

cheers of the entire crowded bar. Victoria and Colin would then offer to provide the nuptials on the house for her efforts right there in front of the crowd to rapturous applause. It would be one of the most momentous engagements since the dawn of time and a great advertising boost for Colin since cameras would be rolling.

Julie returned from freshening up. Nir indicated he had to go to work, and suggested she get a nice massage, steam or sauna while hydrating and relaxing by the pool. They fist-bumped as he departed.

Julie was amped up. She would get her massage and steam, then relax by the pool going through the choreographed moves in her head. Reginald was due to check-in at three. It was best Julie be off the grounds so he would not spot her coupled up. Ross suggested they go to nearby Cable Beach after her spa time, and head back to the room with an hour to spare.

Nir gave Julie a burner phone to receive texts to keep tabs on where Reginald was and when he was heading to the lounge. Nir wished them good luck and said, "Don't worry. When you are prepared, there's nothing to be nervous about."

"Ross, I've to go into town and get boots. Shit-kicking boots for later. Maybe some whorish perfume."

While Julie got her massage, Victoria called Ross, who suggested they come over at about four, to go over a few things. She assured Ross that Julie would say yes to his proposal, and the odds were good they might feature it on Australian news, as Colin was eager to get publicity for his wedding destination resort. Ross might have a wonderful wedding in three days. Dress fittings, makeup sessions at the spa, photographers were ready to go shared from Victoria's wedding crew. All Ross had to do was pick out a tux and show up.

The text came in to Vicky about four-thirty. A dusty and unshaven Reginald Dodemaide checked into the Broome Royal Pearl Resort and was greeted warmly by the front desk. "Mr. Dodemaide, we're a relatively new resort and we appreciate your business. We have selected a few random guests for special upgrades. We would like to treat you to dinner and drinks tonight and have made a reservation for you at our Cable Beach lounge. Here are six drink coupons for you to use at the bar, including our top-shelf liquor selection. It's our way of saying thank you. We hope to earn your repeated business."

"I'm here for the jeweler's convention. Much obliged. Hey, I got me satchel here and need to know there is a safe in the room."

"Yes, Mr. Dodemaide. It's in the closet. If you need a larger one I can get maintenance to come by and swap it out for a larger model."

"That would be great, Love."

"Okay Mr. Dodemaide, we have you at our lounge at seven and your dinner table will be ready at 8. Please be prompt, we have a lot of guests and want to make sure we take care of our VIPs."

Colin himself prepped the reception staff on Reginald's impending check-in. The clerk from Indonesia played a scripted conversation like an actress. The generosity overwhelmed Reginald, and he checked out the property. He had a satchel and dusty backpack. Ruggedly Australian, he had about three days' worth of stubble and a toothpick dangling from the left side of his mouth. His Aussie Akubra hat dangled by its chinstrap to the middle of his back. He had on a tight black tee, where sweat pockets were visible. A silver belt buckle in the shape of a cobra adorned his jeans, wider than normal. He wore a pair of dusty boots, and a shark's tooth necklace he picked up in the Gold Coast hung around his neck. An unbuttoned leather vest completed the look. He looked forward to a nice hot shower, kick his feet up for a while and catch a brief nap.

Reginald couldn't believe how well things were going. In just a few hours he would mingle among dozens of Chinese, Indonesian, Malaysian, Filipino, and Japanese jewelers looking for local deals on pearls. He had several diamonds, gold, and heirloom silver that could net him seventy-five to one hundred grand Australian.

In just a few days, the merchandise would be untraceable thousands of miles away. After boozing and whoring around town he could put a tidy down payment on a station a hundred miles west of Alice Springs, or maybe a dusty watering hole, a new motorcycle, and a big-ass truck.

He entered his room. Impressive view and decorated with class. Smelled of the ocean and reeked of class. He put the satchel on a chair, the silverware service was wrapped so as not to make a noise and he looked for the safe, too small, and called the front desk. It was a call they were waiting for.

"Yes Mr. Dodemaide, we will get right on it. If it's okay with you, we can get a guy up there around seven. I noticed we have you set for an appointment in our lounge under our VIP program, at seven. If you like they can have things finished for you while you are eating dinner. I'm sorry for the inconvenience. Is that okay or would you like to switch rooms?"

"No, that won't be necessary."

"How about you stop down at the front desk, ask for me, Soraya? I'll have the guest services agent give you a ticket and it'll be locked up. By the time you come back, your safe will be ready."

"OK, love, I'll do that on my way to dinner,"

From the second he checked in, Reginald had done everything possible to fall deeper into Vicky's trap. They would open his satchel and examine the contents in police presence. Victoria had compiled a list of her jewelry as had Melba, and as long as her descriptions matched those examined in their presence, they could take possession after some brief paperwork.

There were a few loose diamonds too, one of which she would give to her friend Ross for his upcoming wedding. They would add the stone to the ring Ross would use in his wedding ceremony. While unaware of her pending wedding, Julie, with TV cameras rolling and high on adrenaline, would surely say yes. Vicky alerted Julie and Ross of Reginald's arrival. The trap was set.

Reggie plopped his arse down on that comfy bed. He'd be at the lounge and dinner for a maximum of two hours. What harm could come to him during that window? Tomorrow he would head over to the convention center and hob knob with Asian buyers. Tonight he could get drunk with a clear mind and thanks to his good fortune to enjoy a delightful meal comped by his swanky hotel.

It felt good to use a fresh razor and the body wash on his skin, which hadn't seen a shower for three days. He wrapped himself in the fluffy hotel towels before spotting the bathrobe hung from the inside of the door. His hair was now shampooed, and he dug Q-Tips in his ears to remove the remnants of his trip. Reginald was ruggedly handsome and if some foreign babe at the resort wanted a real Australian experience, he'd surely oblige. A souvenir of their stay in Broome. He slapped cologne on for good measure.

Reginald took a swig of the flask filled with Irish whiskey and set his alarm for six-thirty, at which time he would get dressed and head downstairs. Reginald dozed off, and after what seemed like only a few moments his phone rang beckoning him to wake up.

He was tired but eager to get his drink on with some

grub. He slipped on a pair of jeans, an open-collared shirt, shark's tooth necklace, and suede vest. Looking like an Australian croc wrestler at a roadside attraction, he headed downstairs. The dangling toothpick completed the look. He had the leathered skin of a bloke that worked much of his life outside.

He spotted a few Asian tourists speaking what he assumed was Japanese. Tomorrow one might just buy his entire stash, but business was for another day. Tonight was about relaxing. As he turned the corner of the lobby, he spotted an attractive woman that drew him into the nearby pub.

Julie waited at the bar dressed in a long, black skirt, stylish boots, and a scoop neck top that sunk to reveal her perky breasts unencumbered by a bra. She made small talk with the bartender while waiting. She spotted him as he entered. She swallowed a momentary bit of trepidation. She could do this. He headed straight for her as Vicky said he would.

"Mind if I sit down?" Reggie said as he pulled out the stool from the bar.

"No, be my guest."

"Waiting for anyone?"

"Depends. Think someone better will come along?"

For a second Reginald thought she might be one of those working girls working the convention. If the price was right, and she was game, he wouldn't mind paying but didn't want to guess wrong. What would a girl from somewhere on the North American continent be doing turning tricks halfway around the globe? Whatever her reason for being there, he wanted to bed her for the night.

"Not likely, love. What brings you to this neck of the woods?"

"Well, I got out of a marriage of some fifteen years, and I thought what's the farthest place that has beautiful beaches and still speaks English. Google said Broome, Australia, so here I am."

"Traveling with girlfriends? Sorry for prying, just curious. It's a long way for a girl to go by herself."

She was getting a whiff of mansplaining, making her up her acting game.

"The area seemed nice, and you only live once. I needed a place to let loose and be happy before heading back to the real world."

"Well, let's get the pahty stahted then. Got me some freebies from the front desk. Bahtendah, a drink for the lady."

"What are you drinking ma'am?"

"Tequila straight up." Julie's tequila was a twenty-eighty mix of tequila and apple juice. Identical in color, but enough tequila to smell authentic. It would take her at least a dozen shots before feeling the slightest effect. Vicky had assured Julie that Reginald was a Jamison's whiskey guy and would not depart from his habit.

As if on cue, "A shot of Jamison's, make it a double and an Emu Export, mate."

Nir was sitting at a bar table across the bar glancing over to make sure things were going as planned.

They toasted to Broome and new friendships. On cue, the bartender motioned to ask if it was time for another.

"Sure mate."

Julie was ready to go in for the kill.

"Are all Australian guys so ruggedly handsome, or did I get lucky?"

"You're quite the babe yourself. We're a nation of convicts. Brits made this into a penal colony."

In a matter of a few moments, Reginald too would be a criminal, busted on national TV.

Julie was laying it on thick as he became cockier. Eager to hear his head hit the floor like a coconut, she played along for maximum effect.

She chuckled and put her best Southern charm on display. The more he drank, the thicker her drawl, and he loved it.

"Y'all are so damn much fun. I bet you've done some serious shit in your life, Reggie."

"Oh, you don't know half of it. I love hunting and have lived in the bush for weeks at a time. I'm a loner. Got a few businesses going. Have a few hundred herds of cattle, a restaurant pub, do contracting work, electrical. Been fortunate but got divorced."

"Was it painful?"

"No, she thought her shit didn't stink. She was a flight attendant and wasn't around much. Thought she was as high-class as her first-class passengers. A city girl, tryin' to be all tall poppy. Me, I love the wide-open spaces of the interior. Give me a walkabout any day."

"What's that?"

"It's wandering through the countryside and wilderness. Meeting with Bush People, getting in touch with nature. Unplugging from all the man-made crap."

"Reminds me of the movie "Deliverance," four guys from my hometown of Atlanta went canoeing and ran into some hillbillies. One gets tied to a tree and screwed in the ass. That's a Redneck walkabout. No thanks."

"Never seen the film but heard of Atlanta. CNN, Ted Turner, Jane Fonda, 'Gone with the Wind', The Olympics, giant airport, right?"

"Sort of."

"Walkabout's not like that. A campfire under the stars with no lights for miles. Exotic sounds of wildlife. Dingos, kangaroos, koalas, and an occasional scorpion. Hunting your food. It's getting back with nature."

Julie lost count at about eight drinks. Reggie was matching her two for one. He was over a dozen minimum. With the coupons exhausted, the bartender was putting two on the table but charging for one. Reggie was getting more suggestive with slurred speech. It was minutes away from show time. A lively crowd watched the local West Coast Eagles play Australian Rules football on TV.

She could tell he was a louse, just as Victoria said. He

made cracks about her ass, Americans, Asian tourists, immigrants, and gays, interspersed with flirtatious advances. Nir had taught her how to think and choreograph the fight. Her chances were best when he was certain he would get in her pants. A relaxed target increases the element of surprise, and the more surprise, the lower the probability of the suspect gaining the upper hand. Her heart pumped a mile a minute, courtesy of adrenaline.

"You are so damn sexy. If I can't have you tonight, I might just go crazy."

There was no mistaking Reginald was drunk, legless in Aussie-speak. He would wish he had those legs in a moment. The bartender, alerted to the plans, looked at her with a knowing glance, fairly certain she was about to strike like a cobra. Julie looked backward and made eye contact with Nir.

She put her arm around his shoulder and placed his hands on her thighs. She glanced at her phone, and some forty minutes had elapsed. More than enough time for the police to search his room and examine his satchel. Shit was about to get real.

"Such slender and sexy legs babe," Reginald said and rubbed the tops of her thighs, inching closer to her lady bits.

Showtime.

It was just as they practiced it, except Julie let out a resounding, "You motherfucker!" as she channeled every asshole guy she encountered since puberty.

Sinking the rear-naked choke, she bounced his head by the bridge of his nose on the bar not once but twice the second time catching his forehead, and in another motion pulled his head backward while kicking the stool out from under him. His hands yanking at her arm around his neck, he had nothing to break his fall except his noggin, which made the sound of a coconut falling from a tree onto a parquet floor.

In the commotion, his beer bottle had fallen on the floor, and as he grabbed at it to defend himself her boots stomped his outstretched wrist. She heard a cracking noise like a tree branch snapping. He let out a yelp like a wounded hyena. Time was moving at glacial speed with every second like an hour. It couldn't have been over ten seconds since her profanity-laced battle cry.

She kicked him in the ribs, then his ear, and as he swiped the broken bottle at her legs with his now feeble hand, the bottle fell farther out of reach. She hopped to the side, recoiled, and unloaded on his crotch. She felt a measure of pity for the man as he clutched his groin.

"You bitch, you! What did you do that for?"

In one fell swoop, Nir had straddled his torso and had Reginald's hands behind him as he lay face down. "Stay calm, people. You've just witnessed what happens when an asshole tries to force himself on the wrong woman."

"You, my friend, just used a broken bottle as a weapon, adding to the severity of your charges," said Nir.

"Fuck off, pig," Reginald said, as blood trickled from his lip.

Ross ran into the pub, gift-wrapped jewelry-box in hand. Julie grabbed a dinner napkin to apply to her bleeding calf. It was a minor and superficial wound, but the bloody napkin had added to the dramatic effect and Reginald's charges.

Nir teed up the ceremonies.

"Ladies and gentlemen, sorry for the inconvenience. The police will be here to deal with this piece of human garbage, but this woman is lucky, not because of the fight, but because a man who loves her has something to say to her."

"Julie, you've been my superhero from the moment I met you. You make me happy like no other, and I can think of no better way to spend the rest of my life than by your side. Will you marry me?"

Julie gasped. "Yes, Ross, a thousand times, yes!"

The police entered the room as Nir stood, lifting his knee from Reginald's back. "This one will need an ambulance," Nir said to the officers.

Five-foot five inches of dynamite. Ross reflected on what had just transpired.

It was like a scripted movie set, Nir choreographing the moves, Colin providing the bit actors, and stagehands, and Victoria directing the script. Ross was perhaps the best supporting actor, playing the perfect foil to Julie and putting the cherry on top with his well-timed proposal. With dozens of patrons in the bar, a YouTube video was a certainty.

Broome is a compact resort town that had local news alerted via police scanners. To be certain, Colin tipped them off. There was a disturbance at the town's biggest resort, and it was a juicy feel-good story that would put Broome in the limelight.

Erin Parke, the town's cub reporter known for her in-depth investigations, was having dinner at the resort, told to wait for a brewing story by Colin. She smelled a winner, and her camera crew was dispatched post-haste. The timing was such that it could be edited and prepped for the 11 p.m. news and rerun with promos the next day. "Woman Foils Jewelry thief with her Bare Hands, followed by marriage proposal" doesn't come around often, and is a story that wins awards.

The scuffle ended with the perp bruised and in handcuffs and the hero getting a ring on her finger from her kneeling fiancé. Erin Parke smelled 'Logie,' the Australian version of the Emmys. Erin had a solid history of investigative reporting, but this would be her Picasso and a stepping stone to a national slot in Sydney or Melbourne.

The sirens had died down as Erin rushed toward the pub to interview patrons and the principals, camera crew in tow. Julie looked the part of the heroine as she was still out of breath. She couldn't tell whether it was her thirty-second beat down of Reggie or her unexpected proposal that took her breath away. Erin did not understand how juicy the story was about to become.

"Well, you see my friend Victoria had asked me for a little favor, seeing as her ex was trying to fence some of her stolen jewelry, and I was happy to oblige. What I did was nothing. Nir the head of security here, has been an absolute ace in showing me what to do, and my dear fiancé, to arrange a trip like this and our hosts Victoria and Colin. It has been like a dream. I can't wait to get married. This is the happiest day of my life."

Vicky and Colin appeared at Julie's and Ross's elbows. "Ross has been a dear friend for a few years. He has been like a brother in helping me navigate through some issues I've had with my abusive ex-spouse who is now under arrest. When told that after so many years Ross met the love of his life, I felt fortunate Qantas allowed me to give them a few tickets. My fiancé was kind enough, having never met either of them, to invite them to his resort. I couldn't be happier for both of them. Ross is like a brother and I feel a special kinship with Julie, who didn't flinch when I asked if she could do a little favor for me."

"I'm a blessed man, and as many in the town know I'll wed my amazing fiancée Victoria in just a few days. I can think of no greater tribute to the bonds of friendship than to share that day with Ross and Julie, who traveled so far to get here, and who offered without hesitation to assist in the recovery of some very sentimental family heirlooms of Vicky's. I've gotten to know them and couldn't have asked for better mates. I count them among my family. Starting first thing tomorrow morning, I'll have my event planners get them in the mix, and we'll celebrate in a way this town has never seen before. We'll get married together," Colin said.

The story just morphed into a Hollywood screenplay

and Erin felt beside herself trying to figure out how to package this prized piece of reporting for her corporate bosses. As soon as they shot the story, she phoned her producers at the head of the news bureau. They told her to get a cursory story for eleven o'clock and they would get a more in-depth version for tomorrow that the ABC would run on its prime newscast. They would milk the story and the run-up to the wedding. They would work on getting the story viral, and a special segment on 'Sunrise' or 'A Current Affair.'

Ross overheard a conversation in Mandarin from some Chinese guests mimicking a karate chop to the neck. Ross's fiancé was a celebrity. A teaser ad popped up on the bar's TV listing "American tourist woman helps foil a jewelry heist by subduing the criminal at Broome's swankiest resort. Only on ABC News, Broome." The crowd erupted in cheers. Colin couldn't buy better publicity.

Colin moved to the edge of his chair, cleared his throat and said, "Ross, Julie, when this thing is over, I couldn't have paid for better advertising than what just happened. That you helped my Vicky get her family jewels back is something I will always be thankful for. So, before you rush to say thank you for what I'm about to say, let me start by saying you've paid for it a hundred times over. We want you to be part of our wedding celebration and get married alongside us. It's from the heart, as I'm grateful, but it'll put this place on the map. And when your lawyer gets hitched to her partner, I'll be the go-to resort for same-sexed couples too. The marriage-equality issue was only recently settled. There is enough pent-up demand to keep me busy for years."

The gang clinked glasses when Julie asked for permission to address everybody. "To our hosts Victoria and Colin, who couldn't have asked for a more incredible experience. To Nir, who instilled confidence in me with one day of practice, to do something I never could have imagined doing, thank you. To my future husband, I couldn't have asked for a better person with whom to spend the rest of my life."

Chapter Twenty-Four
Steph Aside

Nicole used her secret key to stay at her dad's apartment. She found his itinerary printed out. It wasn't upsetting she was out of the loop but knew her mom would flip if she knew Ross was heading to Australia without informing her. Nicole knew to leave well enough alone with her mom, but was not, however, so quiet with her friends. Stephanie heard her mention something about Australia while she was talking on the phone and swiped her phone while she was showering. Texts back and forth describing her dad's itinerary with his current girlfriend. Paydirt! It was the same small resort town that Henry had traced his via IP address and the emails that busted him for cheating. It was an odd coincidence, the same small Northwest Australian resort town. She was all ears to what Henry and his PI son had to say.

Narcissists love to keep exes around via social media. One never knows when they can make an existing partner jealous, or in moments of low self-esteem to give effusive compliments or adulation. Stephanie, despite the contentious breakup, would send periodic feelers to Henry, to let him know she had a boyfriend but with red flags. She wanted Henry to never get over her. He hadn't. He wanted the much younger Stephanie to be his arm candy and an antidote to aging. She needed him to make sense of this coincidence. His discovery of the Broome Australia IP address gave credence to Stephanie's self-absorbed theory that Ross was jealous and sought to sabotage her relationships out of jealousy.

To Henry, this renewed contact would provide the perfect opportunity to get in her good graces and remove her current beau. Travis, his son, was a Private Investigator and computer whizz.

Two could play this game, he thought. All he had to do was convince her to go to Australia and solve the mystery together, to prove his devotion.

Dave quickly got wind as she informed him of her need to go halfway around the world to bust her husband. He tipped-off Ross before the two headed for Australia, and then fired off an email about this unwelcome development. He vowed to get their flight numbers. Vicky also pulled a few strings and got the manifests of all the Qantas flights leaving from the US in the next 48 hours with American passengers. The two would arrive later the next afternoon, having bought a flight from Atlanta post-haste.

It elated Ross to get engaged, but he was nervous as a tick about his entire world crashing down. The front desk alerted him to the fact that Rebecca Harrington had checked in and requested he call her room.

"Becky, thank God you are here. I'm panicking. My ex-wife is on her way here with her former boyfriend. The old guy she was dating got an IP address and traced it here from an email Vicky sent to break them up and clear the way for Dave. Steph's on to the whole thing. She doesn't know the entire story, but somehow Nicole got my itinerary from my apartment, and somehow Stephanie found out. She put two and two together with this Henry guy, and they're both coming here. I'm supposed to get married in two days. There are too many people here. Julie beat up Vicky's ex-husband last night, and it's all over the news. It's too fucking much. There are just too many things that can go wrong. I'm getting a terrible feeling so close to everything working out."

"Ross, slow down. You're talking like you just snorted meth. I got this. Last time, you calmed me down and talked me off a ledge. Now it's my turn."

"What do you mean I got this? I'm almost ten thousand miles from home. I thought I was getting away and now every character in my fucked-up life is here to screw it up. I'm not cut out for this. I want to marry Julie and live happily ever after. I thought I could find peace here. It's been anything but peaceful. My fiancé beat up Crocodile Dundee in a bar fight."

"Ross, get a hold of yourself. I got this. Never underestimate someone that has nothing to lose. I'm no longer constrained by what the bar will think or what my peers will say. I have Eunice over a barrel, and she knows it. Right now your ex is about to find out that her attorney is so radioactive that no judge would give her the time of day. The entire city hates her guts. I may never practice law again, but neither will she. I'll make Stephanie an offer she can't refuse. I'm looking forward to setting her straight on a lot of things, including how she comports herself with your daughter. I guarantee you I'll fix this to your liking. It's my wedding gift to you. I'll talk to Julie. Trust me, I got this."

Becky sounded so sure of herself. Ross didn't have a clue how she could prevent someone intent on damaging his life from doing just that. Dave was a few weeks into cohabitation, and this would blow their entire relationship to smithereens. Right now, Dave was watching Nicole while Stephanie flew around the world. Her ex-boyfriend was tagging along to get back in her good graces and pants. Ross might die of a heart attack before everything could be worked out.

Stephanie was not a great traveler and with business class on brief notice priced at a six-thousand dollar round trip price tag, she went for a coach ticket for half the price. She had an eight-hour layover before the flight to Broome, the only combination that got her to the resort within thirty-six hours.

Fuming with anger, she and Henry had arrived at Broome airport only to find their luggage had been delayed.

It would be a good twenty minutes before Stephanie's and Henry's luggage arrived. In the meantime, a driver arrived to take them to the resort, just enough time for Colin to send over a driver with a hand-held placard with Stephanie's name. That driver would be Nir, who would bug their entire conversation. She would then be whisked to the priority check-in and presented with an envelope welcoming her to the property.

At the check-in desk, the resort concierge informed Stephanie that their stay was comped until the following Sunday as part of a promotion and handed her an envelope. The concierge said the enclosed letter would explain everything. Stephanie was hardly in the mood for fun and games and thought there must have been a mistake, but she opened the letter, hoping it helped her understand.

"Dear Stephanie, it's Becky, your ex-husband's attorney. Yes, I'm in Australia too. You got us. I don't know how your superhuman detective skills figured out that Ross was here, but he was so worried about your pending trip, he flew me out here on the next flight. He's quaking in his boots and as a result, is too nervous to talk to you in person. He asked that I meet with you on his behalf. If you do this, he's prepared to make you a very generous offer. This offer is contingent on you meeting privately with me. If afterward, you wish to consult with your attorney, we will grant you twenty-four hours to do that. Meanwhile, as a goodwill gesture, we have paid for your stay and whatever tours you wish to do. All we ask is that you listen to our proposal. Meet me in the Roebuck Bay Salon at four-thirty. Freshen up, take a nap and I look forward to seeing you then. We're trying to make this up to you.

Sincerely, Rebecca B. Harrington, Esq."

Stephanie was self-congratulating at how she had cracked her husband's web of deceit. "Nothing I hate worse than being lied to, and I always find out. That dickhead thought he got the best of me. I'm way too smart. He's scared to death, scurrying around trying to pay me off. It better be large. I bet he will have to liquidate his entire pension. I know him. He'll do anything to keep me from humiliating him. I can't wait to tell my mom how I handled this situation. I've grown so much since the separation," she said to Henry.

What should I wear? Maybe something businesslike? Shit, I might as well find somewhere to go clothes shopping. The money will be no object after this is done. I knew he was hiding assets, and now I'll get it all.

"Henry, I appreciate your help on this, and I'll try to make it up to you. I hope you'll always be in my life."

Stephanie had a few hours before making Ross's high-powered attorney eat crow. Eunice was the perfect attorney to intimidate Ross and his lawyer, an expert in making men pay.

Ross must've pissed his pants. Dave was a work in progress, but he would be a decent provider, was complimentary and trainable. She would get some huge lump sum payout from Ross to avoid making trouble. Then she could get married and have Dave pay her way. Maybe she'd insist on the continuation of alimony despite their relationship? Either way, Stephanie wins. Wait until all the other divorcees and unhappily married Facebook friends heard about her triumph.

Stephanie wanted to shop for the meeting. Since Broome was a pearling center, perhaps a necklace would be appropriate. She would bleed her ex-husband dry and would soon be flush with money. She would make Henry pay for dinners, and he would comply willingly if she stroked his ego. Make him think she's having second thoughts about Dave. Upon returning to the states, she'd keep him at arm's length and have Dave pay her bills.

Nothing animated Stephanie more than exacting revenge. Schadenfreude was in her DNA. Stephanie had Karma on speed dial. She would soon use those powers for maximum effect.

Broome was gorgeous. Shops sold pearls for prices a fraction of what they were in the states. Stephanie asked Henry if he could put a deposit on a necklace. She would pay him back right after Becky the attorney cut her a check. There'd be plenty left over. A present to herself for being so resourceful.

She bought a summery outfit, half-business, half-resort wear. She wanted to look intimidating for her meeting. Down the street, she picked out shoes to match, and a designer bag for good measure. Her account dwindled to near zero. Henry kicked in some dough with the proviso she would pay him back after Ross's lawyer made her whole. She showed Henry the letter too, proving there would be a windfall.

They went back to the room for a quick change, and to get some late afternoon sun. After ordering poolside sandwiches and drinks, it was time to get ready. Ross lied to Nicole. She intended to let Nicole know what a louse her dad was. Nicole would see his deceptive side obscured by their father-daughter bond.

She asked the concierge for a hair and nail appointment. They responded that they'd make time for her. Someone was pulling out all the stops to make sure she was happy. But it would take a lot more than a new hairstyle or French tipped nails to make her forget the dickhead and his bullshit. She would take a selfie to post to Facebook and tell all six hundred of her social media friends that she received a windfall and was in Australia. She would be vague enough to arouse interest but specific enough to signal she was winning.

Stephanie was having a fantastic hair day as she rode down the elevator to head towards the room where she would meet Becky. For the first time in her life, she felt as if she could handle whatever life threw at her, self-assured as she ticked off all the people that tried to pull one over and failed.

Stephanie entered holding the hotel stationery and a pen. Becky was seated with her legal pad and a leather portfolio open.

"Hello Stephanie, I'm sure you remember me from the mediation. I'm Rebecca Harrington. Come in."

"Ms. Harrington, I trust you're prepared to make this situation right, but I need to know everything. I don't want you to spare a single detail. Everything. Got that? I don't know what kind of stunt Ross thought he could pull. He needs to come clean and make everything right. That means paying up. So, first, why was my ex-boyfriend getting emails from this town?"

"Stephanie, I ask only that you allow me to explain everything and wait until I finish before responding. I want to make sure we give you a full accounting."

"You better."

"Please, be seated. Here is pocket money for you. It's a thousand dollars. Take it. I'm sure it was a hassle getting here, and you'll need money to enjoy yourself. We don't want any trouble. Not that there was much left after your attorney got through with my client."

"Now you're talking. He deserved it. She made him pay and now you'll pay again." Stephanie took the envelope with ten crisp hundred-dollar bills. She counted it, smiled a self-satisfied grin, and put the envelope in her purse.

"So, listen here to what I'm about to tell you. I have a rather complicated past with your attorney. She and I were opposing attorneys before on the Grayson Whitcomb case, one of the ugliest divorces I've seen. Like Eunice, I too am a lesbian, and my partner is the head of Psychiatry at UNC Medical Center in Chapel Hill, where the Whitcomb daughter, Melanie, attended college. To the horror of the whole UNC campus, she took her life publicly. It was the lead story in the Charlotte and Raleigh papers for a week. I was mostly private about our relationship and my sexuality."

Becky folded her arms on her portfolio and leaned forward. "A select few knew of my relationship with Dr. Mindy Horowitz, the girl's psychiatrist. My partner was sharing heart-wrenching details of her sessions, and I was sharing details of the divorce. We were hoping to help get the child help. To stop her torment."

"Not to sound cruel, but what does this have to do with me? You've told me nothing about my ex-husband and this whole Australia charade. I didn't fly halfway around the world to hear about some shitty divorce from three years ago. You need to explain my ex-husband's scam."

"I'll get to that, Ms. Parkman. I ask that you respect the sequence of what I'm saying. All the pieces will fit together in due time. It came to my attention that Eunice was using the child as a pawn, a willful strategy to inflict pain on her ex-husband as all this played out in the courts. Eunice tormented the child, urging her to testify to falsehoods about her father, a high-profile executive, knowing full well it would humiliate him, and ruin his career. The daughter suffered the most."

"I'm familiar with the case. I read about it in the Observer. My attorney plays hardball, so what? That's why you're in such a shitty position." Stephanie was losing her patience.

Becky continued unabated. "The child cut herself as a

cry for help, and all the while I couldn't reveal what I knew or how I came to know it. I tried to represent Grayson hoping to out-lawyer Eunice into stopping the below-the-belt tactics while never revealing what I knew of Melanie's privileged medical records."

Stephanie did an eye roll to signal she was in no mood for a lengthy story, "I'm bored. Get to the point." Stephanie felt sure she was in the driver's seat.

"It's relevant, Ms. Parkman, trust me. Being urged to testify about sexual abuse that never took place, promising the daughter a new BMW, and summer in Europe, was about the lowest thing I've ever heard in all my years practicing law. My fiancé told me that Melanie was in Eunice's office pressured to sign an affidavit about sexual abuse that never took place, for a bigger settlement." Becky swallowed and leaned forward. "Melanie said she needed to think about it and finish midterms first. She went back to Chapel Hill, called her psychiatrist saying she had an impossible choice, and couldn't take it anymore. The very next day she flung herself from the Bell Tower. Do you know what she told my fiancé in her last therapy session? 'I don't take bribes.'"

"Well, boo-hoo. It's sad, but you're forgetting what my husband did. What about me?" Stephanie was visibly mad, but Becky was fuming and trying to keep from reaching over and choking Stephanie, trying to maintain composure, enraged by the absence of empathy for the girl whose death caused her such anguish.

"Both my fiancé and I were powerless to reveal your lawyer's depravity, for fear of jeopardizing our careers. I know Grayson Whitcomb. He quit the business world and works in a Micro-lending NGO in Central America trying to make amends and honor his daughter's legacy. Seeing your attorney hog the spotlight for media attention, now he is ready to fight. When I'm done, he'll be mayor of Charlotte."

"So my attorney is a take-no-prisoners type and maybe

did something shady. Her strength is why you are in this predicament. Ever think of that? She has you painted in a corner and outlawyered you. You're the losers. I'm the deceived one here. I'm the victim. I'm tired of being lied to. Pay up. Your story is boring."

"Not so fast, Ms. Parkman. I've wrestled with my conscience every day since, as has my fiancé. We're no longer worried about our careers. That is unfortunate news for you and your attorney. I know what you're doing to Nicole. You never miss an opportunity to rag on my client. It ends now."

Stephanie's bravado slipped. Becky had a face that said she wasn't fucking around.

"I know you've been traveling the past few days. You probably haven't read the Charlotte papers much. You have the most radioactive attorney in North Carolina, or should I say ex-attorney. I may not be practicing law soon, but yours will never set foot in a courtroom except as a defendant. Why is that relevant? Before I left, I ran a full-page ad in the Observer. I've printed a copy for you if you like. Your attorney is now exposed, and Grayson is running for mayor and trust me, he'll win. I sacrificed my career to give his life a new meaning. He wants to give Melanie a voice and so do I. He wants to dedicate himself to public service in her honor."

Stephanie tried to swallow but she had no spit.

"His level of disgust with your attorney is sky-high. He will do whatever it takes to make sure they try your attorney for witness intimidation. He wants to make sure another girl doesn't go through what Melanie went through. That means Nicole. You better mind your p's and q's, Ms. Parkman. Imagine the mayor thinking you are doing the same underhanded things that led to his daughter's suicide. The North Carolina Law Review Board asked Eunice to surrender her license to practice law pending review. The State Attorney General is convening a Grand Jury to discuss a variety of criminal charges, including an inducement to commit perjury, witness tampering, conspiracy, and six other charges. The case is blowing up the papers as we speak. Here are a few articles for your review. Technically, Ms. Parkman, you don't have representation now."

"I can get another lawyer that will just pick up where she left off." Stephanie mouthed off, but immediately wished she had kept quiet.

"Ms. Parkman, if you go to court, the entire city will be watching. It'll be a media circus. They'll see Melanie Whitcomb when they look at pictures of your daughter. A young woman, a chess piece in a divorce, and you, like Rhonda Whitcomb, more concerned with maintaining her lifestyle than her daughter's wellbeing. You won't be able to go to a Bojangles without getting dirty looks," Becky said.

"My client will marry his girlfriend here. You will leave him the fuck alone. If you abide by this, I have some very generous perks for you. If you violate what I'm about to tell you, things will get very difficult. I suggest you watch this video of your ex's fiancé. It's viral on YouTube at eight hundred thousand hits last time I checked. She is beating the shit out of Vicky's ex-husband, a small-time Australian creep. She can do the same to her fiancé's ex if you mess with her." Becky turned her laptop around to tee the bar fight clip up. After the thirty-second fight part, Stephanie had seen enough.

"He can't get married. Technically, we're still married. I get his benefits for another year," Stephanie said.

"Ms. Parkman, I've awful news for you and some wonderful news. The terrible news is you don't have many options except to listen and do as I say," Becky said.

"When you go back to your room, you probably won't find your passport. Maybe a maid took it. It is hard to vet every chambermaid. I'm confident we can find it and get it back to you if you do the right thing and show me some good faith."

Stephanie felt lightheaded. She grabbed the table for

support. Things were going way different from what she planned. Very different. What the fuck was happening?

"If you can't find your passports you must go to Canberra, to the embassy to get a replacement. I can assure you, it's a colossal pain in the ass. If we report it stolen, it would put you on a watch list in every international airport in Australia. You couldn't fly for a few weeks."

Becky's knowing grin sent shivers down Stephanie's spine.

"Guess what? In two weeks when you can get back home, your boyfriend will have lived at your address for over a month, and you'll have legally cohabited for an intimate relationship. No more alimony."

"Wait a second; my boyfriend is crazy about me. He'll wire me money. I can call him now, and he'll move out right away and get the clock back to zero and your plan stops. I need that alimony. I can't work. You know I'm studying physical therapy. That's why I'm getting rehabilitative alimony. You can't do this."

"I'll get to your boyfriend in just a second, sweetheart. You have no passport. If the hotel reports you can't produce it, they must list it as missing. You can't fly home without one. That is a month of you and Henry trying to figure out how to survive, and I know all about your survival skills. Do you think he'll subsidize you for a month without you sleeping with him? He'll go home sorry he ever met such a train wreck, and you'll be all alone." Becky said poker-faced.

Stephanie's tongue stuck to the roof of her mouth.

"Technically, you have no representation since your attorney cannot practice law. I can talk to you about legal matters directly. So here are divorce papers you need to review. Take twenty-four hours to review them. They're boilerplate. Refuse to sign, and you're stranded here with no hotel, no money, and trying to figure out how you'll get through the next month. I give Henry three days before he ditches you like an expired carton of milk."

Becky grinned. "But here's the enjoyable part, and I suggest you listen. Sign the papers and you've another week here, completely comped."

"When this is over, Grayson Whitcomb will be mayor, and everyone will know the story of his daughter, and how your attorney contributed to her death. Keep up your antics and everyone will know you were marching in lockstep with Eunice. There is no payday for you, Ms. Parkman, but if you do as I say, you'll be okay. Make one step out of line, and you're checkmated."

Stephanie's chest constricted. She couldn't breathe.

"Dave is watching your daughter while you're over here. He's taking care of her until you get back from Australia. Dave feels bad for her. He sees how you treat her, lean on her, parentify her, and try to alienate her from her dad. He knows a lot about her because Ross told him. Yes, those two know one another well, I might add."

"I fucking knew it. He contacted my boyfriend because he's just jealous. He can't stand to see me happy with a guy that adores me. What a sicko. Where do you get off trying cheap dime-store psychoanalysis on me? My ex is a fucking liar. God knows what he told you." Stephanie couldn't keep from shooting her mouth off, but it dawned on her that mouthing off might not be the best course of action. Whatever Stephanie thought she knew, Ross's attorney was two steps ahead. Stephanie felt nauseous and was hyperventilating. She wanted to call her mother.

"Oh, it's not like that at all. Dave plotted to cohabitate with you so that your husband would no longer have to pay alimony. It worked. He was never in love with you and can't wait to leave. He's moving out the moment you get back when he knows Nicole is safe, and with a parent who won't use her as a pawn. I'll call him now if you like. You can hear it for yourself. After years of using and manipulating people to get what you want, you are on the other side. How does that feel, Ms. Parkman?" Becky asked.

"It's still not thirty days. I need my alimony to become a physical therapist."

"Seriously, I'm wise to Eunice's tricks. You do this to appear as if you are preparing to be productive, but when you screw up, you'll blame your failures on others. My fiancé has you better analyzed than your shrink. Your passport is missing, remember? Listen to what I say, and perhaps we can find it for you. Let Dave go, sweetie. He never was yours, to begin with," Becky said.

"Dave is in love with me," Stephanie said, on the verge of tears.

"He isn't. He thinks you're a whiny, narcissistic bitch who always puts herself first. If this doesn't teach you a lesson, nothing will. If you choose not to take this as an enlightening moment in your life, perhaps the consequences will keep you in line. Your attorney no longer practices law and will be a felon when the justice system is done with her. Do you want to be known throughout Charlotte as the last client of Charlotte's sleaziest attorney? Trying to pull a Melanie Whitcomb on your daughter? The harder you push, the worse you look."

Becky continued while Stephanie developed tunnel vision. The world darkened around her.

"You're fairly lucky, however. I have a sense of decency. I want to make things easy for you. That guy you are with does probably love you. Don't ask me why, but he does. He's someone you can train to fetch on command while you lounge around all day. I have someone I'd like you to meet," Becky said.

Who other than Ross could she possibly know in Broome, Australia? Stephanie felt like crying but didn't do tears. It was a defense mechanism from her mother's constant criticism, to not give her mother the satisfaction of knowing she wounded her. She remained stoic and robotic. Her pills aided this absence of emotions.

Vicky entered the room.

"Hi love. I'm the hot Aussie engineer your Henry was

cavorting with."

"I have your emails. You slut!" Stephanie blurted before realizing she had a losing hand.

"Watch your language tart, I never met the guy. My fiancé owns this place. If I so much as wink at security, you will be out on your ass. Our head of security is an ex Israeli special-ops agent, and he was also your driver on the way over here from the airport. He's not from Lebanon like he said. He was listening and making mental notes of everything you and your travel companion said. I'd never date Henry in actual life, but you are fresh out of options. He seems perfect for you. Trust me, love, for you that guy is a keeper," Vicky said, dispensing advice with a side dish of condescension.

"Don't mess with Ross or his fiancé. She's feisty. She beat the stuffing out of my ex after I told her what a louse he was. Ross is enjoying being with someone who is a productive member of society. Do not stand in her way. She'll destroy you. She's an attorney also, and a damn good one. For you, love, Henry is your only option," Victoria said matter-of-factly.

"What are you talking about? You people are fucking crazy. How does everyone know everyone? What is this, some kind of Twilight Zone where everyone has been listening in on my life?" Stephanie did not hide the fact she was both confused and overwhelmed by the turn of events.

"Listen, love, you have two days to convince your guy pal here to marry you. He'll be overjoyed when you end it with Dave. Dave can chaperone Nicole here and see her mom and dad get married to other people. The flight and hotel are on me, love. Dave can attend his best bloke's wedding, and yours as well if you like. It'll be a glorious trip for your daughter. But say one negative thing about Ross to your daughter and the deal is off."

"All you people know one another. What the fuck is going on? How am I going to get married here?" Now Stephanie wanted guidance.

"You get him to propose to you, and we will pay for a wedding here, a photographer for your Facebook page, a dress, even a champagne toast with dinner on us, and fly your daughter here and Dave can chaperone. She can see both of you get married. Misbehave and I can get Qantas to put your passport on the stolen list. By the time you get a replacement, you'll have to pole dance in Woop Woop to get airfare home. Surely, you can get Henry to marry you. Manipulate him. It's nothing new, love. Take the deal. Becky already gave you spending money. Shop for some clothes. You have one week here. Enjoy. Just leave your husband and his fiancé alone. Do you hear me? My fiancé is branding this place as a destination wedding resort. Look at the bright side. Your wedding will be on our brochures right beside your ex-husband's. You can look back with fond memories. Becky and Mindy will be on the brochures too. One big, happy family. Aussies friendliest wedding resort."

Stephanie could only stare, open-mouthed.

"I just thought I'd introduce myself. Now if you'll excuse me, I have wedding plans of my own to attend to. First, I just want to watch my ex getting his ass kicked by Ross's fiancé. Best YouTube video ever. It's almost a million hits now, and she will have a segment on 60 Minutes Australia. If I hadn't heard so much about you, I might feel sorry for you. Right now, you need to stay within the parameters we have laid out. Don't step out of line," Vicky said, smiling the entire time.

"Becky, what time do you and Mindy want to go for mani-pedis tomorrow? I have us booked for a hair appointment at four. Run along Stephanie. You have an engagement to facilitate and divorce papers to notarize. Tell Henry I said 'G'day."

Stuff was happening too fast. People knew one another, were marrying each other, and now her grifter boyfriend and Nicole were flying halfway around the world. Stephanie needed a Klonopin. She couldn't juggle stress and responsibilities on a good day, and today was not a good day. Nausea swept through her.

There were a few important points. Ross's fiancé was not to be trifled with. She could physically and legally kick her ass. Eunice's career was toast, and after paying ten grand, Stephanie would have to start from scratch with another attorney. Dave was never her boyfriend, to begin with, and if she didn't pivot to Henry as her love interest, it would strand her in Australia with no money or passport. Henry was her only path to a semblance of financial security. She had a few days to get him on board. She hated Dave now. She wanted to get revenge on somebody but seemed checkmated. Everyone was three moves ahead.

This was surreal. However, she would wind up at the end with an incredible vacation, and a man who would take care of her for the rest of her life. She had one path to security, and if she didn't take it, all roads were dead ends. She felt alone and needed to call her mother, but what could she say? Her mother would criticize her for not having consulted her first and for trying to do things on her own. She would feel weak and stupid with no confidence. She needed Henry to tell her he loved her and that she was great, even if no one outside of Facebook thought so.

If she came back married to a likable guy, she would be the victor, if not in actual life then at least on Facebook. Beautiful pictures, a dream vacation, and a happy new husband eager to show her off. Her bobble-headed sycophants wouldn't be able to push "Like" on her posts fast enough. No one is as happy as they appear on Facebook, so what was the harm in embellishing a little. Henry loved her. She wouldn't spend a moment without a boyfriend, and he would pay her bills.

No one needed to know about the humiliation part. She felt empty inside, but others would think the opposite. Who had a better story than a whirlwind destination wedding in Australia? She was a survivor who did what she had to do. That's what winners do.

Her path was now clear. She was bitter and vengeful, sure, but her adversaries were strangely allowing her a face-saving gesture. It would take a while to process all that the Australian and Harrington had said, but she knew what she needed to do. Two Klonopins would put her in just the right frame of mind to rope in Henry and enjoy the rest of her trip. Nicole at her wedding would make a great photo-op. Who flies their kid to Australia for a destination wedding? Winners, that's who.

Her hair came out good in Australia, and they said she could get it styled and the resort would provide a photographer.

No one needed to know about the humiliation.

She had spending money and a comped hotel room with unlimited tours and a paid-for destination wedding.

Stephanie was pale as she entered the glass elevator to their ocean-view suite. She had to admit for a nightmare of a comeuppance the perks were good. She had to concoct a story that would make her change of heart believable and yet not violate the terms of her NDA with Becky and Victoria.

"I'm so upset!" Stephanie said.

"What's the matter, Stephanie? You look like you saw a ghost."

"Hug me. I need one."

Henry was all too happy to oblige.

"I broke up with my boyfriend. I had my suspicions. Turns out he's just another liar. He wants to come here to win me back, but I don't want him. He was jealous of us. Dave knew I still had feelings for you. When that IP address surfaced, and he knew you were faithful, he knew I'd run back to you. Good riddance."

To friend-zoned guys, hearing a break-up spiel is like music to their ears. It's when they have their opening, and Henry jumped at the chance. There were no teachable moments ever for Stephanie. Becky knew that. Stephanie's focus was getting through life responsibility-free and maintaining her image. If she followed the script, her image would remain, perhaps be enhanced. Like a martial artist, Becky had used Stephanie's momentum against her.

Narcissists don't learn morality lessons. They change their behavior based on what they can and can't get away with. The desire to avoid being publicly shamed is perhaps the only thing tempering their behaviors. Stephanie held no cards. She checked, and their passports were not where they had been. These people were not fucking around.

Stephanie would wind up married and wanted by a man who would give her the adulation and supply she needed. He might croak but had life insurance, and land in the mountains near Banner Elk. She would have an exceptional honeymoon for the world to see. By all appearances, that was a life, others would envy. She wouldn't need to get a job to make ends meet. She was growing more comfortable with Plan B. She could spin this like a major coup on Facebook. #winning.

"Dave was up to no good, jealous you were accompanying me. A friend of mine saw him cheating. I feel so humiliated. I met the woman who wrote those emails. As I suspected, Ross was jealous of our happiness. You didn't know her. She admitted it. You were telling me the truth the whole time. Boy, did I ever rip her a new asshole. I'm sorry for ever doubting you." Stephanie had Henry around her finger.

"Let's have ourselves a beautiful dinner overlooking the water. My treat. Get dressed up. I have a feeling today will be a glorious day. We're in Australia, for Pete's sake. I know we came to bust your ex, but think of the silver lining," Henry said.

The couple locked eyes, then lips, and began a kiss that should have made Henry feel twenty years younger. Stephanie had the power to fake it well enough to fool the old man.

"Stephanie, I love you."

"I love you too, Henry."

Chapter Twenty-Five
Rehearsal Dinner

Tomorrow, The Broome Royal Pearl Resort will host four weddings. The bizarre connections between them were almost too ridiculous to imagine. Ross chuckled to himself as he realized he slept with three of the five brides. The only wedding where he hadn't had conjugal relations with a bride was the Harrington-Horowitz lesbian wedding. If Becky was bisexual, who knows, she might have given him pity sex when he was down on his luck. Such was their friendship. He would be their best man or would give Becky away. How does that work in lesbian weddings, anyway?

Each wedding made Ross happy in its unique way. The Stephanie-Henry wedding would save him thousands each month. Victoria's wedding would give her the fairytale life she so deserved. Becky and Mindy had guided him through his journey and helped him heal. Ross gave their long-term relationship the impetus to move forward. Even poor

Reginald might have a cellmate who would take a fancy to him. Nicole and Dave would soon arrive to help celebrate. Halfway around the world, surrounded by love, but still petrified Julie could piece together how and why they first met.

Colin planned a rehearsal dinner. One of two he would be attending. The first would be for local dignitaries, old family friends, business contacts, and assorted mucky-mucks, but he had another with his American friends. He would thank them, and they would thank Colin for arranging the nuptials. It was a big weekend—the first wedding to take place in the resort, and the pictures would appear on promotional materials.

Ross and Julie walked to the Kimberly Salon for the rehearsal. He would feel a lot more confident if he had his passport back with the Sydney hotel receipt, but it was still in Julie's purse.

Mindy and Becky were already there and greeted the couple at the door.

"Hey, there is a guy here that says he knows you," Becky said.

"Meester Ross, boss. You changed my life. I just start last week. Maria too. We love it here. Gracias amigo."

"Holy cow, I figured it would take months for everything."

"No, Señorita Victoria and Señor Colin help to take care of everything. My son Ernesto is playing soccer in high school. We're thrilled. I want you to meet my wife, Maria, and my son."

"Con Mucho Gusto, Mr. Ross," Maria said as she hugged Ross. She was emotional, holding back tears.

Their son Ernesto was tall, handsome, and athletic looking. He looked Ross in the eye, like well-raised boys do, and thanked him for everything he had done for his family. He gave Ross a firm handshake. *Fine young man.*

"Happy to help. How about those Australian girls, Ernesto?"

"Let's say soccer isn't my only extracurricular activity," Ernesto smiled.

"Who are they?" Julie asked.

"Marcelo worked at a hotel I used to visit in LA. Nice family."

Nir arrived with his wife. A leggy Gal Gadot type. She spotted Julie and wanted to introduce herself.

"Well, if it isn't Wonder Woman. You're quite the celebrity."

"I owe it all to your husband, Nir. He had me ready for anything."

"Hopefully, you are ready for marriage."

"That depends on Ross over here."

After grabbing a cocktail, Victoria and Colin arrived dressed to the nines from their previous engagement. She looked radiant, and he looked dashing. They would be the power couple in Broome and looked the part.

They exchanged hugs all around.

"I thought I'd surprise you with Marcelo and Maria. Colin loves them. They're settling in. We're setting her up with a Salvadoran/Mexican food truck business on the side. Ernesto is working part-time here. They're a lovely family."

The clinking of glasses signaled it was time for a few toasts. Julie insisted on going first.

"To my life partner and soulmate Ross, I've some important things to say. There were things as we got to know one another that gave me pause, but your spirit won the day. Thank you for your friendship with Vicky. She's a beautiful and amazing woman. I count her as among my closest friends. Colin is lucky to have her, but if there is anyone in the world that deserves her it's him, for there is no nicer, more accomplished gentleman in this continent or any other."

Julie smiled at her soon-to-be husband. "Ross, you have an incredible capacity to assemble a cast of characters in your life. Your attorney Becky is one. As one attorney to another, she's the real deal, intelligent and sharp as a tack. I even got to talk to her partner Mindy, who was of great help to you in managing your ex and your journey to a joyful life. I think I got a measure of you and your unique ability to get people to root for you. To help them as they help you. That is empathy so essential for a healthy marriage. I found out so much about you, I thought there wasn't anything more to find out. Then, the pieces just kind of fit together with me, the circumstances of our meeting, the frantic trip halfway around the world by your ex, and this, the hotel bill in Sydney with Dave's cell number on it. So, I had to come right out and ask Vicky and Becky what was going on."

Ross got a whiff of where this was going and couldn't believe something that had gone so right appeared to have unraveled at the eleventh hour. The rehearsal dinner for Chrissakes. It seemed Julie knew everything. She had just accepted his proposal because of the reporter's mike in her face.

"I can explain, Julie." Ross's rubbery legs could barely hold him up. This was not the speech he was expecting.

"Ross, allow me to explain. I was raised in a wonderful family. My mom adapted to her new surroundings in Atlanta, having come from Panama. My dad built a business from the ground floor up and always taught me I could be whatever I wanted. He taught me to be strong. I also should have taken more lessons from my older brother Brad. While he gave me my love of music with his hippie friends, I always looked at him as lacking for not getting this competitive streak that my dad ingrained in me."

Ross leaned on the table and waited for Julie to finish. Maybe somehow he could salvage this relationship that had grown so dear to him.

"Brad had a balance in his life. Sure, he was a screw-up, but he still goes to concerts and has held on to his inner youth. He refused to just follow what they expected of him. While I was consumed with winning and proving myself." Julie's hands were shaking as she held the paper with her notes. "I lost perspective along the way. I was obsessed with winning during the divorce, to protect the family business. I wrecked my marriage because I wanted to prove myself and make my husband handle my family responsibilities to the business." Julie continued, her hands trembling as she read.

Ross swallowed past the lump in his throat.

"We never missed an opportunity to remind Dave he was an in-law and not blood. It hit him where it hurts, and it wasn't fair. There are few things harder on a man than the mental beat-down he must have received by being embedded in my dad's company."

"I must admit that when our marriage was breaking apart, I wasn't as compassionate a human being as I should have been. I was competitive, I was vengeful, and I chose sides as if I were in a war. I made his life after our split worse than it should've been."

Ross was even more perplexed. She was veering way off course and now had the passport with the hotel receipt in her hand. He was unsure whether she wanted Dave back or would excoriate him for coming up with The Plan.

"But Julie..."

She shushed him and continued unabated. "Ross, please allow me to finish. I want Dave to find happiness. I'm glad you're friends, and I'd like to be too. I figured out your little plan. At first, I felt betrayed, but then the whole YouTube hoopla happened, and I kind of put it aside. Kicking the shit out of Reginald was a catharsis for me. Vicky, Nir, Colin, thank you for that. I'm done trying to prove myself. To win the affections of my daddy, to be the outsider that won everyone over like my mom, I want to have a life partner, and to be a wonderful life partner. That's all I want, and I want that person to be you, Ross. You can tell your friend Dave he's off the hook. I don't want to soak him for another dime. I want him to find his soulmate like I found mine." Julie was sobbing "Just don't deceive me again, okay? You've seen me on the YouTube video. It would be pretty ugly." She regained her composure, wiped her eyes, and continued.

"I applaud you for the rather unorthodox manner in which you got me to this place. It doesn't matter how the journey started. Both of you get points for creativity How the fuck did you come up with such an idea and pull it off? I wouldn't have met the man of my life if not for you two knuckleheads, and your ridiculous plan. When I think of you huffing and puffing at the gym to meet me, getting beat up, I just smile. This lovable and endearingly stupid guy jumped in the middle of a sparring match in a gym to rescue me from a punch that he thought was dirty but barely grazed me."

She laughed. "With a month's worth of experience, he jumps in to save me in a gym with half a dozen black-belt instructors. They threw him out like yesterday's newspaper. They had him on the ground tapping out before I even put my mouthpiece back in. No one does that for someone they are trying to scam. Genuine feelings and cupid's arrow can only cause that kind of stupidity. You are a nut in the most endearing way. For having the fortitude and gumption to pull it off, it must be some divine intervention that led me to you. Now let's find someone that makes Dave happier than I could, and as happy as you make me. Your plan worked, and I'm glad it did. I love you."

Vicky was crying and put her hand in Colin's. Nir, the military man, even looked moved. His wife grabbed his hand. Julie uttered the words, "Group hug," and the table all huddled together and seemed ready to call the tumultuous night to an end.

Colin seemed to be the only one composed enough to say anything. "How the hell do you follow that speech? Drink up everybody, it's all on me. There is a lot of love in this room and Vicky and I are just damn glad you're here. Not an inauspicious start for a wedding resort, eh?"

Chapter Twenty-Six
Wedding Bells

Julie opened the curtains on another beautiful Broome day. She, Becky, Mindy, and Victoria were all scheduled for a make-up session followed by a mani-pedi and lunch. After, they would dress for their big day. Julie loved her Broome girl-posse. *Such a cool group.*

Ross was still sleeping. He had only to pick up his tux and then meet Dave and Nicole at the airport by eleven. Nicole would quickly change and get ready for her mom's 2 p.m. wedding, hurrying back to attend the triple nuptials at 7 p.m. Colin, through representatives, gave Stephanie and Henry the choice of where in Australia they wished to celebrate. He wanted them out of the hotel during the other weddings. They decided on Perth. It was a quick flight from Broome and had good connections back to the states. They would be on their way and out of the hotel by 6 p.m. and be in Perth by nine, in time for a late dinner to celebrate their impromptu wedding if Henry could stay up that late.

Ross roused himself from the bed, still groggy from drinking and digesting the day's events. Julie was wise to his plan, and it didn't matter. He had no secrets anymore, except maybe sleeping with Victoria, but Julie probably wouldn't care about that one either. He was a lucky man.

Ross grabbed breakfast downstairs and thought of calling Marcelo, or even Nir to join him, but being alone with his thoughts would suffice.

He headed over to the airport and waited for the arrival from Sydney carrying Dave and Nicole.

"Come here, babydoll."

She sprinted into his arms. "Dad, this is the coolest trip. Listen, I know mom will probably hate his guts now that she's marrying Henry, but you will still be friends with Dave, right? He's kind of like my uncle now."

"Yes, sure. Guess what. Julie is Dave's ex-wife."

"I know dad, Dave told me on the plane. You were worried about screwing up my view of marriage? This is some serious Gerry Springer stuff."

"It's all good. Julie is looking forward to seeing Dave too. They're friends, but just don't want to be married anymore. We can all hang out together."

"Dad, I saw Julie's YouTube video. It popped up on my Facebook screen. She's like *Xena, the Warrior Princess.*"

"Don't go that far, Nicole," Dave said.

The trio grabbed the luggage and settled into the resort.

"Hurry and get dressed, Nicole. You can order room service but leave by 1 p.m., no later. Your mom is getting married on the beach at 2 p.m. Be back by six or you'll miss mine."

"Love you, Daddy. This is amazing. I know Uncle Dave isn't going to Mom's wedding, but will he be at yours, on account of his ex-wife being the bride?"

"Yes, he will be the best man."

"Cool. I decided you were right. I'll need a therapist, Dad. This is bizarre."

"I need therapy at least as much as you do, Nicole," Ross said.

"Me too," Dave said.

Nicole, Ross, and Dave laughed. Ross decided everything would be all right.

Dave and Ross grabbed a quick burger and caught up.

"You will not believe this. Julie figured out The Plan and is fine with it. She thought it was funny. She's sorry for putting you through the wringer."

"No shit? Can't be."

"It's true, and that bar fight thing, it's all over YouTube. The biggest story here in some time. Colin said he was splitting the YouTube royalties with us as a wedding gift. Says he couldn't buy publicity like this for a million dollars. Plus, Stephanie has got to be scared shitless of her. Now go get your tux. Julie doesn't know you're the best man yet, but she will probably be happy when she finds out."

"The video was playing on CNN when I was changing planes in Atlanta. You sure about Julie?" Dave asked.

"Yep. Two more hours, and we are alimony free. Do you fucking believe it?" Ross asked.

"We pulled it off. It's been a helluva ride, buddy."

Ross couldn't wait to make Julie his wife. He and Dave strolled to the ballroom.

Vicky and Colin had decked it out in grand style. Some four hundred guests packed the area. They set up three separate podiums, one for each couple. Nir agreed to walk Julie down the aisle while Dave stood next to Ross as best man. Maria, Marcelo's wife, had agreed to be the maid of honor, something she pointed out was an ironic twist on her humble start in the hotel industry. Nicole looked quite the young lady as Ernesto walked past her to stand alongside her dad on the podium.

Palimony

Local TV cameras were rolling. A year ago, Ross had
been a virtual nobody. Now here he was in a huge social to-
do. This was an enormous deal in Broome, Kimberly, and
the rest of Australia. The LGBTQ angle had attracted
attention throughout Australia too. The Charlotte Observer
sent a reporter, and no doubt local Charlotte news would
request footage from the Australian Broadcasting Service.
Grayson Whitcomb was leading by almost twenty points in
the polls after Becky launched his campaign.

The do-you-take-this-bride spiel was repeated once,
then a second time, then a third. With each affirmative, I
Do, the crowd erupted into applause. First Becky, then
Julie, and then Victoria. Everyone stood as the three
couples walked to lead the audience to the reception.

They served each elegant course to the orchestral
sounds of a ten-piece band.

"Congrats, Julie, you look beautiful. You got a helluva
husband there."

"Thanks, Dave, all because of your ridiculous scam.
Congrats to you. You pulled one over on me. I guess we're
even. You got a raw deal in the divorce, and I'm sorry.
You're a wonderful guy. I hope we can be friends. My mom
always asks about you."

"I'd like that. I'm happy for you too. Give Blanca my
love. So, you're a kind of internet celebrity now. How does
that feel?"

"Oh, that. It got things out of my system. I've
mellowed. I want you to know I hope you'll continue to be
friends with Ross and have a friendship with us as a couple.
I want the best for you."

"Thanks, Julie. I feel the same. I was far from a perfect
husband. No hard feelings. We're good now? Gimme a
hug."

Julie leaned in and hugged her ex.

"Okay, you two, that's enough. Julie's my wife now,"
Ross said.

Dave and Julie laughed.

Julie kissed Ross's cheek. "Sorry, sweetheart. This may take a bit of adjusting, but we'll get the hang of it," Julie said.

The band had a request and launched into "I knew the Bride When She Used to Rock-and-Roll." The entire table emptied, dancing with no one like a giant ball of happiness.

Ross watched as Ernesto asked Nicole to dance. She said yes to the handsome teen, wanting to join in the celebration. "Adults are crazy, you know. Both my parents got married. I should be confused, but I'm happy. This entire thing makes no sense, but for the first time since my dad left the house, I feel like everything will be okay. My parents are getting along."

"We should keep in touch, swap emails. My Dad said Victoria and your dad were great pen-pals, advising each other on relationships. I moved eight-thousand miles from California. I could probably use an internet friend."

"Sure, I'd like that. Hey, check this out." Nicole opened her Facebook page on her phone. It was a video her mom had posted. She was singing "I will Always Love You," the Dolly Parton song made a mega hit by Whitney Houston, as a late entrant in "Australia's Got Talent."

"I'm the luckiest girl in the world today marrying the love of my life. My soulmate Henry Graves. After taking me on a vacation of a lifetime that most people could only dream of, he proposed and flew my beautiful daughter here to be with us. I'm so grateful to have found genuine love."

"Ernesto, your family. Is it 'normal'?"

"I'm not sure how to answer. They're good parents if that's what you mean."

"Okay, it's settled then. I must keep in touch because mine are nuts. I need the opinion of someone with normal parents."

"Cool. I'd like that. Your dad helped us out. He's a magnificent man."

"He's much cooler than I thought he was." The two teens walked away to the dance floor.

Ross was happy Nicole would be eight thousand miles away from Ernesto. He liked the kid, but Nicole had a lot more growing up to do. Internet friends would be fine for the present. He'd deal with anything more later.

Stephanie's video already had twenty-nine likes, a million shy of Julie's fight video. Nicole showed Dave her mom's YouTube answer to Julie's video. Soon there were high fives all around the head table as everyone stared at the video and Facebook post. Everyone told Nicole how happy her mom looked. "Facebook Stephanie" was radiant, courtesy of the professional photographer and makeup artist Colin provided.

"Oh my God, Ernesto."

"Check out this text. 'Australia's Got Talent in our hotel in Perth. Going to enter. Million YouTube views, here I come! #winning."

"Your mom?" Ernesto asked.

"Yes! She just doesn't get it."

"Get what?"

"Life. Hey, you want to dance?"

"I'm Latin, what do you think?"

Mindy motioned to Nir as if needing to speak with him. He was curious and came over to her and Becky.

"Nir, we went to Chinatown for lunch yesterday. The food is excellent."

"Yes, very good actually," he said.

"The restaurants. Are they open on Christmas?" Mindy asked.

"I believe they are. Chinese restaurants are almost always open on Christmas," Nir said.

"Is there a movie theater in town?" Mindy asked.

"Sure," the wiry ex-commando said.

"Then it's settled. Becky and I are moving here. If you aren't doing anything on Christmas, we'd love to go out for Chinese and a movie with you and your wife."

"Jewish Christmas in Australia, I'll put it in my calendar."

"Seriously, this is the place we can have the relaxing life we always wanted. We are stepping off the treadmill."

"I'll talk to Colin for you. He knows people that can get visas. You will love it here. Mazel Tov on your wedding neighbor."

The dancing lasted until two a. m. Colin worked the room. Ross knew this multiple wedding event had set his resort on a trajectory that would keep him busy for years.

"Colin, thank you for everything you've done. It's been amazing. You've got a magnificent girl in Victoria. I'm glad she found you. We love you both. Promise me when the brochure comes out with all the four weddings in it, you'll send me a copy," Ross said.

"You got it, mate. Congrats to you, too. You got quite a little feisty one there. Treat her right, and she'll keep you happy for the rest of your life. I can't wait for the brochure myself."

"If only everyone knew the story behind all these weddings," Ross said.

"We do, mate, our little inside joke. That's what makes it so special. I'll always smile when I think of your improbable plan and how it all worked out."

9 781633 635074